About the author

Alan M Keef has a business building small railways for the industrial and leisure markets that he describes as a hobby that got out of hand, but for all that, it has taken him to some of the less glamorous countries around the world.

He is widowed, remarried and lives and works in Herefordshire. He lives in the village of Lea in the ecclesiastical parish of Ariconium, on the edge of the Forest of Dean, Gloucestershire. This book started life as a (long) short story related to the ancient iron mines at Clearwell, with Puzzlewood being almost next door. The lower River Severn and the Bristol Channel are his home waters for sailing - a crazy place for such pursuits with its huge tidal range.

This is Alan's second full-length novel.

BY THE SAME AUTHOR

The Finding

SLAVE TO ARICONIUM

Alan M Keef

SLAVE TO ARICONIUM

Vanguard Press

VANGUARD PAPERBACK

© Copyright 2020
Alan M Keef

The right of Alan M Keef to be identified as author of
this work has been asserted by him in accordance with the
Copyright, Designs and Patents Act 1988.

All Rights Reserved

No reproduction, copy or transmission of this publication
may be made without written permission.
No paragraph of this publication may be reproduced,
copied or transmitted save with the written permission of the publisher, or in
accordance with the provisions
of the Copyright Act 1956 (as amended).

Any person who commits any unauthorised act in relation to
this publication may be liable to criminal
prosecution and civil claims for damages.

A CIP catalogue record for this title is
available from the British Library.

ISBN 978 1 784658 96 0

*Vanguard Press is an imprint of
Pegasus Elliot MacKenzie Publishers Ltd.*
www.pegasuspublishers.com

First Published in 2020

**Vanguard Press
Sheraton House Castle Park
Cambridge England**
Printed & Bound in Great Britain

Dedication

For Lin

Role model for Helen of Troy

Author's Note

Slavery has existed since time immemorial, and up to and including the era of the cellphone and the iPad. It is for this reason that the Anti-Slavery Society, first founded in 1823, still exists and remains active to this day. In the popular mind possibly the two best-known and well-documented times of slavery are those of the Roman period and the transatlantic slave trade to the Americas. In Roman times, slaves did all the donkey work that made the empire what it was. This included virtually all the day-to-day jobs that make a society function, from the most menial of tasks to positions of very considerable trust and authority. Slaves were made up of all the captured races, and slavery could be a punishment for crimes committed. Equally to become a freed man, or woman, was a reward for exceptional service to state or master.

The transatlantic slave trade of Africans to the New World is better documented, especially in its later stages, and was rather more simply a means of supplying cheap labour. Again slaves could and did rise to positions of trust and even relative wealth, but the norm was unremitting hard labour for both male and female, as of course it was for the so-called lower orders in what was fast becoming an industrialised society. One also needs to remember that several million Africans were transported in the other direction, across the Indian Ocean, to service the Islamic states of the Middle East from long before the transatlantic trade started and for a hundred years or so after it had finished.

The hallmark of all slave systems seems too often to have been unprovoked brutality by master to slave. Near starvation rations were equally normal, from which a longer than normal day's work was required. This latter was especially true of Hitler's treatment of his Russian prisoner slaves and, in turn, of the Russians to their prisoners in the Gulag. One can but wonder at the irrationality of the mind that, for some relatively trivial offence, gives a slave a flogging that then leaves that slave incapable of any work at all for days or weeks. Never mind the morality of it, the economics don't add up either, as the slave still has to be fed and, at least to some extent, cared for.

As a result, rebellion and running away amongst slaves was a perpetual problem that in turn exacerbated the violence. There are recorded instances of a more humane attitude towards slaves however, and whilst this improved the lot for all concerned, it didn't solve all the problems. Slaves still ran away or rebelled and suffered the consequences most grievously. Freedom, if and when it ever came, often produced an endemic lethargy, with it being very much the exception for a one-time slave to become an industrious and self-supporting member of society.

***

This story is set at the tail end of the Roman occupation of Britain, with its more perceptive characters, such as Julius Octavius, seeing the writing on the wall. He may have had it in mind to retire to Rome but the bloodletting and chaos there makes him decide that his future, such as it was for a cashiered army officer, lies at Ariconium. His return is as fortuitous as it is instantaneous. Marcus comes from a family that is high-class and well educated, but is still a family of slaves. The random disposal of his entire household is typical of the instability of slave life, both then and later. Most of his compatriots – Clio, Mahout, even Sparticus – have similar tales to tell. As he admits in the letter to his brother, his good fortune is more luck than judgement, a major contributing factor being his happening to be in the right place at the right moment.

It is probably his military ability to judge men, together with a good manager's intuition, that causes Julius Octavius to send Marcus back to sort out the mine after the riot. There is, however, the overriding caveat that the ore must keep coming, to which is added the further complication that the supply of slaves is erratic at best. Both are aware of instances both militarily and domestically where kindness and common sense have wrought dividends. Nevertheless Marcus knows he has to be as brutal as the age in disposing of the ringleaders of the riot, *pour encourager les autres*, if nothing else. It is necessary for him to have his gang-masters with their whips and to deal ruthlessly with any deviation from the rules, but for all that he can sometimes be the benign *dominus* that he wants to be. It is a very fine line that he has to tread, and how well he succeeds is amply demonstrated when Tiberius takes charge.

Christianity should have changed all that but it didn't. The Empire couldn't exist without its slaves, and a compromise had to be accepted. The change was just too great to contemplate. Benedictus brings the basics of the new religion to this outpost of empire, and those, such as Marcus, who listen to his words have to get by on however little they know. Indeed it was to be many centuries and almost within living memory before the rigmaroles of 'Church' were to be introduced into the Forest of Dean, where this story is set.

Having said that, most of the places herein do exist. Clearwell Caves and Puzzlewood are now tourist attractions. New Hamm is a corruption of Newnham and probably didn't exist in Roman times. The temple of Nodens at Lydney Park can sometimes be visited. The one-time stationmaster at Mitcheldean Road (in the village of The Lea) was called Noden, so his family didn't move far in a couple of millennia! Ariconium has been described as the Sheffield of Roman Britain, although only a very small part has been excavated prior to the laying of a major gas pipeline across the area. However, the surrounding group of six parishes have resurrected the word as a collective name for themselves, so your author could be said to be a resident of Ariconium.

***

I have to confess to a certain amount of 'author's licence' with this story. The biggest act in this direction is a telescoping of history. The Romans didn't finally leave Britannia to its fate until 411AD, but no doubt the process was gradual and the more distant parts lost their military protection well before that. In a similar vein, Christianity became acceptable and official in Rome close to a hundred years before the timeline of this story, but maybe it took that long to reach this backwater of the mighty Empire. Thus Benedictus could not have experienced the miracle he claimed, but it made his point nevertheless.

We, none of us, have any idea of how the Romans spoke. As a consequence I have endeavoured to use so-called 'plain English' with the addition of a few Latin words in order to keep the reader in the right era. However Latin seems to lack versatility and I have found it necessary to adapt words to suit the context. For example, *bulla* is correctly the boss in the centre of a round shield, but it seems a useful word for the boss of a situation. Whilst tempted, I have avoided using any serious use of accents for lower class or foreign persons as this may just confuse. I have avoided the swearing that must have existed, not least because I have yet to come across a dictionary of Latin swear words, partly because it can become very repetitive and largely because it seems hardly necessary. I hope readers will not find it all too anodyne as a consequence.

The likes of Tiberius exist in every walk of life, and in the army in particular. It should also be possible to identify with other characters. Moreover, they all suffer from our common fear of the unknown.

Glossary

I have generally put the English word in brackets after the Latin but have only done it once.

Place names
Aqua Sulis	Bath
Corinium	Cirencester
Deva	Chester
Eboracum	York
Glevum	Gloucester
Londinium	London
Mare Internum	Mediterranean Sea
Sarum	Salisbury

General glossary
bulla	boss
Caelum	Heaven/Nirvana (literally sky)
calend	month
cubit	Approx. 18in, 450mm
dominus, domina, domini	master, mistress, personal
Hades	Hell
lavare	washing
latrina	lavatories
mater	mother
mille, millia	mile, miles
nummus	penny
nobiles	gentlemen
nutrix	nurse
optia	assistants
pater	father
pronuptia	bridesmaid/matron of honour
sesterium	silver coin
Styx	river that has be crossed between this world and the next
vigiles	police

The rankings of a centurion in the Roman Army, from lowest to highest, are:
- Hastatus posterior
- Hastatus prior
- Princeps posterior
- Princeps prior
- Pilus posterior
- Pilus prior

Chapter 1
Rome

Hello, my name's Marcus. I'm twelve years old. I'm a slave. In Rome. At least I was in Rome. I know that life as a slave can fall apart quickly. But not this quickly, surely?

Ten days ago I had been living what – for a slave and especially a child slave – was an idyllic life attached to prosperous family where my pater (father) kept the establishment in sweet running order. Now, here I am dressed in a coarse tunic that makes me sore all over, and sandals that don't fit, plodding down the mountains into Gaul along with a rag-taggle of other slaves watched over by lazy guards. We are being taken somewhere, but I have given up bothering about that. Anywhere will do. However, it does give me time to think about how in the world, and by all the gods, I've come to be in this predicament.

The house had been beautiful, and well suited to the lavish entertaining that our lawyer owner did in his efforts to woo the best clients in Rome. That things were not as they should be had become apparent in recent weeks and months. I had heard Pater and Mater discussing the matter in quiet voices. Obviously it was not for my ears, nor those of my younger brother. Something to do with a senator and the lawyer's wife. More ominously, a serious case that had gone badly wrong for the lawyer. I almost laugh to think that my parents were naïve enough to think that I didn't know what was going on. But it had been no laughing matter. Oh no, most definitely not.

Unexpectedly the dominus and domina (master and mistress) were no longer there and the house was full of soldiers. All of us slaves were rounded up and taken off to the dungeons under the Coliseum. So far that had been the worst bit. Everyone knows what happens if you land up there. You're very unlikely to come out alive. So perhaps I'm lucky to be plodding across Gaul. It doesn't feel like it.

I know that my mater was beautiful. She had once been taken for the lady of the house by a high-ranking dignitary, and that had become no laughing matter either. From the dungeons she was instantly shipped off to Tarsus and all the world knew what went on in Tarsus. Anything and everything in the way of sex, but somehow I knew she would survive – although I also knew that I would never see her again. The next to go was my brother. They said to a farm that made wine, though somehow I don't believe that. Again he just went, with barely time for a tearful goodbye. He may not survive and, again, I'm unlikely to see him again. But the worst thing was Pater. They simply took him out and fed him to the lions – alive. They said it was cheaper than buying meat. I heard one scream and that was it. That scream will stay with me for the rest of my life.

'Not enough meat on you,' they leered at me, but it was no consolation.

So I sat in a corner hoping I could become invisible and, yes, I cried until I could cry no more. A few more miscreants came and went – at least one, a fat one, the same way as Pater. Then I was kicked out of my corner, stripped of my clothes and dressed in what I am now wearing. I imagine the decent clothes, supplied by the lawyer when times were good, were sold by the guards for a few copper coins to spend on strong drink. But if that was what they were after, why, oh why, had they not sold Pater out of the back door for good money? That would have been silver, not a few miserable pennies. The lions might have missed a meal, but to whom would they complain?

Then they hustled me out into the blinding light to join a group of other slaves.

'Where am I going?' I wailed at them.

'Dunno, kid. We got our orders,' was all I got from them.

Chapter 2

I watched those overweight, callous thugs waddle back to the sanctuary of their stinking haven. I was actually quite sorry to see them go. Brutal they may have been, but they were something solid, very solid, to hang onto in a life that was changing fast – very fast. Butcher me, bully me, bring me out here; they would do exactly as they were told.

I turned to see if I could find out what was going on. I was in a gaggle of slaves of all sorts – young, old, tough, superior, but surrounded by another cordon of bully boys all armed with swords, whips and clubs. At least I had left the stench of the arena behind, which was a small consolation. There were a few other boys of my age all hopping nervously from one foot to the other in anticipation of whatever might come next. The superior and snooty slaves amongst the group appeared to know what was happening but were not telling anyone they considered inferior, and certainly not a mere child dragged from the dungeons.

When it happened it was a bit of an anticlimax. With much cracking of whips and shouting, the column moved off and at a pace that I had to run to keep up with. However, it had slowed to a fast walking pace by the time we reached the city walls. By the time we were a couple of millia (miles) on from there, it had reduced to a smart amble and some of the guards had disappeared as well. The pace slowed further and it was obvious that the guards were not as fit as they were cracked up to be. By the time it was dusk we had reached a village with a compound into which we were all hustled. Then we were abandoned.

Here the group separated out into its component parts. Us boys, both younger and older than I was, sat down together. The superior brigade sat in snooty silence in a corner to themselves. The rest sorted themselves out into those who were skilled craftsmen and those who were just muscle. There came to be a bit of interaction and swapping about both within and between the various groups but it was precious little and stayed that way for most of the rest of the journey.

I just sat and tried to be brave but couldn't quite manage it. A very small boy who turned out to be only slightly younger than me came and sat very close beside me.

'They call me Atticus,' he said.

On the one hand I was glad to have this diminutive person for company but on the other I would have preferred to be left alone to try to sort out what had happened to my life.

'What's your name?'

I didn't answer.

Atticus nudged me in the ribs with a very sharp elbow.

'I said, what's your name?'

I tried to ignore him but that elbow was very painful.

'Marcus,' I mumbled.

'You stink,' he said.

'That place...' I couldn't say any more.

'Yeah.'

'What... what's happening?' I stuttered. The bravado that had kept me going up to now was rapidly running out.

'How should I know?' replied Atticus.

'Just thought you might.'

'We're being taken somewhere.'

'Where?'

'Does it matter?'

'I suppose not.'

Silence ensued.

This was broken by a lot of shouting when a cauldron of tepid soup was deposited in the middle of the compound. One guard stood over it with a ladle and another with a whip. The snooty crowd had bowls, as did a few of the others, but the rest, including all of us boys, could only hold out our cupped hands and make do with what little we could get. The cauldron was then taken away.

The march started again at first light. I must have slept but it didn't feel like it. Again there was a bit of soup but that was all. Again we were thrown into a compound at night. It was a pattern that was to continue for day after weary day, and still nobody would tell us where we were going. The only change came when we started down the mountains into Gaul and one of the 'muscle' men escaped. It wasn't until nightfall that he was missed. That delayed us for two whole days until he was handed in. That was bound to happen and, no doubt, someone received a good reward for doing so. There was no food at all for those two days. The whole group was made to stand and watch him being flogged. Most seemed impervious, but, whilst I had heard of all sorts of floggings, I had never actually witnessed one before. The guards made him start the day's march, but obviously he couldn't keep up, so they tied him to a tree, broke his legs and left him – for the wolves. I was physically sick at this point, but nobody took any notice of that either. The only good thing was that there was perhaps silent agreement that no one would try to escape from then on.

So we continued to put one weary foot in front of the other. The nights were the same. The compounds were the same. The soup was the same. But a change was in the air. The road became flatter and busier. The guards became more vigilant. They hurried us along as though they needed to be somewhere. In truth we were actually arriving somewhere: Lutetia (Paris), the capital of Gaul.

I had heard of the place but it meant nothing to me. What now? Again a compound but bigger, split into sections, and properly guarded. We were divided up – apparently at random but I assumed there was some order to it. There was. Some of the snooty crowd were leaving us here and going to their new owners. We lost most of the craftsmen and muscle as well. There must have been some major building works going on to require all these slaves. The rest of us just waited. And waited. The soup was slightly better but I still didn't have a bowl. It was while we were in Lutetia that Atticus seemed to be attaching himself to a couple in what was left of the superior slave group.

'What's that all about?' I asked him.

'They know where we're going!' he said, without answering my question.

'Where?'

'Britannia, or so they say.'

I wasn't impressed. Just more walking. But there was a glint in Atticus' eye that couldn't be ignored. I looked at him.

'And?' he said.

'So,' I said.

'They want to take me with them to wherever it is that they're going.'

'They can't do that.'

'They say they can.'

'How?'

'Money talks.' He rubbed his fingers together in the time-honoured way.

'I suppose,' I said.

It wasn't so impossible. If my pater had been with us and we were merely being transported from one owner to another with no other trouble involved, then he would almost certainly have had money with him and the authority to make a decision like this. Atticus and I had borne each other's company. We had never really been friends but had helped each other along the way. I would miss him for that.

'So, when do you go on with them?'

'No idea,' he said.

He never did have an idea and it annoyed me.

What we were waiting for happened the next day. A similar column of slaves arrived from the south of Gaul. The usual chaos arrived with them. We had a mixed bag put in with us and, if what Atticus said was true, I guessed we were all destined for Britannia. I was right. Two days later we were on the move again. Back to the plodding along and back to the poor-quality soup. Once again the guards were vicious while we were still in Lutetia, but once they had made it clear who was in charge it all settled down again.

It wasn't until we had reached it, that we realised that we were going to have to go in a boat and cross some sea. We were all horrified. We were bound to drown, but the guards and sailors just laughed at us.

'How did you think you were going to get to Britannia?' they asked.

'Can't we walk?'

'Don't be stupid. It's an island!'

That shut us up. I did remember Pater saying something like that but had taken no notice at the time, like a lot of other things that I should have been more interested in. So we embarked on a leaky old ship that was apparently only used for the transport of slaves. Because of the state of the ship I don't think our guards were any happier about this bit of the journey than we were. We knew that some of them had been off to the nearest temple to pray for a safe crossing – and this despite their having made the trip before. At least the weather was kind, and a tattered sail was raised to help those slaves who would otherwise have to row. We were kept well away from them just in case we should all try to make a break for it, but that wouldn't have been easy in a small boat like this. Just like our being moved out of Rome and Lutetia, it was all a bit of an anticlimax. When we were still in sight of Gaul there was a shout that Britannia could be seen, and it seemed we had hardly got onto the ship before we were getting off it again.

Then there was the big hold up. Having got us onto Britannia's soil, none of the guards seemed to know what was to happen next. A number of the superior set were due to go on to a place called Londinium, which we gathered was the capital of this region. That was only a few days' march away and they were anxious to get there and start living what they called a respectable life again. I understood what they meant. Others, including the couple who were taking Atticus with them, were due to go much further north to towns called Deva (Chester) and Eboracum (York). They were equally anxious to get moving, as they knew it would be colder the further north they went. That left a few boys like me in limbo, with no idea of what was supposed to happen to us. Nobody else seemed to know either, still less to care.

But our cosy world of lazy guards and compliant slaves was about to be blown apart.

Chapter 3
Mahout

It's been a hard life and it doesn't get any better. By some cock-up between the Romans and the Egyptians, my family got sold to a poncey Roman merchant who in turn thought he could turn a good profit by shipping us off to Rome itself. I doubt he made much out of it by the time he'd paid to have us transported down the Nile and across the Mare Internum (Mediterranean). I hope he lost a fortune!

My family came from Nubia and should never have got themselves involved with the Egyptians. We're a proud race who've been around for millennia before Rome was even thought of. We had cities and writing before they did and yet they think they're a gift from their gods to the human race. Now, the people of the lower Nile are a two-faced lot. They persuaded many of my race to go to live and work for them on what seemed very good terms, but when the contract to build whatever monument it was came to an end, instead of sending us back they simply absorbed us as slaves. Then we couldn't go back.

Many people consider us to be black-skinned, but we're nowhere near as black as the curly-haired men from further south. Some of us, myself included, are quite fair of skin.

Generally we are a tall people and strong with it, which suited the Egyptians just fine. They kept building these enormous monuments, pyramids and tombs all over the place, so good strong young men were at a premium. But when we got to Rome it was different – very different. At least in Egypt we worked on prestigious projects for the Pharaoh, but in the Roman Empire we were just so much muscle to work on any hard-labour project that came along. Worst of the lot was mining, which became mostly what I was doing after my group got split up, with my family going one way and me another.

Because we were tall and strong, the gang-masters were afraid of us and would use the whip or worse at the slightest provocation just to show us who was in charge. My back is a ragged mess from too much of that and, yes, I'll admit it, it's made me very cynical about the whole system. The consequence is that I'm always pushing to upset it and have a reputation as a troublemaker. It doesn't help me. Also I've never really learnt their Latin language, so I can be in the wrong without even knowing it.

Now, the Egyptians would provide us with women; it was one of the perks of working for the Pharaoh. But the Romans – no way! Too tight-fisted. So I have to make do with young boys instead when the opportunity arises – and I'm usually big enough to get first choice! And to add insult to everything else I have to wind up in Britannia, where it's so cold it could freeze your important bits off!

I'm not sure just how much longer I can put up with all this, but then there's no obvious way out. I've no intention of killing myself, as so many have who could stand it no longer.

Chapter 4

We were all shut up in a compound that would have been easy to get out of, but none of us thought it worthwhile. We were fed tales, true or not, about the ferociousness of the local population, and we knew from experience that to escape meant a certain and unpleasant death if you were caught, and that was considered as good as inevitable. Anyway life was fairly comfortable even if the future was uncertain, and slaves cannot ask for much more than that. So we were content to sit tight and see what happened next. Unusually there was not much friction in the group.

Then one morning there was much shouting and getting us sorted out into the groups to be sent to different places. It soon became obvious why. The sail of the slave transport ship had been sighted and the next consignment was due to arrive within hours.

And, oh dear, what a consignment!

The sweepings of Rome's lowest-class slaves, sold off because they were incorrigible and uncontrollable. They came with twice as many guards as we ever had, and all of them armed to the teeth. Even so we gathered that three had escaped on the journey and had suffered nastily in their dying. One had jumped off the ship and been left to drown.

Of the boys in our group, Atticus had indeed managed to go off with the couple going to Eboracum, and nobody seemed to mind, least of all the guards. The remainder of us tried to keep ourselves to ourselves, but with this crowd of toughs thrown in it was going to be impossible. This looked almost worse than being shut up in the Coliseum.

The sighs of relief from their guards were almost audible once this lot had been allowed in with us and the compound gates locked and barred behind them. The guard towers were suddenly fully manned – something we hadn't seen before as it hadn't been necessary. An enormous man with dark olive skin, black hair and a black beard seemed to be their leader, if they had one. He now drew himself up to his full height of at least four cubits and surveyed us puny little people. The rest just stood waiting to take their cue from him. His eye roved over us and kept coming back to me. It was unnerving. Very much so.

'You,' he barked, staring at me.

I jumped and looked around hoping he might mean someone else. He didn't. I made some sort of hopeless gesture to query whether he really meant me. He did.

'Yes. You. Here.' He pointed to the ground in front of him.

I shuffled to stand where he indicated, expecting to be treated as a cat treats a mouse before killing it. My time was up. I knew it.

Instead he asked, 'How did you all get here?' He waved an encompassing arm.

'Well, we came from the Coliseum. Marched in a column. Across Gaul…' I was getting faster and faster in what I was saying, to the point of being incoherent.

He cuffed me across the head, and none too gently.

'Slow down,' he said. 'Now start again so that I can understand you.'

I discovered later that it wasn't really my fault. His knowledge of the Roman language was not that good and one had to speak slowly for him to make sense of it. Also I think his brain was pretty slow. So I started all over again and tried my best to explain it slowly for his benefit, winding up what I said with, 'So here we are with no idea of what happens next, and least of all where we're going.'

'I'll find out,' he said. I obviously looked surprised, but all he did was tap the side of his nose in a conspiratorial manner.

He nodded and the rest of his tribe descended on our poor lot like vultures in order to appropriate their own personal slaves. Whilst they were deciding which of us they fancied, two of these ruffians got into an argument about something or someone and it got to being serious. Harsh words turned to a fist-fight, which in turn became a fight with no holds barred. Their supposed friends stood round in a circle and cheered them on. We boys were horrified as they just seemed to be egging the two of them on without any partisanship for either contestant. The guards did nothing to prevent it and stood in their watchtowers cheering with the rabble in the yard. It was simply a fight for the sake of a fight: fundamentally what the Coliseum and other amphitheatres were all about. It only came to an end when one of the contestants was injured to the point that he could no longer stand up. It was a sobering reminder of what us boys could expect from these louts if we should be unlucky enough to fall foul of them.

But my man was speaking again.

'Now, pretty boy, my name's Mahout and you're mine. Got it?' I nodded. 'You do as I tell you and as I want you to do and life will be OK for you. Got that?' I nodded again. 'If not…' And he made a gesture of wringing a chicken's neck. 'Got that too?' I nodded even more vehemently. 'Now let's see what you're made of.'

I wasn't at all sure what he meant, but it was soon obvious that it was my body that he was after.

'Not been allowed any women since we left Rome so you'll have to do.' I was disgusted and afraid of what was going to happen next, but he was surprisingly gentle for such a bull of a man. I was of an age when my manhood was just beginning to wake up and he gave me some really very pleasant sensations, even if some of the other things he did to me were painful in the extreme. As he said, all in the name of education. It was his little joke.

We weren't to stay in this place long. Somehow Mahout had found out where we were supposed to be going.

'Glevum (Gloucester),' he said.

'Where's that?' I asked.

'Don't mean nothing to me but it sounds bad. The guards think it's a huge joke us being sent there. "That'll cool you down" is all I can get out of them.'

It didn't sound good for the rest of us either, but it was obvious he didn't really care. For him one place was going to be as bad as any other.

'Can't be any worse than some of the places I've been,' he said.

'Not north, I hope,' I said. 'It'll be colder up there and I'm fed up with it getting colder all the time.'

'Pansy!' spat out Mahout. 'Think it's west if that helps you at all.'

'Not much. How long's it going to take us to get there?'

'They say twenty days but maybe we can make it longer.'

I didn't like the sound of that either. It meant they were going to make trouble in order to delay us. Like with our domini, trouble from this lot spelled trouble for the rest of us, who were only anxious to get where we were going, wherever that might be.

'So when do we leave?' I just didn't understand where this crowd got their information, but they were usually right.

'Tomorrow.'

If he was right then things were moving faster than I had ever known them. As predicted, the next day started early and in a state of chaos, but for sure the lackadaisical days of our journey from Rome were gone for ever.

There seemed to be guards round every corner. Whips were cracked and shoulders slashed but the rabble were adamant that they would not move without their injured comrade going with them. The guards were happy to leave him behind to die, but no, Mahout and his friends wanted to make a litter so that they could carry him. I was astounded that these hulks could be so concerned about someone whose near death they had themselves orchestrated so recently. It was all so different from the world from which I had come, but I just had to get used to it if I was going to survive – and that I was determined to do.

And so we started the weary march. It was slow, as Mahout had intended. We were moving west; I could tell that from where the sun rose and set. We spent a long time in a place called Sarum (Salisbury). I think the guards hoped to get rid of some of the troublemakers here as there seemed to be a steady procession of well-to-do citizens climbing the guard towers and then wrangling with the guards.

'You can't have the young lads!'

If I heard that once I heard it ten times.

'Any of the big ones, but not the boys.'

It seemed that we were booked for somewhere, but to lose a few of the rabble would make the guards' job easier. And I guess there was money in it too; they could surely think up an excuse for being one or two short at the end of the march.

But again – no, it didn't work for them and we all moved on as a unit. Now we were moving more north than west, and the next place we called at was Aqua Sulis (Bath), because the water here was special and could heal your ills and ailments. Taking it in turns the guards all went off to try to cleanse themselves. Mahout wanted to take their injured companion to see if the water could help him. That caused a great to-do amongst the guards. On the one hand if he could walk properly again it would speed the process up, but on the other they really couldn't let this rough and ready lout into the wonders of the baths. In the end they agreed to let him bathe, under guard of course, in the river in the hope that the water there would have some healing properties. There is no doubt that he was holding us up and also that Mahout and friends treated him as a wonderful delaying tactic. Especially as we were less than four days march from Glevum, where our fates were to be decided. As the guards hadn't managed to get rid of any of us in Sarum they had another try here. Apparently there was mining in the neighbourhood for the creamy-coloured stone from which all the posh houses and the baths were made. Mahout dreaded it: he had been in mines before and considered it the worst of all possible fates.

'Even the Games are better,' he said. 'At least there you stand a chance of survival but in a mine there is none.'

As matters turned out it might have been better here than where we did wind up, although I surely would not have been as lucky as I was to be ultimately.

It was in a corner and in the quiet of the evening when Mahout was in a soporific mood after having had his way with me, and before we left Aqua Sulis, that I asked him how he got his information, especially as it was usually right. He laughed and tapped the side of his nose again.

'Just use your eyes and ears.'

I must have looked puzzled because he went on, 'The guards want to know where we're going just as much as we do – see? They want to know when they're going to get back to their women. And they also want to know, when they do get back, if they're going to be shuffled off to some battle or another. Much safer to be guarding the likes of us than getting your head chopped off in a fight, and if it looks that way, then they'll spin the journey out. See?'

'But they don't tell you any of this, do they?'

'No. Course not. But they talk endlessly amongst themselves about mostly the same things as we do. Women, food and where we're going, in that order. Just you listen to them.'

'I shall,' I said. 'From now on.'

'You do that and we can compare what we hear. You're a bright lad, I'll say that for you, and you'll probably understand them better than I do. I just act stupid and they think I can't make out what they're saying. Truth be told, sometimes I can't.'

'We could make a good team then,' I ventured.

He looked at me, laughed and gave me a friendly shove that bowled me over and left me sprawling on the ground.

I did listen and he was right. Because I was young and no trouble I could walk close alongside the guards and they ignored me as though I wasn't there. By the time we reached Glevum I had a pretty good idea of what was going to happen next. Mahout and I talked it through and then waited for it to happen. And it did.

We were herded into the usual sort of compound when we got to Glevum, and then nothing happened. We were obviously waiting for something or somebody. This was where we were to be sold or otherwise disposed of. In due course some superior-looking domini arrived and walked around the guardwalk looking down into the compound and talking about us. I couldn't catch all they said but it went something like this.

'So, Gaius, how many of these do you want?'

'Well, ten or twelve would help. Many more than that would be a nuisance. What about you?'

'I could take the rest but I need the tough ones.'

'I know that, but these young boys can't manage a decent day's work. Absolute rubbish they send us nowadays. Their only real use is that they can get into places that a man can't.'

'That's true enough. So how are we going to split this lot up then?'

'The centurion suggests that we keep that huge bull of a man with the beard and the young lad, who's his pet dog, together.'

That was me they were talking about!

'Say he's much more manageable that way. After that it's up to us.'

And so it went on until they were satisfied. The guards came and daubed us with colours relating to where we were going, just like cattle in the market. The next morning these two were walking round again to check if they thought they had it right and a few had their colours changed. Whether they got it right even then was anyone's guess. They both looked as though they'd had a very good time the night before. Most of the boys were coming with Mahout and me, and their 'patrons' were not amused at being separated from their comforts. The injured one was coming with us too. He could just about walk by now. Once again there didn't seem to be any rush. We wondered what it was that required what the two domini had described as 'real men' and therefore where the rest of us were going and what we were to do when we got there. In a few short days we were to find out.

Chapter 5
Bouncers All

'Did either of you two ever fight in the Coliseum in Rome?'

It was Sparticus who had spoken as he, Caligula and Porcius sat around in their hut drinking the local ale.

Caligula spat on the floor. 'By the gods I hate this stuff. I wish they made some wine somewhere hereabouts. But to answer your question – yes, I did,' he said.

'If you hate the ale, why do you drink it? You say the same thing every time. You know full well it's too cold here for wine. Gets boring too, listening to you.' This was Porcius' contribution to the conversation.

Caligula blinked as his brain registered that he had another answer to deal with. 'I suppose it could be worse.' But whether that referred to the ale or fighting in the Coliseum was anyone's guess.

'They tell me it's a bad job. One of you has to die so the big man can feel like he's had a good afternoon out.' Porcius again.

'Yeah. More or less. Sometimes they let both of you off, but it's only so as you can get killed another day. Can be easy if you get a load of Christians in the ring. They hardly ever fight back, just stand there and let you kill them. Mostly. Not very exciting.'

'Cor. Glad I only ever fought in the regions then,' said Sparticus. 'I was only ever just good enough to survive. And we never had any Christians to make it easy. My heart was never really in it, I suppose. Only got into it by accident when two of them killed each other and they were a man short. Some prat thought I had the right physique!'

'Yeah. It could be a bit of a bastard,' said Caligula, 'but if you were on top, the money could be good.'

'You mean there was money in it?' cried Porcius in astonishment.

'Oh, yeah, if you were good enough. But you had to be pretty good. One man I heard of saved it all up and went and built himself his own fancy villa with it,' answered Caligula.

'Never!'

'Yeah, but he was canny. He did it over in the north of Hibernia where them from Rome hardly ever got to, so there was no chance of them being able to drag him back and get him killed off. And I did hear later that he'd become a Christian as well, so all the more need to be careful.'

'So how'd we all wind up here then?' asked Porcius. 'You especially, if you've made your fortune in the arena.'

Caligula looked a bit downcast. 'Have to admit,' he said, 'I drank most of it and the rest got pinched.'

'Much the same with me,' said Sparticus, who didn't want to admit that he'd ever had any money.

'You two are a pair,' said Porcius. 'Me, I'm well pleased to be still breathing! But how did we get here?' he asked again with some vehemence.

'Well, I got a job as a minder outside a brothel, which was good, as you got the odd one as a bonus now and again if they weren't too busy,' explained Sparticus. 'We could do with some decent women around here too.'

'You're telling me. I did just the same.' Caligula beamed at his fellows. 'And then this fancy man comes along and doesn't want any girls but wants me to come and beat Hades out of his slaves in some place called Britannia. Never heard of it but he was offering good money, so I thought it would make a change, so I took it. And here we all are,' he finished sarcastically.

'So how did you get here, Porcius?' asked Sparticus.

'The hard way. I had a half-decent job guarding money at a bank when some local guy got me drunk. Then he robbed the bank. Lucky to be alive I suppose. I found myself first on a ship, then in a gang of slaves with no idea where we was going. Kept my head down so as not to attract attention in case of something worse – and here I am. Had a word when I got here and they took me off the hard labour and gave me a whip. Good enough by me. But I agree with you, Spart, we could do with some women.'

'Yeah,' grunted Caligula. 'But it's my job to keep control of you two as well as the rest, so don't get ideas. Just play it quietly and be grateful for the ones you've got. They're so bloody particular about anything upsetting their supply of ore, you wouldn't believe it. Otherwise I'd join you in raping every woman for millia (miles) but then we wouldn't have any carters to take their bloody ore to Ariconium!'

But Porcius wasn't finished. 'So are you two freed men then?'

'Yeah, but we might as well not be for all we get paid. At least as a slave you get looked after. We have to pay for it!'

'So Caligula here and me, we could walk away,' added Sparticus smugly.

'Yeah, but where to?'

'That's the problem!'

Chapter 6

The next morning it was the usual chaos of our getting started away from somewhere where we had stayed a few days, except that this time we were being split up. Some of the 'real men' were cutting up rough about not being able to take their boys with them, and in the meantime trying to sneak them out instead. Mahout was philosophical about it.

'Looks like we might have got the easier option,' he said. 'Although I doubt it will be easy for all that. You stick around with me. There's no telling what some of these silly buggers might get up to now.'

He was referring to the lesser slaves in his lot who had not been able to appropriate a 'boy'. They would now be out to catch any of those left behind without fear of retribution. Mahout was obviously not going to let anyone make a mistake where I was concerned.

'We could even escape!' he muttered.

I was appalled. I thought there was a tacit agreement that no one was going to escape, because the consequences were too awful. It must have shown.

'Only joking,' he said.

I wasn't laughing.

Four days later the guards came back from wherever they'd been. The wisdom of Mahout came to the fore again.

'You watch,' he said. 'They'll be in no rush to get us to wherever we're supposed to go. It's the end of this job and, like I said before, there's no knowing where they'll be sent next.'

He was right. We, and they, idled around for several days before they could string it out no longer and we had to move on. Mahout thought they were just being lazy, but once we did get going, I could understand some of the problem. We had a big river to cross and it was in two parts. The first bit we could wade across when the water was low, but even then the current was strong. The second bit was wider and we had to cross in small boats, which was a nightmare for the guards as it meant we were split up and might escape. They'd get the blame, even if we died. They needn't have worried but they weren't to know that. Thus it took all day – and we were still in sight of Glevum.

We were off sharpish the following morning and pushed along as though we were suddenly in a hurry. We crossed low-lying, marshy land before coming to some steep hills and a huge forest with only a few tracks through it. Despite their bravado our guards were jumpy about the locals, who we gathered were quite likely to attack a group such as ours. Knowing the punishment that might be meted out to anyone being so stupid, I couldn't understand this, but apparently they were able to just melt back into their forest and never be found again. This was something I was later to learn all about. It was the tempered iron in the guards' weapons they were after. They weren't bothered about us. That was some consolation but not much.

'Here we are,' said Mahout suddenly.

I wasn't really watching – just putting one foot in front of the other. We had come to a large open clearing with a stockaded enclosure in the middle of it. We were bundled inside and the guards became cheerful all of a sudden. We were somebody else's problem from now on and it was our turn to be edgy. First the dominus, referred to in Glevum as Gaius, came to see that he'd got what he'd ordered, and to sign various tablets to that effect. He seemed satisfied.

'Oh dear, here come the bully boys,' commented Mahout as two or three men who looked remarkably similar to those I had left behind at the Coliseum appeared, carrying whips over their shoulders and strutting about as though they owned the place. They didn't speak. They didn't have to. It was all too plain what their function was and how they were going to enforce their will. I was terrified, but the old lags of Mahout's gang merely shrugged and let life go on. What we were to do here, in this strange place in the middle of a large forest, we had no idea. There didn't seem to be any other slaves around, so why all this muscle power? We were fed and left to tremble overnight in the open compound with no shelter. I certainly didn't sleep much and I don't think anyone else did.

Certainly there was none of the oversleeping we had become accustomed to on our travels from Rome. With the first light in the sky the bully boys were out cracking their whips and telling us to make the most of the daylight as it was the last we would see of it for a while.

'Mining,' said Mahout, in despair. 'I might have known.'

'How?' I queried.

'Somebody must have said and we missed it. Say your prayers to your favourite god, Marcus. This is going to be a killer. We'll be lucky if any of us survive. May the gods preserve the others if whatever they're doing is worse.'

This was quite a speech for Mahout. He was not usually so downhearted about anything.

'Is it really that bad?'

'It is.'

There was no time to think about this. We were led off into a building apparently built against the hillside but which in reality was the mine entrance, or one of them. This one might have been termed the administrative entrance. We entered a long, wide passage with rooms off either side, some of which appeared to be offices, and others just compartments dug out of the surrounding rock for storing a few tools. There was a steady blast of hot, foetid air coming towards us. In short, the place stank – especially after we'd been living in the open for so long.

We were penned in and herded like sheep by the bully boys from yesterday.

'Stick by me,' said Mahout. 'I'll do what I can for you.'

I nodded. That was what I had intended to do. I was too scared to do anything else. Glevum seemed like heaven now. It was hard to believe it had only been a couple of days ago. One of the gang-masters, or bully boys – take your pick – was speaking. He was known as Caligula. Needless to say, this was not his real name, but we were soon to discover that he revelled in it, along with its connotations of cruelty. He cracked his whip in order to get our attention, as if we weren't waiting on his every word anyway.

'Now, you lot, if you had any other ideas forget them. You're here to work. If it kills you, that's tough. If it doesn't, that's going to be tough as well. We,' he continued, indicating his companions, 'are here to make sure you do work, and these very good friends of ours will assist us.'

Here he held up his whip and then caught one of the boys a stinging blow on the chest with such speed that none of us even saw it happen. The boy concerned jumped and yelped as he wondered what had hit him.

'You see, you don't even have to be close for us to give you a little encouragement.' He leered at us. 'Now move.' And he started cracking the whip again but without actually touching anyone.

I determined then and there that, even if it killed me – and I knew full well that it might – I was not going to be on the receiving end of that whip. Whatever I had to do, whoever I had to bow and scrape to, whatever ignominy I had to suffer, whichever of all the things that could happen to me, I was not going to be whipped by these hooligans. Apart from the obvious immediate suffering, a serious whipping could come close to killing you anyway, and would simply lead to a lingering and pretty unpleasant death, because you would still be expected to work as though nothing had happened.

So, move, but where to? Quite obviously we were not going to be allowed outside again. So the only way was forward and into the depths – apparently in total blackness. Caligula led the way, followed by one of his henchmen who lit a brand on a stick that at least gave off some light around him. He left it to us to work out that the only way forward was to put a hand on the man in front and hope he knew where he was going because even a few cubits back from the light it was as dark as night.

In no time at all we came into a large cavern. It was lit by just the single flaming brand that we had with us and the glow from a charcoal fire over which hung a large pot on a chain suspended from the roof. Two men were tending this contraption. They looked very old and bent, but they may have been younger than they seemed.

'This is where you live,' announced Caligula. Again he leered his toothy grin at us.

I looked around.

There was nothing.

Nothing at all but a few bundles of rags in a corner and a hard, compacted earth floor. Oh, and the rocky shape of the roof above. I looked up at Mahout and, to my surprise, he put an arm around my shoulder much as Pater would have done. I all but cried at the memory, but this was no place for sentiment.

'We'll survive,' he said through gritted teeth.

I looked up at him with a lop-sided grin. It was all I could manage.

'Move on!' yelled our guide.

We moved out of the chamber on its opposite side and started downwards. To our surprise a stream of water appeared beside us as we stopped again.

Caligula pointed towards where it started.

'That end you get water,' he said, adding with a wave of his arm in the opposite direction, 'and at that end you shit.'

His instructions were to the point.

'Move on.'

We carried on ever downwards, stumbling and slipping on the unfamiliar ground that was mostly dry but every now and then wet and slimy. Soon there came the sounds of voices, shouting, curses, banging and hammering. Then the overpowering smell of dust reached us. 'Smell' is not really the right word, except for the fact that it got into your nose. Actually it got everywhere. It was something that we would never be free of from now on. It would be in our noses, our ears, our eyes and other places as well. We somehow scrambled down to the level where all this activity was taking place. Work stopped and slaves already here stood and stared at us through dust-caked eyes.

We stared back.

'This is where you work.'

He needn't have said that. Any fool could have figured that out.

Some lesser gangers came forward to sort us out.

'This is where we get separated,' said Mahout. 'But don't worry, we'll meet again in that living place, if nowhere else.'

'Must we?' I said. 'Can't I just tag along with you?'

'At this stage, no. We just do as we're told until we see how the land lies. Then maybe.'

It was good advice but I was going to feel very lost without my protector at my side. But it could have been worse. I was put alongside another boy of my own age whose name was Hadrian, and who was going to teach me all about this place. There wasn't actually that much to learn but, for the time being at least, he was to be a good friend, if in a very different way from Mahout.

We were set to work filling baskets for the likes of Mahout to carry away. We were shouted and bawled at to work faster and I instinctively tried.

'Slow down,' said Hadrian. 'No need to kill yourself sooner than they will.'

'But…' I began, indicating the man shouting at us.

'I know,' he said. 'But like the rest of us he's only making a show. The secret of surviving here is to do just enough to make it look as though you're doing what you're supposed to be doing.'

It was good advice. I was learning.

'Mind you,' he added, 'we have to do enough to keep the carriers loaded – but they're doing the same.'

My problem was that I had never had to work. Physically, I mean. Yes, I had waited at table from a young age and I had walked all the way from Rome. But actual hard work like this? No. Never. So I soon began to tire, and felt sure I was not doing my share. I didn't want Hadrian covering for me, but he was having to.

There suddenly came a great clanging, followed by a dropping of tools and a rush for the entrance passage. I got swept along, guessing correctly that this was to be the midday meal. It was in the living area we had passed through, and the old men with their cauldron had obviously been preparing it.

'Keep with me!' yelled Hadrian above the frenzy. I did my best.

From somewhere about him he produced a wooden bowl and managed to get it filled. We retreated from the bedlam and he shared it with me. I said he was to be a good friend.

'Now you go and get a refill. They won't recognise you.'

'Would they recognise you amongst all this lot?' The idea seemed impossible.

'More than likely, and that can mean trouble.'

So I did as bidden. I had played this sort of game before on the road from Rome with Mahout, and I knew the rules: there weren't any.

When I returned, Hadrian looked pleased. 'My, that was quick, and a full one too. With none spilt.' A bit of praise from him was music to my ears.

'I've been a waiter since I was six,' I laughed, adding, 'Where's Mahout? I'd have thought he'd be pushing his way in by now.'

'Possibly he was outside when the clang went. If so, he's probably missed out for today.'

That was bad news. Mahout without food was going to be trouble, and trouble meant that he might well take it out on me. Despite his pledge to take it easy and see how the land lay, this could put him on the rampage. Then anything could happen.

We were soon sent back to work and the back-breaking routine continued. Mahout did indeed miss out on our meal, such as it was, but seemed remarkably unconcerned. Maybe he was just going to wait and see, as he had said. It seemed unlikely, but in this madhouse anything was possible.

Chapter 7
Bad Boy

'Polonius,' my parents would say, 'you must be nicer to Jason. You can't always have your own way, you know.'

He was my brother, but I knew better. I could have my own way.

Inevitably I got into trouble. I could usually fight my way out of it, and the surprising thing is that I never got involved in any criminal gangs. I would have been ideal guard or attack material for them. I did hear a whisper that they didn't want me because, being so violent, I'd cause them more problems than I solved. I took that as a compliment.

Alas, one day the trouble was bigger than I could bully my way out of, and I got taken in by the soldiers, who passed me on, no doubt for a few sestertii, to fight in the games. This was not good. I knew nothing of sword work or that sort of thing. I had always relied on sheer brute force and the power of my arms and fists. I needn't have worried. I was to fight bare.

So I found myself up against this supposedly clever man who had a sword and a net – in which he managed to get me tangled up. Now that's pretty serious. He can prod you and poke you with that very sharp sword and you die slowly. Of course you can be lucky and the crowd wants you dead quickly so that they can get on with the show. Now I don't know if it was sheer rage or whether his net was poor, but I just ripped it apart. That's not supposed to happen. In the few seconds it took this fellow to take it in, I had brought my fist up under his sword arm, and, by the way his sword skittered away in the dust, I probably broke it. I then just simply knocked him down and stood with my foot on his neck. I got the thumbs up and put all my weight on it. Once he'd stopped thrashing about and was dead, I was the hero of the games.

Didn't do me any good though. Decided I was too dangerous – that's a laugh, that is! So they shipped me off as a slave to the mines in Hispania. Now, I took to this mining thing. By a mixture of throwing all my weight about and being savvy with it, I got to learning about how you mine, what to look for, and how to dig safely. On top of that, I seemed to have a nose for following the seam of whatever it was we were after. Then I got into a fight about something stupid. I won, mind, but this time they shipped me off again and I wound up here. Said they hoped I would either drown on the way or that it would kill me when I got here.

Chaos it was. Nobody had a clue what they were doing, or barely what they were mining. I calmed myself down and made myself indispensable. It worked. I've never looked back. Everyone looks up to me – or looks the other way. Got a nice wife and kids now too. Still a slave, but that's worth a lot, that is – having a wife and kids I mean. Only snag is I never could get my head into that reading and writing bit.

Cor. Then I got lucky. Just when it really mattered, along comes this kid Marcus. He knew all about reading and all that – may his god bless him. So he's had to write this for me. He's my dominus now, but he's OK, he is.

Chapter 8

Now Vulcan is a Roman god but I've never been too sure about the gods of Rome. There seem to be far too many of them, and people choose whichever one suits their needs at any given moment. Those amongst us who thought they knew about these things, prayed to Vulcan as being the one perhaps most closely concerned with our predicament, and I sort of tagged along. Mahout would have none of it. He said it was up to each of us to cope with what life threw at us. Maybe he had a point, but if he had any gods he wasn't talking about them.

But Vulcan it was who came to my rescue. It's true that I'd hardened up a bit, indeed quite a lot, but I was never cut out to be a miner. I just didn't have the stamina. I was healthy enough, but the everlasting scrabbling around in the half-dark got to me. It was Hadrian who always seemed to be carrying me and, although he steadfastly denied this, I knew better. Still, on the rare occasions when we were let out into the daylight, he didn't always beat me at wrestling.

With the exception of Caligula, the gang-masters weren't too impossible to cope with either, once you got used to their little foibles. After all, when it came down to it, I think they were slaves too, just like the rest of us.

It happened a few days after my first getting here.

'Keep working hard, but watch this,' Hadrian had said to me.

A great bull of a man appeared in our working area. It was perhaps surprising that I had not seen him before. He scowled around him but, not seeing anything obviously wrong, allowed himself to be taken to the end of our cavern, where he then fell into a deep discussion with the gang-masters.

'Who on earth's that?' I whispered to Hadrian. There was no need to whisper but it had gone very quiet in the presence of the great man and all three principal gang-masters.

'That,' said Hadrian, with great emphasis, 'is Polonius. He's the only one here who knows anything about mining and, more to the point, he's the only person here that Caligula's afraid of.'

That was a surprise. I thought Caligula was omnipotent, but apparently not. Certainly this Polonius looked like a man you didn't trifle with. One blow from his mighty arm would have probably put any one of our immediate masters on the floor.

'Watch out,' hissed Hadrian.

Polonius was coming back with his minions in tow. I had great difficulty in not laughing.

Hadrian looked at me, as they passed. 'And what was so funny about that?' he demanded.

'It's just like Rome with the emperor and his train of ministers behind him, all trying to ingratiate themselves with the great man – and that I have seen.'

'Well don't laugh next time you see him,' he scolded.

Now Sparticus was the best of the gang-masters. While he wasn't afraid to use his whip, he only did so with genuine reason. At least genuine in the sort of life that we were leading. So you can imagine how I panicked when, some time later, he singled me out from the crowd.

'Marcus,' he said, 'you're to go and see Polonius with this message.'

If he noticed me turn pale under the perpetual layer of dust that covered us, he didn't say anything, and carried on.

'Tell him that the ore appears to be running out in Seam Seven and does he want to see for himself. Also ask him if he can hurry the blacksmiths up with the picks we were promised. Have you got that?'

I repeated it to him.

'You know where to go?'

'Along the passageway where we came in?' I queried.

'Second door. Now move yourself.'

My, I was nervous. If Caligula was afraid of this Polonius, what was I supposed to feel? And why didn't Sparticus go himself? Why me? Perhaps he thought that, with me being not much more than thirteen, the man wouldn't take it out on me if he was in a bad mood. Or perhaps he would and I was expendable. I got to the door, which was open, and knocked – nervously.

'Yes?' he said.

I relayed my message.

He grunted and continued to pore over a wax tablet, oblivious to me while he pointed at the letters with a stubby finger. Vulcan must have been on my side because I must have been insane to say what I did, but I put everything, including life itself, into a few short words.

'I can read that for you if you like,' I said.

He whirled round.

'You can? But you're just a slave, and slaves can't read.'

'Yes,' I said, 'I can – and write. My pater was head slave in a large house and he taught me. I haven't done any for a long time, but I expect I can remember.'

'Well? What does it say?'

He shoved the tablet at me.

'Polonius. Is that you?' He nodded. 'Greetings, he says, and then he compliments you on the running of the mine.' Out of the corner of my eye I saw Polonius beam. 'But he wants another hundred baskets a day of quality ore, and is afraid he hasn't any more slaves for you until the next shipment in three calends' time.'

Polonius looked aghast.

'He says,' and I didn't like this bit, 'stop any slacking and get the whips out is my advice. And then he signs off, Gaius Maximus.'

He slumped onto the table in front of him.

'I'll Gaius Maximus him, I will,' he growled. 'He's been here barely a year and he should have the guts to come down and tell me to my face. Like his predecessor would have done. 'Cos he's afraid I might break his bloody neck, that's why! And I would too. To be crucified might be better than what could happen to me if I got too rough with them down below.'

He sat gazing at the wall for a long time and then seemed to realise my existence as if for the first time. 'Anyway, who are you and what are you doing here? You young toad!'

'I'm sorry,' I said. 'I was sent with a message.'

I repeated it to him.

It was time to grovel. 'I'm very sorry. I shouldn't have interrupted you by saying I could read.'

'Indeed you should,' he stormed. 'I'd be back down below in double quick time if you hadn't. And I may be yet. Go back and tell them that I'll be down to look at that seam later today and that the blacksmiths are doing their best, but are waiting for some more iron from Ariconium. Got that?'

I relayed it back to him, word for word.

'Be quick about getting that message down below and then come back. Tell them it's my orders but don't say why. Understood?' And, like Mahout, he tapped the side of his nose as he spoke.

'Yes, dominus,' I said, and was gone at the double. He wasn't really a dominus, but to use the word wouldn't do any harm. Maybe my life was going to change!

To my horror Sparticus seemed to have vanished when I got back and there was only Caligula there shouting his head off, cracking his whip about the place as usual, and not in the least concerned as to who might be in the way.

'And where in Hades have you been?' he stormed at me.

I explained as best I could and gave him both the questions and the answers. He grunted.

'Now back to work and make up what you've lost running about like that,' he yelled into my face.

I had no idea what the effect might be but having heard Polonius' reputation I had to say it.

'I have orders to go back.'

'You've what?' he screamed.

I could sense everyone else within earshot holding their breath and waiting to see what would happen next.

'Dominus,' I began. (Flattery again!) 'Polonius said I was to go back, and if you queried it I was to say that it was his orders.'

'Why?'

His rage was palpable but clearly the word of Polonius was law.

'I don't know,' I said and truly I didn't, although I guessed it had something to do with the message I had read. Better if Caligula didn't know I could read – he'd only take it out on me.

'Go then,' he growled, 'but come back quickly. I'll be waiting for you.'

I went, with a sting in the middle of my back where his whip flicked me for not moving quite fast enough. The threat was plain enough, but Vulcan was still on my side. Polonius was sitting where I had left him just staring at the wall. He roused himself.

'Good,' he said. 'I'm off. You can sleep under the table. Suggest you drop the bar over the door. We don't want anybody finding you here, do we? I'll bring you some food later if I can.'

He left me in near total darkness, but at least the air was a bit fresher up here. To my surprise he was as good as his word. He came back with food and drink – the local ale he called it, and poured out his troubles to me. I listened as I ate. As a slave, you always eat when you have the chance. You never know where the next meal will come from, if it comes at all. It seemed that he had been to see this Gaius Maximus, who had recently taken overall charge of the mine. While he was willing to listen to Polonius' arguments, he was under orders from someone even higher and somewhere else altogether to get this extra production. These must be the two we had seen at Glevum.

'I could up it a bit,' he concluded. 'But go too far and all I'll get is injured slaves, which reduces what we can get, or I have a riot on my hands. Then I get slaughtered by them down there or by him up here.'

He pointed appropriately as he glumly reviewed his chances.

'My pater always said to try food.'

The work must have made me go crazy. Who on earth was I to go making suggestions like this to a man feared even by the gang-masters for his sheer physical strength? It must have been Vulcan again putting words into my mouth.

'And what's that supposed to mean?'

'He said that if you want them to work harder, to do something unpleasant, or whatever it is, give them extra food. So, if you want the extra baskets of ore, say you'll increase the rations.'

I could virtually see the idea going round in his head.

'Might work,' he admitted. 'I'll talk to Gaius M in the morning.'

And once again he left me. As instructed I slept under his table but at least I had a full belly. There was a fearful rumpus outside during the night. I just kept very quiet and hoped that the bar held.

The next morning, Polonius was as near to being in a happy mood as I guessed he could manage.

'Spoke to him up there,' he said. I presumed he meant Gaius Maximus. 'Surprising, but he seemed to take my point. But you, Marcus, and I have got some serious work to do.' He had never asked me my name but somehow he seemed to know it. Scary.

Like a good slave I waited to be told what was going to happen next.

'He says, and may Jupiter do him a nasty, that I – me if you please – have got to put in writing what I said to him this morning and then take it to the really big man for him to consider. I told him it would be dangerous if I left here, no telling what might break loose. So he says no doubt I could find someone trustworthy to take the tablet. So you, young man, have to remember how to write pretty damned quick and then find your way to Ari… whatever its blinking name is.'

'Me?' I was appalled.

'Yes,' he said, 'you. Or you go back down below and we're all in trouble.'

Truly I would be glad to get out of the dust and labour of the mine but I was only thirteen, well a bit over, and probably wouldn't make twenty if I stayed down there, but this was silly. Even allowing for the fact that there is no harder taskmaster than one slave to another slave, I had no choice, and anyway, I was beginning to like this Polonius. Tough he may have been, but at least he'd thought to bring me some breakfast. What was I saying about extra rations?

'OK,' I said resignedly. 'So, whatever you told Gaius Maximus, now tell me and then we'll see if I can work it into something I can write.'

It took all morning and well into the afternoon, not least because I had to remember how to write. It was the best part of two years since I'd done anything like that. But in the end we worked out something that Polonius thought he could make work. It would increase the production without igniting the tempers of the likes of Mahout and others down below. Caligula would have liked nothing better than to use his whip, but even Polonius could see that it wouldn't really help. The message covered a sizeable tablet and he went off to get Gaius Maximus to approve it.

When he came back he was almost pathetically grateful.

'Cor, you got me off the hook with that one!' he said. 'He asked me if I'd done it myself and I had to admit I'd had some help. "You've got somebody bright over there," he said. "Look after him." So I brought you an apple. But you've got to leave in the morning.'

I was mightily pleased with the apple, though shaken by everything happening so fast. But tomorrow, as always, is another day.

Chapter 9
Once an Army Man

Here they know me as Julius Octavius and, although that's not quite right, it will do. I was in the army once. I was a senior officer. Legatus Legionis, no less. Well respected – until it all went wrong. And the Empire's system decrees that there has to be a scapegoat when that happens. My good friend and tribune Gaius Maximus and I, between us, became that scapegoat.

I was the officer in charge of a whole army unit in what history knows as the Battle of Adrianople. Half the time we weren't sure which tribe we were fighting or defending ourselves against, but in this case it was definitely the Visigoths and the Alans. Like all good army people we just took our orders from on high and did as we were bidden.

Prior to the battle we'd been told by our generals, by our intelligence people, and by our own spies, that this particular collection of barbarians were more interested in fighting each other than taking on the power of Rome. That made entire sense to us on the ground. We were well organised and well equipped, and there were plenty of us. We knew precisely when they were going to attack and had laid our defences accordingly.

I guess the truth of the matter is that we were complacent, blinded by our own cleverness if you like, and didn't believe that such a rag-tag enemy could organise itself properly. They came at us like a thunderbolt from all the gods of war put together. They just drove straight through us! And then had the temerity to circle round and cut the two halves off from each other. Then the slaughter began.

But that's history now. It's what happened next that brought me here. I took the blame for what happened and was chucked out of the army in disgrace and given a choice. I could either be exiled for ten years to wherever they chose to send me or I could make myself useful by coming to Britannia in the Western Empire and running this ironworks where I might – only might – be able to rehabilitate myself.

I took Britannia for the principle reason that I could bring my dear wife Aemelia with me. My friend and colleague Gaius Maximus chose to go wherever they sent him. Mistake. However, once I had got myself organised here I went to a lot of trouble to get him back from the island to which he'd been banished. I claimed I needed a good manager to run part of this organisation, and for that, as we'd had experience of each other's abilities, he was the obvious choice. The powers that be believed me, and now he runs the mine where our ore comes from.

Whilst everyone knows we're army people, we're technically civilians, even if we're in control of what the soldiers do here. It can be a little bit tricky at times, but diplomacy – buttering up the army ego – usually works.

I have a problem, however, and Gaius Maximus is that problem. Despite my good opinion of him in the past and my recent efforts on his behalf, he just doesn't measure up. He still believes himself to have been slighted and he can't adjust to his new situation. He wishes he was still in Rome, and in the Roman army in particular. He tries to live that lifestyle here and it doesn't work. Aemelia and I have made that adjustment. We've made the most of living here and only occasionally hanker for the life that was. Much as I like Gaius, I fear for him. If anything goes wrong for him, he'll be done for.

Chapter 10

So, the next morning I was equipped with a special satchel to carry the tablet, together with a special small tablet that gave me free passage if anyone should think I was a runaway slave.

I didn't realise it at the time but this was a very real possibility and there was a sizeable bounty to be had for turning in a runaway slave. This was particularly so for soldiers, who stood not only to earn the reward, but also to be awarded a promotion. I was also given a clean tunic, not new of course, but at least not thick with dust.

Perhaps the strangest thing was that nobody seemed to have any very clear idea as to how one actually got to Ariconium.

'Can't I go with one of the carters on a load of ore?' I asked Polonius. It seemed obvious to me.

'I would agree,' he said, 'but strict orders from Gaius M. He doesn't want any chance of this tablet going astray. So you've got to make your own way there even if it takes a bit longer. Anyway I should guess you'll be quicker. You can walk faster than the speed they go!'

I shrugged. At least I wouldn't be scrabbling about filling ore baskets.

In fairness, one of the carters did at least point me in the right direction, saying I should follow the cart tracks and it would be obvious. I doubted that, and it wasn't, or at least the first part wasn't.

From somewhere a bit over halfway, and by then the following day, it became plainer as not only were there ore carts on the move but also ones carrying wood to make the charcoal for the smelting. The men with these were local, not slaves like the rest of us, and some weren't too happy to give me directions, but most were willing to help a young lad. Eventually I came to an area with no trees at all – they had all been felled for charcoal – and then it did become obvious where I was going. I could see a great pall of smoke in the distance and all roads led in that direction. The getting to Ariconium turned out to be the easy bit.

The whole place seemed to be some sort of military establishment and obviously the iron being produced was sought after and valuable. My instructions were simple: 'Go to Ariconium and deliver this message tablet to Julius Octavius.' My simple request at the guardhouse to see this man caused consternation. You would have thought that the next lot of Punic wars had broken out.

It seemed that no one, but no one, just came asking for Julius Octavius, least of all a thirteen-year-old slave. I had to show my pass several times as I was gradually ushered up the hierarchical tree. I also had to show the tablet I had brought to prove that it really was addressed to him and then given another small one to certify that the seals had been broken officially by the soldiers protecting the place. I had been nervous when first sent to see Polonius, but that was nothing compared with what I was doing now. Eventually I was brought into the presence by a sycophantic eunuch who I guessed was also a slave, though he may not have been. I explained my business to the man I presumed to be Julius Octavius.

'Ah, word from my good friend Gaius Maximus,' he said.

I handed over the tablet. He read what was written on it and a scowl appeared across his forehead.

'This I have to think about,' he said, and to the sycophant, 'Find this slave somewhere to stay overnight and be sure that we can find him whenever he's needed to carry a message back.'

The eunuch bowed and scraped and we left. He took me to some sort of hostel for visiting slaves and it had to be said that the food wasn't so bad, even pretty good. The next day I spent hanging around waiting to be called, and it wasn't until another night had gone by that I was finally fetched. Hanging about was tedious, especially because I was forever being accosted by soldiers hoping to get promoted for finding a slave sitting around doing nothing. My pass got me by with those that could read, except for one smart-arse who dragged me before his superior and got a right telling off for his trouble.

The eunuch seemed even more deferential than before. I soon found out why.

'Who wrote this?' demanded Julius Octavius, pointing at the tablet I had brought.

'It has Gaius Maximus' name on it, dominus major.' I could bow and scrape too, and hopefully dodge what I suspected was coming.

'I know that, but who wrote it?'

'Well, Polonius is the foreman, dominus. He produced it.'

'But I know that he can't write, so who wrote it?'

I had no choice.

'I did, dominus.'

'Huh. So who composed it?'

I had no choice but to tell the truth, whatever the outcome might be. On the positive side he did not now seem to be quite so imperious, or acting as though he was about to bring my life to an untimely end.

'Dominus, Polonius had a discussion with Gaius Maximus, who asked him to put his ideas in writing. As you say, Polonius cannot write, so he told me all about it and together we composed a proposal.'

'So have you read what has been sent to me?'

'Oh no, dominus. I only know about what I wrote for Polonius,' I said, quietly transferring any blame, if there was any, to Polonius.

'Just as well.'

What was that supposed to mean? But he was carrying on.

'You're Marcus, aren't you?'

I had to admit that I was, although how he knew my name I had no idea.

'Well, Gaius Maximus, who, I would remind you is a very good friend of mine, has sent me exactly what you wrote.'

I was both astounded and appalled.

'Separately he explains that not only did you write that for Polonius, but also that some of the ideas are yours too.'

So that was how he knew my name, but, dear Diana, why didn't Polonius tell me? Maybe he didn't know that Gaius M was going to add his own comments.

'He says you are to be commended.'

Wow!

'So you are to get back to the mine with the clear water with my answer as soon as possible, which – and this is for your ears only – is favourable. Now go!'

'Yes, dominus, and thank you, dominus.'

Bowing and scraping again!

'Go, Marcus, and quickly.'

I went, with his order to do so ringing in my ears. The eunuch was pleased to see me go and gave me a supercilious look as I passed him. I suspected that this one could be a jealous individual and eventually I was to be proved right.

It was at this point that I discovered that I must have a pretty good sense of direction, because I was able to recognise where I had come previously and thus found myself back at the mine later that same afternoon. However, the problem I did have and had been thinking about all the way back was to whom I should give this return missive. On the one hand I was working for Polonius, but the tablet was directed to Gaius Maximus. In truth it should go to him, but what would Polonius say if I bypassed him? Telling him that he couldn't read it anyway would put me straight back down the mine, there to be the butt of Caligula's wrath. Did I have the courage, as a very lowly slave, to take it direct to Gaius Maximus? Especially with him being the friend of the great man in Ariconium. I finally decided that I didn't and I would go to Polonius and he could take it on.

As it turned out, I needn't have sweated about it. They were standing together talking in the mine yard when I got back. I took the bull by its horns and handed the return tablet to Gaius Maximus. Instead of instantly dismissing me as I expected, he invited me to listen to whatever reply he had received from Julius Octavius.

'You had a big hand in writing the request, Marcus,' he said, 'so you might as well hear the answer.'

He read it first and smiled.

'Good news, Polonius. Julius Octavius agrees to our proposals and, in a nutshell, we are to do the best we can for him without creating a riot.'

Despite his bulk I swear that Polonius stood up straighter and taller with that news as though it had been entirely his own doing.

Then Gaius M turned to me.

'As for you, Marcus,' he began. I didn't like the tone of this, but at least he was still smiling. 'I didn't read the tablet out verbatim as it might have upset Polonius here.' He winked at Polonius. 'But you seem to have impressed my friend at Ariconium and I have as good as an order to look after you.'

Now what was that supposed to mean?

'You will continue as a scribe to Polonius and act as a runner to Ariconium, so that we shall keep in better touch with them and hopefully know in advance what they want. That way we should be able to meet their needs without too much trouble.'

'Thank you, dominus,' was all I could manage to say to him. To myself I said, 'May all the gods be praised!'

Gaius Maximus' apparently simple statement precipitated a tug of war that threatened to get very unpleasant, and which I found centred on me. Gaius M departed, obviously feeling very pleased with himself and thinking it had all been his idea. Polonius then dragged me into his office, also thinking it was his idea. There he shook me warmly by the hand and pronounced that he would be forever in my debt.

When I looked doubtful he said, 'Look, you got me out of that one with being able to write and with your ideas about the food.'

I still looked doubtful.

'Listen,' he said, 'Without you I'd be labouring back down in the mine by now. Me and you are going to make a great team.'

He was euphoric. I still needed convincing.

'But I owe you just as much,' I said. And I did, too. 'Without what's happened, I'd definitely still be down the mine!'

'Forget it,' he said, and then became practical. 'You'd better continue to sleep in here. And make sure you keep the bar across the door. I don't want anyone dragging you out.'

It turned out to be very good advice. The next morning, soon after work had started for the day, Polonius gathered his gang-masters together and harangued them about wanting more production from the mine and said they had to ensure that all slaves worked their hardest. Caligula beamed at the thought of being able to use his whip more generously.

'But lay off the whip unless it's essential,' said Polonius. I saw Caligula's face fall. He even looked aghast. 'To encourage them, more food is to be provided. I don't want any, and I mean any, slaves injured by whips or by accidents. I want to have a full tally available for work all day, every day. Is that understood?'

Caligula looked deflated.

'Then I want him back,' he said sullenly, pointing the heel of his whip at me.

'So you may, but you're not getting him.'

'And why not?'

'Because he can do one thing that neither you, nor I for that matter, can do.' Polonius was giving like for like. 'He can read, and he can write!'

'Pansy!' Caligula was scathing in his attitude as he spat the word out.

'I've said you're not getting him. And what I say goes.'

But Caligula wasn't giving up easily. His sort don't.

'You're asking for more production,' he said. 'And you're taking away from me a good strong young slave so that you can keep up with the dominus in the big villa. Is that it?'

He had a point and I wondered how Polonius was going to overcome it. I certainly hoped he would. I really didn't want to find myself back in the mine.

But it was obvious from the colour of his face that Polonius was losing patience with Caligula. Also the other two gang-masters had moved away slightly and were rather too obviously trying to avoid getting dragged into the argument. Perhaps they too relished the idea of a bit more food – not that they actually needed any!

'Because I say so.' There was finality in Polonius' tone. 'And if you don't like it, I'll have your whip back now and you can join the team carrying up baskets of ore!'

Caligula knew when he was beaten. He shook his whip, his symbol of authority, at me and headed for the door.

When they were gone, Polonius looked at me and said, 'Be careful.'

'I will be,' I replied.

What else was there to say? If Polonius had carried out his threat, I shudder to think what nasty retribution might have awaited Caligula if Mahout and his cohorts were given their opportunity. They would not have worried about the consequences, but it was not to be – yet. And in the meantime, through no fault of my own, I had made a bad enemy.

I only had to be within a whip's reach of Caligula and a stinging strike like a snake biting would land on me. He knew I was avoiding him and he relished his cleverness. There were times when I couldn't sidestep him, and then it was best to get in really close so that he couldn't use the whip, and there were others when I had to see him on official business for Polonius. On these occasions he was sullen and uncooperative, although he knew full well that an order from that source had to be obeyed. We both knew where we stood, but it didn't help. Ultimately the problem of Caligula was to be solved, but not in a way that one might have expected.

Chapter 11
Serving Wench

I think I come from Hispania, but I really don't know. It's sad because I should like to know where I came from. I don't remember having any parents, though obviously I must have done. But were they parents who loved me, or was I a baby to be got rid of as rapidly as possible?

I don't even know how I got my name. I've always been Clio but I've never come across anyone else with that name. Was it given to me by my parents, whoever they were, by someone who looked after me, or by other kids on the street? Come to that, I don't even know how old I am! I can only guess from the fact that a couple of years ago I started to bleed, as all women do, and they tell me I must be at least twelve to do that, so let's say that I'm fourteen now.

So, how did I get here? Well, like I say, we kids were living off the streets and one day a crowd of us got rounded up by the soldiers. Where? You may well ask, but I don't know. It was just the city where we lived, or rather existed. Anyway, as I was saying, we were rounded up and sold to whoever would pay something, however little, for us. The head soldier kept me for himself. All he wanted was sex with a little kid. He wasn't bad in so far that he fed and clothed me – quite well too – but he wanted me at any old time of the day or night. And he was big in me, especially at first. Still, you get used to anything.

It was him who brought me to Britannia. Got posted to Londinium and got promoted in rank, then asked to stay. So he sends for his missus and you can guess who has to go. I think he'd got fed up with me by then so I'd have been on the move anyway. By the time he knew his wife was actually coming, he had to get me out of the way in double quick time. He couldn't wait for a decent auction in which to sell me, so he gave me to a mate of his that he owed a favour to. This man was being sent to some place that nobody had ever heard of, called Glevum, and expected to be there a while. That suited both of them just fine as then I'd be well out of the way and there was no chance of his wife coming across me.

But this man was different. He had a nasty vindictive streak in him. Typical soldier – thought the world owed him something. Always wanting to pull rank on someone. He fed me just about enough to stop me being too skinny when I was in his bed, which was actually not that often. Nothing like his predecessor! He never bought me any new clothes and I had to make do with those I'd brought with me. He seemed to prefer the local girls he had absolute power over, with no possible comebacks. After all, as I was his slave he did have some responsibility, be it ever so small, for my welfare.

The only good thing about this arrangement was that I simply didn't have enough to do, so I started cleaning his lodgings. With that he got grandiose ideas and had me wait at table for him. It was a bit of guesswork on both our parts as neither of us knew how the posh lived. At least we could laugh about it. It all sounds very cosy, doesn't it? But then, like everything else in my life, it suddenly went wrong – or, actually, right!

My soldier man wasn't a great gambler and usually came out on top when he did, but this time it went disastrously wrong. There was no way he could pay his debts, and I would have to go, and at a good price too. How he knew I shall never know, but the real boss man around here heard about it and called my soldier owner in. This fellow had a reputation for knowing exactly what was happening everywhere around him.

He gave my man a father and mother of a dressing down that must have made him feel like a tiny insect, but the upshot was that he offered to buy me for enough to pay off his debts. The soldier didn't have a choice. Me? I was scared silly. I mean, this man, and I didn't even know his name then – it was only later that I discovered it was Julius Octavius – he really was somebody, and I had just been scraped off the streets. He had his wife with him and rumour had it that they were very lovey-dovey together, so I doubted if it was the sex he wanted.

I was right. He wanted someone to serve food and drink in his office, and more particularly if he had business visitors or guests. I needed a bit of training but soon got into it, and for the moment at least he seems well pleased. More important, he feeds me well and I have a whole range of new clothes to wear. The downside is that the soldier man – Tiberius is his name

– is still here and he's just as nasty as ever. In fact more so, as he hates to see me with the chief dominus, and there's nothing he can do about it. However, I do have to be a bit careful and not be about anywhere in the dark.

And a bonus to all that: there's this young fellow who comes to see him pretty regularly. Now that *is* good news.

Chapter 12

And so there began what was to be one of the pleasantest periods of my life, even if it didn't last more than a year or so. I started making regular trips to Ariconium, at least once a week and very often more than that. With the route having become second nature, I could make it there and back in a day – if I didn't get held up when I got there. This of course was in the summer time. Being so far north the days get very short in the winter and the domini didn't want their courier being out after dark with, possibly, important information about him. The natives were never entirely trusted hereabouts, and there were cases of slaves going missing even if they were going about their legitimate business. There was in fact no chance of them being able to read the messages I was carrying. They seemed to have no writing ability of their own, never mind being able to read the Roman script. But that was not the point. I might have been expendable but the messages were sacrosanct. There was, I suppose, the off-chance that they might have fallen into the wrong hands. Even then, the safety of Rome and its empire was hardly likely to be jeopardised by what I was carrying. But once again that was not the point.

Oxen are, I think, possibly one of the slowest-moving beasts in the firmament, but they can pull a tremendous load, and go marginally faster with an empty cart than with a full one. I got to know a few of the carters passably well, and I even think some of them felt sorry for me trudging to and fro along what they considered 'their' route. As a consequence I occasionally got a ride on one of the returning carts. This saved my legs and my feet, and could be ideal when the weather was wet or cold. The downside was that walking did at least keep one warm. The other interesting side of doing this was that I got to learning a smattering of the local language so that I could talk a little with the driver of whoever's cart I was on. It was to stand me in good stead in the future although I didn't know that yet.

All the troubles I had getting into the place on that first occasion disappeared. I had simply become part of the scenery, the everyday life of Ariconium. Occasionally a new arrival in the guardhouse would have to refer to his senior but that was all of it. I got to being expected in the hostel and even, I think, got the pick of the food.

This hostel was run by a remarkable woman who was known as Helen, or, to give her her preferred title, Helen of Troy. I can only think that she acquired this name because she was big enough to contain a whole army! She was not someone to be trifled with and I loved her dearly, even if she was about as different from my own mother as it was possible to be. She had arms like a blacksmith's, a raucous voice, and a command of bad language that would have put a Pilus Prior centurion in the shade. Underneath this rough exterior was a heart of gold, and she was later to effectively save my life.

Surprisingly too, the sycophantic eunuch who guarded all Julius Octavius' business affairs thawed a little to my presence. Only a little bit, mind. In truth the whole scheme was working out. Gaius Maximus did indeed produce more and better food. Polonius used his mining skills to find another seam of ore and also to streamline the winning of it. Production increased and everyone was happy, with the exception of Caligula, who continued to try to reclaim me to where he thought I belonged and where he could take out his frustration on me.

Despite my slightly elevated situation I did see Hadrian on occasion, and he would tell me how things were 'down below'.

'We're working harder, but with better food, life is more bearable.'

I listened but didn't say anything.

'And the gang-masters aren't as vicious as they used to be. Now that's a real improvement.'

'Things have changed then,' I said diplomatically.

'Yeah,' he said. 'Something must have been said because even Caligula is laying off his whip. He's so frustrated that there are times when I think he'll blow up with not being able to use it!'

'Then that has to be good.'

'By Vulcan it is. If we can keep the ore coming then maybe it'll stay that way.' As an afterthought, he added, 'Until some idiot does something really stupid and the beast gets his chance to go back to doing what he does best.'

Overall this was sheer joy for me to hear and I passed it on to Polonius, particularly the warning about Caligula. He grunted and changed the subject very much as though he was not really in agreement with the new regime.

Polonius was actually the one who surprised me most. He seemed wholly content with his lot, seeing no reason for improving it, not even by being able to read the communications himself. He didn't want to go anywhere, least of all to Ariconium to see the ultimate product of his labours. Even when his wife was sick with some local malady, probably brought on by the cold wet weather in these parts, it was me he sent to the shrine of Nodens with an offering on her behalf. She recovered, so I suppose it was fine. I didn't mind because it gave me the chance to see the great river Sabrina that flows through these parts and was much talked about by both Romans and locals alike, although the latter called it the Severn. It certainly was big and more like a sea than a river. One of the locals explained to me something that it took me a long time to understand but apparently it has a thing called a 'tide', and twice each day the water comes in and goes away again! He also said that, usually in the spring or autumn, the river comes up in a great wave but I think that's just nonsense. Apparently I saw it with the water there, otherwise it's just banks of sand and mud with a trickle of a river in the middle.

I spoke to Mahout about this, simply because I saw him shortly afterwards, and asked whether he had ever come across anything like it. To my surprise he had, and he seemed to take a particular interest in what I was telling him.

'On the Mare Internum,' he said, 'there is a little, perhaps half a cubit, but once when I was in Hispania I saw the endless sea that goes on to the end of the world and there, there is something similar.'

'And does it do the same?' I said, 'Come in twice a day?'

'I don't know because I only saw it as we passed by from one Hades hole to another.'

'And did it come in a big wave like the man told me?' I was intrigued by all this.

'Oh, for goodness sake, Marcus!' And he ruffled my hair like he used to on the march. 'You're always wanting to know the impossible! But I'll tell you this, there were some very big waves in that sea. I wouldn't have wanted to be in a boat on them.'

I laughed.

'But, if you find out any more about how it all works, you let me know. I could even be interested myself.'

'You? Interested in something other than food and causing trouble?' It was my turn to pull his leg.

'Must be catching from you!' he said, and went off to load up some more carts, calling over his shoulder very much as an afterthought, 'If you find out any more about it, tell me. I should like to know.'

I couldn't think of a quick reply so shrugged my shoulders and went off to do whatever I was supposed to be doing. Nevertheless I recalled his comments some calends, maybe nearly a year later, when I was sent with some urgent messages to a small town a bit further inland than Nodens' place, a new settlement on a high point overlooking that great river. This time the water was what they described as 'out'. It was true: there seemed to be no water at all. The centurion in charge of this new town laughed and told me to come back next week and he would show me something.

'Not up to me, centurion,' I said. 'I'm only the messenger slave and go where I'm sent.'

'Bit like being in the army,' he muttered. 'But come if you can.'

As luck would have it, Polonius did send me back there a week later and the centurion was as good as his word. The place was chaotic with everybody moving their possessions back from the river.

'Whatever's going on?' I asked.

'You'll see,' he said and took me up to the highest point of the place, overlooking the river. All I could see were millia of empty sandbanks with a smallish strip of water amongst them. Then there came a roaring sound like thunder in the distance and the centurion looked down at me.

'Watch,' he said.

Then I could see it coming, a wall of water at least four cubits high taking everything with it, tumbling and crashing as it came, sweeping over its banks and into the lower parts of the town. Now I understood why people were moving their goods up the hill. At best a good many of them must have lost their huts and homes.

'How do you know when this is going to happen?' I asked, awestruck by what I had seen.

'I don't,' he said, 'but the locals do and, despite what my superiors would say, I'm always happy to listen to them. They say it's always biggest and best, or worst, in the spring and you can tell by the river being almost empty of water – like today.'

But I was still curious.

'Whatever happens to any boats that are on the water?' I asked him. 'They must get smashed to pieces.' He seemed keen to educate me in these matters.

'Ah,' he said, 'they do, but if you look down there…' and he pointed downstream of where we were standing, 'you'll see some masts sticking up on the bend of the river.'

'Yes,' I said.

'Well that's where all the smart merchants who have moved into this new town keep their boats. It's only like a little stream runs in there but the entrance is so narrow that the waves outside don't affect the pool of water on the inside. Bulla Port, they call it locally!'

He laughed at the pun.

'Harbour for the domini,' he smirked.

I laughed too, but I was intrigued and promised myself a visit one day when I had the chance.

I had been amazed by this whole phenomenon and was in some haste to get back to tell Mahout about it, but I was to be disappointed in him. Whilst he listened intently enough, he didn't seem as excited as he should have been if he really was taking an interest in these things. He was soon back to grumbling about food and life generally.

This local god Nodens turned out to be quite good. I have no idea how Polonius knew about him, but then he kept a lot of things to himself, such as his mining knowledge. Certainly his wife recovered from her illness and seemed as good as new. In the winter my feet used to get very sore with the endless walking on wet, muddy tracks – I wouldn't deign to call them roads – and I used to stop by a shrine to Nodens in the lea of the woods just before I got to Ariconium. Being a slave only just above the bottom of the slavery tree, I was never able to make any sensible sort of offering, but I used to pause, wash my feet in the spring water, and ask for help with my feet. It seemed to help or maybe it was just the effect of having a break in my walking. Or washing my feet!

However, far more efficacious than anything Nodens could contrive were the ministrations of a girl who waited upon Julius Octavius. On one occasion when he was in an expansive mood, in a back-handed way he introduced us and put us together.

'Clio,' he said. Now I knew her name. 'Whenever Marcus is here…' And thus she knew mine. 'Make sure you find him something to eat and drink too. He will have walked a long way.'

As to why he was taking this interest in my welfare I neither knew nor cared, but if it gave me access to Clio that was all that mattered. Oh, and the extra food. And good food it was too, fit for a dominus! However, despite a slight thawing in relations, the eunuch wasn't best pleased with my familiarity with his bulla and still less my getting friendly with Clio. He made it plain that Julius Octavius had no business to be discussing the details of the mine with the likes of me, and still less offering me the services of his handmaiden. From then on I always seemed to have to wait a little longer before being allowed into 'the presence'. I should have been more aware, but then I was young and more than a bit cocky.

For me, Clio was Venus and Diana rolled into one. We were both slaves, so had no control over our lives, but she always did her best for me. In particular she somehow managed to obtain a salve of some sort that helped my poor feet greatly. She said it was a local remedy made from the herbs to be found in the forest. It was a good excuse to get her to rub it on.

Quite obviously we met when I was there on business, as it were, and very occasionally outside of Julius O's office. These meetings were fleeting but great for both of us, and I had high hopes that we might come together more permanently. I had no idea how that could possibly happen, so just played along. After all I had time on my side – or so I thought.

Chapter 13
No longer a man

It's not so much the being castrated, although that's obviously painful and bloody. It's what it does to your soul. It's what you become. It's what you then have to be. The butt of everyone's jokes, whether they be man or woman.

I'm a tall man, and I was a big man, and a proud man, before... well, you know. I was captured in a riot in Carthage. We were young and silly and thought that a few hundred of us could get the better of the Roman invaders garrisoning our country, but then youth can be pretty stupid. We all know that. Most were slaughtered in the riot, and a large number of those who survived were killed off later by disembowelling, crucifixion, burying alive, and other unpleasant methods. A very few, twenty at the most, who were uninjured in the fighting were taken away and castrated. I was one of the lucky ones to survive that process. If you can call it lucky! We were then sold off to the women of the town and the soldiers made a few gold coins for themselves.

These women then made a few more gold coins, without their husbands' knowledge, by selling us on again to their friends in Rome. So there was a consignment of eunuchs shipped to Ostia and then walked to the capital of the empire. Again we were distributed amongst a selection of the ladies of the city. It was pretty obvious that we were going to be sold on yet again and some more gold made out of us with which these ladies could preen their hair or buy themselves jewellery. However, I had always been good with numbers, so I became useful to my lady, who was being fleeced by her bailiff.

She kept me until that bit of nastiness was sorted out and the bailiff had killed himself so that his children could inherit his ill-gotten gains instead of them being appropriated by the state. Because of this she was able to sell me on to her friend Aemelia for a considerable extra number of gold coins because the latter's husband was being posted to an administrative job in Britannia and thought that somebody good at numbers might come in useful. Eventually I came to this place – for which I feel an all-consuming hatred. It's cold, it's wet and, because I'm the only eunuch here, I'm the standing joke for everyone from the meanest slave upwards. They won't even move out of my way – I have to walk round *them*!

It was on the journey from Rome that my body fell apart. My voice changed to something more like a woman's and I lost the urge to assert myself. I became flabby and had no will to be any different. I do as I'm told without question – it's easier that way. But my brain still functions. Oh, yes, that still works. If I can find out what's wrong in the bookkeeping, I can also cover up what I want to be wrong. I may have no one to pass on *my* ill-gotten gains to, but I can use them to bribe others to do my bidding.

And soldiers will do anything for money.

Chapter 14

The Fates had been good to me. I was enjoying life. A slave has to savour what pleasure he can from his lot. Take each day as it comes, for tomorrow he may be sold or die, or both. So I had made the most of my trips across the Forest and elsewhere. I had learnt a lot from the carters who had kindly given me rides on some occasions and I had become quite friendly with some of them. They knew I was a messenger slave and was unlikely to harm them, as a soldier would almost certainly have done. I had learnt a lot about the Forest and its ways and, more usefully, how to find my way about in it. It no longer looked all the same to me. I recognised its hills, some of them quite high, and its valleys, equally deep, despite the almost continuous tree covering. Chance had also taken me a bit further afield, for example to that new town of New Hamm, and to the temple of Nodens. I had taken an interest in the area and in its way it had repaid me.

But it couldn't last, and one beautiful spring morning it came to an abrupt end.

I had just left Ariconium when I saw Sparticus, the gang-master, coming towards me very much out of breath and in a state of great agitation.

'Marcus, thank the gods I've found you,' he gasped.

He was the best of the bunch and had done well to find his way this far.

'By all the Fates, what on earth brings you here?' I asked him.

He struggled for breath.

'Five messages,' he wheezed. A long walk in a hurry was patently something he was not used to. He held up the fingers of his left hand.

'There's been a riot,' he panted, pulling in his thumb. 'Gaius Maximus is dead.'

'Dead?' I echoed. He nodded and pulled his index finger down.

'Polonius is injured but should live.'

'That badly?'

He pulled his second finger in and I had visions of Caligula seizing his chance to get me back in the mine and using his whip very much to my disadvantage. I shuddered.

He pulled the third finger down. 'He sent me. Said you'd know what to do.'

That I would know what to do! Polonius must have been badly injured to think that.

He stood panting, with one finger left up and a worried look on his face.

'And what's that one for?' I nodded towards the upstanding finger.

He still hesitated.

'Come on,' I said. 'You must have been there.'

'No,' he said, 'I wasn't. Had the shits. Must have been something I ate. Heard a commotion and crept out to investigate only to find that most of those who should have been underground were up top on a killing spree.' Again he hesitated. 'Sorry, I crept back into my hut and kept quiet.'

He would have been well aware of what the sentence would be for admitting to that, but I suppose he trusted me.

'And Caligula and Porcius?'

'Dead.'

The final finger went down.

I wasn't in the least surprised. It was inevitable that in any sort of uprising those most hated would be the first to die. At a personal level I was glad to see the back of Caligula. It would suit me very well to keep Sparticus' secret.

'Come with me,' I said. Who was I to start ordering him about? But I was only mildly surprised to find that he followed me as though he was my pet dog. He was out of his depth in these surroundings and overcome by what he saw around him. I took him into the place – it was neither city nor town, nor even village – took him to the hostel where I always stayed when I was here overnight, and asked Helen of Troy to find him something to eat.

"Ere,' he said. 'How do you manage to walk into this place and nobody says you nay? And with all these soldiers guarding it. And then go ordering food like you owned it as well?'

'You forget, Sparticus, that I've been coming here regularly for a while now. Most people know me and, hopefully, trust me not to do anything stupid. Now you stay here, and don't for any reason go off anywhere. There's plenty here only too quick to take advantage of a stranger, especially one without any passes.'

'Na, so help me, I shan't.'

And I believed him. He was scared and overawed, much as I had been on my first visit, and he didn't have the authority that I'd been given.

I went to find Julius Octavius, who was not pleased to see me back again. I knew he wouldn't be, but I liked even less the snide grin of his sycophantic eunuch. I explained what had happened and how I had heard.

'Who's this Sparticus?' he asked.

'The last of the gang-masters. The others are dead. He was sick and not at work this morning, although – if I might venture an opinion, dominus?'

He raised an eyebrow in acknowledgement. There I was sticking my neck out again!

'He is, or rather was, the most humane of the gang-masters and, for what it's worth, I think he may have been fed something to keep him away.'

'Really. Honour among thieves, eh?'

'Something like that, dominus. And if I might venture a further opinion?'

He looked at me quizzically. I could get myself executed for doing this.

'I think it might also have been timed for while I was away. That way there would be no quick way of reporting to you.'

He was gently nodding his head as the impact of what I was suggesting made sense to him. I carried on.

'The final part of his message from Polonius was that I would know what to do. I think that must have been some sort of joke, but I've reported everything that Sparticus told me.'

'Hah. That Polonius is no fool. Somebody has to go and sort this mess out. Now I'm going to venture an opinion, as you so politely put it, and take a guess at what his thinking is.'

He paused and looked very hard at me. I had to work equally hard to meet his stare.

'I think,' he said – very slowly, 'that the best person to do that is you.'

'Me!' I squealed like a stuck pig.

'Yes, you, Marcus. It must have been very pleasant for you wandering to and fro carrying messages, but I've thought for a while that you're wasted as a messenger – as, incidentally, did my late good friend, Gaius Maximus.'

'But, dominus, I'm not yet sixteen…' I trailed off. I was a slave after all. I knew only too well that he could have me do anything he wanted and just as easily discard me if his idea didn't work. Feed me to some lions, if he had any here! I didn't have a choice and there was always a chance that the food might get better.

'Then we had better decide between us what you're going to do. Sit down.'

This was unheard of – that a slave of my rank should sit down with a man like Julius Octavius! Even the sycophant wasn't allowed to sit, for all his bowing and scraping. I hesitated but remained standing.

'Oh, for Vulcan's sake, Marcus, sit!'

Like I said, he could have me do anything.

We sat, with me very much on the edge of my seat so that I could leap up and not be seen casually sitting around with such a man as this. He even called for Clio – my Clio, as I thought of her – to bring us drinks and pastries. I must admit she did look a bit surprised to see me sitting there, for all the world as though I was part of the furniture. And the expression on the eunuch's face when he happened to pass by was worth all the anxiety that was to come. I was being treated as an equal by no lesser a personage than Julius Octavius himself!

So we discussed what was to be done. As neither of us knew exactly what had happened or who was behind it, Julius Octavius could only give me guidelines as to how I should deal with it all when I got there. He was, however, adamant that he was giving me the authority to do so and that he would back up whatever I saw fit to do. Another consignment of slaves was due but he did not know when, and in any case he would need a good many of them to keep his furnaces going. To this end he would provide a chariot to take Sparticus and me back as quickly as possible. He wanted us back there that same evening.

The important thing was that I had to get the mine back into production again, and I had to keep up a supply of ore to Ariconium. That was the first essential and that was the sting in the tail to my sudden promotion.

'One final instruction,' added Julius Octavius as I stood to leave, 'and this is personal. Assuming they really are dead, send the bodies of my friend Gaius Maximus and his wife here with a reliable carrier, so that I can bury them properly with full honours. And shut up the house so that it can't be damaged any more than it probably is already.'

'It shall be done, dominus,' I said.

I left him and went to find Sparticus, who had indeed not budged from the hostel, although he had taken advantage of the food. I explained to Helen of Troy more or less what had happened and that she would see less of me from now on, which resulted in a bear hug that could have killed.

So Sparticus and I hung on like grim death whilst a snooty charioteer drove his horses hard to get us back to the mine in time for him return to Ariconium before dark. I let him take us right into the yard just to make sure that anyone who might be watching knew we had come with a serious amount of authority. The place seemed deserted, but we must have been seen because it wasn't long before one of Polonius' children appeared, asking me to go and see him straight away. I made the charioteer wait, even though I knew he was wanting to get back, but I did allow him to water his horses.

I found Polonius barricaded inside his hut with logs and branches. The child who had come to meet me scrambled underneath them and, once he had got permission, moved enough away so that I could scramble underneath too. I made Sparticus stand guard outside. He was not too keen to do this, but he realised that in our revised circumstances he took orders from me.

Polonius was looking very sorry for himself. His injuries were indeed serious but, as Sparticus, had said, he'd live. He had a broken leg and a gash on his arm that must have nearly cut it off. His wife had splinted his leg and had effectively done the same with his arm so that he couldn't move it. He was pale as pale but very much alive.

'Left me for dead, they did. Bit of luck the family came looking for me.' He smiled at his wife. 'Got her to roust out Sparticus to tell the world what had happened. Good job he found you. By the way where is he?'

'Standing guard outside and not liking it one bit.'

'So what happens now?'

I had to laugh, even though I knew it was no laughing matter.

'Julius Octavius wants you and me to sort it out.'

'Me! Us!' he gasped, much as I had done but in a deeper voice, and then nearly collapsed with the pain.

'Who else is there?' I asked.

'But – but aren't they going to send somebody?'

'They have.'

'Who?'

'Me.'

'But... but you're little more than a boy, and a slave like the rest of us. He can't do that.'

'He has,' I said flatly. It took him a few minutes to assimilate this information.

'So what are we supposed to do? You, what hasn't shaved yet, and me, who's no use to man nor beast!'

I ignored both comments. 'Is anyone still here?'

'No idea. Maybe a few left who didn't follow the mob.' He wasn't being helpful.

'Then we wait.'

'Wait!' he ranted. 'What – for the sky to fall in to put us all out of our troubles?'

'No,' I said patiently. 'To see who comes crawling out of the woods when hunger gets the better of them.'

He tapped the side of his nose.

'You ain't silly, are you? I can see now why that bulla man sent you back. Yeah. It could work.' He mused on this for a while.

I went outside and personally dispatched the charioteer with a simple message for Julius Octavius.

'Tell him,' I said, 'that the situation here is as bad as it sounded and that I'll send a report within a few days.'

'And don't forget to tell him,' I yelled, as he whipped up his horses and left in a cloud of flying gravel. He didn't like taking orders from me!

I gave Sparticus orders to go down the mine and see if there were any slaves left down there who might not have joined the general rampage, or who at least were still alive and could be used.

'Feed them,' I said. 'Tell them that because they didn't join the rabble they will live and that tomorrow they will be clearing up this carnage and burying the dead. We need to get things back where they belong.'

I would have started there and then but it was nearly dark and we were all of us afraid of what darkness might bring. Sparticus set off – a bit hesitantly, for which I didn't blame him – with a heavy leather whip in one hand, a very sharp sword in the other, and a dagger in his belt for good measure.

Some time later, he came back looking pleased with himself.

'How many have you got?' I asked.

'Six,' he said, 'but I reckon there's at least as many again hiding deeper down. This lot wouldn't say, but you get a feeling for these things. Know what I mean?'

I nodded.

'Puppies they are! All of 'em got their tails between their legs waiting to be whipped. I doled out food like you said and left 'em to think about it. I put an extra chain on the gate too, by the way.'

'Well done,' I said. 'Polonius wanted us to stay with him for protection. His, not ours, I think.' Sparticus smiled. 'But I said no, we'd sleep in his office like I've always done and it would look like no one was here. I don't think anyone's likely to attack us anyway. What would be the sense in it? More to the point, do we have any food for ourselves?'

'A bit of stale bread and some nearly gone off meat. I should have some in my hut but they've probably pinched that while I've been looking for you. But, to tell the truth, I don't fancy going outside the compound to look.'

'Bread and rancid meat it is then.'

I don't think anybody slept much that night. The place was abnormally and eerily quiet. Ordinarily there was always some shouting coming up the walkways from the mine. The noises of animals in the surrounding forest were hardly there and those that were seemed unnaturally loud. I had always been on my own in Polonius' office. What's more, Sparticus snored. Not to mention my head was going round in a whirl thinking about how I was going to exercise my new authority and, at the same time, manage to keep up a supply of ore to Ariconium.

For me at least, the dawn simply could not come quick enough.

Chapter 15

'Now what?' were Sparticus' first words the following morning.

'You go and get as many as there are out from down below before they have a chance to go hiding themselves again. Go quietly so they don't hear you coming and then harry them out just so they know who's in charge around here.'

He nodded his head in appreciation of the strategy, grinned and was gone. Remarkably soon there was a mighty shouting, cracking of a whip and scurrying of feet as twelve slaves (yes, there were, as he had guessed, some extras hidden away) erupted into the yard, blinking in the dawn light only to find me waiting for them.

'Hey, Marcus,' somebody jeered. 'How come you're still around? You missed all the fun. Not running errands today then? It's changed a bit since you were last here!'

'It most certainly has,' I said. 'For a start, I'm the new dominus in this place. I've taken over from Gaius Maximus...'

'You've done what?'

Words to that effect were spoken or whispered by each and every one of them.

'Indeed I have. And I have full authority from Julius Octavius, who was dominus to Gaius Maximus, to do as I like here and to treat you in any way that I like or you deserve.'

That sobered them up, for they well knew what penalties could be meted out to them. I carried on.

'There is, however, one proviso: the supply of ore must keep coming.'

There were gasps of amazement.

'And my first orders are that this place be cleaned up. Bring all the dead bodies together and dig a grave for them all. Keep the bodies of Gaius Maximus and his wife separate, wash and clean them up, wrap them carefully. My instructions are to send them to Ariconium for proper burial.

Wash away the blood and guts that are splattered everywhere. Start repairing anything that's broken. We'll have a break at the breakfast hour and then it's going to be back into the mine to get some ore moving again. Remember, Sparticus still knows how to use a whip!'

And he cracked it for good measure.

There was some grumbling, but most were glad they were still alive, and apparently with no retribution coming their way.

Sparticus voiced their obvious concerns to me after they had been set to work. 'How are you going to start getting any ore out with only this lot to do it? These are the old, the injured, or those too young to work full time. Jeer they might, but they were too scared or too infirm to have gone with the rest.'

'I know, I know,' I said.

'So?'

'We wait.'

Sparticus looked at me as Polonius had done – as though I was mad.

'We wait,' I said again.

He moved off, scratching his head.

In fact we had to wait much less time than I had expected. Within an hour of my having rousted the slaves out, and before the morning meal that I had promised them, one had come back in from the forest, thoroughly frightened, nearly naked, scratched and exhausted. He had spent the night up a tree. He was quite prepared for any punishment due to him and was astounded that I simply set him to work with the others. I needed them back if I was going to send any ore to Ariconium and I just hoped that word would reach those outside that retribution was not inevitable, and that more would turn themselves in.

Maybe it was the smell of cooking that reached into the trees, but by the middle of the day we had a further four, and by nightfall this had increased to ten. The following morning one of the first to come in was my old friend Hadrian, and I was mightily glad to see him. He had been a good friend to me while I was filling baskets, and I wouldn't have wanted to be obliged to bring any of the available penalties down on him just because he had gone with the crowd. While I showed no particular favour to him, and sent him off with the rest, I knew I was going to need a replacement for myself.

Hadrian was more than a little surprised to find me in charge.

'By all the gods,' he said, 'how did you become dominus around here?'

I had to repeat what I'd told the others. It was becoming a chore, this having to explain myself to everyone, but I was a bit more forthcoming with Hadrian.

'To be truthful,' I said, 'I really don't know. I happened to be leaving Ariconium when Sparticus turned up all out of breath.' Hadrian grinned as I continued. 'Polonius had sent him with news of a riot here. I went back to see the big man and the next thing he says is that I've got to come over here and sort it all out.'

'It's all right for some,' he grumbled, managing to look completely dumbfounded at the same time.

'Well,' I said, 'You know as well as I do that as slaves we have to do as we're ordered, with no question about it. How long it lasts for me remains to be seen, but my prime job is to get some ore on the move again, so get yourself down below and doing your usual job.'

I was distracted by another bunch of slaves coming out of the woods and I admit that I said it a bit more sharply than I would have wished. He picked up on this.

'Hey, steady on, old friend, if I can still call you that.'

'Of course you can, but remember how you once told me that we all have to keep up the appearance of what we're supposed to be doing.'

He nodded, but he too had noticed the influx and looked back at me.

'That one,' he said, 'second in the line. Xerxes he calls himself. He's the one that planned all this. The sharp end of a sword would be too good for him.'

Hadrian seemed very bitter about it.

'Thanks,' I said and winked at him. 'We're still friends. Remember that.'

He didn't look as though he believed me, but time would tell. Meanwhile I went to see what Sparticus was doing with this lot. They were different from the ones who had crept back in up to now. Those knew they were in the wrong and would be lucky to get away with their lives. These, on the other hand, had a *look at us, weren't we clever* attitude. Obviously being on their own in the woods didn't suit them as well as they'd expected, so they thought they could follow the example of the others and just come back to where there was food, and carry on where they'd left off. Some hope!

Sparticus came over to me.

'These are the ones who started it all,' he said. 'That Xerxes, not his real name, mind, is the real bad one.' He pointed with the heel of his whip. 'By Mars, I don't know how they've got the nerve to come back all so jolly and cheerful like.'

'Nor me,' I said.

'Well, you're the bulla now, so what are we going to do with them?'

'This Xerxes character, bind him, gag him and bury him alive.'

Sparticus' eyebrows shot up.

'You can't do that. Even you haven't got that sort of authority.'

'I think I have and I'm going to chance it. If he was the cause of all this mayhem, I suspect there's quite a lot of the follow-ons who might be glad to see him out of the way, and it'll cool the others down a bit when they see what happens to him.'

Sparticus shrugged his shoulders. Although he wasn't actually a slave, orders were still orders. He was plainly aware that it was my responsibility and I'm sure he fully expected to be doing the same thing to me before too long if this was what I was going to do. Ever practical, he said, 'That's him dealt with, but what happens to the rest of them?'

'You put them down below, separate from the rest, and you work them as hard as they've ever known. Julius Octavius promised to send over some soldiers to take away the likes of these and work them even harder at his furnaces back in Ariconium. You know, and I know, and probably they know, that there they'll be worked to death and the world will be a better place without them. Unless…'

'Unless what?'

'Unless you want one or more to help you as a gang-master.'

He considered this for what to my mind was too short a moment, before saying, 'For the time being I'm fine. I'll manage. When I want assistance, I'll tell you. I wouldn't thank you for any of this lot.'

'Well, at least think about it.'

'I will, and I've got one in mind. If, that is, he comes back.'

'He will, you can be sure of that!' I said as he went off to carry out my draconian order.

We got others to dig the hole on the pretext that it might yet be needed. Sparticus clubbed the so-called Xerxes hard on the side of the head when he was shouting it off about how nice it was outside. He went down like a felled tree. He was bound and gagged in seconds, and they waited till he became conscious again before tipping him in the hole and filling it in. It certainly brought his cronies to heel and sent a ripple around the place that said: young I might be, cocky I might be, too clever for my own good I might be, but I'm certainly not to be trifled with.

Later I went down the mine with Sparticus to see what his arrangements were down there and to see where we might have a bit of ore we could send off. There was already a bit of stock on the surface and if we could get a few carts sent to Ariconium it would prove to Julius Octavius that we were at least trying. It would have the added advantage of showing the locals who provided the carts that we were still in business, despite what had happened. Their livelihood would be secure. I was also able to arrange with one of the carters that I knew fairly well to take the bodies of Gaius Maximus and his wife back to Julius Octavius. All proof to him that we were creating some order out of the chaos.

Sparticus continued to surprise me, and had some good suggestions to make. That evening I went to see Polonius, who was still in pain but a bit more his normal self. He seemed to be healing without any poisoning of his wounds.

'Sparticus is suggesting,' I began, 'that we could scrounge a bit of ore from round the pillars that are left to hold up the roof without too much risk of collapse. If you think that's feasible it would keep up a supply fairly easily for a while, which could be useful. I don't have to tell you, of all people, what the demands are from Ariconium.'

'Pillar robbing,' he grumbled. 'Always a sign of a failing mine but when the gods aren't helping as much as they might, there's not much choice in it. Actually, I think that with care there are places where you could take out some of the pillars altogether and leave a big open cave, provided the roof continues to be good sound rock. But you're going to have to go deeper and follow the seam down.'

'We both know that – you were talking about it before all this mess arose, but we can't do anything about it until some more decide to come back out of the forest – and some good strong ones too.'

'If they do!'

'Oh, they will. What else are they going to do?'

'Hole up in the woods and live their lives as they want.'

'No, Polonius, they've got to come back. Nowhere is very far from anywhere else just here. The native population is largely with us because of the work we give them, so they won't stand any nonsense from slaves who have a useful bounty on their heads anyway.'

'If you say so.' He obviously wasn't convinced.

'I reckon another riot led from outside is more likely,' he said.

'I'm convinced otherwise,' I said, and had to pull his leg a bit. 'You've sent me all over this area with messages and I've seen just what it's like. The woods aren't as impenetrable as they look and there's a lot of people live in them. Then there's the Sabrina to think about. They can't cross that, and I'm told there's another big river somewhere towards where the sun sets. So, you see, they really can't escape.'

But Polonius was only going to believe me when, hopefully, I was proved right. So he changed the subject.

"I wish I was well enough to start having a look at these pillars for you.'

'You will do. I shan't do anything drastic until you get to see what we're doing. A disaster here would land me working at the furnaces, and we both know where that leads!'

For me it was the plain truth, but it made him laugh. He also seemed relieved by the stance I was taking.

And that is exactly what we did for a week or so. As we all agreed, it kept the supply going and, good as his word, Julius Octavius left us to our own devices. Slaves continued to crawl, some of them literally, back out of the woods, and we soon had enough to keep up a regular supply. Out of these Sparticus found his potential gang-master, Trojan by name. He described him as, 'Big, a bully, but he works hard and he's fair.' And he thought someone like that would appeal to me.

'OK,' I said. 'Just as long as he's not a Caligula or the cause of another riot.'

We also buried another ringleader, but, slightly to my surprise, this did not cow the remainder with fear. If anything they seemed to rejoice that another troublemaker was out of the way. With nearly all our slaves back it was time to report officially to Ariconium, and I sat down to compose a lengthy tablet to Julius Octavius. The next morning I sent for Hadrian. Despite hoping that he was still my friend, he was as mystified and fearful of his summons as I had been of the one from Polonius.

Before I explained what I wanted, my first question was as to whether he could read or write.

'Just about know my letters but, read properly – no.'

'Fine for now, but I might just have to teach you.'

He didn't seem pleased by that suggestion.

'It's all right for you high-class slaves.'

I'd never thought of Hadrian as a grumbler but it seemed as though he was becoming one.

'Well, it's done me no harm.'

He grunted. I was beginning to wonder if he was a good choice for my runner, but just now I didn't have much choice.

'What this is about is that you'll have to start doing what I was doing. I have here a tablet with a report for Julius Octavius. I'll send you with one of the ore carts to Ariconium even though it will be slow, but you can take note of the route and come back as quickly as possible.'

He was wide-eyed, but whether with alarm or pleasure it was difficult to tell.

'Now, Julius Octavius is a powerful man but he's OK. You're my messenger and he'll take my tablet and have to think about it. You'll wait for a reply. There's a hostel there that will give you food and accommodation while you wait, but don't wander far. He won't be pleased if you're not close by when he wants to send you back.' I made chopping gestures to illustrate my point. 'Understood?'

He nodded. 'But how will I know where to find him?' he asked. It was a fair question. I'd had enough trouble the first time I went there and I'd had the authority of Gaius Maximus behind me. Hadrian only had the authority of another slave!

'I'll send word with the cart before yours,' I said. 'And then, hopefully, they might be expecting you.'

Hadrian didn't look convinced and I didn't blame him. I wasn't.

'Besides, I also have a rather personal reason for sending you.'

'And…' he said, cocking his head in my direction as though he knew what was coming.

I couldn't help blushing, but I'd started so I had to go on. After all, as he had pointed out, Hadrian and I had been close friends and much the same age, so he should understand.

'Julius Octavius has a servant called Clio, who makes drinks and things for him. I should be glad if you could find the opportunity to tell her that I still think of her and hope I shall get back to see her one day. And not too many words about it around this place. OK?'

It all sounded awfully formal.

Hadrian grinned. 'Whatever you say,' he said. He was cheekier than I would ever have dared to be but I had to go along with him.

When Hadrian got back, having only got lost once on the way, I heard that my system had worked. Apparently the soldiers were expecting him and he was taken straight to see Julius Octavius. As I expected, he had had to wait overnight before a tablet was put together for me. His biggest worry was that he wouldn't see my Clio, but fortunately he did just before he left. He said she seemed pleased and sent back her best wishes to me. Also very formal!

'Nice one there,' he said. 'I wish you well with her, but look out if she takes to me.'

'I can pull rank on you any day,' I said.

We both laughed and I sincerely hoped that we were both joking.

The tablet from Julius O didn't tell me much, although in fairness it was complimentary about what I was achieving. It was nice to be appreciated, but then it simply went on to exhort me to produce more if I could. Not much that was new or helpful there!

Chapter 16
Helen of Troy

Helen, Helen of Troy, they call me, after that Greek myth. It has to be a myth, doesn't it? I mean, how could they possibly have got a whole army inside a horse? However big it was! No, I think they call me that 'cos I have a habit of turning up places just at the moment when I'm not wanted. But, like the real Helen, it's stood me in good stead. That's how I come to be here. Let me explain.

I was a slave, like everyone else. Always worked in kitchens and people's houses. Nobody very posh but reasonably well-to-do folks. Businessmen, minor politicians, army officers and the like – generally solid people. Got myself a good reputation so that, when time came to part company, I got sold on to someone decent. Comfortable sort of life it was till I got given to this head centurion fellow. Took me to Londinium, he did, and that's where it all went wrong – for him that is! Don't know what it is about these centuria, but once they get to Pilus Inferior, like Tiberius here, or Pilus Prior like this one in Londinium, they think the sun shines out of their arses and the world owes them something.

Anyway, back to the story. This one decides he doesn't like living in army quarters and needs to set up house on his own. Well that was fine by me. It gave me a bit of responsibility 'cos then I bought the food and could have a bit of what I liked rather than what the army thought was good enough for me. And a bit more of it too! Suited him as he liked to entertain a bit and he could do so in his own house with as many men and boys as he liked. Horrible it was, but then some men are like that. Honest, I'd have let him have me rather than all these young boys who didn't know the ways of men like him. And then it fell to me to nursemaid them after he and his mates had done their worst. Poor kids, they didn't know what had hit them.

Now, to get to the point, he started to get short of the readies for this sort of lifestyle and started to borrow money wherever he could. I knew because, like I say, I happened to come across him when he was talking to people. Then he started to borrow money to pay back money he'd already borrowed somewhere else. It couldn't go on and it didn't. He finally lost his temper with one of these moneylenders; they had a row and he killed the fellow right there in the atrium of the house. And, wondering what the rumpus was about, I walked in just after it had happened!

'You've got to help me clear this up,' he says, as calm as though it was a bird the cat had brought in.

'I should be going straight to the vigiles,' I told him.

'You do, and you go the same way!'

'You got to catch me first!' says I, heading for the door. 'Slave I may be, but I don't have to be party to this sort of thing.'

He was a big man, all paunchy, and I knew I could outrun him if it came to it. And to see him chasing me down the street would soon make others want to know what he was at. It must have dawned on him just in time.

'OK,' he says. 'How much?'

'You haven't got any money and you know it.'

I think it shook him that I knew what state he was in.

'What then?'

I stood up straight and I might have been just a bit taller than him.

'My freedom!'

'Don't be ridiculous,' he says. 'You know I can't give you that.'

'I do, but I reckon you might know somebody that can.'

He pondered this and looked at the body on the floor.

'Maybe, but two conditions.'

'Try me.'

'One, you help me clear up this mess. Two, you get out of here within a day of getting your freedom and go as far away as you can – perhaps Northumbria, or somewhere up that way. And, I suppose, three, we never see each other again.'

'How long will it take?'

I had him on the run, but I needed to know.

'Two days, maybe three.'

'I agree.'

I saw him relax.

'But...'

I saw him tense up again.

'Once we've cleared up this mess, as you call it, you give me some money.' I saw the alarm in his face. 'Not much, but enough so that I can leave here today and not have anyone ask me why I can't pay for my food. I'll call every day until you can give me the documents that prove I'm free.'

In fairness he was as good as his word, and four days later I was on my way to these parts. He thought I was going north but I was afraid he might try to catch me, so I came west and landed up here when the money ran out. I have to say he was quite generous, and, as I'd kept 'my share' of the food money, I was pretty well off. And I'm possibly the only person who came here of their own free will. I love it. I enjoy running this hostel and seeing all the interesting passers-by that come through. Not to mention the gossip!

Chapter 17

There was one slightly curious request in the tablet from Julius Octavius. He confirmed that he wanted me to close up Gaius Maximus' house, but to maintain it in good condition. 'In case it was needed,' as he put it. I couldn't understand this, but perhaps one day I would. In fact the house hadn't been badly damaged – knocked about a bit was a better description – and we had cleared up the blood and gore. The snag was that it took slave power away from my main priority.

The house was situated a little distance from the mine, and it was of no use to anyone unless they had business in the immediate vicinity. But, if that's what he wanted, that's what he would get. It wasn't a big house anyway, but it had an adequate number of rooms, heating, a kitchen and slave quarters. Some of the house slaves had been killed and a couple were amongst the early ones to return. Quite reasonably they felt that the riot was nothing to do with them. They would now be working in the mine, and I knew only too well how hard they would find it. In due course I weeded them out to cook and clean for the remainder, but first they had to work and learn who was bulla. It seemed that Gaius M had been a bit of dilettante where food was concerned and it was almost an equal shock for them to be cooking stews and soup for hungry men.

After about a week we had all our slaves back – well, except those we'd executed. However, there was one notable exception. At least to me it was notable: Mahout. The strange thing was that no one else seemed to have missed him. Sparticus was cock-a-hoop that we had them all back. Mahout must have been working hard to make himself invisible and that was not like him at all. It made me ponder the whole question of the riot and whether Xerxes was in fact the ringleader that everyone proclaimed him to have been. Friend or not, we were probably better off without Mahout.

It was not too long before Polonius was hobbling about on a crutch and had his children remove the barricades from his hut door. He obviously felt safe again. Similarly Sparticus had moved back into his hut and taken Trojan with him.

'If there's any trouble coming my way, at least there's two of us,' was his comment.

I continued to live in Polonius' office, where I could be well-barricaded in. I knew I was going to be number one target in case of any further trouble. Once Polonius had had a look at what we were doing underground and had set out a way forward, we were able to relax a bit and look slightly further forward than where the next cartload of ore was to come from.

'I've heard talk of some other old workings somewhere near here that we might be able to use,' he said quite casually one day.

'Why ever didn't you mention it before?' I asked him.

'There didn't seem any need. We were working steadily, keeping them at Ariconium busy, and always had a bit in hand here.'

'So where is this other mine?' I asked.

'Oh, it's not a mine,' he said. 'Or at least I don't think so. I believe it's an open quarry.'

'Where?'

'Now that's where you have me. I don't really know!'

I groaned.

'Marcus,' he said, 'you know how to talk to these natives, the carters and such like. Why don't you have a word and see if they can tell you anything?'

'I'll try,' I said. 'But I don't really know their language.'

'You know more than I do,' he grunted.

For both of us, if this place actually existed then it would be a real boon. The problem was that ideally the mine needed extending downwards and that was going to take extra slave power and time in the form of an interruption to our production. So I did as he suggested: I spoke to one or two of the carters that I'd got to know when I was cadging lifts to and from Ariconium. I struck lucky with the third one I asked.

'I think I know where you're talking about. But mind, it's not been worked for a long time. Come with me now and I'll show you. It's not far.'

And it wasn't. A bit more than a mille. And I'd walked past it regularly for the last two years or so without realising.

I bade the carter get on his way and plunged into the woodland. Everything, but everything, is covered in trees and bushes hereabouts, and it all looks the same, so getting the lie of the land is always difficult. What I found was a maze of cuts and holes into the hillside that were patently not natural. There were also low heaps of spoil that had been dug out. When and by whom was another matter altogether. Pools of dirty brown water lay in the hollows. I got back to Polonius as soon as I could.

'By Jupiter,' he said, 'I wish I could walk a bit better. I'd soon know if you had the right place. But it sounds spot on.' This was encouraging for me.

'Don't worry,' I told him. 'We've got enough to do here at the moment, and then I'll get a cart to take you over there and we can have a closer look.'

I startled myself with this. Here was I giving instructions and making arrangements for someone even Caligula had been scared of!

So about a week later Polonius and I left the mine in Sparticus' care for a few hours to go and look more closely at this overgrown area. Having been scornful of the cart, he hobbled, and I walked. I looked around at this and that to answer his questions. He stood scratching his head and muttering to himself for a long time. Finally he pronounced, 'Provided there's some ore left here, we should have a go at it.'

'Are you sure?' I said. 'I can't see anything that looks like a mine, or iron ore or anything.'

Polonius grinned. 'Maybe I've got to start teaching you a bit about mining!' he said. 'There's more to it than just organising a few people to dig the stuff for you.'

He was right, of course, and I knew it wasn't said unkindly.

'Start away,' I said.

'Well you can see that somebody's dug for something here, can't you?'

'Yes, it looks like it but it could be for anything or nothing. You know what the locals are like round here.'

'True,' he said, 'but look at it this way. These trenches they've dug in the rock might seem haphazard, but I reckon they were following a vein of something – could even be the same vein of ore that we're following. It was a while ago judging by the size of the trees. And look just here where there's some water coming out: it's brown. Now you spotted that but didn't realise what it meant. Sure sign of iron ore.'

I looked, and sure enough he was right.

'So?' I said.

'I reckon we get a few reliables that won't try to escape or butcher one of us, and we dig a few holes and see what we find.'

'Hang on a bit. We haven't got so many that we can put a gang over here, very possibly for nothing.' I wasn't yet totally convinced.

'Not a whole gang. Just five or six and you or me to tell them what to do.'

'That's more like it,' I said. 'But I need to clear the idea with Julius Octavius first, and he might be able to tell me when we can expect some more slaves.'

So Hadrian's next dispatch to Ariconium included a lengthy proposition as to what I, or more truthfully we, intended to do, and a request for permission to do it. I also asked when we might expect another consignment of slaves, as that would markedly help the whole scheme. The reply came back that we could spend some time on working out how to do it, but no labour was to be diverted from the main task until the next batch of slaves arrived. As to when that might happen Julius fudged. It was obvious that he'd had word that some were on the way but equally obvious that he had no idea when they might arrive. Even then it depended on what sort of quality ore we got. I was actually quite glad about this delay as it gave Polonius a better chance to recover from his injuries, and without him I should have been lost, not having any real idea of what I was supposed to be looking for.

In fact, the new batch of eighteen slaves turned up much sooner than anyone had expected, and, as far as I was concerned, they were a good mix of young boys with a number of old lags to do the heavy work. I confirmed with Ariconium that we could start on the proposed exploration, and got permission to proceed. Polonius insisted on going himself, even though he wasn't as well recovered as he thought he was, and I put Hadrian with them to act as runner if they needed anything from the mine. After a week Polonius was depressed.

'Nothing,' he said. 'A lot of work, and nothing. Better for all of us to have left them in the mine.'

'Are they reliable?' I asked him.

'Seem to be, but what's that got to do with it?'

'And do they know what they're looking for?'

'Should do by now. What are you getting at?'

He wasn't usually as testy as this.

'Trust them then. Let them spread out over the whole area. Further than you can walk, especially at the moment, and let them see what they can find.'

He was very dubious. 'What happens if one of them takes off?'

'They all know what happens to them if they're so stupid.'

'Not to them – to me,' he growled.

'You?'

'Yes, me. I'm responsible for them and if I lose one it could go badly for me.'

'Oh, Polonius, I hope we know each other better than that. Nothing happens. You're working on my instructions to help increase production. Don't worry. Remember you got me where I am now, and I'm not likely to forget it.'

He gave one of his grunts but seemed mollified.

And it worked. None of them ran away and one of them did find what Polonius was looking for. At the end of one particularly deep gouge between the rocks he came to an old working face where there was ore to be got and in useful quantities too, but as to quality we had no means of telling that. It was time for me to go and see Julius Octavius. I was nervous about leaving the mine to Polonius, but I had little choice. I just hoped that I had so stamped my authority on the place that any unrest could be contained. I sent Hadrian off a few days beforehand so that Ariconium would know I was coming and I could be away for as little time as possible. In any case it would make a pleasant change to be walking my old route again, and I might see Clio!

Nothing much had changed. The sycophant ushered me in as before and the great man was waiting for me. He called for Clio to bring us some drinks and seemed amused that we both blushed at the sight of each other.

It was embarrassing. I had to get down to business, and quickly, but I was not quick enough.

'I'm very pleased,' began Julius Octavius. 'You've done very well to keep up the supply as you have. I thought you could, and you have.'

If I was embarrassed before, I was even more so now, and didn't know which way to look. Certainly not at Clio.

'Well, thank you, dominus. I've tried my best.'

'And succeeded. Now, you wanted to see me.'

'Yes.' This was feeling better. 'We've found the other source of ore that I wrote to you about. About a mille away from the mine and, most importantly, it's on the surface. In fact it was Polonius who'd heard about it and was ultimately responsible for finding it.'

'If it's so handy, why are we mining and not working this anyway?'

It was a fair question. I went on to explain about how we needed to work the mine deeper to reach more ore and how that would require apparently unproductive work, but if this other place could produce ore easily it would keep up the supply while the expansion work was being done.

A scowl started to spread across Julius Octavius' face. I became distinctly alarmed and I couldn't work out what was upsetting him until he finally burst out, 'You've done even better than I thought to work all that out in the short time you've had. But why in the name of Vulcan didn't Gaius Maximus do all this before? Maybe that riot has done us all a favour!'

I had no answer to that and, as a slave, was certainly not going to give any opinions of my own. I kept quiet.

'Go on,' he said.

'There are a couple of problems.'

He groaned. 'Only two?'

'I think so. First, we do have to spend quite a lot of effort in clearing this other place. It's covered in trees and all of a muddle. But it looks as though it could be useful. Second, I only know what Polonius has told me about ore quality so I can give no opinion on what this may be like. It's been abandoned a long time and that's maybe why. I thought perhaps we could send you some sample loads before we make too much effort and you can let us know what you think.'

'Then that's settled.' He was certainly living up to his reputation for being decisive. 'How shall we know one from the other?'

I hadn't thought about that problem. After a moment's hesitation I had a solution.

'We call the mine Clearwell, because despite the iron in the ground the water in the stream and in the well always runs clear, so loads from there will be clear of markings. Loads from the other place, that I've named Puzzlewood because of the problems we had finding anything there, will carry a tree branch preferably with leaves on it. In fact you could send burners over to make charcoal for your furnaces out of the wood we're going to cut down.'

He laughed.

'Marcus, you're a genius, but I think that would be a step too far.'

I rose to go, my business completed.

'Wait a minute, young man, before you go we must drink a glass of wine to your success in these matters.'

'But dominus?' I questioned, 'I'm just your slave.'

'So? I'm asking you to drink a glass of wine with me to your success.'

'But this just doesn't happen.'

'Why not?'

'Well, if you order it so, dominus.'

'Clio,' he shouted, 'bring us wine and glasses.' He continued, 'That's as may be. If you insist then this is an order! You've done well and learnt fast. A little celebration is called for.'

And he tapped the side of his nose very much as both Mahout and Polonius did when they were being conspiratorial. So Clio brought us wine and glasses as she was commanded, and Julius Octavius and I, yes, me, drank a glass of wine together as though we were old companions. It was all very amicable, but very strange, and I wasn't sure whether it boded good or ill. When I left, the sycophant's usual smile was more of a sneer, and that certainly didn't bode well.

On the other hand I did manage to have nearly an hour with Clio. I bet Julius O knew what we were doing as he didn't miss much. On both counts only time would tell. Feeling well pleased with myself, and not a little cocky, I got back to the mine late, but the same day.

Chapter 18

The next morning it was time to put plans into action. I'd had plenty of time to think about it on the walk back the previous night. Once everyone was at work and any problems sorted, I left Trojan in charge and called Sparticus and Polonius together in the latter's office.

'I have permission from Julius Octavius to go ahead with this additional operation at Puzzlewood.'

'Where?' asked Polonius, even though he knew damned well what I was talking about.

'Sorry. I had to think of a name for the place on the spur of the moment and came up with that because it was such a puzzle to find and then work out what had been going on.'

I got one of his grunts for that and a smile from Sparticus.

'I also have a plan as to how we're going to do this thing. Polonius, you'll be in charge of the mining operation and all the technical stuff. Sparticus, you'll be in charge of supplying and supervising the labour in use over there. I think that may be trickier than you think, and you may need an assistant as well as Trojan.'

Both considered this for a few minutes. It was Polonius who spoke first.

'How are we going to separate the ores?' he asked.

'Ah. Number one question from Julius O! You two should get on well.'

He almost blushed as I went on to explain my spur of the moment method of identification.

'Well, there should be plenty of branches around to put on the carts. That's if the locals can be persuaded to leave them there.'

'We'll deal with that when they don't,' I said.

'How many are you planning to put over there?' asked Sparticus.

'I reckon eight or ten for a start to get the place cleared so that we can see what we're doing, and after that we'll just have to see.'

'How do you suppose we're going to guard them. With trees all round, what's to stop them just disappearing? Even with extra help I can't be everywhere.'

Sparticus had a point.

'Perhaps I'm being too trusting, but if it's made very clear that anyone who does run will certainly be caught and then publicly flogged with fifty strokes for every day that they're away, I don't think you'll have too much trouble.'

'I don't want *any* trouble,' he shot back at me.

I would have to choose my words with care in future.

'Neither do I, or we've all got problems. My thinking is that you need to pick your slaves carefully and possibly change the gang there each week.'

He raised his eyebrows to the sky in exasperation.

'The reason is so that they don't get too comfortable over there and learn too much about the immediate neighbourhood that might tempt them to run.'

I think he saw what I was getting at.

'And what about the long-term plan to deepen this place?' asked Polonius.

'That will have to wait and may depend on what sort of quality of ore comes from Puzzlewood.'

'There's certainly ore there, but I'm dubious about its quality.'

'So am I, but until they've smelted some we shall none of us know.'

Despite putting some of our toughest men onto the work it was nearly two weeks before we were ready to send a load of ore with its green-leafed branch off to Ariconium. I sent Hadrian to warn them it was coming and to get an answer as to whether it was any good. He came back with the dispiriting news that they were going to wait until they had a bigger quantity before smelting any. The only good news was that Clio had said that she wished it was me still going with the messages.

We persevered and Polonius got more and more grumpy as we weren't getting any information back on what we were sending. Eventually we did, and it wasn't good news. They said it was producing very poor quality iron with a lot of slag. This might be good enough for domestic ironmongery but not good enough for swords and edged tools, and we all knew that was their principal business.

'Tell them to mix the two lots of ore about equally with better quality stuff from the mine and use a higher temperature if they can,' said Polonius.

'What's that going to do for it?' I asked, curious.

'The good ore will improve the poor. It'll only make it better, never first quality, and the higher temperature will burn off some of the rubbish and slag.'

I sent a message to this effect to Ariconium and a few days later had a grudging reply that Polonius had been right. He didn't seem particularly surprised by his small success and kept on at me, saying that we had to do something or the supply of good quality ore would run out – and then where would we be? In the Styx, he reckoned! I told him to decide where he wanted to dig and we'd make a very tentative start on it.

However, viewed from my position things looked good. Although the ore was not of the best, we were meeting our commitments to Ariconium. The dire warnings had maybe had their effect as we hadn't lost any slaves to the surrounding woods. We could have done with a few more but those we had were in good condition and worked hard. Sparticus and Trojan seldom had any trouble to put down. I was on good terms with the local population and had become more proficient in their language, which I think pleased them. I was sure it couldn't last, but at that moment I could see no trouble round the corner.

It was Trojan who saw it first. It was a day that I was at Puzzlewood to keep myself up to date and resolve any problems there might be. There was very little to worry about here; it was a case of follow the ore vein wherever it went. There was no roof to fall in and all the accommodation and feeding was provided at Clearwell.

'Look,' he shouted.

I followed his pointing finger. A great column of smoke was rising from the woodland.

'It's the house,' I said.

'Oh, Hades!' he said.

'Who can run fastest here?'

He thought for only a split second.

'Antinous.'

'Get him and send him to Clearwell and raise the alarm just in case they don't know already. Then find Sparticus, tell him to lock down and make sure he's got everybody. You check everyone is here who should be here. Nobody missing. Nobody added.'

As it happened, Antinous appeared at that moment, as if he knew he was needed, and went off at the double. I followed him but he was out of my sight almost immediately. When I got there the alarm had already been raised but possibly we saw it before they did. Sparticus had, of his own volition, locked the mine down for those inside and had taken the loaders and a couple of carters to see if they could do anything to stop the fire. It was a forlorn hope. The water supply for the house was from a fairly small stream that was useless for our purpose. All we could do was let the fire burn itself out and worry about the consequences.

Julius Octavius would not be pleased.

And he wasn't.

I sent word as to what had happened and got a peremptory message back to come to Ariconium myself immediately. *And I mean immediately*, he had written.

So I went and the atmosphere was very chilly with all of those with whom I normally had to do business. The eunuch was particularly insufferable.

'Read that,' Julius Octavius shouted at me when I arrived and he shoved a very small wax tablet across his desk at me. The writing, his writing, was almost illegible.

The walls have ears. Will shout at you. Grovel. We talk later.

If I looked surprised I hope no one else saw my face. He took the tablet back and erased it.

'By what incompetence did you allow the house of my late friend Gaius Maximus to burn down?' he screamed at me.

This was a wholly different Julius Octavius. I did not like it.

'Dominus, it is less than two days since it happened and we have not been able to get near the place because of the heat.'

'Did you not have it guarded?'

'No, dominus, there was no need. Or at least there seemed to be no need.'

He continued in a very loud voice.

'And what, may I ask, gave you that idea?'

'Well, we... no, I... I should blame myself, I thought there was no one who would want to do it any damage. We did have two of his slaves keeping it tidy, but not guarding it.'

'There is always someone wanting to get their own back on the power of Rome.'

He was getting very red in the face.

'That is true and I'm making excuses. The fault is mine but we were short-handed even if we do have our full complement of slaves, but we're on good terms with the natives so there seemed no need.'

'I thought you said you were one slave short.'

Mahout. Back to haunt me!

'Yes, dominus. It's true we are one short, but my opinion is that somehow he has got right away, or is dead, and that he will never be seen alive again.'

'You should know you can never trust the natives, however good they seem.'

'Yes, dominus.'

'And you might not have been short-handed if you hadn't allowed a riot to happen.'

'Yes, dominus, but at least we got rid of the troublemakers.'

He seemed to have forgotten that the riot had happened while I was still a runner and nothing more. Had I grovelled enough? It looked as though his fury might have blown itself out. He stood and pointed at the door by which I had come in.

'Go,' he said. 'And consider yourself very lucky you're still alive. But do not leave this site. I shall want to speak to you again when I have had time to think about what to do about you.'

I went, very cowed and wondering how much of this was real and how much was for the benefit of anyone who might have been listening in – and he obviously thought there would be some. His voice had remained very loud to the last words he said and the eunuch was even more supercilious than usual as I left, so he must have heard what was said. Or at least what Julius O had said, even if not my replies.

Word, even verbatim word, of what had been said seemed to have travelled round the camp faster than the lightning of the gods. Even Helen of Troy knew all about it by the time I got there.

'Don't worry, luv,' she said. 'His bark's worse than his bite. Firm but fair he is. He'll have forgotten about it by tomorrow.'

'I doubt that,' I said.

'Yeah. You'll be all right.'

I couldn't agree with her, but only time would tell. In the event Julius Octavius sent for me late that evening – to be taken to his house, no less. He had an office in his house and he sat me down there. His wife Aemelia brought us food and drink. What was going on?

'Welcome, Marcus,' he said. 'I'm sorry about this afternoon's little charade but there are people here who don't like the way I, and therefore you, are running this operation.'

I was literally speechless and it must have shown. He smiled.

'You're naïve, Marcus. You know that?'

'I thought I was pretty realistic,' I said.

'You can be, but you don't understand the Roman way.'

I must have looked puzzled for he carried on.

'Rome lives on intrigue and backbiting; and the biting can be lethal, literally. I've seen too many good men die for no good cause. It's one reason why I'm happy to be stuck on the margins of Empire out here.'

'Although, I should like to see the great city again before I die,' he added wistfully.

'But the burning of the house must have been some sort of accident. Sun on a piece of glass. A lightning strike perhaps.'

'I told you that you were naïve,' he laughed. 'A lightning strike on a fine summer's day?'

He was right. I had no answer. I could only look sheepish.

'What I want you to do is go back, dig around in the ruins and see what you find. I think that house was fired deliberately, but by whom, and why, is what I want to know. And think deviously! They won't have left a notice saying, *I, Postumous, set this place on fire!*

'I'll try,' I said.

'Good. Now go. Can you find your way back in the dark?'

'I think so.'

'I guessed you could. Tell Helen that you've had another dressing down from me and that you're not staying for a third one, slave or no slave. That'll be all round the camp by first light and some people will pray for the wolves to have got you on the way!'

Like a good slave I did what he had told me to do. I found it much more difficult than I expected to find my way back, and dawn was just breaking when I got there, which was just as well because otherwise I might have had trouble getting in and been attacked by Sparticus!

It also gave me all night to think about what had happened and to puzzle about why this was such an issue. I knew what I had to do but my thinking and the terrors of the forest at night did not sit well together.

Chapter 19

Everyone at the mine was surprised to see me, and even more surprised that I had managed to come back in the dark, but I wasn't explaining much. All I required was an hour or two's sleep and something to eat. Then I wanted to see Polonius. I had come to the conclusion that I needed his expertise in order to dig into what had been Gaius Maximus' villa. It wasn't so much the digging – we had plenty who could do that – but knowing what to look for. Of that I wasn't at all sure.

Polonius' leg injuries were giving him trouble as they did periodically and I found him in his hut.

'Couldn't go in my office with you asleep in there,' he said. We both knew it was an excuse but I let it pass. I had more important things on my mind.

'I had a very strange meeting at Ariconium yesterday,' I began.

'Thought it was odd you being sent for like that. Tell me.'

So I did, in as much detail as I could remember, especially regarding the strange behaviour of Julius Octavius. Polonius thought for a while.

'You've got a problem, young Marcus,' he said. 'Somebody's got it in for you.'

'I was rather afraid of that.'

'Anyone particular you've upset?'

'Not that I know of. The eunuch doesn't like me but there's not much he can do about it.'

'Himself, probably not, but he might get others to do his dirty work. They can be devious, that sort.'

I thought about this man. No, I can't bring myself to call him that, even if it isn't his fault. He had always had a very slimy expression and his bowing and scraping to Julius Octavius was puerile in the extreme. He looked as though he had plenty of bad thoughts but was incapable of carrying them out. Polonius had a point. Maybe he was in a position to bribe someone else to do what he couldn't do himself. And if he did, I would have bet that it wasn't his own money he was using.

To Polonius I said, 'You could be right, so where do we go from here?'

'Do as the man said! Dig the place over and see what you find.'

'And what will I find?'

'How do I know? Pull yourself together, Marcus. You've got an order; all you've got to do is carry it out. You may find out how the fire started, you may not, but you'll have done what you've been asked.'

'I suppose you're right.'

'I know I am! And if you'll take my advice you'll hand-pick a couple of them that are reliable and can keep their mouths just about shut.'

'Not more?'

'No. Like mining a new level. Go at it slowly, then you can hear if the roof's going to fall in.'

'But I'm not mining.'

'By all the gods you are obtuse this morning! Must be being out all night. I know you're not mining, but the principle's the same. Go at it slowly, see what there is to see, don't miss the obvious, don't let anything fall in on you, and I'll warrant you'll find something strange in there.'

'Any ideas as to who should help me?' I had some myself but I was interested to see who Polonius had in mind.

'The lad who helped you out when you first came here. Hadrian, you use him as a runner now. That's a start.'

'I'd thought of him. Only thing against him is that he seems to think I owe him something for old time's sake. I'm getting a bit fed up with him.'

'Now's your chance then. Special job and all that.'

'OK and then Antinous for the other. He seems pretty reliable.'

'Don't know much about him, but I'll take your word for it.'

'And finally you.'

'What you want me for?' He sounded almost offended.

'Advice as to where to start.'

I got one of his grunts, which normally meant that he agreed with me.

The next morning the four of us set out the short distance to what had been Gaius Maximus' house. Sparticus was not best pleased at losing two of his labourers, even if Hadrian was not there all the time anyway. I had to explain what I'd been told to do and he did at least understand that I had to do it or we'd all be in trouble.

'Quick as you can then,' he said. 'Don't make a meal of it.'

I didn't explain to him that Polonius said we should take it slowly. In fact I didn't tell him that Polonius was involved at all. I did, however, swear both Hadrian and Antinous to secrecy. It would soon be obvious what we were doing. But why? Well, the small world of the mine would have to guess at that and would no doubt very soon guess correctly.

The house was certainly a mess when we got to it. In reality there was nothing left except a few bits of wall. Everything that would burn had burnt. Polonius surveyed the wreckage.

'No question – this has been fired,' he pronounced. 'Doubt it would have burnt like this if it was an accident. Still hot too. Shan't be able to dig much until it cools down a bit.'

'We've got to do something,' I said. 'To prove we're doing what we came to do, if nothing else.'

It was Antinous who came up with a good idea.

'Let's just stand back, walk around a bit and see if there's anything that doesn't look right,' he said.

Polonius nodded his head in agreement.

So we did just that. We stood and looked and saw only a still-smouldering heap of ashes. We walked about and quite well into the surrounding woodland but were not much the wiser. The surrounding trees were severely scorched from the heat, and their leaves hung in blackened tears. There had been a lot of trampling of the grass and undergrowth when they came from the mine with ideas of extinguishing the blaze.

'Do any of us know how the house was arranged?' asked Polonius. 'I mean where the rooms and out-houses were. You can't tell from this mess.'

The rest of us looked at each other and shook our heads blankly.

'Hadrian,' I said, 'go back and fetch one of the household slaves. And tell Sparticus that it's on my orders!'

Hadrian was gone and back again shortly with a slave named Gallus, because he came from Gaul, and he was as appalled as the rest of us at the destruction. In fact he was nearly in tears.

'Such a nice house, such a nice house,' he kept saying, 'And especially for here.'

'Never mind about that,' I said, irritated. 'Where were all the rooms?'

Gallus started to explain the layout of the house, but Polonius cut him short.

'And where was the heating hypocaust fired from?' he asked.

Now I knew why he wanted someone who knew the house intimately.

'Round the back. Here.'

He ran round to the other side of the wreckage anxiously gesticulating. He, like everyone else except me, was afraid of Polonius. The latter grunted and limped his way round to where Gallus was pointing. From my experience in Rome I knew how a hypocaust worked, which was more than could be said for either Hadrian or Antinous, both of whom tagged along in apparent wonderment.

'There should be some steps down to a fireplace,' I said.

'No. Not this house,' said Gallus. 'See, the hill slopes down and you could walk in. It's full of ash now but it's just here.'

Polonius took a branch and poked it into the ashes that lay about. It went in a long way. He pulled it out and felt the end.

'Not very hot,' he said. 'Could be where the fire started and so it's had more time to cool than elsewhere.'

'Brilliant,' I said, and I thought it was.

'Don't get too excited,' he said. 'It could just be that being in this trench has let the ashes cool quicker than in other places!'

My hopes of an instant solution were dashed. 'But it's a good place to start digging. For one thing, it's not too hot.'

This produced another of his grunts.

'You three,' he said, for Gallus seemed to be one of the party now, 'Go back and get baskets. I want to see everything that comes out of this place, especially just here.'

'And?' I queried.

'My best guess is that if, and it's still very much if, this fire was started deliberately, then it was started here where there could have been a fire anyway.'

'But there was no one here to have a fire. There was nobody living here,' I objected.

'They might have known it was being kept shut up and thought the slaves might have had a fire to keep it aired.'

'That's as feeble as my lightning with Julius Octavius,' I laughed.

'Well, it was an idea.'

He seemed dispirited but revived when they came back with baskets and started to excavate the ashes from the entrance trench. He sorted each basket with care and made me join him in what seemed to me to be a fruitless exercise. The day dragged on and, apart from all of us being grey with wood ash, nothing new was achieved.

It was Hadrian who found it. The next day had started off the same but with more grumbles from Sparticus. Polonius did not come, saying he had better things to do and we could get filthy without his assistance. We were continuing with clearing out the drift that Gallus assured us led to the fire hole for the hypocaust when Hadrian suddenly shouted and bent down to pick something up. It was a buckle off a sandal. But not just any old sandal! It was a military one and, just like it was not just any old sandal, it didn't come from just any old foot soldier. I sent Antinous to fetch Polonius as he probably knew more about soldiers' rankings than I did. His opinion was the same as mine.

'Nice,' he said. 'Centurion, I reckon. Could be someone making his way up, hastatus to princeps perhaps but with ideas above his station. He'd have to have a bit of money behind him to buy this sort of kit. No sign of the sandal to go with it, I suppose?'

'Just the ashes, no more.'

'You're right, but look over very carefully where you found it. Hadrian and all of the rest of you, go steady, no telling what else you might find.'

But we didn't. However, we did get to the fire hole and found the wood store, all ashes, and the metal parts of rakes and shovels for pulling ashes back out of the fire, just as Gallus had said we should. These had been all bent by the heat and the pile of ash was still almost too hot to approach. I decided to abandon it at midday as, like Polonius, I had things I needed to do, and Sparticus might be a little appeased to get some of his labour back, even if only for half a day.

The buckle I hid where I hoped nobody could find it and swore my three companions to silence. I had decided to leave it another day to cool down and I debated about sending Hadrian with a message to Julius Octavius but decided against it. I would risk his wrath in the interests of keeping what we had found secret.

The fourth day of our digging revealed what had happened; or at least I thought it did. We managed to dig our way round onto the heated floor and there found that a hole had been made in it and the flue blocked with broken bricks and earth. Any fire in there would have burnt straight up into the house. To add to that, it also looked as though furniture had been moved to where it would burn nicely.

It was clever, but it must have taken a while to set up and was almost too neat a solution. Polonius and I discussed it at length.

'You've got to go and see him over there,' was his conclusion. He rarely called Julius Octavius by name. 'And then it's over to him. You've done your bit.'

'I know, but I'd still like to find out who's behind it and whether it's me they're getting at, or the system in general.'

'Wouldn't we all.'

'And why?'

'You being put in charge hasn't helped. Not that I'm saying you haven't made a good job of it, but that only makes it worse. If you'd fallen on your nose straight off, whoever it is would have been able to say "I told you so" and laughed his head off. As it is, he's stuck with you.'

This was quite a speech for Polonius and very shrewd too.

He added, 'Have you told any of the locals that you know about this?'

I shook my head.

'Worth a try. Have a look for footprints too – one shoe on, one shoe off.'

'Now that's brilliant,' I said.

'Except that it's been so dry there won't be much to see. That's also why it burnt so well.'

I was deflated.

'I'll try both and then it's off to see the dominus, but not very confidently.'

'Good luck,' he said, and I think he meant it.

I sent Hadrian off with his weekly report to Julius Octavius and also a tablet saying that I was coming to see him myself in three days' time to talk about the burning of the house. I then made it my business to 'happen' to talk to some of the carters who were waiting to load. One, Chad, was somebody that I knew quite well, and I asked if there had been anything unusual in the forest recently. He scratched his head and then said that some kids had been playing in the woods (where else was there?) and thought they had seen a patrol of soldiers. The children gently disappeared into the undergrowth and ran like madmen for home. There nobody would believe them.

'We haven't seen any patrols in years,' he explained. 'Since you lot have brought a sort of prosperity and kept all those from Cambria out, there hasn't been any need. But you'd better come back with me later 'cos Iden won't understand your language, and you don't understand ours that good.'

I took the jibes about language and prosperity in the manner in which they were given and so it was arranged.

Perhaps surprisingly, or not, I hadn't been to their village before and was intrigued as to what I might find. These people were always considered to be next best thing to savages and only capable of existing, not living. It turned out to be a small place, just a few huts, maybe six, arranged round a central area. The surrounding scrub had been cleared both to give them space but also to give warning of any unwanted visitors or animals. There was excitement at the return of one of their menfolk and alarm when they saw who he had with him. The whole population seemed ready to run or hide, or both. They stood nervously in their hut doorways trying to decide if this man Chad had brought back was good news or bad. He hailed them as we crossed the clearing and told them to fetch Iden. A tall, bedraggled man appeared from one of the huts, leaving his wife and two boys peeping round the edge of the door.

'I come to do you no harm,' I said. 'But Chad here says that your two boys saw a patrol in the woods recently.'

This was translated, with the addition that I was well known and to be trusted. I could understand the gist of what was being said. Iden tugged at his beard and lank hair and then yelled for his two boys to come.

'Better as you hear it direct from them,' he said.

The two boys came across the open space slowly and in obvious trepidation.

'Tell the man what you saw,' said their father.

They started babbling away together and then arguing with each other, as boys do, until I held up my hand to restrain them.

'Chad,' I said. 'Listen to them and tell me generally what they're saying. I can't understand a word.'

'Told you!' he said triumphantly and then listened closely to the boys before relaying it to me slowly so that I could understand.

'It seems,' he said, 'that they were playing about halfway from here to the mine, and this patrol of soldiers came by. Four of them and one in charge.'

'Is there a roadway there?' I queried. I had a fair idea where all the roads were in the immediate vicinity of the mine.

'No. That's the funny thing. They were following a sheep track and, it seemed to the boys, trying to do it quietly. Didn't seem quite sure where they were either.'

'Did they see them go back? Or anyone else see them?'

'Now that's why nobody believed the boys. They soldiers don't often do anything quietly. Usually make a big noise so's you can tell half a day's walk away that they're coming! Gives you time to get out of the way, though,' he added.

While we'd been talking, the villagers seemed to have realised that I meant them no harm and had come to gather round and listen. An old man pushed through the crowd.

'Listen to this,' he said. 'I was down by the stream yonder…' He waved an arm that encompassed the horizon all round. 'And there were footprints in the mud by it. Not our feet, Roman feet!'

'You can tell the difference?' I asked.

'He probably can,' said Chad and there was a nodding of heads in agreement from those standing around.

'And there's more,' he cackled. 'One of 'em only had one shoe on. Hobbling he must have been. One shoe on, one off!'

And he gave a demonstration to which there was laughter all around. But I wasn't laughing. I knew just what this was about and my meeting with Julius Octavius was not going to be easy. It was going to earn me enemies, even if I didn't have them already.

Chapter 20
Tiberius

The rankings of a centurion in the Roman Army, from lowest to highest, are:
- Hastatus Posterior
- Hastatus Prior
- Princeps Posterior
- Princeps Prior
- Pilus Posterior
- Pilus Prior.

At the moment I'm a Pilus Posterior. Risen right up from being a common soldier I have, so I haven't done too bad for myself, now have I? I want to make it to Pilus Prior, then I can retire. The snag is that there's not much chance of that here. As it is, I'm the highest-ranking soldier about the place – proper soldier that is, not one who's been cashiered 'cos he got it wrong. That Julius Octavius, he's a civilian now, but orders us all about like he was still in command of an army. Trouble is, he's within his rights. Somehow that's how it's been organised in this benighted place. We – the Roman army – have to take orders from a mere desk lackey!

If I'm truthful I don't know how I got to being here, guarding these furnaces and all that. The funny thing is, that seems to go for most of us: from the top, Mr High-and-Mighty himself, down to the slaves what does all the work. Mind you, they has to go wherever they're sent, no choice in it, and get the Hades beaten out of them wherever they are. Now there's another funny thing. Mr H&M don't want us to beat it out of them to make them work harder. Says it doesn't help. Says an injured slave can't work as well as a fit one. Added to that, his theory is that he's always short on slaves and doesn't know when he's going to get any more, so he can't afford to lose any for any reason at all. Rubbish, I say. Whip a few good and hard and force the rest to make up for the ones that can't take a beating. They should try being in the army for a bit, then they'd know what discipline really is, and how to enforce it!

But then again, there's a few that's in command of full-blown armies that takes his line – be nice to the ranks and they'll fight better when they has to. If I'm honest with you, I have to say that I have seen it work. Just once against the Huns. But that's the only time, and I reckon those Germans was off colour that day. Eaten too much sausage probably.

Then there's this eunuch here that keeps saying he can get my promotion for me if I help him with 'one or two things'. Don't know what he's up to but he paid well enough for setting a perfectly good house on fire. No idea why or what was in it for him. Or where he got the money from. And he got me out of trouble when I lost a sandal on the job. Got me another when, Pilus Posterior or not, I would have had all sorts of bother with the records being wrong.

Long may it last!

Chapter 21

I retrieved the buckle from its hiding place in the crack in the wall and, with it securely in my pocket, made my way to Ariconium. It was a nice sunny day – we'd been having a better summer than usual – but I was unable to appreciate it. My mind was elsewhere, rehearsing what I was going to say to Julius Octavius. As so often, I was expected, and was shown into his presence rapidly.

The eunuch was particularly ingratiating. It put all my senses on the alert. Was he behind all this, trying to create a problem for me? And if so, why? I could understand him having a grudge against a system that made him the way he was, but why should he have anything against me? Was I being naïve again, as Julius Octavius had said before? Possibly. My rise from labouring slave to being in charge had been pretty instantaneous, but how did that affect *him*?

After the usual pleasantries, and on the spur of the moment, I opted to say nothing. I just laid the buckle on Julius Octavius' desk.

There was a very sharp intake of breath behind me and the eunuch stumbled and almost fell. My natural instinct was to go to his assistance, but he brushed me aside. This little scene was not lost on our mutual dominus.

'And what's this?' Julius Octavius enquired, quietly and at his most imperious. After our last meeting I was not intimidated by this but I could feel that the eunuch was.

'Dominus, you asked me to dig into the ruins of Gaius Maximus' house to see if we could find anything to give a clue as to how the fire started.'

'I did give you those orders, and it appears that you consider this buckle to be of some significance.'

'You, dominus, would know. I'm only going on what Polonius has to say, but the suggestion is that this belongs to a military sandal, not necessarily to someone of high rank but certainly above foot soldier level.

Perhaps a centurion rising in his ranking, but also someone who could afford better than standard issue sandals.'

'Do you know anyone like that?' He threw the question at the eunuch.

'Oh, no, dominus.' His voice sounded even squeakier than its normal high pitch.

'I'm afraid there's more,' I said. 'According to Gallus, who was a house slave for Gaius Maximus, there were no shoes or sandals in the house that had buckles like this one. We didn't find any sign of the sandal or shoe to which it should have been attached, but that would certainly have been burnt to ashes along with everything else. However, one of the locals that I know quite well…'

There was a snort from the eunuch behind me, and Julius Octavius didn't look too pleased either. Knowing the locals was apparently something of a crime. I ploughed on.

'A few soldiers were seen in the area at about the right time but whether they were part of a larger force I don't know.'

I carefully omitted the fact that this was reported by mere children.

'However, one of the elders of the village noticed footprints in the mud by a stream that suggested someone walking with only one shoe, or sandal, the other foot being bare.'

Julius Octavius' face was impassive.

'What else?' he asked in a very hard voice, but for whose benefit I couldn't judge. I began to get nervous. Was I being too clever?

'When the heat had subsided a bit, we dug into the hypocaust. It looked as though it had been deliberately blocked and a hole made so that the heat and flames would have gone up into the room. Gallus, again – and I'm sorry – said that it was in good working order when last used.'

I stopped at that point because anything further would be pure conjecture. There was a long silence. I stood my ground but the eunuch was breathing heavily and noisily. It was for Julius Octavius to make the next move, and it was directed at the eunuch. I almost felt sorry for him.

'Check the records,' he said. 'Check the inventories. See if there are any discrepancies in the number of centurion's sandals. Check with the sandal makers to see if anyone has asked for a one-off favour.'

'And send Tiberius to me!' he shouted after the departing eunuch as he wormed his way off.

Silence descended again. I just stood. I had not yet met, but had heard of, this Tiberius. He was the Pilus Posterior here, or the next to highest rank of centurion, and had an unsavoury reputation in what was otherwise a well organised and efficient operation. There came the sound of rapid footsteps and a short but nevertheless imposing man entered the room. His uniform was immaculate and his sword hung at his side. Without moving my head I swivelled my eyes to see his feet and from what I could judge one of his sandals looked brighter than the other!

'You called, dominus!' he shouted, as though they were on opposite sides of a parade ground.

Julius Octavius turned to me.

'Tell Tiberius what you've just told me,' he said.

'I would rather hear it from you, dominus,' said Tiberius. Obviously it was anathema to him to be told anything by someone as inferior as me.

'Better that you hear it first-hand, Tiberius, rather than you getting my version and Marcus here having to correct us.'

Tiberius stood very straight and erect. The idea that he, or even Julius Octavius, might have to be corrected by a mere slave was inconceivable. I gulped and said my piece again, only leaving out Polonius' name and emphasising that my digging in the ruins was at Julius Octavius' instruction. At the conclusion, Tiberius continued to stand very upright but said nothing.

'Well?' said Julius Octavius.

'Am I supposed to believe what this young idiot is saying?' he enquired.

'It would be well for you if you did!'

It was the first time I had seen Julius O use his authority.

'It's absolute rubbish. Pure drivel. I know where my soldiers are at all times and I know what they're doing. If there'd been a patrol out I would have ordered it – and I didn't.'

He shut his mouth with a snap like a trap. Julius Octavius seemed unperturbed.

'And what do you make of someone having to walk back with only one sandal?'

'Well, if you're going to believe what the local people say then…' He left his comments unspoken, which was perhaps more eloquent that anything he might have said. 'And in any case there was no patrol out. As I have just said,' he added unnecessarily.

'So you say.'

Tiberius stood his ground and said nothing.

'You will go and check the footwear of all your centurions to see if there is any evidence that tallies with what you have just been told. I will have your report within the hour! The records and the inventories are being checked.'

Tiberius sniffed, expressing his opinion of the eunuch.

'Now, go.'

Tiberius turned smartly and marched out with his head held high. Silence returned.

'Marcus, you will go to the hostel. You will stay there. You will not move out.'

'Is this that serious?'

'It might be, so you will follow my instructions to the letter.'

'Of course, dominus.'

'I will send Clio to you with a message if needed.'

I blushed and he laughed, which made me blush more.

'You'll be quite safe to get there now – they all have other things on their minds at the moment. But later – well, just be careful.'

Rumour and gossip, true or not, flourished in Ariconium. I hadn't had time to finish a bowl of soup and eat some bread before Helen of Troy came and said coyly, 'Who's been upsetting Tiberius then?'

'Not me,' I said.

'Not what I heard!'

'Only doing my job like I was told, and reporting back what I found.'

'You're naïve. You know that?'

'You're not the first person to say it.'

'There you are then, but seriously, you want to be careful. Pilus T could make a very nasty enemy. He wants to make the final grade as a centurion and he doesn't stand much chance here as there are no battles going on –

may all the gods be praised. He knows that and is out to do anything that he thinks might improve his chances.'

'That fits, sort of.'

'He's got himself in with that eunuch, even though he hates his guts, and I reckon they're up to something – although a fat lot of good I think it will do either of them.'

'That also fits.'

'Yeah. Well you be very careful. I like you, and I don't want to see any harm coming to you.'

This was praise indeed and from an unlikely quarter, not that it was going to help me much just at the moment. She had her hostel to run and I had my mine to run, and that was all there was to it. But it did set me thinking.

If I was right, why on earth would Tiberius have gone all the way to Clearwell with possibly as many as four soldiers and set fire to Gaius Maximus' house? As likely as not he was scared of the local population, so felt he needed some protection if he should meet any of them. He wouldn't have had the rapport with them that I had. As for his soldiers, they would simply obey orders. If he said to burn down a perfectly good house, they would burn it down. If he said to dig up the hypocaust floor first, they would dig it up. In the army, discipline is everything. If an officer gives you an order, you follow it or you're dead meat.

But none of this answered why. OK, two people have now called me naïve, but I can see no good reason why Tiberius should want to get at me. Our paths don't cross. His job is to guard the furnaces, mine is to provide the iron ore that gives him something to guard. No connection. To my mind at least. Even if, as Helen of Troy said, he's in cahoots with the eunuch, how is that going to help his promotion? I went round in circles on this one and finally decided it wasn't a problem I could solve. It was one for Julius Octavius, and he would no doubt tell me eventually if it in any way affected me.

I would just have to wait for Clio to fetch me, and thinking about her was much more to my liking. But when she came she was nervous and on edge. I don't think she had been to the hostel, at least officially, before. She was more upset that there had been a further row between Julius Octavius,

Tiberius and the eunuch. The latter pair insisted that there was nothing amiss and that no patrols had been sent out. Julius Octavius was convinced otherwise but was unable to prove anything. She was alarmed that I was caught in the middle and seemed to be making an enemy. We tried to chat about more pleasant matters, but it was no use; we both had weightier matters on our minds. In the end she went back sooner than either of us would have wished, and nearly forgot to give me the message that had brought her there in the first place. I was to wait until a messenger came to fetch me.

In due course the messenger came and I was taken to Julius Octavius' house. I was certain that the whole place was watching and waiting, and that Tiberius would be the first to be told of my movements, but I couldn't do anything about it. Julius Octavius was in charge and his word was law. Everyone should know that! As last time I was ushered into the office in his house and, again as last time, he apologised for the apparent subterfuge. He came straight to the point.

'I don't believe a word they're telling me,' he said.

What was I, in my position, to say to that?

'Dominus?' I queried.

'The eunuch and Tiberius like to give the impression that they hate each other's guts but why is it that I'm sure they're in this, whatever it is, together?'

Again I was stuck for an answer but fortunately he carried on.

'In fairness, I think Tiberius dislikes the eunuch for what he is rather more than anything else. I'm not that fond of him myself but he has his uses where keeping all the records are concerned.'

'And he didn't come up with any missing buckles or sandals?' At last I could make a constructive comment.

'No, but I don't wholly believe him.'

'And Tiberius?'

'I don't believe him either, but he's adamant that he hasn't sent out any patrols. And the eunuch backs him up as he says he would have had to issue stores, weapons, and so on if he had.'

'Dominus, may I venture a suggestion?'

'You know you can, Marcus. Don't be a fool.'

'Thank you, but what I want to suggest is treason coming from a mere slave like me and I would rather be a live slave who had said nothing than a dead one who had said too much.'

'Go on, get on with it. You have my word.'

'I think Tiberius led the patrol that fired the house. So, technically, he's telling the truth when he says that he didn't send out any patrols. He was that patrol! Also I'm not alone in thinking that he and the eunuch are in this together, although what's in it for them I have no idea. But if so, it would have been easy to cover everything up. Even the loss of one of his own sandals.'

Julius Octavius leant back in his chair and eyed me in a way that I found very uncomfortable. He had given me his word and I trusted him, but it looked as though it was going to be a close run thing.

'Are you suggesting to me that Tiberius himself burnt that house down?' His voice was icy.

'Yes, dominus.' What else could I say? I was.

There was a long pause.

'Now I know I did the right thing when I told you to go and run the mine!'

'Thank you, dominus.' I was running out of things to say.

'I shall give you your final orders tomorrow on the assumption that others will hear them. Where are you living at the moment?'

'I'm still sleeping in Polonius' office – it's safe and secure, but I eat elsewhere.'

'I want you to rebuild that house and live in it.' This was outrageous. 'Do it slowly and make sure everyone knows that it's on my orders. No need to do it to the standard that my late friend Gaius liked, but adequate for yourself or visitors. I'll think the details through and we'll talk again in the morning. And I'll send two of my staff back with you to the hostel. I think one or other of our two friends has got it in for you.'

It was dark by this time and I was glad of the escort. It did seem very dark indeed around the settlement.

True to his word he sent Clio for me the following morning and barked orders at me that repeated what he had said the night before. The only addition was that once I had a building that was complete and habitable I was to have a guard to protect it from any marauders who might want to set it on fire again. Whether this order was for others to hear or was for real I couldn't work out. In any case it would be a while before I reached that stage.

I only had the chance to make the appropriate noises of acceptance, like 'Yes, dominus,' and 'Of course, dominus,' all in the spirit of the charade he was enacting.

I left then, with the eunuch gloating at my discomfiture. I think he really did think I'd had a strip torn off me, but I have to say that I was very unsure what the future held. This all smacked of the sort of intrigues that led Pater to the lions and Mater to Tarsus.

Chapter 22

So I had another weary walk back to the mine with a thousand and one thoughts whirling round in my head. The only consolation was that it wasn't dark this time. It was becoming increasingly apparent that mining for iron ore was the least of my worries. The fact that I couldn't see the point of rebuilding the house in any form appeared to be irrelevant. And as for my living in it – that was just ridiculous. Nevertheless Julius Octavius had ordered it, so it had to be done. This was where his military background made itself known, but that wasn't peculiar to him: virtually anyone who was anyone within the Empire had a military background.

When I got back, both Polonius and Sparticus wanted to know what had happened, but I side-stepped the question by saying that all was well and that we would talk the following morning. I also wanted to know if all was well with them. It was, except that Polonius had his usual grouse about wanting to dig down in the bottom of the mine to try to find another seam of ore. Equally, as usual, I had to fudge that one.

The following day we sat down so that I could explain what needed doing and for us to work out how to do it.

'He wants us to rebuild the house,' I said.

'He wants what?' shouted Polonius.

'Who with?' said Sparticus.

I could see where their priorities lay.

'He says,' and I indicated that I didn't quite believe him, 'that he doesn't want it done to the high standard it was before. Just so that it's habitable and might be suitable for guests, although who in the world is likely to want to visit us I don't know. Unless he's thinking of coming himself.'

'And what do any of us know about building?' said Sparticus.

'Probably not that much different from mining,' commented Polonius. 'At least you're only holding up a roof not half a hill!'

'Yeah, but it needs to be a bit more sophisticated,' I said.

'And how many men are you going to take out to do this?'

'Probably not many. Again, he says,' I rolled my eyes upward, 'that he's not in a hurry to see this done.'

'My arse,' said Polonius. 'If he wants it done at all, he wants it done soon!'

'My thinking exactly,' I said.

'Well, how many do you want?' said Sparticus resignedly.

'Initially, not many. The first job is going to be to clear the place of rubble, ashes and half-burnt timber, then we can see what we've got. But there's more.'

They both groaned.

'Once we get to having anything like a building, we're to guard it, especially at night.'

They groaned again.

'Who's going to do that?' demanded Sparticus. 'I can maybe spare a few to help with the house, but guarding it – that's another thing altogether.'

'I know, I know. It's not immediate but I think you'll have to find another Trojan, if not two, to be able to do that successfully.'

'Any new slaves due soon?' he asked.

'Might be by the time we need them.'

'Then, like you said once before, we wait.'

'So who can you spare for a start? How about the ones I had when we found the buckle?'

'Gallus…'

'Yes, I want him because he knows what the place was like before.'

'Antinous?'

'Yes, he's quite bright and keen.'

'I know you and Hadrian were pals but he's got to being a bit of a troublemaker. He's become a big strong lad and inclined to throw his weight about. I'd be careful there.'

'Guard duty?' I suggested.

'Maybe,' was all I got in return.

'OK. I'll use him for the initial clearing. If he causes trouble then it's back to the mine for him. If you need him either here or at Puzzlewood then you can have him back instantly and the same goes for the house slaves, although I doubt they'd be much use.

I turned to Polonius. 'What about materials?'

'What was it built of?' Typical Polonius – trying to catch me out.

'I don't know, do I?' I could give him as good as I got.

He gave one of his derogatory grunts to put me in my place. 'It's mostly stone so we can get that from the mine or possibly easier from Puzzlewood. For timber we'll have to fell a few trees – there's plenty of them!' he added, surveying the surrounding forest.

'When do you want to start?' said Sparticus.

They both seemed reasonably enthusiastic, which boded well.

'Not for a few days. I want to have a thoroughly good look at what's there and then set about it with some sort of order.'

'You're learning,' grunted Polonius.

'Thanks to you,' I said. He seemed pleased.

And so it came about that I spent most of two days just wandering round the ruined building trying to work out what I was going to do. I didn't know much about building but then I hadn't known anything about mining either, yet somehow I'd coped. I was certain that Polonius knew more than he was letting on, and if Gallus had any real idea of what the place had been like then maybe, just maybe, I could pull this one off as well.

But I knew I had to be careful. Two very different people had now called me naïve and I could only presume that they had a point. If those at Ariconium thought they were in a backwater, and for their own reasons either loved it or hated it, then I was in an even more remote stretch of countryside where absolutely nothing happened – apart from arson and the odd riot! Because of my traipsing round the neighbourhood as a runner for Polonius I had built up a rapport with some of the local people. Thus I had a good relationship with most of those in and around Clearwell but had obviously ruffled some significant feathers elsewhere.

Three days later we started.

'So what are you doing this for?' asked Hadrian. He was almost certainly speaking for all three of them when he said it.

'Simple,' I said. 'Because I've been ordered to do it.'

'Why?'

'No idea. You know as well as I do that we do as we're told or the consequences get unpleasant.'

The other two nodded their heads in agreement, but Hadrian wasn't taking it that easily.

'What's the point? Who's going to live in it when it's done?'

'No idea.'

'You?'

'Don't be daft. Me? In a house like this was?'

'Could be.'

He was taunting me and I could see what Sparticus meant. Maybe I had made a mistake in bringing him out here.

'Silly talk. Now let's get at it. First I want all the ashes moved into a pile over there, well out of the way. Then we can start on the ruined materials. Separate out stone, wood, even if it's part burnt, anything that's metal plus any odds and bits that might be useful. Hopefully Gallus will be able to tell us what we're getting to and what it is.'

Some serious work would perhaps bring Hadrian to heel. It seemed to have a good effect but I wasn't entirely sure about him. In any case he was still acting as runner to Ariconium and had to go off for a while during that first week. He wasn't actively difficult, but we seemed to get more done without him. Interesting!

The fire had been very intense and very destructive. I wondered what Tiberius, assuming it was him, had used to make it burn with such intensity. Had he brought oil or very small dry wood with him? There was little for us to salvage. Effectively all the wood had been totally burnt and any that hadn't was in such small pieces as to be useless. The stone walls of the main block had partially collapsed and would have to be rebuilt. Gallus said that there had never been any fancy mosaics, but the heat had seriously damaged the stone-flagged floors. As we knew from our previous excavations, the hypocaust had been deliberately damaged, but beyond that it was repairable. The earth walls of the outbuildings barely existed. It was going to be some job.

Once we had cleared up a bit I sent word to Julius Octavius questioning whether he wanted us to continue, given that this would be almost like building a new villa. I also pointed out that the cost was likely to be heavy in respect of materials, and especially manpower, which would have to be taken from the mine.

His answer was terse and to the point: *Get on with it but keep the ore coming.*

More or less what I expected. Neither Polonius nor Sparticus was pleased. Also as expected.

'How does he intend us to do that?' they both grumbled.

'We need to get digging down to a lower level, not wasting time on fancy houses that nobody's going to live in,' said Polonius.

'And we're already tight on numbers for doing what we have to do,' added Sparticus.

'You know how it is,' I said. 'The big man says and…'

They knew. I didn't have to say more.

'Do we have any builders amongst your slaves, either underground or among the loaders?' I asked Sparticus.

'Not that I know of,' he said, 'But I'll ask.'

The next day he came to me with one, Lepidus, who he said had been on building work. The poor man thought he was in big trouble to be brought to me, but although he seemed a bit doubtful about how much he knew, he had indeed worked on building houses.

'I was mostly on digging foundations an' that,' he tried to explain. 'Did a bit of stone work but never nothing with wood, like.'

'That's why I have him loading carts,' said Sparticus. He tapped his temple, suggesting that the man was not quite all there, which seemed quite likely. But it was a start, even if my main concern was for a carpenter. I knew that there was at least one in the mine who did shoring up with timber baulks where necessary. I got onto Polonius about him.

'The main thing is that I can't spare him,' he said, 'but on top of that, he's good with tree trunks but hasn't got much idea with anything smaller. Now, we used to have a very good man but he got killed in a rock fall.'

'No help then!' I said.

'No. You're going to get stuck.'

He seemed to be gloating, which was unlike him.

I had no option but to see if they had anyone at Ariconium that they could spare. Yes. One of Tiberius' soldiers did all the woodwork there and had a full kit of tools with him. Julius Octavius would have him released to me if I wanted. I most definitely did not want. Tiberius spelled trouble and if he thought he was doing me a favour he would be insufferable. I had another idea.

On the basis that he had some idea of what the finished building should be like, I took Gallus with me on a local tour. Of course I had some knowledge myself from the houses where we had lived in Rome, but I was only a child then, and those tended to be very grand houses where slaves of Pater's ilk could be afforded. Whatever else I was doing, it was not replicating that sort of establishment. We went to the shrine of Nodens first, where I knew there was a grand villa more on the Roman style. They were very snooty and wouldn't even let two slaves through the door, despite the fact that I had put on my best tunic and had personally scrubbed Gallus so that he didn't look too much as though he had just come out of a mine – which of course he had!

So we moved on up the big river to the new settlement where I had met my friendly centurion some years before. Needless to say he had been moved on, but his successor and his soldiers, the local traders and the local natives were friendly enough. Or maybe it was simply that somebody building a house meant a bit of profit for all of them. More to the point I found a competent carpenter who claimed he could do all that I wanted, from felling the trees to putting a roof on our buildings. Whilst he was a freed man himself, Drusius by name, he employed a number of the local people to help him. I liked this because it kept the locals on our side. Those of us who belonged to the Empire, whether slave or freed, were a bit thin on the ground in these parts and could easily be outnumbered in any argument.

The only problem with Drusius was that he would have to be paid in actual money. I couldn't just lose his costs in the running of the mine. That was going to be down to Julius Octavius, but guessing from the way he was carrying on it wouldn't be a problem. The settlement had ceased to be a little village beside the great river and had become something of a town. As such, it now had available many of the fittings and items of furniture that I knew we would need as the building progressed. I was surprised that I had never heard Julius Octavius mention it, but then it was so new that he probably didn't know it existed. Especially as it didn't really have a name yet. Some called it simply the New Town and some New Hamm, but where they got the Hamm bit from I don't know.

When we got back to the mine, Hadrian and the others were just arriving back from their day's work at the house.

'There's a strange one there waiting for you,' he said.

'What do you mean?' I said. 'I'm not expecting anyone.'

'Maybe not but he's expecting you.'

'Sorry?'

'This man – at least I presume it's a man,' the others laughed, 'came by and asked for the dominus.'

'So we told him,' continued Antinous, 'that you were away for three days and could be back tonight. So he said he'd wait.'

'Wait? He could have been waiting for days.'

'We told him that but it didn't bother him. He just sat down and watched us – and waited!'

'What's he want?'

'No idea.'

'Is he dangerous?'

'Shouldn't think so. He's got nothing with him to be dangerous with.'

'Nothing at all?'

'Only the clothes he stands up in, and they're weird too.'

'I think I'd better go and see,' I said.

'Best of Roman luck,' they guffawed.

I was tired from my travels and had many things to think about but I knew I had to go and investigate this. If nothing else, Julius Octavius' insistence on guarding the place started to ring in my ears. I had done nothing serious about this on the basis that up to now there were only a few half-destroyed walls to guard.

What I found was going have a profound effect on my life from here on, and it was going to be not only for the better but also for the worse.

Chapter 23
Benedictus

The crowd in the Coliseum roared their approval for the next item of the afternoon's bloodletting. Lions were going to eat Christians. It wasn't quite such fun as seeing gladiators kill each other, because for that you could bet on who might win and in turn win a bit of cash yourself. No good betting on the lions because they always won as the Christians weren't given anything with which to defend themselves. In fact these Christians weren't much good anyway; even if they were given weapons and put up against the rawest gladiatorial recruit they rarely fought with any conviction. But to see the lions treating them as a cat plays with a mouse was good sport and they always got eaten in the end.

I was on the menu for the lions' afternoon snack. There were six of us. Christians we may have been and sure of our place in God's Kingdom, but the prospect of being mauled to death by a huge beast of a lion simply for the amusement of the crowd was not a pleasant one. It was only marginally better than being crucified, as Our Lord had been, and then only in so far that we would die quicker. We knelt in prayer, but what could I say in those prayers that could be helpful in the circumstances?

The time came and we were chivvied out at spearpoint. One of our number fought back and was speared on the spot. It was a quick and possibly blessed release. In the arena there was a huge lion and three lionesses all supposedly hungry for human flesh. They gathered on their haunches like cats about to pounce, which of course they were.

I fell to my knees and prayed for the crowd, the Emperor and my fellow Christians. I shut my eyes. I had decided that I preferred not to see into the lion's mouth as his jaws encircled my head. I heard screams, and roars from both lions and the crowd. And then it went quiet. And I mean quiet. So quiet I could hear something moving up to me. This was going to be the end. But no! I could smell and feel warm breath upon me. Lion's breath. It couldn't be anything else. Then I felt a rasping like a grater on my skin. It was a lion, *the* lion, licking me! The quiet continued and I could hear him padding away. I heard the crowd release its collective breath.

Then a great voice shouted: 'The man lives!'

They told me afterwards that it was the Emperor.

After that I'm a bit confused about what happened, but I gather that the spearmen were sent in to get the lions out of the arena and one of them was killed in the process. Somebody came and gathered me up, took me forward and told me to bow to the Emperor for saving my life. I did of course, but it wasn't him who saved my life, it was the Lord Jesus. I was told I was free to go. Just me out of the six who had started out.

My salvation must have had some effect as it was not long after this that Christianity became allowed, and ultimately became the official religion of the Empire. But I didn't wait for that: I moved slowly away from Rome, almost as far as I could go, to Britannia, and even then buried myself well away from the centre of things. I did not want a repeat of that experience. Indeed it was very unlikely that it would be repeated!

Chapter 24

I found what had been described to me. Sitting cross-legged amongst the detritus of a part-built house was a man who scrambled to his feet as he heard me coming. He had close-cropped hair but a long and straggly beard. He was dressed in a long cloak-like garment that reached to his ankles with a piece of old rope tied around his waist. Worn-out sandals more or less covered his feet. His only possession seemed to be a staff that was longer than he was tall. However, his most striking features were piercing grey eyes and a laughing face.

He spoke before I had the chance to do so.

'Welcome,' he said, very much as though the house was completed and he was greeting me at his own front door! I was considerably taken aback.

'And who are you that you choose to welcome me thus?' I said with some asperity.

'Oh, it doesn't matter who I am.'

His tone was casual, as though it indeed did not matter.

'You can't just come here, stop my men from working, hang about waiting for me – I might not have been back for days – and then say it doesn't matter who you are!'

A cloud visibly crossed his smiling face.

'Oh, dear me. I'm sorry. I didn't mean to stop your people working and indeed I didn't think I had.'

I let out a Polonius-style grunt but I don't think he was as impressed as he should have been.

'I'm sure it is you I want to see and I'm prepared to wait. In fact I can wait as long as you like.'

This was getting silly.

'You mean you would have waited until I got back, whenever that might have been?'

'Yes,' he said, but did not elaborate.

'So what do you want to see me about?'

'That is important, to me anyway, but you've had a hard day, so that too can wait. Tomorrow or the next day, or the one after that will do.'

'Do you have a name?' I asked in exasperation.

'I do, but that doesn't matter for now either.'

'So what do you want?'

He looked at the sky.

'For now somewhere I can sleep without getting too wet, and a morsel to eat, be it only a very small morsel.'

He was certainly not slow in coming forward, and I was about to turf him off the premises with a serious warning not to come back, when I remembered how grateful I had been to Polonius for the food he brought me when we first met. This man obviously had something to tell me that, while important, could wait until I was in a better frame of mind. I relented.

'Come with me,' I said brusquely.

We went back towards the mine. Noting that he followed me, not trying to walk with me, and that he did not speak at all in that time, I mellowed a little towards him. I pointed towards an open hovel in which we kept a bit of hay and told him that he could sleep there. He turned a thankful face towards me.

'Bless you,' he said.

'I'll bring you some food,' I said. This was getting embarrassing.

He bowed his head towards me but said nothing.

I returned after a while with some old bread and dripping for him to eat. I would see how fussy he was!

He took it from me, held it up and said, 'Bless you and this food.' Then he retreated into the hay to eat and sleep.

I was mystified but intrigued at the same time. I went to find Sparticus and tell him that our visitor was allowed to be where he was, but nowhere else, in case anyone should come across him.

'I heard about him,' said Sparticus. 'What you going to do with him?'

'Hear what he has to say and throw him out,' I said.

'Best thing too. Good night.'

Intrigued I might have been, but the following day did not get off to a good start. I had only been away two nights and from the problems that had arisen I might as well have been away for ten. I arranged for some small amount of food to be sent to my visitor and then immersed myself in the affairs of mining iron ore. Polonius was in one of his grumpy moods about having to dig deeper, especially as the ore quality from Puzzlewood seemed to be getting worse. I was going to have to face up to a confrontation with Julius Octavius about this one. Sparticus had two slaves off sick and one who had dropped a large rock on his foot and broken it. We agreed that it had not been deliberate. I had to send Hadrian off with a message to Ariconium about all this, so it was past noon before I got to seeing my visitor.

I took two fresh baked rolls with me, one for him and one for me. I found him more or less precisely where I had left him, still sitting cross-legged, but now leaning back against the wall while watching all that passed in front of him. On seeing me coming he jumped to his feet with an alacrity that belied his appearance.

'Well?' I said. I was determined to play hard to get.

'Do you have time?' he asked.

'As much as I shall ever have.'

'Good. Shall we talk here?'

'It's as good as anywhere.' I was certainly not taking him inside.

'Excellent. Pray be seated!'

He made a sweeping gesture. Again he was welcoming me into my own premises! We settled ourselves into the hay.

'So what do you want with me?' I asked.

He thought for a moment.

'Not necessarily you in particular, but you're a good starting point.'

I said nothing.

'Who's your favourite god?' he asked.

'Vulcan.' I didn't think about it, which I later realised I should have done.

'Why?'

'Because he's good for mining and metal-working and that sort of thing.' I became a bit vague.

As though reading my thoughts, he said, 'And what about the rest of them?'

'To be honest I don't know much about them.'

'But you still use them?'

'When it seems sensible. Like Nodens from down the road.'

'Is that all?'

'Yes.' I was bemused. 'Look, what's all this nonsense about?'

'Suppose I told you that you only need one god, not all this pantheon of gods for every little need?'

'Are you…?'

The light was beginning to dawn.

'Yes,' he said and his face lit up with a laughing grin.

'But that's illegal!'

'Not any more it's not. A few years back Emperor Constantine allowed us Christians to worship openly without fear of death.'

'I hadn't heard that, but then we're a long way from the centre of things here.'

'Exactly why I'm here.' There was a triumphant note in his voice. 'And you're halfway to being a Christian anyway.'

'Don't be ridiculous. I'm sure I can't just be a Christian.'

'True, but what I'm saying is that there are two main things about being a Christian. The first is to love our God very dearly, and that comes with time. The second is to love your neighbour as yourself. Well, you've done the second by providing me with shelter and food. See what I mean?'

'I shall have to think about it.' I was playing for time.

'You do that. You've got enough to think about for a start. We'll talk another day, assuming you don't mind if I stay and sleep in your hay.'

'You can stay,' I said, still trying not to be too friendly. 'And I'll send some more food over.'

'Bless you again.'

I got up and stumbled away. This strange man seemed to have got into my innermost soul. I turned and shouted to him, 'Now tell me your name!'

'Benedictus,' he called back and turned away from me.

I still had nowhere to call home. I ate with everyone else and still slept in Polonius's office. I had nowhere to just sit and think. I bumped into Polonius on my way back.

'Who's that fellow you've got in the hay shed?' he growled.

'I wish I knew,' I said.

'Well, what's he doing there then?'

I jerked my head in the direction of his office and we walked there in silence.

'This man got something on you?' he said once we were inside and I had ensured the door was shut.

'No, far from it. He's a Christian and he's trying to convert me!'

Polonius snorted. 'Get you killed more likely.'

'He says that it's allowed now.'

'First I've heard of it.'

'Me too.'

'So what about him?'

'You've always been good to me, Polonius. What do you think of these Christians?'

'You know I haven't got a lot of time for any of this god bit. Life's always been too hard for me to believe in anything beyond the next meal. I leave it to the missus. She's keen on it. Always got a candle in a shrine or a sacrifice to one god or another. They say these Christians have only got one god so that must make it easy.'

'That's sort of what he said and he said that I was halfway to being one anyway. And,' I pointed a finger at him, 'if I am, you are too!'

Polonius looked distinctly alarmed.

'Whaddya mean? I don't know nothing about them.'

I laughed.

'You remember when we first met and you brought me some food and I was more than grateful?'

He nodded.

'Well I remembered that and gave him some stale bread last night and took him a roll this morning. He says that being nice to everyone else is part of being a Christian. So that makes you one too.'

'Rubbish!' he exploded. 'That was a reward for getting me out of a hole. I can tell you this: I was more grateful to you than you ever could have been to me.'

I laughed again.

'No matter, we're both Christians now!'

He turned very serious. 'Now you watch out, Marcus. You get into that, legal or not, you could find yourself in bad trouble. Talk to him if you must, but keep whatever he says a secret that only you know. There's plenty about here would like an excuse to pull you down a bit.'

'I know, I've been forcibly warned.'

'Well, take notice of it. Don't be naïve.'

'Oh, don't you start! You're the third one to tell me that.'

'Third time. Must be true.'

'At least you're superstitious, Polonius, even if you don't believe in their gods.'

He wagged a finger at me. 'Don't treat it as funny. It could be serious for you.'

'I know, I know. I'll be careful.'

'Good.'

This was followed by one of his notoriously dismissive grunts and he went off back to his hut. I was left to lock myself in again and think about what I should do next. I wanted to talk to this man and hear what he had to say. I didn't know why, but from what little he had said and from what I had heard about Christians they seemed to make some sort of sense. I just about remembered Mater and Pater talking about them when I was younger. They dismissed them as being harmless and no threat to anyone unless you were cruel or enjoyed taking too many bribes. And of course there were plenty of those in Rome. I determined to leave him for a few days but I would ensure that he was given food so that he didn't trouble anyone else. He might get fed up and go off to bother somebody else, although I doubted it.

Over the next few days there were problems underground, not least of which was that for some reason we were short of carters, and that was blamed on the locals needing the carts to get their harvest in. I was sceptical about this and had to do some serious persuading to get the right quantity of ore moving again. A slave was seriously injured when he fell off a rock face at Puzzlewood. The number of slaves allocated to us was always only just enough, so to lose even one could be critical.

As a result it was nearly a week before I got to speak to Benedictus. In fairness he had been no trouble. He had been content to stay in the hay shed and eat whatever was given him, and always with profuse thanks and blessings to whoever happened to bring it. He took the trouble to ask Sparticus if he could walk a bit in order to get some exercise, and I think even the hard-boiled gang-master softened a bit towards him.

'So,' I said, 'we can finally talk to each other. Whatever is it you have to say that makes you to wait about for so long? And why me?'

'Well,' he said slowly, 'I heard that your pater had a spot of bother at the Coliseum. I did too, but I survived.'

I was floored. Very few people here knew about that and yet it seemed that it was common knowledge somewhere.

'How did you know that?' I spluttered.

'It doesn't matter,' he said, 'but it gives us a sort of a bond, shall we say.'

'So what do you want? Are you here to blackmail me? I'm not worth it. Do you know that?'

I could hear and feel my voice rising.

'Now you have offended me.'

'Well, what then?'

'Ever heard of Jesus Christ?' he continued, as though not a harsh word had passed my lips.

'Yes,' I said sullenly. I was not being drawn.

'Ever heard of Saul, or Paul, from Tarsus?'

I didn't reply. I couldn't. This man knew too much and was playing with me. After a long pause I said, 'Mater was sent there when Pater was…' I was unable to finish.

'Oh,' he said. 'I'm very sorry. That, I didn't know, or I wouldn't have mentioned Paul.'

'Who is he anyway?'

'Was he.'

'Who was he then?'

'He came from Tarsus. He was sent out to persecute those who believed in Jesus and called themselves Christians, but he saw a vision on his way to Damascus and was blinded. He wrestled with himself and eventually became a believer. Then his sight returned.'

'A miracle then.'

'Yes and I am a miracle too, but we won't talk about that. Are you a miracle?'

'Me? No, I'm just a slave doing his job.'

'A fairly important slave, by what I hear. They tell me you can read and write, so, for a slave, you must be a miracle!'

And his face broke into a ready smile.

I was embarrassed. 'There's plenty that can read,' I said.

'Not out here there's not. In Rome maybe, but here even the ones you'd expect to be able to read can't. Or maybe only just. And that goes for freed men too.'

'Tell me about Rome,' I said. I needed to change the subject and he had made me feel nostalgic for my childhood. 'You've obviously been there since I have. Even then I was only a child.'

'Christianity can wait till another day, eh?'

I nodded.

'Rome gets worse. In fact if I were to try and predict the future, which I don't do, I'd say Rome hadn't got long to live. There's always been intrigue and backbiting in Rome but it's got impossible for an honest man to live in the place. The only good thing that's happened recently is Christianity suddenly being permissible, even becoming the supposedly official religion. But it won't last. The Empire's getting ragged round the edges and could cave in on itself. Are you getting any trouble round here?'

'No, it's very quiet. No need for any soldiers, and that means they're bored and cause more trouble than anyone else.'

'If they were on the edge of Gaul near the Germans and the Huns they'd know differently.'

'And if the Empire collapses as you suggest will happen, then what?'

'We're all on our own. But it won't. Not in my lifetime anyway. Perhaps in yours, but you'll cope.'

'I'm not so sure about that.'

'You have done, so far. Have faith!'

'That's maybe where you have to help me.'

'Amen to that,' said Benedictus.

Chapter 25

I was unsettled by what Benedictus had had to say, in fact, as much as anything by what he hadn't said. The possibility of the Empire being on the point of collapse was not new but had largely been the province of disgruntled soldiers and others who thought the world owed them something. Coming from a thoughtful person like him lent it a credence that it didn't otherwise have. More disconcerting was the fact that, whilst he proclaimed himself to be a Christian, and undoubtedly I thought he was, he didn't seem to be doing much to convert me if that was his purpose in life. And as a side issue, how had he found out about Pater?

My life was becoming very busy. The mine was my principal anxiety as Julius Octavius never missed a chance to exhort me to keep the supplies to Ariconium coming in a steady and uninterrupted stream. But then he also wanted the house built, and that seemed to have almost as high a priority in his thinking. And now I had Benedictus to think about. I realised that that was my problem, not his, but I did really rather want to know what this Christianity thing was all about and why it had been such an issue. After all, with the numerous gods that the Romans worshipped, what difference was another one going to make?

It was time to move on to something that had been on my mind for a while, and that was to sort Hadrian out. As Sparticus had complained, he had been surly for a while, although I think he was worse with others than with me. I called him in to see me.

'What's this all about then?' he began before I even had time to say anything. I waded in.

'A change of job for you,' I said.

'Suppose I don't want a change of job?' he said.

'You know as well as I do that you don't have a choice. That's being a slave.'

'So how does "Emperor" Marcus get away with it then?'

'With what?'

'Doing as he likes, going off for days at a time, too good to actually work!'

He was needling me; I was struggling to keep my temper – and he knew it.

'For an answer to that you might have to ask Julius Octavius when next you see him. You know damned well that I too am only doing what I'm told to do.'

'I might just do that.'

'More of this attitude and you'll find yourself loading carts rather than scrabbling around underground or building houses in the fresh air. Worse still I could send you off to Ariconium. They like big strong men like you.'

'OK. Sorry. So what's this new job then?'

He subsided into a sullen silence. I accepted this as peace, at least for the moment.

'One of the things that Julius O was insistent about when he gave orders to rebuild the house was that it should be guarded when we weren't actually working there. I haven't bothered much up to now as there've only been a few walls, but now we're going to start on roof and woodwork I have to do as my orders tell me.' I was rubbing that point in hard. 'And I want you to be guard.'

'What, like Sparticus and them?'

'Not really.'

'Sounds like it to me.'

I wasn't sure whether he was being deliberately cussed or if it was just the way he was, or rather, had become. He had been a good friend when we both worked underground.

'No, they guard and bully people; you just have to guard a house or a part-built house.'

'At night?'

'And when it's deserted.'

'I shall need help. Can't be on duty all night and all day, just because you've decided to have a day off the job.'

He was getting at me again but I ignored him. He was riding towards a much more serious dressing down.

'We'll sort that one out in due course. I'm giving you a choice: carry on working in the mine or guard the house. I would remind you that choice is something slaves don't often get.'

But he was not finished.

'What about wild animals at night? Wolves and that, and the locals. They could be worse than wolves.'

'We don't even know if there are wolves here.'

He changed tack.

'And what about my messenger job? I can't do that as well.'

I knew that and was surprised that it was so late in coming in his arguments. Maybe that confirmed my instinct that a change was needed there as well.

'That too will have to be sorted.'

He pondered for what seemed an interminable time.

'I'll do it,' he said finally. 'At least I'll be out in the fresh air.'

'Good,' I said. 'Now get back to what you're supposed to be doing and don't do anything silly to cause me to change my mind.'

I think he got the message. This gave me the chance to move onto the rest of my reorganisation plans, but first my curiosity got the better of me and I had to talk with Benedictus. I found him, as usual, sitting in the hay apparently staring into space.

'What do you do all day, just sitting here?' I asked him by way of an opening.

'I pray,' he said.

'You pray?'

'Yes.'

'What for and who to?'

'The second part of your question is easy. I pray to the one and only true God and his son Jesus Christ. The first part is more difficult. Often it's very simple. Just that someone will have mercy on me and give me some food. At other times, like now when you've been a good Christian and provided me with food and shelter, I can pray for better things in the world. Like that there were more good people around, like you for instance, or that there could be an end to the so-called Games, or an end to slavery perhaps.'

'That'll never come,' I interjected.

'No, it won't, but there's no harm in hoping – and praying.'

'This Jesus Christ that you mentioned. Wasn't he the one that was crucified in Judaea?'

'He was. I'm surprised you've even heard of him.'

I grinned.

'You forget that I was brought up in Rome and in a household where these things were known about, even if ignored.'

'I inadvertently mentioned Paul the other day.'

'You said he was some sort of miracle and that you were too.'

'Never mind about me, that I'll tell you one day, but I'm trying to be like Paul – going round telling anyone who'll listen about Jesus. Not sure that I'm very good at it.'

'Well, I'm listening.'

'Yes, but you've got brains and can think. Not like most of them round here who only think of food and women. And the local population is the worst of the lot. Pig-headed and don't want to know!'

It was quite an explosion from this quietly spoken man. I tried to change the subject a little.

'This man, Paul – you say he came from Tarsus? That seems unlikely.'

'It does, doesn't it? Supposedly a tent-maker there. I imagine somebody there has to have a legitimate occupation,' he ruminated. 'But then that's the whole point. If somebody, or something good could come out of a place like Tarsus then maybe there's hope for the rest of us!'

He had a point.

'Go on,' I prompted. 'What happened to him?'

'Well he went all over the place until the Empire caught up with him. He had the merit of being a Roman citizen, so when they did he demanded to be tried in Rome, as was his right. He found himself in the same position as Jesus. He hadn't actually done anything wrong, so they had to dream up some charge that a rigged court could accept. As you might guess, that took a while, and in the meantime he was able to carry on spreading the Word, so that when he finally had to die there were enough of us around to keep the beliefs alive and well. They crucified him too, but at his own request upside down, so that it was worse for him than for his Master.'

That was a sobering thought.

'But what chance does someone like me have of competing with men of that calibre? Or even to be like you?'

It was impossible for a mere slave who had to make his way in the real world!

He put his hand on my arm. 'You don't,' he said. 'The best you can do is to try and live your life better. To try and do better by your fellow man. As for me, I may die of starvation yet, or be robbed and killed on the road somewhere. Only God knows. But you've heard enough and had enough shocks for one day. Go back to your hut and think and pray. May God bless you.'

With that he turned away from me and our conversation was at an end. I got up and wandered away. I did indeed have plenty to think about. Tarsus, Mater, this man Paul, and Jesus Christ, who seemed to be the beginning and end of all their thinking. I had let myself into this and I would have to get myself out of it!

The following day I left early to go and see Drusius at New Hamm about the carpentry work on the roof of the house. By that time the walls were nearly rebuilt and he could at least find some trees out of which to cut the necessary timber. I knew I would have to haggle with him over what he might charge because, whilst Julius Octavius was willing to pay for the work, he was not going to let himself be overcharged for it. It was not going to be an easy day. As usual I arranged for some food to be sent to Benedictus with word that I would speak to him again when I returned.

I liked this place, New Hamm. It had a bustle and enthusiasm about it that was lacking elsewhere. I think it was because it was not a military town like most others were, and Ariconium in particular. That was quite simply a place for producing iron, very largely for the military, and was guarded by the army at all times. In New Hamm the soldiers kept a minimal presence just to remind the population who was ultimately in charge. I found Drusius at his workshop.

'I'm ready for you to start on the roof of the house,' I said after the usual greetings.

'Can't at the moment,' he said bluntly.

This was not what I was expecting.

'Why's that?' I asked him.

'Got too much work on.' He picked up a piece of wood with some writing scrawled on it. 'Going to be at least six weeks.'

It sounded as though there was almost a note of triumph in his voice.

'Six weeks!' I echoed.

'Might be eight, even ten. Depends on the weather.'

He was definitely feeling pleased with himself about my discomfiture.

'So how do we get over this problem?' I asked, being pretty sure of what the answer would be.

He looked at the sky and down the street, stroked his beard and finally drawled, 'Well, I suppose I could get some more fellows onto it so as to speed things up a bit. Cost you though!'

I was spot on.

'You know I can't authorise any higher prices on my own. It's been bad enough getting this cleared as it is.'

'Then you'll have to go back to your dominus, whoever that is, and get him to dig a bit deeper for some gold in that mine of yours.'

I think he was serious and genuinely thought we were digging for gold!

'Don't be daft,' I said. 'You know we're not doing that.'

'You could try.'

I ignored it. 'If I can get something extra allowed, how quickly then?'

'Maybe we fell some trees in three weeks and then go from there.'

'I'll see what I can do. No promises.'

'I shall have to come and measure up, whichever way,' he said.

That sounded a little bit more hopeful. 'Come any time you like. Now, perhaps?'

'Can't today.' No surprise there. 'Could tomorrow. How about you spend the night here and I come back with you in the morning?'

I was getting as bad as Polonius. Possessive about my mining operations and didn't want to be away from the place any longer than I had to be. But it made sense. I could show him where to find us, he could do his measurements, we could look for trees together, and I could then check that there weren't going to be any problems with the locals, who could be equally possessive of their trees. Maintaining peaceful relations in that quarter was vital to keeping Ariconium supplied. So it was arranged, and I spent a pleasant evening in his company, eating and drinking in this vibrant new community.

The next morning we went straight to the house, he decided what he wanted, and we chose trees in the immediate vicinity. We agreed a price for him to do the job and when he could actually start. I told him I would send word when I had cleared the cost with my superiors and was sure in my own mind that he would be paid. There were two reasons for this, the first being that I had to agree actual figures and times with Julius Octavius before work could start. That was obvious to anyone; I was just a slave after all. My second reason was slightly more devious and might well have raised eyebrows in some quarters. I was all too well aware that Ariconium required its supply of iron ore without any sort of interruption and I wanted to check with the local population that we were not about to cut down trees that were sacred to them. The regime would normally have ignored the locals' wishes, but if they withdrew their carts and carters then we were in real trouble, me most especially.

Before returning to whatever problems the mine had thrown up in my absence, I went to see my friends Chad and Iden to talk about trees.

'We need a druid,' they said as with one voice.

As luck would have it their druid was close by, so they went and found an old man who was nothing if he was not simply an older, white-haired version of Benedictus, who I also wanted to catch up with that day. The main difference was that he was very deaf and we all had to shout at him to get him to understand what I wanted. When it did penetrate, he looked very alarmed and fairly dashed into the woodland and his beloved trees.

In his own language he kept saying, 'Which ones? Which ones? Show me! Show me!'

I had visions of having to get Drusius back and sort out different trees, but all was well. When shown the trees, his shoulders relaxed and he went back to being an old man again. He then took my young hand between his two old gnarled ones and looked into my eyes as though he could see right through and out the other side. He said quite a lot but it was unintelligible to me in spite of my having some idea of the language. I looked to Chad.

'He says that he thanks you for being so considerate about our trees. It is not like your race.'

I presumed he meant the Romans, but I understood and was glad of what I had done, even if I did have an ulterior motive. But there was some discussion going on with the old man.

'I'm not sure whether we should tell you what else he says,' said Chad.

'Try me,' I said and laughed.

'No, don't laugh, it's serious.'

'All the more reason that I should hear it,' I answered.

'He says that you will find yourself very alone, but that you will survive.'

'What's that supposed to mean?'

'No idea, but he's very often right when he says things like that. I should just be careful if I were you.'

'I will,' I said, and shook my head in disbelief. We all parted the best of friends and I headed back to speak with Benedictus before the day was out.

Chapter 26

I expected to find Benedictus sitting in his usual place in the hay shed, but he was not there. Oh well, he might be stretching his legs, but all the same I went to ask one of the slaves who provided us all with food.

'I thought you knew,' he said.

'Knew what?'

'He's gone.'

'Gone?'

I was incredulous. I was sure Benedictus had wanted to say more to me, just as I had wanted to learn more about this Jesus Christ man from him.

'Did you give him food as I told you?' I asked.

'Oh yes, dominus.'

'When did he go?'

'After I left food with him yesterday morning.'

'Did he say anything? Or leave me any message?'

This was becoming hard work.

'Yes, dominus. He said to thank you for being so considerate to him.'

I thought of the druid who had used precisely the same words.

'He said to bless you, and all of us here, and that he would see you again sometime.'

'That's all?'

'Yes, dominus.'

'You're sure?'

'Yes, dominus.'

This was also getting repetitive.

I was completely taken aback and it must have shown.

'Are you all right, dominus?' he asked.

'Yes. Yes,' I said, 'I was just hoping to speak to him again. And at least wish him well with wherever he was going next.'

I was stumbling over my words and probably not making a lot of sense.

'You wasn't thinking of becoming one of them Christians, was you, dominus?'

'No, well, er, yes, possibly.' I was getting myself into deep water here. 'I only wanted to know a bit more about it.'

'Wouldn't blame you, dominus. Makes a bit more sense than all these other gods they have.'

Now where had I heard that comment before? And what did this man know about it? Had Benedictus been talking to him too? And, if so, with what result?

'Interesting comment,' I said. I knew this lad well enough but wasn't absolutely sure of his name. 'What's your name?'

'Lepidus, dominus. I hope I haven't spoken out of turn, have I, dominus?'

I smiled. He had good reason to be frightened of having said too much. Some domini would have thrashed him for it.

'No, Lepidus, you haven't. Now is not the moment but we must speak together about this Christianity thing sometime. Get on with what you're doing.'

I smiled again and he seemed to relax.

'Yes, dominus.'

I had greater things on my mind to worry about than Benedictus and what he might or might not have said to Lepidus, or anybody else for that matter. After all he had had more or less free rein of the site, and even if he had not moved far from his place in the hay shed, there was nothing to stop someone coming to talk to him if they so wished.

I had got the all-clear from Julius Octavius in double quick time so there was now only a bit of walling to finish before Drusius could come and fell his trees prior to starting on the roof. Hadrian would become the guard and I had told Antinous that he would now become the messenger to Ariconium. He was eternally grateful to me.

'I don't think I could have stood being down there much longer,' he said, 'I really think I would have killed myself!'

I had known that he would be glad to get out of it but not that he was that unhappy. He was small for his age but was very fast when either running or walking, so I thought he would be good for the job. Hadrian was scathing.

'Only a runt,' he said. 'Wanted to get out of doing any real work.'

I kept my opinions to myself. Hadrian was riding for a fall and I wondered how long the guard duty would last before I had to get rough with him and send him underground on a permanent basis. With or without a flogging on the way.

The walls of the house were done and I was impatient to get on with the timber work because I knew I would have Julius Octavius chasing me. The fact that Drusius had other customers to serve meant nothing to him. Julius O was used to dealing with either soldiers or slaves who did exactly as they were told – now! And in both cases argument only led to more or less serious punishment. The last thing I wanted to do was to go to New Hamm, pleasant as that might be, to chivvy Drusius, as I was sure that it would be counterproductive. Out of sheer cussedness he would simply find more excuses for not being able to start. I was getting increasingly edgy about this when his men appeared armed with axes and the intention of felling trees.

'You got permission?' was their first question before they had even set up camp.

'From their druid, you mean?' I said.

'Yeah.'

'Yes, and he's quite happy with the ones that are marked. Don't cut any others down and be careful where they fall so as not to damage other trees.'

This was obviously not the answer they were expecting. I suspected that what they were really looking for was an excuse not to actually start work, although I could detect a certain respect in their expressions.

'Think we ought to check with 'im anyway.'

'There's no need; I've done that,' I said flatly, adding, 'But you can if you want to. I don't know his name, but if you ask for Chad or Iden, they'll find him for you.'

This seemed to disconcert them further. I think it was the fact that I actually knew some of the local people by name. It was not the normal way for the Empire to carry on.

Looks passed between them. A decision was made.

'Better get set up then.'

And they did, but not with any great enthusiasm. I thought my previous surmise had been right. I determined that I needed to keep a fairly careful eye on what they were doing, and it was as well that I did, as the very first tree they set about was a 'wrong' one. I caught them out by being there at first light the following morning as they were clearing the scrub around the tree.

'Wrong tree,' I said amiably.

''T'isn't.'

'Show me the mark cut into it then.'

They looked all round the tree and then the leader took his axe and cut a mark into it.

'Well, it's got one now,' he said triumphantly. 'Anyway what's one tree or another tree? And while we're at it, what's it to you? You're only a slave at best.'

'If you don't fell the right trees, you'll be wrong by Drusius, who won't want to employ you again; you'll be wrong by the druid, who may well bring all sorts of trouble down on you; and you'll be wrong by the local people who live here, and what they might do to you I wouldn't like to think. Finally you'll be wrong by me, and I shan't have you anywhere near the place again.'

This seemed to subdue them a bit.

'And as for my being a slave, you're absolutely right, I am, but I'm in charge around here. If you were one of my slaves carrying on like this, I'd have at least one of you flogged sufficiently to make you think twice about being so stupid.'

They glowered at me.

'Just to make sure you don't try any further tricks, I'll send Sparticus over to keep an eye on you. I doubt you'll try anything silly with him!'

I turned and walked away. I heard much grumbling behind me but I could definitely hear that they were moving in the direction of one of the trees they were supposed to cut down. I did indeed send Sparticus to watch over them, armed with his whip and a sword for good measure. He thought it was the funniest thing that had happened in a long time.

Later when our differences had been settled and we were all good friends, on the surface at least, I heard about it.

'By all our gods and yours, who was that you sent over to keep an eye on us?' I was asked.

'Oh,' I said, 'that was just Sparticus. Nice fellow, as long as you keep on the right side of him. Why?'

'Shouldn't want to meet him in the dark and argue with him.'

'Not a good idea,' I said.

'And 'is whip!' one of the others chimed in.

'Yeah, knock the acorns out of the trees, he could! And one at a time too. Made my back feel creepy just to watch him.'

I laughed.

'He's OK. Just don't upset him.'

They raised their eyes skywards and we parted good friends.

Having felled the trees they then set up to saw them into beams and planks in accordance with a list that Drusius had provided. They were patently not as stupid as they liked to seem. At least one of them could read or had an exceptional memory for what he had been told was needed. True to his word, and much to my surprise, Drusius did turn up when he had said he would, and they all set about building the roof on the walls that we had built. Hadrian took up his post as guard and, whilst he was nowhere near as intimidating as Sparticus, I think everyone had a healthy respect for him. That I intended, as word would no doubt get round that the house was guarded and by whom, which would hopefully prevent trouble from even starting.

I was proud of what I – we, really – had achieved in the rebuilding of what had been Gaius Maximus' house, and I thought it was time that Julius Octavius made a rare absence from Ariconium to have a look at it. After all it was him that had been pressing to get it finished, and as quickly as possible. It was always something of a puzzle to me that he never came to see what was going on. The only time had been a visit soon after the riot, and he had left almost as soon as he got here on the pretext of having urgent business in Glevum. I hadn't believed him but I had had too much on my very new hands to give him the attention he deserved. I supposed that I could take it as a compliment that he was happy to leave it all to me, despite my youth and my being a slave. Nevertheless I did want him to see the house, so I sent word with Antinous on his next trip to Ariconium that I expected my dominus at his convenience. I got no direct answer from him but the result was startling and not at all what I might have expected.

A week or so later someone came rushing into the mine with a smirk all over his face to find me, to say that there was a returned cart with a load of stuff for me and, oh, as an afterthought that someone had come with it as well. Yes, I was needed and fast! My first thought was that Julius Octavius had arrived unannounced in order to catch me on the hop, but then I realised that he was most unlikely to come on a cart. A fast, light chariot was more likely. Either way I scrambled out from what I was doing, dusted myself down just in case it was Julius O, and went to investigate. There was indeed a cart in the yard loaded up with a mass of household furniture, beds, benches, pots and pans. And sitting in the middle of it was Clio! She appeared pleased to see me, not least because I could protect her from the gawping faces all around her. I was sure she would cope but I sent them all packing so that I could try to find out what was going on and why she was here, not to mention all the rest of the contents of the cart.

'What in the name of creation are you doing here?' I asked, when I had got my equilibrium back and felt in a position to speak sensibly to her.

'Julius Octavius sent me,' she said. That was all she said and it left me in the air.

'Why?' was all I could think of to say.

'To look after you... I think,' she added as an afterthought. 'Oh and to set up house for you.' She gestured to the contents of the cart.

I was even more taken aback. 'But who said anything about me living in that house?'

'Your friend Julius, of course!'

'There's no of course about it. He told me to rebuild the house and I've done so,' I replied petulantly, adding, 'And it's not finished yet either.'

I wasn't too happy with this 'my friend Julius' bit. I had always had a good working relationship with him but it had been very much a slave–dominus relationship and I had been happy to keep it that way. It was all too easy to get into too cosy a relationship with one's dominus, and that could lead to disaster if there was a change at the top.

'Oh, Marcus,' she replied, 'stop being high-minded and take it as your worth.'

I hadn't noticed Polonius come quietly up behind me, although I might have expected it; as he rarely missed anything that was going on about the place.

'You tell him, girl,' said his gravelly voice, making me jump. 'We can't get it through to him that he's worth a lot more than anyone thinks, although perhaps your dominus does after all.'

'Yes, but…'

Clio cut me off.

'Here,' she said and handed me a sizeable tablet. 'He said you wouldn't believe him so he's written it down so you can't get it wrong. Read it to me.'

'And me!' said Polonius.

I raised my eyebrows and took the tablet from her outstretched hand. I skimmed through what he had written and was embarrassed. I was undecided as to whether to tell anybody what it said. On the other hand it would explain why I was apparently giving myself airs and graces. It was certainly Julius Octavius' writing, so I read:

My dear Marcus,

You will be a bit surprised to get this message from me along with Clio and what should be on the cart. You have done well with the mine and have kept up supplies through difficult times. You have rebuilt my late friend Gaius Maximus's house with virtually no outside assistance. Not just as a reward, but because I intended it from the moment it was burnt down, you are to move into it and live there. That is why I have sent over your good friend Clio, not only to set it up, because I think you may not be too good at that sort of thing, but also to look after you and turn it into a home for you both!

In truth I am just an old man doing a bit of match-making but I hope you will be pleased.

Your dominus and friend,

Julius Octavius.

PS I have also included a set of superior-class tunics for you to wear with your new status.

Despite the grime I was sure my face was burning with embarrassment from this public spectacle of my promotion. Because I was facing her I could see that Clio was grinning all over her face, but imagine my shock when people behind me started clapping. I thought only Polonius was there, but when I whirled round I found I had an audience of Sparticus, Trojan and several others from the mine who had 'happened' to drift by as well. They all stood grinning stupidly at me.

'The man knows when he's got a good'un,' said Polonius. 'Good for him.'

'And so say all of us,' added Sparticus, which prompted another round of applause and caused my face to redden even more, if that was possible.

I had to take some sort of control.

'Get back to what you're supposed to be doing!' I shouted, which only produced some good-natured laughter, although they did move off.

'And, Sparticus, send over a couple of men to help unload this cart. Give me time to get the small stuff off first though.'

This was going to be a whole new lifestyle for me, and for Clio. For us.

Chapter 27

So I rode with Clio to the new house. She was overcome by her surroundings and intimidated by the all-pervasive forest. I suppose I had got used to it gradually, with my travelling to and from Ariconium, whereas she was basically a town girl, and even a smelting works was more like a town. It had a fair number of houses, none very special it has to be said, a few shops and a bit of a market. Its surroundings were unpleasant, smelly with smoke from the furnaces, noisy with people shouting to make themselves heard above the perpetual banging of iron on iron, and in bare countryside where all the trees had been cut down for fuel. Still, it was a sort of a town for all that. If it had to be a town, I much preferred New Hamm!

'Are there no other houses here!' she asked in alarm when we reached the nearly completed building.

'No,' I said. 'What did you expect?'

'Julius Octavius told me that it was a big place with all modern facilities and that I'd like it here.'

'You will, but I suspect he was referring to the house not the place. As far I know, he's never been here so I think he was having you on a bit. Just so that you'd come. He's clever like that.'

She hummed doubtfully. 'So where do you live? Where does everybody live for that matter?'

'Some of us, those that can, live in huts. Most live underground. It's easier for us that way as they have virtually no means of escape, so we keep what slaves we have.'

'And what about you? Do you live underground as well?'

'I did until very recently. At least not quite underground, but I've slept under the desk in Polonius' office ever since I started coming to Ariconium. And even after Julius Octavius put me in charge. Especially since Julius

Octavius put me in charge. It has a good strong door with a heavy bar to go across it.'

'But why? Weren't you safe here in your own little kingdom?'

I could have taken that the wrong way, but there was a smile on her face as she said it.

'No. I don't think I was. Lots of those here weren't at all pleased with my being given authority – and still less so when I used it. They shouldn't have been able to reach that door, but more than once I've heard people banging on it in the night. Not nice, I can tell you. But in the last year or so it's been much better. I've weeded out most of the troublemakers and the rest seem to have realised that if they do things my way, the dominus in Ariconium is happy and we can all lead a reasonably trouble-free life. So I've moved out and built myself a bit of a hut.'

'But those who crept up on you by the cart seemed pleased enough for you.'

'Ah. That was Polonius, who incidentally nobody messes with, and who's been like a puppy dog to me ever since I got him out of real trouble once, years ago. But he's also the best and most straightforward man I know, here or anywhere else. The other was Sparticus. He's chief gang-master and would have got killed in the riot if he'd been around at that moment. He's good and reliable too.'

At that moment Antinous and Hadrian turned up to help unload the cart. One thin and wiry, the other hulking and tough. I wasn't entirely pleased to see Hadrian as I wasn't too keen on him knowing what had been sent over from Ariconium. However, he had passed on messages to Clio for me and maybe they were about to bear fruit. In fact there wasn't as much as there seemed to be and it all looked a bit lost in the unfinished rooms of the new building. I made a decision.

'Come on,' I said to Clio. 'It's no good us thinking of being here tonight. You'll have to come and stay in my hut for the time being.'

'But what will they think?' she wailed.

'Silly girl!' I chided. 'By now everyone knows you're here, and whatever they might think, they've already thought it.'

She didn't look as though she saw it that way. We went to my hut. I don't think she was impressed. If I'm truthful, I know she wasn't.

'Being as you're in charge here I'd have thought you would have had a bigger and better hut than everyone else,' she said.

'I don't want to push it,' I said. 'I've been lucky and don't want too many people to resent it. Like I said, most of those who might have done so have gone, but people could get ideas that I don't want them to get. Besides, it's adequate for me.'

She pursed her lips and sniffed. It was more eloquent than anything she might have said.

'And now it seems I'm to move into the big house. There will be plenty of room for both of us in that.'

'Hmmm.'

'Either way, we'll have to cope for tonight. Tomorrow will have to look after itself.'

Again, 'Hmmm.'

So we did sort ourselves out. As I believe is the way of these things, I slept on the floor and she slept in my bed, such as it was. I organised some food. Again she wasn't impressed, obviously being used to something better than our plain fare. I began to see her slipping away from me and all the sweet words we had spoken having been to no avail. I silently prayed to all the gods and to my new God, Jesus, to help me keep her. Whatever it cost me. Of course, thinking about it wholly pragmatically, she had been sent here by no lesser person than Julius Octavius, so she couldn't go anywhere else even if she wanted, but that was not entirely the point.

The following morning I went off to finish what I had been doing, when Clio appeared on the scene to upset my well-ordered existence before going to the new building. I still hesitated to call it a house, and certainly not *my* house. When I got back I found that Clio had been tidying up my hut. I wasn't best pleased, but I contained myself.

It was a pleasant walk, but I was nervous. Clio seemed to have regained her usual high spirits, which was good, but I had the feeling that I was abandoning the mine, including Polonius and all the others who had aided my good fortune. I was becoming possessive about the place. Was that good or bad? I didn't know.

We had soon created some order out of the muddle we had left the night before, when Clio started to be particular.

'What about washing and latrines?' she queried.

'Well,' I said, 'I've been concentrating on getting the main building back together again and in truth, not all of that. I wasn't expecting anyone to actually want to come and live here as soon as this.'

'I can see that, so what are we going to do?'

'Water we can have in a bucket and—'

She cut me off. 'Where from?'

'It's all overgrown at the moment, but there's a trickle of a stream that runs just outside, and a pool's been made so water is easy to get.'

'Good. And latrines?'

I wasn't quite ready for these intimacies, or practicalities, depending on how you looked at them. I waved my hand at the surrounding foliage. 'Or we could dig a pit,' I added.

'Hmmm.'

Again not impressed! It was time to change the subject.

'You haven't mentioned cooking but I think we could soon build an oven outside and then put a roof over it afterwards.'

'We could, but until it's ready do we starve?'

'No, we eat with everyone else. Like I've always done.'

'And I get mentally undressed, or worse, by every man there!'

'I shall ensure that all Hades will descend on anyone who actually tries it. Anyway you'll soon be part of the scene and no one will take any notice of you.'

She didn't like the idea of being ignored but she could see my point, and asked me to treat cooking arrangements as urgent, to which I agreed. Her next requirement, and I began to wonder if her arrival was a good idea after all, was about where she could have a shrine to her gods.

'I didn't see one in your hut,' she said. 'It worried me.'

'Ah.'

'Ah, what?'

I hesitated. She cocked her head on one side and looked at me.

'It's not very obvious,' I said and rushed on. 'Did you see two bits of wood lashed together like a cross?'

'No,' she said, and then realisation dawned and her hand flew to her mouth. 'You haven't become a... one of them?'

'Yes.'

Whilst I had been careful not to make any issue of it, there was no other answer, and I finally had to admit it to someone.

'How could you?' she asked, with a full measure of reproach in her voice,

'It makes so much more sense,' I answered. 'And it's so straightforward. Do to everyone else as you would have them do to you.'

'Hmmm!'

'I had this man Benedictus come by and he stayed a bit and we fed him and he told me about this Christianity. I had heard of it and he said that as it was now legal I didn't have to worry on that score. I don't really know much but, as I said, it makes a lot of sense, so I suppose I'm a Christian now.'

'It could be bad for you.'

'I know, but for the time being at least, I'm a Christian.'

It made me feel quite good to stand up for what I was doing, but I have to confess there was a bit of bravado in it.

'But to answer your question, you can have a shrine to whoever you like and wherever you like. I shan't force you to be a Christian.'

'I'm glad about that and you can tell me about it sometime.'

'Not much more to tell than I've already said.'

'Sounds too easy.'

'It is, until you try to live by it!'

And thus it was all arranged. So we started and continued to pull together to turn the new building into a house and then into a home. Despite the fact that neither of us really wanted to, we made a big effort to move in and to prove to those around us that even if we didn't like it we were obeying the orders from Ariconium. Clio was frightened by the forest and was quite certain that one of the locals would break in on her at any moment. For my part I was worried about the mine – that something might happen that needed my immediate attention and I would be too far away. But in the end we both became used to the idea and shook down into a very companionable state. I got a fair lot of ribbing from all and sundry that I was the only person on the place with his own woman to make love to, and it was close to being true. Polonius was the only other man with a woman, and most thought that he and his wife were well past it. So long as it was all good-natured, I let it pass.

Into this state of domestic bliss came a message that was to change everything. I was requested to go to Ariconium to discuss the digging down to a lower level that Polonius had been carrying on about for some considerable time. There were no surprises there, but the instructions were to arrive at a time of day after his office had closed and to go direct to his house without going into Ariconium first. Now that was different! And to make it even stranger, I was to arrive by a devious route so as not to be seen. Oh, and bring a smart tunic but don't wear it. Had he taken leave of his senses? I discussed it with Clio, thinking that she might have some thoughts as to what was going on. She was blank on the subject.

So I sent word as to when I would come, and duly arrived at his house at dusk. One of his servants had been posted outside to meet me so that I could be taken indoors immediately and with minimum fuss. Julius Octavius was waiting for me.

'Ah, Marcus, my good friend. Come in. Let us drink some wine together.'

What was all this? I thought the late Gaius Maximus was his 'good friend'. He was never slow to remind me of that, but Gaius M was dead!

'But dominus,' I said, 'this is all very mysterious. I am honoured, but just what is this all about?'

'All in good time, Marcus. Let us drink and then let us eat, and finally we will talk business. First things first, eh?'

None of this boded well, but I could only go along with it. More alarming still was that his wife Aemelia joined us for the meal. I had to dredge up my childhood memories as to how one behaved in polite society! I breathed a sigh of relief when that was over and we retired to his office for whatever he had in mind.

'You must be worried silly as to what this is all about,' he said amiably.

'I am indeed, dominus,' I said, hoping I wasn't being too familiar with him.

'I hope this is going to work,' he said, with a hint of worry in his voice, 'but you will understand that I don't have much choice.'

I stayed silent and worried even more. There was a long pause.

'Aemelia and I are going to Rome.'

'Permanently?' I asked in some alarm.

'No. Oh no. We are very happy in our isolation here but we both feel we would like to see Rome again before we die…'

'Oh, dominus.'

He held up his hand.

'Marcus, it's true. Neither of us is getting any younger. From what little we hear of Rome, things are not too good there and we would like to see it again before the whole pile of oranges collapses.'

'You jest!'

'No, I'm afraid I don't.'

This was news indeed, although Benedictus had mentioned something similar; and coming from the one man I trusted implicitly it was very worrying news indeed. Where did any of us stand if what he was suggesting came to pass? I collected my thoughts and became practical.

'How long will you be away?' I was doing arithmetic in my head as to how long it had taken me to get here in my long column of slaves.

'Probably about four calends. It will take us about three weeks each way travelling and the rest we hope to enjoy in our home city.'

'And who is to be in charge while you're away?'

I was hoping against hope that he wasn't going to throw me into this one. I knew absolutely nothing about the smelting end of the operation. But it was worse.

'Tiberius.'

The colour must have drained from my face for he carried on, 'I'm sorry Marcus. I knew you wouldn't like it but I don't have any choice in the matter. This place is basically a military base, even if I'm technically a civilian.'

I nodded. Glumly.

'Tiberius is the most senior army man here and trying hard to get his final push up the rankings. While I have anything to do with it, he'll never make the grade!'

'That doesn't help me much.' I was being horribly familiar but I didn't care.

'I know, but you'll have to make the best of it.'

I grunted. I was really out of sorts. He became brusque.

'You will spend the night here. You will leave before sun-up and make yourself scarce until mid-morning; you will arrive at the hostel as you well might; you will change into one of the tunics I sent you; you will come to my official office and we will discuss business exactly as we would normally. Tiberius and the eunuch will be present so that all those who matter will know what my orders are. Do I make myself clear?'

'Yes, dominus. All too clear.'

'Cheer up, Marcus,' he said quietly. 'The charade has to go on until I get back, then we shall see. You'll cope.'

And I think he meant it.

I did exactly as ordered. Helen of Troy was pleased to see me in her hostel again but put out because no one had told her that I was coming. We had a good-natured grumble about that and she found me a late breakfast before I went to see the great man. He should have been an actor, he really should. He greeted me as though we hadn't met in months. Then he called the eunuch and told him to fetch Tiberius, and produced hot drinks for all of us. I noticed that he had a replacement for Clio and that she wasn't half so pretty, not to me anyway.

Tiberius bustled up in all his military pomposity and we all sat, at Julius Octavius' instruction. From the expression on his face it was obvious to me that Tiberius did not think that I should sit when in 'the presence'. So I sat, very determinedly.

'Now, gentlemen,' began Julius Octavius. Tiberius was visibly shocked. Of the three of us he was possibly the most high-born, having always been a free man. The eunuch none of us knew about, and I certainly wasn't. He probably thought that he was having his leg pulled, something he always resented, and the dominus may well have been doing it deliberately.

'I have an announcement to make,' he continued, 'that will affect everyone here and everyone at Marcus' mine as well.'

The other two patently didn't know what I did and were all agog to know what was going on – Tiberius waiting to see if he could make his Pilus Prior, and the eunuch to estimate how much money he could filch out of it. We all expressed surprise as one man.

'I am going to Rome for a holiday!'

This was not what the other two expected, but the obvious questions came first. How long for? Who's in charge? When was he leaving? And so on.

'As the most senior military man here, you, Tiberius will have overall charge while I'm away.'

Tiberius nearly exploded with pride. 'You do me a great honour,' he began. 'I shall do my utmost to maintain the high standards that you have set, my dominus—' He would have gone on but Julius Octavius held up his hand, bidding him cease. Tiberius was only slightly deflated.

'You, eunuch,' he said, pronouncing the word with a certain distaste, 'will keep your records and accounts up to the minute as you always do, and you will keep a tight rein on expenditure so that costs do not rocket while I'm away. Are you listening, Tiberius?'

The latter came back from his dreamland of being in charge with a jump and nodded his head in acceptance.

'Certainly, dominus.' In fairness he made no more fuss about it than that.

'Now, Marcus.' He turned to me. 'And you two listen as well.' He pointed at Tiberius and the eunuch. 'Your man Polonius has been getting at you, and thus at me, to be allowed to dig down to another seam of ore that he is convinced lies below where you are working now. Correct?'

'Yes, dominus.'

'I am now giving permission for this to be done. Doing it will almost certainly upset the steady supply of ore coming here, but you should be able to manage. Orders for iron are not large at the moment, so with a bit of forethought you should be able to provide enough without difficulty. Now, have the two of you understood that?'

He looked piercingly at Tiberius and the eunuch. They both agreed that they had.

From there we moved on to discuss other matters relating to his being away. Most of that did not concern me but I was amazed by what a grasp he had of the tiniest details of what went on around him. I was glad to be left on my own at the mine! Afterwards we all went our separate ways, and I'm sure all were preoccupied with thoughts as to what would happen next.

I cogitated it all the way back and then discussed it, first with Clio, then with Polonius. We were all agreed that the omens were not good. Polonius was, as might be expected, delighted to finally get permission to dig deeper, even if he was putting his own reputation on the line by doing so. Clio knew too much about the goings on at Ariconium to be at all pleased at the thought of Tiberius being given any more authority than he already had. I was the one who was going to suffer most, simply because I was in charge of the mine.

The probability of problems to come seemed to help Clio and me to come closer together. She managed to overcome her initial fear of the forest, together with the absence of proper washing and latrine facilities, and even managed to accept my being a Christian. For my part I found her fussiness with household affairs and her need to have me around difficult at times, but made a great effort to cope. She took a little time to realise that I was often going to be filthy dirty by the nature of what I did. We were not married – I hadn't even asked her, but it felt very much like a honeymoon.

We kept sending ore to Ariconium as we always had. The quantity and quality could be a bit variable, because I was pushing Polonius to get digging to the lower level.

'If we have to have a serious shortage of ore at some stage,' I told him, 'our friends in Ariconium will not understand, so you need to have the chance of a new seam if there is one.'

'I know, I know,' he grumbled. 'We'll get there in the end.'

'Sooner rather than in the end,' I said.

I was being a bit hard on him but I knew that he knew exactly what our problems might be.

It was the best part of three weeks later before Antinous came back from one of his regular trips to Ariconium with the news that Julius Octavius and his wife had left for their visit to Rome. He also brought the not unexpected news that Ariconium was not a happy place. Helen of Troy was swearing like a soldier at anybody who crossed her, and that was never a good sign. Swear she always did, but mostly good-naturedly. The place tended to be at war with itself at the best of times, and this, to my mind at least, was brought on by the military being too much in charge. Now they, in the form of Tiberius, had free rein. Our time would surely come.

Chapter 28
Soldier, Soldier

If you want to know, my name's Petrus and I've been in the army all my life. Went in as a kid expecting to cover myself in glory and very soon learned that I was more likely to get killed. Didn't fancy that, so I made a career decision that I wasn't going to be. Not if I had any say in the matter, that is.

I was the lowest of the low, completely expendable. If I got myself killed not one person would notice. They probably wouldn't even let my mater and pater know, even though they're supposed to. It took a while to think through. I wasn't allowed much time for thinking, either then or since. But so far it's worked and in a year or two I shall be ready to retire with a bit of cash and maybe start myself a little shop somewhere. Just a little longer is all I say.

So what was this wonderful plan, I hear you asking.

It was very simple really. First try and get yourself transferred to units well out of harm's way. It's not that easy but there are a lot to choose from, like guarding places that are important to the army, such as the pay scribes, bridges and ports. Places where not much happens and as far away from Rome as possible, if you can manage it. Second, be happy to do all the shitty jobs that no one else wants to do. In this line comes digging latrines and, better still, filling them in again, running errands for lazy centuria who can't be bothered to get off their backsides to fetch a glass of ale, and polishing armour for the lazy bastards who won't do it themselves.

Now if you're prepared to do those sorts of jobs, everybody loves you. They'll go off to get themselves killed and leave you behind to fill in the latrines just in case the army should advance a bit. And if you think battle may be called for, you can always get lost when taking a message somewhere. It's surprising how often signposts get turned round! And if you're well away from the action, they're still glad to have you there to do the shitty jobs for them when they get back. Sometimes they'll even pay you a little to clean their uniforms and polish the plates. All goes into the shop fund.

Also I've never been much of a drinker or one for the women. Miserable bugger they call me. But it means I can save what little I earn, officially and unofficially that is. I even got a little bit of promotion out of the plan: halfway up the centurion's ladder I am. Never earned it, but those I've got out of the shit put me up for it and there was no point in complaining, now was there? It got me a bit more pay and even less need to exert myself! I can shout and bawl along with the rest of them and then find some other idiot to do my chores.

Now this place is well off the beaten track and, as I say, that suits me fine. Tiberius is a bit of a bastard but his bark is worse than his bite, provided you've got the rules on your side. And believe me, I know them by heart now! So, just a little longer, Petrus, and you're in the clear. Whether I start my shop somewhere hereabouts where I'm known, or go back home where it's a bit warmer, I'm still deciding.

Chapter 29

It happened, on a beautiful sunny day when we were all stopped for a midday break, that the mine was suddenly surrounded by soldiers, and Tiberius was standing in the middle of the yard all dressed up in his best uniform. I had to give him credit; we had no idea that he and so many soldiers were there until they appeared as if from nowhere!

'Why aren't you working?' he bawled.

'We've stopped for our break,' I said with studied calm, adding, 'We always do.'

'Not from now on!' he yelled again.

'That depends on who's in charge here!' I really was putting myself in harm's way. 'Julius Octavius put me in charge here and so far he hasn't taken his order back.'

'But he's not here now, is he, young man?' he sneered. At least he didn't shout it.

'Does that make a difference?'

'It does.'

'That depends on whether you want ore delivered regularly and in the agreed quantities.'

He started to shout again. 'I do and I want better quality and more of it!'

'Don't you remember the discussions with Julius Octavius? We were going to dig down to another seam so that we had good ore for the future, even if there were difficulties for the time being. You were there if I remember correctly.'

I was trying to be reasonable, even if I knew it would be wasted breath. He just ignored me.

'I want both. Now!'

'Well you can't have it,' I said flatly.

I looked at Polonius, who simply shrugged his shoulders. We both knew it was no good arguing.

Tiberius went purple in the face and I really thought he might have a fit, but the whole charade was obviously meticulously planned. I might have expected as much from the army. He held up his arm and snapped his fingers, whereupon a detail of soldiers surrounded me. At a nod of his head they marched me out of the yard and, without pausing for breath, we headed for Ariconium.

We marched with military precision and at military speed for about the first three miles. I knew I could keep pace with them whatever they did unless they started to run, and that I thought was unlikely. I held my head high and I didn't speak. All I could do was worry about Clio. She would have no inkling of what was happening and it was unlikely that either Polonius or Sparticus would be able to send anyone to tell her. The first she would know was when Tiberius burst through her door, and then I shuddered to think what would happen. I just hoped she would go along with him, as anything else would get her hurt. He could do whatever he wanted with her, and I had a pretty good idea what he wanted. She'd survived living with the military before, so I guessed she'd cope with Tiberius, but I worried all the same.

I imagine the soldiers thought they were far enough away from Clearwell and Tiberius that they could afford to stop for a breather. They stopped by a stream so that they could have a drink, and were good enough to offer me one too.

'Thank you,' I said.

'It's OK,' said their Hastatus Inferior, the lowest form of centurion life. 'Sorry, but we've got our orders to follow too. Nothing personal.'

'I know,' I said. 'Not good for any of us.'

I had heard someone, somewhere, possibly Mahout, say that when you find yourself in this sort of situation, if somebody, anybody, will talk to you – keep them talking.

'You must have had an early start,' I said, by way of polite conversation, even if it sounded daft, but he took my comment for what it was.

'Could have been worse, we came halfway last night. Very particular, he was, as to just when we got here.'

'How did he know we'd all be outside at that moment?' I was curious if nothing else.

'Dunno. Probably had spies watching what you did every day. He's a devious bastard.'

Those last two words were music to my ears. They meant that even his own underlings were not too keen on the high and mighty Tiberius. It might be useful, it might not; they had to obey orders too.

'I can show you the quickest way back,' I offered. 'I've done this journey more than a few times.'

He became very wary. 'That's just what he said you'd say, and then do a runner on us.'

I laughed. 'I could,' I said, 'but what good would that do me?'

'You wouldn't be in the trouble you are now.'

He wasn't very bright, this one.

'If I escape, which you rightly say I could, very easily, what happens if I'm caught?'

He drew his finger across his neck, adding, 'If you're lucky.'

'Exactly. I'm gambling on a chance that I'll survive this. Then I'll be able to go back and see Polonius and the rest of them who work for me in that hole of a mine. Not to mention my nice little girl whom your Pilus Posterior is probably raping as we speak. Even if your lot don't catch me, I could never go back there.'

'They said you were a decent sort and good to work for. I can see why now. OK, swear in the Emperor's name that you won't try and escape and you can lead us back.'

'I swear,' I said, knowing that swearing in the Emperor's name wasn't much use for a Christian, but there was no need to complicate matters. The men under him seemed pleased by the idea of a shorter route home too.

'Come on then, let's go.'

They formed up round me just as before so that I couldn't escape even if I wanted, but they did accept my directions. We marched at a slower pace until we were close to Ariconium, when the stride picked up and they marched with precision. Perhaps my Hastatus Inferior friend was hoping for promotion too!

Once there I was unceremoniously shoved into a very small cell in the guardhouse.

'Thanks,' he said. 'I'll bring you some food. Enjoy it – might be the last you get!'

That didn't sound good, but he did bring me some soup, which had certainly never seen any meat, and precious few vegetables either. And there I was abandoned. I had to face up to the fact that I had had it too good for too long, ever since, in fact, I had come under Polonius' influence and later that of Julius Octavius. Many, many slaves must have died from callous mistreatment while I had been running my own show and hopefully doing the best for those under me. I knew I could endure the hardship. After all, it was only recently that I'd had a bed of any sort in which to sleep. I hoped I could endure the brutality which was bound to come my way, but more serious to me was going to be the jeering at my downfall. And I knew there would be plenty of that. This was an army establishment, after all, and the military didn't let anyone in my shoes off lightly!

It started the next morning. I was to be taken to the cells for the really bad malefactors, of which the place had plenty, or so I was told. I was shackled into the middle of a group of soldiers for a show of 'Look what we've got here!' I was toured round the camp and shouted at by all the soldiers in a manner that only emphasised their lowly rank. When I thought about it afterwards, the jeering only really came from the military. Perhaps they had been ordered to, or maybe there was a tiny bit of sympathy for me. More likely the rest of the population had seen it all before and just couldn't be bothered to take any interest. Just another poor beggar likely to end up dead, although a couple of people did throw me hunks of bread. Alas, being shackled to the soldiers meant I couldn't catch them. The tour was simply for the army's benefit, I ended up in a cell that backed onto the one I had left earlier, except that it was smaller and dirtier. And I still hadn't had anything to eat so far today.

An older, more pompous, middle-ranking centurion, whose name I later learned to be Petrus, appeared at my cell gate and stared at me for some minutes.

'Why are you here?' he asked eventually.

'Ask Tiberius,' I said.

'He's not here.'

'I know.'

He pondered this. 'What have you done wrong?'

'Ask Tiberius.'

'I've told you, young man, he's not here!'

'And I've told you that I know that, and I've also told you that he's the only one who does know why I'm here.'

He was patently not used to having prisoners in his cells who would answer him back and that gave him cause to have to think. 'What am I supposed to do with you then?'

This question was not really directed at me but at the sky or the roof of the cell block or whatever he happened to be looking at.

'Some food would be a good start and a bucket would help!'

Once again I was saying more than was likely to be good for me, but if I could cause these idiots to stop and think then I might be helping myself. Whether he was unused to someone changing the subject so dramatically on him, I don't know, but he drew himself up to his full height of not very much and stalked off. However, a while later a small portion of food did appear, along with a leaky bucket.

As I expected, the eunuch was quite early on in a procession of people who had nothing better to do than come and stare at me. I was actually surprised that I'd had to wait this long for him. He slithered to a stop in front of my cell.

'Well, well,' he said.

With difficulty, I said nothing. I forced myself to just stare at him.

'And what are you doing here then?'

I was getting heartily sick of that question. 'Ask your friend!'

'I am asking him,' he said with intrigue in every syllable he spoke. I was incensed with his presumption. I looked around me as though searching for something.

'I don't see him,' I said.

'Silly boy. I mean you, you fool.'

'I'm not your friend.'

'Oh, but you should try to be.'

I ignored this. 'It's your soldier friend you need to ask.'

He flicked his hand. 'He won't tell me. He's too… too pompous.'

'Well, he's the only one who knows.' I sat down on the floor with my back to him.

'Temper, temper! Upset are we? We should always do as we are told. Has no one told you that?'

He made various other inane remarks but I ignored him and eventually he oiled his way off. Another bad enemy? Possibly. But he probably was one already, and I was in no mood for compromise.

The queue continued but then dropped off to a trickle. I was obviously only a five-minute wonder and interest was soon lost. Most seemed surprised that I hadn't found myself in this exact position a lot sooner, but a great many were sympathetic and wished me as good a time as might be possible.

With the rush over I fell to wondering about Clearwell and all my good and faithful friends and workers there. Mostly I worried about Clio. How would she manage with Tiberius? He would by now have moved into my house; he would consider it his right as his spoils of war. And as part of that right he would have her in his bed – and smartly. I shuddered. But then what rights did I have over her? She had been sent to me by Julius Octavius, almost as a present, to 'set up house' for me. And he could no doubt take her away again. And, my God and all their gods forbid, she might prefer Tiberius! I doubted it, but it was always possible.

That evening Helen of Troy brought me some food. She was about the only person here with whom I had any sort of friendship. She had known me since my first tentative arrival and had always been good to me. I had hoped I might see her. Her raucous voice giving the guards a friendly telling off signalled her arrival.

'Brought you some food, darling,' she shouted. As always, straight to the point and taking life as she found it – me in prison or talking to the dominus – whatever. But she carried on in a much quieter tone. 'Brought you standard prisoner's fare. That's all you're allowed and it's not much, so I brought you some leftovers as well. Sorry about that but I have to account to that eunuch…' she spat the word out, 'for every bit of bread you have, see?'

'My, am I glad to see a friendly face and not just be an exhibit for everyone to laugh at. And thanks for the food. I was wondering when I might be allowed some more.'

'I'll do what I can for you 'cos you don't deserve to be where you are. It's that pillock Tiberius trying to play the big "I am".'

I nodded. We both knew what the other thought so we went in for a bit of friendly ribaldry for everyone else's benefit. We were, I suppose, two of a kind, both having got where we were by luck and shrewd judgment. I wondered when I would be free, if ever.

It didn't look too promising at the moment.

Chapter 30

A couple of days passed and life started to get boring. I had definitely ceased to be the wonder of the minute and the procession of people coming to witness my downfall had as good as ceased. Helen was a laugh when she came, but she had her work to do. I started to think about all sorts of things and, after Clio, it was Benedictus who was most in my thoughts. I wondered what he would do in the circumstances. He had the advantage, if advantage it was, of having nothing to lose. He had intended to die anyway and his God had looked after him. He could afford to take chances if necessary. I, on the other hand, had a lot to lose, and material things at that, so it was unlikely that any God, however well disposed, would bother with me.

By the same token I thought it was unlikely that I was in a life or death situation. I would need to have done something pretty drastic for Tiberius to put me to death. He just didn't have that authority. If I had murdered a soldier, say, or tried to escape, as he may have expected that I would, then he would be within his rights. No, he was going to make my life thoroughly unpleasant and when Julius Octavius came back, which eventually he must, he could crow, 'Look what a good boy I've been. I've raised production, reduced food costs and generally taught that upstart Marcus a lesson. He's back in the mine now! Working!'

A quick calculation suggested that I should have to survive at least two calends, perhaps three but more likely four, before Julius O returned. It could be nasty, and a visit from the fat centurion confirmed that possibility. He didn't waste time.

'Now, young man, tell me why you're here.'
'I don't know. Ask Tiberius.'
'I've told you and I shan't tell you again. He's not here.'
'We all know that.'
'None of your lip.'
'I'm telling you, I don't know. Anyway it's up to you to find out.'

'I shall have you out of there and start making you talk, so tell me exactly what I want to know.'

He wasn't joking and we both knew it, even if I doubted that he would soil his own hands in the process. There were, however, plenty of others for whom it would be a pleasure. I didn't exactly have to grovel but I had to be reasonable.

'I'm sorry,' I said, 'but I really don't know why I'm here. Tiberius made a well organised raid on the mine timed for just as we were sitting outside having our usual break so he could accuse us of slacking. At a flick of his fingers his men arrested me and dragged me off here. No word was said as to why or what I was doing wrong.'

I knew – and probably he knew – that I was here simply because Tiberius was jealous of the authority I had been given and the way in which I had successfully used it. But there was no point into getting into that sooner than necessary.

He contemplated what I had said for a while.

'Looks like I'll have to ask him, whenever he chooses to come back.'

He thought a bit further. I could almost watch his brain working.

'You been paying him off at all – or, rather, not paying him off?'

'No. Never crossed my mind.'

'Ah.'

'Why should I? Aren't we all in this mess together, like it or not?'

'You could have said that and been right, but I dunno. Times is changing and nowadays he's only interested in making a bit on the side. Him and that eunuch thing between them!'

He shrugged his shoulders as though in acceptance of some new unspecified order and continued, 'We shall see. Now you don't cause me no trouble and I'll cause you as little as I can get away with.' He winked and waddled on his way.

'That's a deal by me,' I said to his retreating back. He raised an arm in acknowledgement.

He had surely given me something to think about. What was this about Tiberius wanting to make money on the side? Or me having to pay him off, presumably in return for a quiet life? Did all this have something to do with these rumours of our mighty empire not being what it was? Was it every man for himself now? Was this why Julius Octavius had gone off to Rome? Would he actually come back? I had no answers, but the omens continued very poor.

I couldn't stop Clio going round in my head either. There was no doubt that if Tiberius wanted a woman she was the only one available. He was unlikely to have one of the locals and, if he did, from what I knew of them, he was likely to end up with a spear in his back. I just hoped he didn't hurt her too much, and in particular that he didn't choose to share her amongst his men. I shuddered at that thought. I knew little of her history; we simply didn't seem to have got round to talking about ourselves. Certainly she knew more about sex than I did, so I had to rely on my instinct that she'd survive. As for Polonius and the others, I had little doubt that they would put up with Tiberius in their own ways.

I wished Benedictus hadn't gone off as he had. In my present straits I would have liked to have known how to get some help from his Jesus God. Being nice to people wasn't doing me much good, although I supposed I had got a truce of a sort with my gaoler. Thinking of Jesus caused me to set about scratching a cross in the back wall of my cell. I was sure it would upset someone, almost certainly Tiberius, but most would probably not care. It was to be nearly two weeks before he did appear, and then in a towering rage, mostly directed at me.

In the meantime Helen of Troy provided enough food to more than keep me alive, and also kept me up to date with the latest gossip:

'Can't think where Tiberius has got to. Should have thought he'd have been back by now...?'

'Whatsisname, your runner chap. Antinous – that's him. He called by with orders to see that eunuch, but he wouldn't stop. Said it was more than his life was worth. Think he meant it too...?'

'They tell me the ore's not coming through as it should...?' I could see no reason for that. Yes, there could be a bit less if he allowed Polonius to continue digging down, but somehow I doubted he would.

'They brought a soldier back yesterday. Badly injured, he was. Broken leg and a head injury. Out of his mind too. Said something fell on him...?' Interesting. I wondered if it was deliberate!

'You know that injured soldier? Well, four carried him back and then took ten more and an inferior centurion back with them…?' I hoped it wasn't my 'friend' but she assured me it wasn't.

The prelude to Tiberius' return was a great deal of shouting in the guardhouse. A lot of stamping of feet and then more shouting when he actually got there. I sat back in the straw against the wall and tried to look forlorn and frightened. By what followed, I don't think I did a very good job.

He knew where I would be and the very first thing he had to do was to come and shout at me.

'What are you doing?' he yelled.

'Nothing,' I said, which was the literal truth.

'And why are you here?'

He said it very quietly in a voice full of menace.

'I don't know,' I gibbered, deliberately, adding, 'I'm here on your orders and, honestly I've no idea what I've done wrong. Nobody else seems to know either. Everybody asks me the same question.'

'You're here because you and your lazy good-for-nothings at Clearwell are not producing the ore in the quantity or quality we need here.'

'Ah,' was all I said.

He suddenly went even more apoplectic. 'And what's that?' he screamed, pointing at the cross I had scratched on the wall.

I looked round as though he had found something I didn't know was there.

'Oh, that? That's a cross. You know I'm a Christian now, don't you? It's legal now.'

'That dumb-cluck girl of yours told me some such nonsense. I made, and I mean made, her take down the one you had in your fancy house. She said you wouldn't be pleased and I said "Good!"'

'I'm not.'

'Good! But here's the deal. You take the magic spell off the mine and I'll let you keep this one.'

I hadn't the least idea what he was talking about and said so. He went purple in the face in his rage to the point that I was glad that there was an iron gate between us.

'You're going to sit there and try and persuade me that you haven't put a curse on the place?'

'Of course not. Christians don't believe in that sort of thing.' At least I hoped they didn't, I didn't really know. 'Why?' I asked innocently.

'Because, my dear little Marcus,' he said, his tone full of menace again – despite the way I was brazening him out I was genuinely scared – 'everything those idiots of yours do takes them twice as long as it should. And as for those local carters they don't seem to care whether they work or not.'

'With respect to your rank, Tiberius,' I said, hoping that a bit of flattery might help, 'I can assure you that I have done nothing and, indeed, am quite incapable of doing anything like you suggest. Maybe your gods…?'

He ignored the last bit.

'I've threatened them with the whip. I've personally used the whip.'

I winced.

'And I've threatened them with the wrath of Jupiter so it will be better when I get back.'

He said it triumphantly, spat at me, then turned on his heel and marched away. The guardhouse relaxed and so did I. Too soon. Seconds later he stopped in his marching and looked back at me. Looked hard and looked again. Then he bawled, 'Princeps Inferior Petrus,' at the top of his voice.

My fat 'friend' came running. I didn't think he could! Ah, and I also now knew his name and rank.

'Why is this man not in irons?' Tiberius yelled.

'I had no instructions, sir.' His nervousness was palpable. 'You sent him back with a Hastatis Inferior, sir, and he had no instructions either. In fact he didn't even know why this man had been arrested. I still don't, and he doesn't either.' He jerked a thumb in my direction.

Tiberius was a bit taken aback by this. It could only be his fault.

'Have you gauntleted him?' he asked.

'Oh, yes, sir. We took him all round.'

'And did they whip him, throw things, laugh at him, beat him – what?'

'Er, no, sir.'

'Well, what did they do?'

There was a real threat in his voice and I was almost sorry for Petrus. Tiberius was not going to like this.

'Er, well sir, they wanted to know why he had been arrested… and I couldn't tell them – sir,' he added in the hope of not having to go further.

'So what did they do?'

Tiberius was going to have a fit.

'Well, it was like this, sir…'

'What happened?'

Tiberius was almost nose to nose with his underling and speaking very quietly.

'They gave him food, sir.'

This was overstating it, but nevertheless essentially true.

'They did what!' Tiberius screeched and jumped back as though someone had stuck a spear in his belly. 'They did what?' he repeated, by now scarlet in the face.

In fairness to my 'friend', he now gathered himself up and told it how it was. 'When you gauntlet someone like that,' he said, 'it's up to the crowd. You can't make them hit him and all that, even if you give them the tools to do it with. If they like him or think someone's being unfair to him, they'll just stand back. I've seen it happen before, but only once, mind. And especially with us not knowing why he'd been arrested.'

It was quite a speech and the last bit was a winner. The army works by rules and if the rules haven't been adhered to, then my 'friend' was in the clear. And Tiberius knew it.

'Put him in irons!' he yelled and marched off with his head held high, although, I suspected, with a lot of worries going around in it. The fat one looked at me and shrugged.

'Sorry,' he said.

'Not as sorry as I am,' I said.

He shrugged again. 'I won't rush it,' he said.

Helen of Troy came round later with my allotted portion of food. 'Daren't bring you any more,' she said. 'Himself's in a right royal temper. Lashing out at anything that moves. Even had a go at the eunuch and now they're in conference. Conference, my arse!'

She was always a breath of fresh air.

'I'll see what I can do but you may have to live on your hump for a few days until they all quieten down. We shan't let you starve, not for him, of that you can be sure.'

'Thanks,' I said. 'It might be a bit obvious if I look too well fed.'

She laughed. 'And don't you go getting yourself into trouble. That won't help anyone.' She smiled and left.

The blacksmith came the following morning. 'To measure me up,' as he put it. He was an enormous man, tall with a big bushy beard and arms the size of a wrestler's legs. There was much sucking of air between his teeth, or what was left of them, and mutterings about the fact that he'd got a problem, the import of which I gathered from an overheard conversation with Tiberius in the guardhouse as he left.

'… I got a problem with putting 'im in irons. We're a bit short on iron, like… not getting the ore to make it with. But you knows that… yes, I know we've got some irons in the stores, but they won't fit 'im… Yes, course it matters. To me it does, I'm not having you or anyone else telling me I 'aven't done a good job… Yes, I'll get to it. It's not as though 'e's dangerous. … Oh, is 'e? Well 'ave it your own way… Don't you worry yourself, I'll find some iron and do it when I can.'

He winked at me as he walked away!

I had to ask myself some questions. Was it just sheer luck that everyone was being kind to me? Did they really like me that much? Or was it that they disliked Tiberius even more so that anything to thwart him had to be a good idea? Had my playing fair with all and sundry endeared me to them? Was one of the gods looking over me? More to the point, was this Jesus fellow looking after me? I didn't know and couldn't even guess the answers to any of that.

Chapter 31

A boring day and an uncomfortable night later I was awoken by a major shouting match going on in the guardhouse. I soon realised that it was Tiberius and Petrus, and that I was the subject of the argument.

'I told you to have him put in irons.' Obviously Tiberius speaking.

'You did, but you ordered the blacksmith to do it.' Petrus.

'And he hasn't done it.'

'No.'

'Why not?'

I could imagine the colour of Tiberius' face.

'How should I know?'

Careful, Petrus, I thought. You could find yourself in trouble saying things like that.

'Because you're supposed to be making sure he does what I've ordered him to do.'

'You never gave me any orders about that, sir. Of course if you had, I should have done as you say! Certainly I would.'

So that was why Petrus was so sure of himself!

'Isn't it obvious?'

'No, sir. Not to me it isn't. If I does something that you doesn't say I should do then I'm in trouble and you can shout at me. Same thing the other way round.'

'Why am I surrounded by fools? Eh?'

The question was rhetorical but Petrus chose to answer it. 'I don't know, sir.'

Oh, do be careful, Petrus, I thought. I know you've got my best interests at heart, but don't stick your neck out too far. Tiberius had simmered down a tiny bit.

'I've got to go back to Clearwell immediately, but all Hades will break loose if he's not in irons when I come back. Do you understand what I'm saying?'

I could imagine them almost nose to nose again.

'Oh, yes, I do, sir. Completely I do. I'll go and see the blacksmith right away. Will you be gone for very long, sir?'

'You don't get me that way, Princeps Posterior Petrus. I have no idea.'

He put a lot of emphasis on the 'Posterior'.

'Did you hear that?' he said to me as he waddled round to my cell.

'Some of it,' I said. Best to be cautious and not admit to too much eavesdropping.

'Cheek, he's got. Expecting me to do things what he hasn't asked me to do. Like I said, it'd be different if the sandal was on the other foot!'

'Things not going his way then?'

But he was still into his grievance. 'Blacksmith can't make irons for you if he ain't got no iron and that's Pilus Posterior Tiberius' problem! Well, course he could manage summat really, but he don't want to. We all know you're not dangerous and not done nothing wrong for that matter. Just in the wrong place when Pilus T wants to take it out on someone. So I suppose I shall have to go and talk to the man and get him to make some irons for you, or we shall all be in trouble.'

'Don't hurry,' I said, more in hope than anything else. 'But why no iron?'

I had to get an answer to this.

'I shan't hurry. He won't be back for a few days at the earliest, but to answer your question, I don't truthfully know. All I do know is that the carts aren't coming in as regular as they used to when you was in charge over there. In fact I didn't see one yesterday. Strange, but not my problem.'

Something was wrong, but I couldn't understand what. Helen of Troy was a bit more informative when she brought me some food, even if it was still only the regulation quantity.

'Things are badly adrift over at your place,' she announced.

'How so?'

'There's not been a cart of ore in all day and next to nothing yesterday.'

'Reason?'

'No idea.'

That seemed to be everyone's stock answer. Genuinely nobody knew what was going on, or why, and they were all gloating at Tiberius' problem. I knew that it was always a bit tight. For reasons of its own, Ariconium never held any great stock of ore and relied on us to provide a steady stream of it.

The following day the blacksmith reappeared, very apologetic, but I did understand, didn't I, that he had his job to do and that it would be all the worse for both him, Petrus and me if Tiberius should return and I wasn't in irons by then. If it hadn't been so serious from my point of view it would have been funny the way he couldn't get his words out quick enough.

'I've made 'em as loose as I dare,' he said.

'Thanks,' I said. What else was there to say?

And so I was shackled up. By all their gods and mine they weighed heavily upon me. The only consolation was that I didn't have to work in them. I'd seen men who were just a mass of bleeding sores who'd had to work hard when in irons. Better dead. They couldn't have lasted long and I knew I wouldn't. At least Helen of Troy was sympathetic. But still no carts, or so she said. And no reasons either.

So I settled myself down to a life of doing nothing, thinking nothing and accepting such food as the rules allowed, but it didn't last. Or only for a few days. It was Helen who brought me the story.

'Your runner lad came through today, saw the eunuch, had a meal and was off back again almost before he got here,' she announced. 'Apparently he had orders for the eunuch to send over some carts from here to collect some ore. So he, the eunuch that is, goes over to the army and tells them what Tiberius wants. "Where's the written order for it?" they want to know. Well, he hasn't got one has he? So he shouts at them but, as you know, he only squeaks and they all start laughing at him! And, between you and me, I think Tiberius can hardly write and that may well be why there was no written order. Anyway, in the end they said they'd see what they could do, and they didn't hurry themselves either. Dragged up some old horse and a cart that'll fall to pieces if they put too much in it and sent it off with a driver that didn't know where he was going!'

'That's crazy.'

'I know, and the furnaces will come to a standstill soon if something doesn't happen, and then there really will be trouble!'

Some days later the cart came back with a modicum of ore in it and Tiberius himself in tow yelling and bawling at the driver and the horse to get a move on. As this entourage passed the guardhouse he shouted to Petrus, 'Cage him!'

'Who, sir?'

He was pushing it. I've said it before, Petrus. Be careful!

'Him.'

Petrus looked blanker than usual.

'Him in there.' Tiberius pointed at me as if he could not bear to use my name.

'Oh.'

'And not necessarily you personally. Arrange for it to be done by those who know how.'

He was obviously remembering his previous conversation with Petrus and spelling it out for him.

'Yes, sir,' said Petrus to Tiberius' retreating back as he urged on both horse and man. He turned to me.

'That's bad,' he said.

'I know.'

'And in irons already.'

'I know.'

I did too. I had seen caging a man cripple him for life. It involves making a box of wooden poles all about half a cubit apart and smaller than the size of the man. If he pokes a leg, arm, or worse still his head through the gaps anyone, but anyone, is entitled to kick it, stamp on it or mutilate it in any way. If the crowd is really nasty they can turn the cage over or roll it about, and then arms and legs are bound to protrude outside. And the culprit can't sit or lie down properly because of the poles underneath him. An altogether unpleasant prospect. But why? What additional crime had I committed?

I was pondering all this when Tiberius crept up on my cell from a direction from which he didn't usually come.

'Ha!' he shouted. Did he never talk normally? 'Now we shall see. You have one more chance to take your so-called Christian spell off the place so that we can get back to normal.'

'But there is no spell.'

'Don't come that with me. There must be.'

'Why? What's wrong?' I was almost ready to help him in order to avoid the caging.

'Everything's wrong. And you know all about it.'

'I'm sorry, but I don't.'

'Christians!'

He spat in the dirt, then at me, but fortunately missed. He stalked off.

Over the next few days, by bribery and threats of violence, he managed to rustle up a few more carts and sent a procession of them off towards Clearwell. In the meantime, Petrus had a collection of poles delivered to outside my cell but would say nothing, only tap his nose. Tiberius called.

'Have you taken that spell off yet?' he growled.

'There is no spell,' I said wearily. 'And why are you sending carts from here?'

'Because yours have vanished.'

'Vanished?' I was astounded. 'They can't have.'

'Well, they have.'

'Where to?'

'If I knew that I'd have had them back by now.'

'But…'

'You, young man, must know where they are. You've cursed them, and they've vanished. Find them and I might, just might, rescind the caging. Think about it and send word.'

There was real menace in his voice and I knew he meant every word. But he did set off in pursuit of his wagons and I was left in some sort of peace. There was no doubt I had a problem. Tiberius had convinced himself that I was the cause of his troubles, whatever they were exactly, and that he was going to take it out on me one way or another.

It was Helen of Troy who shed a bit of light on the scene.

'You got a problem!' she announced.

'I know that,' I said in some exasperation. 'But tell me something new about it.'

'Him…' (she seldom referred to Tiberius by name), 'and that eunuch thing are hatching something.'

'Something?'

'Don't know, and probably better not to know, but the two of them have been "in conference", or so they call it, for hours at a time. Nobody's allowed to go near. At least that's the tale from both the office and – listen to this – from the house!'

'The house!' I whistled. 'He's got a nerve.'

'He hasn't actually moved in there yet but he's planning to!'

'And me?'

I couldn't quite see how whatever bit of making money on the side they had in mind affected me. And surely that was what it was. The eunuch was only interested in money; for Tiberius, prestige and money, in that order, were everything.

'The important bit you have to remember is that he can't get rid of you – for which read kill you off! Only if you do something that's treason. And you can't do that shut up in a cell here on your own.'

'I think I'm still missing the point.'

'Look, idiot! He thinks everything he does goes wrong because you've put a curse on him, or the mine, or even this whole place, and therefore that by grinding you down he'll get you to take it off and then all his – and the eunuch's – best plans will work out.'

'Oh.'

It seemed remarkably stupid thinking to my mind, but then Tiberius was pretty stupid.

'You know, I know, everybody knows, that you haven't put any curses on anything. Apart from the fact that they probably wouldn't work, it's not your way. So we're all working out delaying tactics to keep you going until the real dominus comes back.'

'If I survive that long!'

'You will, you've got to. For all our sakes.'

With that she turned her head in the air and walked off as though thoroughly exasperated with me, which she probably was, but I knew that there was a heart of gold under that enormous bosom. And so the weary days passed in discomfort, pain and boredom. The next time Tiberius passed by for one of his sessions with the eunuch, which had by now become common knowledge, he commanded Petrus to get the dreaded cage made so that eventually he could personally supervise my being put into it and that there were no half measures. That depressed everybody, and eventually that day came round as well.

It was afternoon and Tiberius turned up very full of his own importance, strutting about inspecting the cage and leering at me.

'Right, put him in it,' he barked at Petrus.

'Can't,' said the latter in his most sullen of voices with not even a 'sir' included.

'What do you mean, can't?'

'He's got to have his irons taken off first.'

'And who says?'

Tiberius was not liking this.

''Tis regulations, sir. Prisoner cannot be put in cage when in irons.'

'You know this, do you, Princeps Posterior Petrus?'

The low menace was in his voice again.

'Oh, yes, sir. I've read it all up, sir.'

Whether it was true or not, it was another barb to Tiberius, whose inability to read properly was well known.

'Well, get them off then!' he yelled.

'Yes, sir, blacksmith's on his way, sir.'

So we all waited. Petrus was as stolid as a pig, and Tiberius kept dancing about like a bird afraid the cat will get it.

Eventually the blacksmith arrived, winked at me, dumped down his leather bag of tools and started to rummage in it. Then there was much sucking in of breath, as he did with any problem, then he picked up his bag and started to head off.

'Hey, where are you going?'

'Ain't got the right hammer and punch with me. Have to go back and get it. I'll see you all in the morning!'

'What do you mean, "In the morning"?'

'In the morning, that's what I mean.'

It was too much for Tiberius. He might even have begun to suspect that he was being made a fool of. He whipped out his sword and pointed it at the blacksmith's throat, bawling at him, 'You'll do it now with what tools you've got, not go wandering off!'

What happened next would have been terrifying, funny or serious in other circumstances, but left us all a bit ashen-faced. By the nature of his trade the blacksmith was a ponderous man with arms like tree trunks and fingers to match the branches. With the speed of summer lightning he grabbed the wrist of Tiberius' sword hand and squeezed. I didn't hear any bones break but Tiberius went white and his sword dropped to the ground like a child's discarded toy.

'Just remember that somebody, no names, wants an iron gate made in a hurry,' hissed the blacksmith at him. 'So tomorrow it is.'

Tiberius nodded as his right arm fell impotently to his side.

Then, to my astonishment, Petrus weighed in. 'Just what has this man done wrong?' he asked as though in total ignorance.

'You keep asking me that and you know equally well what the answer is.' Tiberius was in too much pain to shout. 'He's put a curse on the whole operation here. Got it?'

'If you say so, sir,' answered Petrus, in such a flat tone, a voice totally devoid of any expression, that it even gave Tiberius pause.

And into that void came a shout of 'Stop! Stop what you're doing!' that caused a string of repercussions.

The blacksmith about-turned and headed back towards us, whistling as he walked.

Petrus found all his efforts vindicated.

I knew that, despite all the odds, salvation had arrived.

Tiberius went even whiter as disaster enveloped him.

Chapter 32

And into our midst marched a slightly out of breath but furious Julius Octavius. He took in the situation in a flash, although I discovered later that he had been forewarned as to what he might find.

'What in the name of Jupiter and the whole pantheon of gods is going on here?' he shouted at Tiberius.

Still nursing his arm, Tiberius seemed lost for words.

'Well?'

Tiberius wasn't the only one who could impute menace into his voice. I was about to say something when good old solid Petrus beat me to it.

'Dominus, Tiberius has had Ma… this man under arrest for a while for a crime he won't tell us about. He wants him caged but I told him that's against the rules while he's in irons.'

A wisp of a smile crossed Julius O's face, although I may have been the only one to notice it. The blacksmith continued to whistle very quietly, and Tiberius started to splutter.

'I've had nothing but insubordination from this centurion, dominus. I shall be wanting to speak to you about him.'

'First you will speak to me and explain just why Marcus is in this cell, why he is in irons, and why you wanted to cage him. Now!'

The last word had the impact of a javelin hitting a door.

'And, incidentally, why are you nursing your right wrist?'

The blacksmith stopped whistling. 'Shall we say I shook hands with him, dominus,' he said.

Julius Octavius definitely smiled at that! 'Well?'

'Dominus, we weren't getting enough ore and I took over running the mine in order to speed it up.'

'You did what?' Julius Octavius' eyes were like balls of fire boring into Tiberius.

'Yes, dominus.' Not so familiar now, I noticed. 'He's put a curse on the place and everything I did went wrong and things went from bad to worse. I needed him to take off that curse, but he wouldn't. So I had to make him take it off. So…'

He looked around him as though seeing the situation for the first time and his whole well-honed military bearing slumped.

'Princeps Posterior Petrus.'

'Yes, dominus?'

'Will you take this man,' he nodded at Tiberius, 'first to his barracks, then to the stores and change all his uniforms for those of Hastatus Posterior.'

If Tiberius could have gone any whiter he would have done. This was the end of all his dreams.

'But…' he began.

'Just don't say a word,' Julius Octavius hissed at him, 'or you'll find yourself back in the ranks. Consider yourself lucky.' He now turned to Petrus. 'Do I make myself clear?'

'Oh, yes, dominus, very clear.'

Then Julius Octavius was all business. 'Good. Now, blacksmith, those irons off as quick as you can, please.'

'Certainly, dominus.'

And once again his leather bag was dropped beside me and, miraculously, all the right tools were suddenly in it. I was free in minutes.

'But…' began Tiberius again. The blacksmith looked at him and just tapped the side of his nose. Now Tiberius knew he had been made a fool of and, although only guessing at the joke, Julius Octavius smiled again.

'One final thing, Tiberius. At first light tomorrow you will leave for the mine and bring back any soldiers you have there. I'm sure you have some. Be back before nightfall.'

To bring back his troops in his much-reduced rank was the ultimate ignominy. That would hurt Tiberius far more than any physical punishment. It was my turn to smile!

'Petrus, when you have dealt with this little matter will you come to my office, collect the eunuch, who is under arrest there, and put him in this cell that Marcus is now vacating. Don't bother to clean it!'

'Yes, dominus.'

He turned to me. 'Come,' he said.

It was a good thing that it was generally downhill to his office as, having been confined for so long, my legs were weak and not used to carrying me. I was panting like a child when we got there. His servants had obviously had a roasting from him and were themselves out of breath from restoring his office to the way he liked it. They were particularly and noticeably obsequious.

'Sit,' he commanded, pointing at a chair. I collapsed into it, the difference in our rank forgotten, for I could hardly stand any longer, whereupon he ordered a boy, who I knew by sight at least, to go to Helen of Troy and bring back food for me – and himself.

'Nothing too rich for him,' he called after the boy.

'Is he still in there?' he asked of another servant.

'Yes, dominus.'

'Checked up on him at all?'

'Yes, dominus. Wet himself.'

Julius Octavius wrinkled his nose in distaste. It was plainly the eunuch they were discussing and he was imprisoned in what I thought was a cupboard.

'We shall be rid of him soon.'

'Yes, dominus.'

'When the food comes, we'll talk,' he said and then proceeded to ignore me.

It was my turn to say 'Yes, dominus.'

What I really wanted to know first was how he came to be back at least a calend earlier than was expected. Usually when the likes of him go off travelling they're much later back than they say they will be. Second, how he managed to appear in the camp without anyone being aware of his arrival and then wreak such havoc with Tiberius' well laid plans. Not that I was complaining about that!

I was lost in these thoughts when the door swung open with a crash and there stood Helen of Troy. Did the woman have no sense of dignity or of whose presence she was in? Evidently not, but more to the point she was carrying steaming dishes of something that smelt good and the boy behind her was carrying warm drinks.

'That was quick, even if you didn't knock,' smiled Julius Octavius.

'No hands,' she said. 'I'd heard what was going on, so I started putting something together for the lad. I knew it was food he'd want.'

'You're a marvel,' I said.

'Well, we did our best to look after you. So now here's some stew, nice and hot, for you both and some warmed wine for the dominus. If he's got any sense he'll let you have some as well to give you a lift up.'

How did she get away with talking about Julius Octavius in this way? I would never have dared, but then I guess he knew her for what she was.

'And when you've finished, send him back to the hostel and I'll make sure he's comfortable and well looked after.'

It was her parting remark as she left, and Julius O simply thanked her. I wolfed into the stew. It was the first decent hot meal I'd had in many weeks. Even when Helen did bring something hot to my prison cell it was usually pretty well cold by the time it got there.

'Steady on, Marcus,' said Julius. 'You really will make yourself ill if you eat as much and as fast as that.'

'I'll chance it,' I burbled through a mouthful of food.

'No. Seriously, I've seen this before, you'll be bent double with cramps in a few hours if you go on like this. If necessary I shall forcibly take it away from you!'

'OK,' I said and looked with longing eyes as the food was cleared away.

'The boy will go with you to the hostel, just to make sure you get there, and tomorrow I will send for you. You and I need to talk about many things, some trivial and others of greater importance.'

'Yes, dominus.'

I was glad we were not going to discuss all of whatever it was now, as I was almost falling asleep. I was also glad the boy was there to get me to the hostel, as otherwise I might not have made it. Helen was waiting and insisted that I should wash myself all over. I could have done without that but nobody argued with Helen of Troy when she was on a mission. She then hustled me off into a bed that was bliss after the bare floor of my cell.

I slept.

I woke when the day was well up, disorientated and ravenously hungry, to find Helen standing looking down at me with a motherly look on her face.

'Thought you was never going to wake up,' she said, chiding me in her inimitable way. 'Come and get something to eat when you're ready.'

How did she know that it was more of that stew that I wanted? She had it ready and waiting. I ate, but with a bit more caution. I didn't want Julius Octavius to be able to say that he had told me so. But the boy did not come for me until late afternoon so I had a chance to eat some more and sleep some more. I couldn't work out how I was so tired when I had hardly moved a muscle for the last... how many weeks?

Helen of Troy was unsympathetic and said that was just the problem – I needed exercise. 'Go and load a few carts,' she said!

When the boy did come I found myself being taken to Julius Octavius' house, which was a bit alarming as I was hardly dressed for that. However, both he and Aemelia were welcoming and, despite the difference in our status, I began to feel very comfortable with them both. They seemed to have changed and to be not be quite as imperious as in the past. We sat down to a good meal at which I was treated as their equal. He refused to talk about anything of importance until it was finished and cleared away and, I guessed, the servants were out of earshot.

'I imagine,' he said, while getting up and very deliberately closing the door, 'that you want to know why we came back early and unannounced.'

'Both questions have been gnawing at me ever since your abrupt and fortuitous arrival. After all, you had gone for four calends and were back in three. I expected you to be away for five.'

He laughed. 'Good estimates, Marcus. The first part is easily explained. It took us the best part of a calend to get there, and another to get back. We knew that. But Rome! Oh dear! We saw old friends, yes, but they had become so superior that we became something of an exhibit: this is what you become if you live on the outer fringe of the Empire! Most of them seemed not to have even heard of Britannia. The infighting between people and factions is worse than it ever was. And the bloodletting in the arena is horrific and pointless.'

He looked at Aemelia, who shivered at the memory.

'So we came back.'

'To what we now consider to be home,' added Aemelia. 'Rome is no longer where we belong. At least we found that out.' She shivered again.

'Why we came back secretly is, shall we say, much less easily explained,' said Julius Octavius.

'It is! Although I have to admit that you were right,' agreed Aemelia.

'Looked at from a military point of view, the current situation in Rome can't last. Yes, OK, it will probably go on for another ten, perhaps twenty years, even more, but there were rumours there that legions were being pulled back from the more difficult border areas. When we got back to Britannia there were more rumours of troops being brought back from the far north of the province. Whether true or not, I have no idea, but it wouldn't surprise me. There seemed to be a state of panic in Rome, with the games being used to keep the plebeians in ignorance of what's really happening.'

He shook his head despairingly. 'It can't last,' he said, and looked dolefully round the room.

This was news indeed and I was having trouble with it.

'Why we came by a back route is quite simple really, provided you trust your instincts. The nearer we got to Glevum, and what Aemelia and I both now consider to be home, the more I had this feeling that all was not as it should be here. I had, as I thought, left everything organised so that it would all run itself while we were away. Call me an old man seeing visions if you will (Aemelia did!) but I knew, I just knew, something was badly wrong. So we came in by the back tracks and arrived at this house without anyone knowing about it. It was quite a shock to the staff!'

'I can imagine that,' I said, thinking that both his way of putting it and my response were understatements of the first order!

'In fairness they rose to the occasion but told me in no uncertain terms that I needed to get up to the guardhouse sharpish. Me, being ordered about by my house staff – and before I even set foot in the place!'

'Thank God they did.'

'Which neatly brings me on to my next point. I hear you've become a Christian.'

'Yes,' I said without further explanation.

'Legally there's no problem with that but locally there can be, as you've found out to your cost. I have clipped the wings of a certain centurion but he will be very bitter about it and will want to get his own back. Just be careful. I might not be around at the vital moment next time.'

I nodded.

'What does Clio think of it?' he asked.

This took me by surprise. 'She tolerates my whim. She has her own shrines to various gods and can't understand why I'm content with just a cross hanging on the wall. At the moment it seems an easy and accommodating religion, if you understand me.'

'Not sure that I do, but I heard a lot about it in Rome, where it's become the "in" way to be different. Apparently there were so many Christians that the Emperor didn't have much choice but to make it legal. Even the Coliseum didn't have the capacity to put them all to death, and that's saying something!'

I shuddered, remembering what Benedictus had said, and his escape from the lion's jaws, but now was not the moment to tell Julius Octavius about that.

'Talking of Clio,' he continued, 'isn't it time you two got married? Either traditional or Christian, as you wish!'

I was flabbergasted. I knew he had sent Clio over to Clearwell supposedly to do my housekeeping, but this...? I was lost for words. Then I noticed Aemelia smiling in the background and realised that this was something of a well organised trap.

'But dominus,' I began, instinctively being formal about it. 'Yes we have talked of it but not much more than that. In any case it requires your permission – for both of us. And not only because we are your slaves but also because neither of us have any parents that we know of to give us away and do the other honours. And goodness knows what may have happened there while I've been imprisoned here. And...'

I ran out of ideas at that point.

Julius Octavius laughed and Aemelia laughed quietly with him.

'Marcus, you are impossibly naïve. Do you know that?'

'You've said that before, and, I have to admit, you're not the only one to have said it.'

'Well, it's true. You've had a soft spot for Clio for years, haven't you?'
'If you put it like that, I suppose I have, but as for getting married…'
'Why not?'
'Well…' Again I was lost for words.
'By all the gods, Marcus. I can see I've got to be a pater to you! I don't want to raise a sore point but what would yours have said? Eh?'

I thought about that. 'Probably much the same as you're saying. I hadn't thought of it like that,' adding wistfully, 'It's so long ago.'

I must have struck a chord because the mighty Julius Octavius became positively pater-like, saying quietly and persuasively,

'Listen to me, Marcus, you're a grown man now. You've lived together for, let's call it a year now, so you're entitled to get married if you wish. Parents or no parents.'

'But I've been imprisoned here for calends. That doesn't make it a year.'

In the nicest possible way Julius Octavius nearly lost his temper!

'Just listen to me, will you! I backed my own judgement, my instinct if you like, as to what you were capable of, and I was right. By your own efforts and your own character, you've made quite a name for yourself.'

I looked up in surprise.

'Don't look so astonished. It's a fact; you have. By your own good judgement you have been able to manage and get the best out of a very tough collection of slaves, and more importantly you have managed to keep the local people on your side so that they have been willing to work for us without problems or arguments.'

'I suppose so,' I said, 'but I haven't done anything special, just what seemed natural to me.'

'Well it worked and you can be proud of yourself. If what I've been hearing today is true, you're going to have quite a mess to clear up when you get back and you'll need all your charm to get the locals on side again.'

'I shall do my best.'

'And I've no doubt you'll succeed! More to the point, get something sorted out with that Clio. We can all guess what Tiberius may have been up to with her, but she and you will cope.'

I had thought this would be the case but had forced it out of my mind. Like Julius Octavius, I was sure that Clio would have coped. 'Now, let's be practical. I asked for word to be sent to me if and when Hastatus Tiberius gets back, and it's not come yet, so we must presume he's not hurrying. You need to be out of his way so you will spend the night here.'

'But dominus…?' I expostulated. Slaves like me just didn't spend the night in a villa like this with people like Julius Octavius and Aemelia! He held up his hand.

'If you insist, it's an order! And you will stay here tomorrow and tomorrow night, and once I'm satisfied that I have Tiberius and his men under proper control then you can make your way back to Clearwell by a route on which you will not be seen by anyone here.'

'And I'll find some more respectable tunics for you, so that your authority will be assured,' said Aemelia, smiling kindly at me.

'Thank you, domina,' I said. 'I shall certainly feel more comfortable in better clothes, but the old ones might be better while I'm on the road.'

'As you wish,' she said. 'I understand.'

'And finally you and Clio both have my permission to marry, if you so wish, and I hope you do. And before you try to think up some other excuse, as far as I'm concerned you've been living together for over a year!'

'Thank you, dominus.'

Chapter 33

I think Julius Octavius must have had a guilty conscience about how I had been treated, or maybe it was Aemelia who had. Perhaps they simply didn't realise that a slave's life could go up or down at a moment's notice, and that this could occur without said slave having created any cause for whatever happened. His putting me in charge of the mine and Tiberius putting me in gaol were wholly typical of what could and did happen. One just had to accept it. Thus in compensation I was given a guest room for the night, complete with a slave to dance attendance on me. Luxury indeed, even if I did want to get back to that little world of the mine that I understood so well.

Julius Octavius came back to the house during the following day to report to me on what was going on. Him reporting to me!

'Tiberius got back very late last night,' he said with an amused smile. 'Doubtless so that not too many people would see him coming back in his reduced rank and with his scruffy band of minions all laughing themselves silly. This morning he's slow off the mark and livid with Petrus ordering him about.'

I had to laugh.

'And dominus,' I said, 'since you mention Petrus, any small reward you can put his way, and the blacksmith too for that matter, I should appreciate. Within what the rules allowed, they helped to make my life a bit more bearable simply by delaying Tiberius' orders as long as possible. Hoping you would come back I think.'

He smiled. 'I can imagine Petrus playing the rules to his own and your advantage. He hasn't much more time to serve in the army and I know he wants to open a shop somewhere when he does leave. I'll see. As for the blacksmith, nobody in their right mind messes with him. Again I'll think about it.'

'Thank you,' I said. I was beginning to understand why Julius O had had such a high command whilst in the army. He knew everything about everybody!

'The eunuch is occupying your cell and whining to anyone who'll listen, which isn't many, about how badly treated he is. He claims he was "only obeying orders from his superiors". I now have to waste a lot of my own time going through the books to find out just how much he and Hastatus T have filched for themselves!'

He updated me again in the evening but not much had changed. He was planning on having a showdown with Tiberius the next day and he would send word so that I could leave when that was happening and there would be no chance of my being prevented. Thus it was that I set off the following afternoon carrying a large bundle from Aemelia, with her best wishes to Clio and myself, not to mention a large kiss to seal our friendship, as she put it. Very embarrassing!

My journey was slow, very slow. If I had had trouble with walking to Julius Octavius' office two days before, now I had millia to cover and a large parcel to carry as well. I lost count of how many times I had to stop and rest but I got there in the end when it was nearly dark. To make it worse I had to take a circuitous route to the house as I didn't want to bump into anyone from the mine until I had seen Clio.

And then it was something of an anticlimax.

The whole place appeared deserted. The doors were only too obviously barred and bolted. There were no lights on but there was a wisp of smoke from the cooking area. I picked up a rock and went round banging on the doors and window shutters, all the while listening for any sound of movement. Eventually I heard something and called out, 'Clio, it's me, Marcus.'

I heard a squeak from within so I said it again.

'Marcus? Is it really you?'

'Yes.'

'Speak to me so that I can recognise your voice.'

So I started to tell whoever was there – and I was pretty sure that it was Clio – about what had happened to me, but I was cut off in full flow.

'Marcus. Thank the gods, it is you. Go to the door and I'll open it.'

I did as she said but, whilst I knew from her voice that it was my Clio, I was totally unprepared for the person that I could hear lifting off the bars and finally pulling the door open. Gone was my trim little Clio, and here was a wretch of the worst appearance. Haggard, hair all dishevelled, no shoes on her feet, clothes torn, hands chapped and bleeding, smelly and thin – oh, so thin. She threw herself at me so that I had to drop my bundle in order to remain standing, for I was just about done in myself. The tears streamed down her face.

'He said you were dead,' she wailed in my ear.

'I could have been,' I said.

'Has he really gone? He's not out there somewhere waiting to pounce back, is he?' She looked around me and shivered in her distress. 'And is it true he's been demoted?'

'He's very definitely not out there and, yes, he has been demoted to Hastatus Posterior.'

'Wow! That bad?'

'Yes.'

'So it must also be true that Julius Octavius has come back?'

'Again, yes, and literally in the nick of time to prevent serious injury, at best, happening to me.'

She looked at me with eyes that I could at least recognise, even if the rest of her was a mess. She became businesslike.

'What are we doing standing here? Come in, come in. The place is a mess, like me, but I might find just about enough oil to light a lamp.'

'What do you mean? We always had plenty of oil about the place.'

'Not any more, we haven't. I tell you there's nothing. No food, no ale, no wine, no nothing!'

She started to cry again. 'Oh, the gods be praised that you're back, Marcus. Life might get back to normal.'

This was no time to embark on telling her what Julius O had told me and that 'normal' might be going to be a very different sort of normal.

In her excitement she carried on. 'I'll see what there is in the way of food. Maybe some bread and perhaps vegetables. Just about keep you alive.'

'But it's you who needs food. I've done all right – at least for the last couple of days!'

More like her old self, she bustled off in the darkness of the house and obviously found a lamp and some oil because I could see a glow of light from it. She came back looking downcast.

'Bread is all there is,' she apologised.

'You eat it,' I said, and without more ado she wolfed it down.

Then it occurred to me. 'Why are you doing this?' I asked. 'Where are the house slaves, Gallus and Lupus?'

'In the mine. Where else?'

'But why? They'd be useless in there.'

'Right, as always, but you'll have to ask Polonius for all those details. Then you'll have it right, rather than me telling it to you all wrong.'

It was a valid argument, and at that moment I was much more interested in finding out how she came to be in the state she was rather than worrying about the mine.

'So what did he do here, and to you?'

'Do you really want to know?'

'Yes,' I said, 'because he could lose even his Hastatus Posterior position and find himself back in the ranks!'

'How long have you got?'

'All night if that's what it takes.'

Apparently Tiberius had acted exactly as I had expected and Clio had become his own private sex slave. I had not been too worried about that because I knew that she had found herself in that position before and could accommodate men in the manner that they expected. It was not for me to be prudish about it: as always, it was survival that mattered. She described Tiberius as being like a ravening beast; there was no love or kindness attached to him. She was there for just one purpose and he was going to use her accordingly. But then he had had some problems in the mine. ('Talk to Polonius,' she said again.) The house slaves were taken away and she had to do all the housework herself, get food and drink and make herself available for Tiberius' lust whenever he felt like it.

I was horrified and said so.

'It gets worse!' she said.

It seems that the problems in the mine spilled over into the locality and the supply of food almost stopped. What was available was also at exorbitant prices. Added to which, just where certain things came from was something that poor Clio simply didn't know. But Tiberius couldn't or wouldn't understand. He merely shouted at her more loudly. That was when she started to let herself go, she said.

'If I was going to be the kitchen slut, then I was going to look like the kitchen slut, and it might just curtail his lust a bit.'

'And did it?'

'No – made him worse if anything!'

This coincided with the sudden urgency back at Ariconium for carts, any carts, to carry the ore. Tiberius must have upset the locals badly. Like me, she had been doing the reckoning as to when Julius Octavius might be back and, also like me, wasn't sure whether she could survive another calend, or possibly two. Quite apart from anything else, she did not have the time or resources to keep herself smart. Also, apparently money came to be in short supply along with everything else. She would implore Tiberius to bring plenty back when he went to Ariconium but latterly he had returned with only minimal amounts. Hence the lack of oil, food and so on. With my knowledge of Ariconium I guessed that the eunuch was siphoning off money for both of them and quite possibly not letting Tiberius have his share. She had heard that he had been back in the last few days but was more than surprised he had not come for 'his usual' and that he had set off again for Ariconium the same day along with all his soldiers.

'They weren't bad,' she laughed, the first time since my return. 'They hated him as much as everybody else and didn't go out of their way to help him if they could avoid it. But soldiers are soldiers and have to do as they're ordered.'

I smiled, thinking of the prevarication of Petrus whilst studiously obeying his orders. Then she became businesslike again.

'I must tidy myself up, now you're back.' I couldn't argue with that. 'And we must sort out somewhere to sleep. Then you must tell me what happened to you.'

'Except for the last three nights I've been sleeping on the floor, so anywhere will do. As to what I've been doing, well… Let's get organised before we start on that. Final thing, in the morning can you get word to

Polonius that I'm back? I think I'd rather talk to him here first before showing my face in the mine.

'Might not be that easy, but we'll see what the morning brings.'

Although our night was not of the best, for many reasons, it was good to be back with Clio and where I felt I belonged. I had yet to talk to her about Julius Octavius' plans for us. The following morning I was bursting to talk about those plans, but, reluctantly, I had to put duty first, and I wanted to find out the state of things before making plans for both of us that might never materialise. Accordingly, I asked her to go and fetch Polonius for me so that I could find out what I was up against. To my surprise she was doubtful about doing this.

'I haven't been to the mine in all the time you've been away,' she said. 'That man always kept me too busy in one way or another.'

This was the beginning of her never being able to say his name.

'Then how could you get a message to him without anyone else knowing that I'm back?'

'Difficult. I suppose I could get whoever I met to fetch him for me. That's if I'm lucky enough to meet someone who knows who I am.'

I considered this. 'Just go and if you have to give away that I'm back, so be it, but do your best.'

'I have to tidy myself up a bit first.'

Typical Clio!

'It's hardly a state procession,' I laughed.

'It is for me! I've hardly been out of the house.'

As luck would have it she met Polonius just outside the mine compound so was able to talk to him without any eavesdroppers. He instantly came back with her at as near a run as he could manage. To have seen a man his size running would have been worth a lot! He was overwhelmed to see me.

'We were told you were dead, or if not actually dead, that you soon would be. Some rubbish about how you'd put a curse on the mine and wouldn't admit it. As though you would do such a thing!'

So I had to set to and explain to him what had happened and how I had been saved just in time by the return of Julius Octavius before matters got really bad. Clio was able to listen in, so I was at least saved from having to repeat it all.

He nodded sagely.

'You look like somebody who's been locked up for a while,' he said. 'Lost a lot of weight and I guess not got a lot of energy.'

I nodded. Sympathy from this hulk of a man brought tears to my eyes.

'So what's been going on here then?'

I wanted to get back onto more businesslike territory. So this is his account of events as he told it to me.

'*After they took you off, Tiberius really started throwing his weight about. He wanted the ore deliveries back at the levels they'd been at last year and all good-quality stuff, none of the rubbish that we'd been having to send. I tried to explain to him that we had permission to dig deeper so that the long-term supply was kept up, even if it was down a bit just now. Also that we had to keep sending the Puzzlewood ore, or there'd be times when he got none at all. But he wouldn't listen. Obviously knew nothing about mining and didn't want to.*

'"*So how were we supposed to do it," I asked him. Cor, I thought I'd be the next one carted off to the cells, but I think he had just enough savvy to know that without me here he'd get nothing.*

'"*Get the whips out," he said. "And use them! Make everyone work harder, sharpen the discipline, cut the food so they know they have to work to get fed!"*

'"*It won't do," I said. "It was giving them a bit more food and laying off the whip that got the production up to the figures we've had. And that was Marcus' idea. I didn't believe him but it worked."*

'*I really thought I'd said too much then, but I was trying to convince him, see, of what you had achieved and how you'd done it. He even reached for his dagger, but I stood up and he realised that I was lot bigger and heavier than he was and he backed off. I'd have killed him if he'd tried it on. At least I'd have done my best to; I'm not as fit as I used to be. So we came to some sort of tacit agreement between us, and each knew that if he made life too impossible all round, one of us could, and probably would, kill the other. It concentrated the mind.*'

He laughed heartily when I told him the tale of when Tiberius took his dagger to the blacksmith!

'*First thing he did was move into your new house. I was afraid for your little Clio and didn't want to see her get hurt, especially by him, but she assured me she had put up with worse than him in the past. I haven't seen much of her until just now, so obviously she's got by somehow or other.'

'Just about,' I said.

He grunted.

'Second thing he did was to get down the mine and start ordering Sparticus and his gangs about. He wasn't too happy down there. It showed. Especially when some time later on they deliberately lost him down a blind passageway. He did find his way out but I think they hoped he wouldn't! He wouldn't listen to anything I told him. Just shouted for more iron ore – it was our problem how we got it. Couldn't, or wouldn't, understand how we had to leave pillars to support the roof or, if not, put wooden supports in instead.

'Third thing was to go over to Puzzlewood, stop work there and bring all that lot back to work in the mine. He said that those over there was having a holiday being out in the sunshine with nobody to seriously whip them. I admit it can feel a bit like that, but as we change them round everybody gets a bit of fresh air occasionally, and that can only be good for their health. Anyway, in the winter it's warmer underground!

'Final straw was to stop me digging down for another seam of ore. I know you know how essential that is because you've worked hard to get me permission to do it. So the only thing that could happen was that production would fall. OK, it rose a little for a start because we had more slaves working in the mine, and for a week or so he could say, "Look, I told you so!"

'But it couldn't, and didn't, last. Not least 'cos they all kept asking him where you were and all he would say was that you were locked up out of harm's way. It was only later that he said about a curse, with the implied suggestion that you could be dead already. As though we were expected to believe that, and with you being a Christian, and all! Now, they'd got used to your way of working and being treated fair, even if you could be hard if they stepped out of line. They weren't going to have his way of doing things. They just went slow.'

'Really?' I said.

'Yes, really, I should take it as a compliment if I was you!'

'Go on,' I said.

'Sparticus and I knew what was going on and we looked the other way. So he gets down there himself and whips a couple till they're nearly dead, so that's two who can't work despite how he shouts at them. It was to replace those two that he commandeered those two house slaves of yours. They were no good for hard work. You know that, I know that and that's why they're in the house. And the rest, they just went slower! I don't think they cared what he would or would not do to them. If he killed them they knew that was that much more ore he wouldn't get. And I think he knew it too 'cos he tried to make it easy for them. Started to cut a bit more round the pillars!'

'Idiot!' I couldn't restrain myself.

'You're right.'

'"Well," I told him, and he wanted to know how I knew. Where was it written down! That was almost a laugh, but I guess that's the army way of doing things, everything written down. I said it was just experience that told me. He never took any notice and we had a bad roof fall. Killed six slaves, including your friend Hadrian.'

'No!' I was sorry to hear that, even if he had got a bit above himself.

'So then he'd lost eight slaves by his own stupidity and there was no way he was going to keep up production. He went rushing back to see his mate at Ariconium to see if and when some more slaves was due or how many he could filch from their operation. Don't think he's liked much there because they wouldn't release any of theirs and supposedly there aren't any new ones due for a couple of calends at least. And they got at him about there not being enough ore getting to them. What was he going to do about it?

'Then it got worse. He started bawling at the carters to get across to Ariconium quicker so's they could get another load in during the week. First they took no notice of him. Then he threatened to flog them as well. We had to laugh at that too, even if he was dead serious. They just turned round and took their empty carts home! Then he gathers up some soldiers and sets off down to their village and when he gets there, there's no one there. They've abandoned it. Must've seen trouble coming and took everything and melted into the trees. Clever, eh? I think he was going to burn the place down, but it was so dead and spooky down there that they all come back in a big rush, blabbering tales about ghosts and strange noises in the woods.

'We laughed even more, behind our hands of course! They're not a bad lot from that village and they don't have to put up with the likes of him. So he really had a problem by then. No carters, no ore to Ariconium. No ore, no iron produced. No iron, no swords or whatever! And – no money! Then he had to have another trip back to Ariconium to find some carts from there. Cor, you should have seen them! All falling to pieces and never built for carrying heavy stuff like iron ore in the first place. I suppose he got some ore back that way, but I did hear tell that it was only at a price that was well over the odds.

'And all the time he refused to tell us what had happened to you, and it wasn't for want of us asking. He gave the idea to anyone who listened that you were either dead or *soon would be. But the gods be praised, now you've come back and all's well with our world again.*

'Mind, the first thing you've got to do is sort out some carts. No, I tell a lie. First, some decent food and then some carts!'

Chapter 34

Polonius was, of course, quite right that my first priority was to get food and carts organised, but I wanted to see just how bad the situation was here first. If my understanding of what Clio had had to put up with was anything to go by it was not going to be good, and more likely very bad. However, I had to find out a bit more background first.

'I know you've said that the food situation's bad, but how bad?' I asked.

'Bad. All the usual people have vanished and what we can get is poor quality and expensive.'

'Exactly what Clio told me about the house. Bread only, if we're lucky.'

'That's about it.'

'How have you kept the place going then?'

'We've sort of let it run itself. Everyone knew that we had to produce some ore, at least enough to fill what carts Tiberius could find and at the same time have an increasing pile of the stuff waiting for carts that he couldn't get. That way the problem was all too obviously his, and no one got flogged.'

'Logical,' I said and laughed.

'It was nothing to laugh at,' said Polonius, reverting to his most lugubrious tone.

'I know. Let's go and look at the worst of it.'

As we walked back towards the mine, a slave I didn't recognise slipped out of the wood with a bundle of vegetation under his arm, looked at us and ran for all he was worth.

'Scavenging for something, anything, to eat,' commented Polonius. 'You can't blame them. One thing though, the whole place will know you're back by the time we get there!'

And he was right. Slaves were spilling up out of the adit with Sparticus and Trojan in the vanguard. But what a ragged lot of men presented themselves to me and cheered as loudly as they could, which was not very loud. All slaves, it was true, but where I had left a reasonably fit and healthy lot of men behind when Tiberius carted me off, now they were thin and haggard, and many were covered in sores. No wonder he wasn't getting much production.

'Praise the gods you're back,' cried Sparticus. 'Even that funny god of yours. Now we can all live again!'

I then made an instant decision that I knew would upset Polonius, who always liked to see something happening.

'No work today,' I shouted. 'Get yourselves washed! Wash your clothes! Wash and cut your hair! In the meantime I'll see if it's possible to get something decent in the way of food for tonight but don't put too much hope in that.'

Another ragged cheer went up.

'And Sparticus,' I said rather more quietly, 'make sure none of them try to run. Make it very clear what will happen if they do!'

'Don't think you'll have any bother. Most of them can't run far anyway.'

'There's always one,' I said.

He nodded.

Polonius grunted and walked off towards his hut. A sign of approval and disapproval all in one!

***

So now I had a problem of my own. I had promised them food and, truth be told, I didn't have much more idea of where our food came from than Clio had. I went back to find her. I was touched that she had made an immediate effort to improve her appearance and, more importantly and with huge energy, had started on tidying up the house.

'Why don't you get Gallus and Lupus to do that?' I asked. 'Once they've cleaned up a bit Polonius will be glad to see them out of the mine.'

'You don't understand, do you?' she said as she swept with even more vehemence.

'No,' I said in my ignorance.

She stopped for a moment.

'Because, my dear Marcus, I can't possibly let them see what a state I've let the house get into.'

'But you could at least let them do the heavy work.'

'No. No. No, I couldn't.'

And she started off with the broom again. I shrugged my shoulders. I certainly didn't have time to stop and help her; much as I would have liked to have done.

'What I came to ask you is, where did you get food from? I have to get food for the men.'

'You mean you don't know either?'

'No. It's never been my problem.'

She found this hilariously funny and roared with laughter. It was good to see her a bit more cheerful but it didn't help me. When she had subsided she became helpful.

'Recently I've managed to get enough to keep himself alive – why I bothered I don't know – from a woman who lives in one of the few huts along the road towards New Hamm. Charged me a fortune, she did, but I didn't blame her. I'm sure she didn't want to be helpful but I think she sort of took pity on me. Kept the peace anyway.'

'Doubt she can help with the sort of quantity I want.'

'No. So you'll have to try the village. If they're still living there, that is.'

'I need to see them about carts anyway.'

'But make sure you take someone with you.'

'I know them well enough,'

'You *knew* them well enough. Things have changed. We may not be popular nowadays, and besides, you're supposed to be dead. And I, for one, don't want you dead!'

And with that she came and gave me a resounding kiss.

'Hmm. Maybe you've got a point. Perhaps I'll take Antinous with me.'

'You do that,' she said, and set to with her broom again.

Antinous always did things quickly, so he was washed and half respectable before any of the others. Thus we set off into the woods wondering what we might find, if anything. The locals could have moved out altogether; it was, after all, the best part of a calend or even more since Tiberius had upset them. It didn't look good as we trudged down the hill in the direction we needed to go. The track had started to become overgrown and it was obvious no one had come this way for a while. The village, when we got to it, was deserted. I had expected that but it didn't look abandoned. True there was no sign of smoke or fire or life of any sort, but certainly somebody came here at least occasionally.

Antinous and I walked around somewhat aimlessly with no idea what to expect. We walked into the woods a bit but kept the village in sight all the time. Basically nothing.

'Now what?' said Antinous.

'We wait,' I said. My, how those words brought back memories from the aftermath of the riot.

'What for?'

'I'm not sure.'

'You're not sure?'

'No.'

'To get killed, perhaps?'

'I don't think so.'

'Then what?'

'They know we're here. You can be sure of that.'

'I'm not. Sure we could get killed is more like it.'

'You're as bad as Hastatus T's soldiers.'

'I can understand their problem. It's creepy here.'

It was, but I wasn't going to tell Antinous that! 'We wait,' I said again, stoically.

Antinous didn't say anything, just looked at me as though I was crazy. Suddenly there was a crash from the edge of the wood, and a branch fell into the clearing. He was on his feet and about to run as only he could.

'Well, come on!' he said, as I continued to sit.

I cupped my hands together. 'It's Marcus!' I shouted in the local language. 'I come as your friend, as always.'

Antinous was more than a little surprised that I could speak their tongue, but again said nothing.

'Come on,' he repeated.

'Sit down,' I said.

Reluctantly he did.

A small child, a girl, ran into the clearing and back into the woods again.

'We make progress,' I whispered. 'They would sacrifice a girl if necessary, but not a boy.'

I shouted again.

Briefly a man showed himself from the trees and was gone. Then another on the other side of the clearing and a third slightly further away. Spooky was the word for it and my companion remained poised to run.

'Chad! Iden! If you're there come out and talk to me. It's Marcus,' I shouted again. 'We need to get back to the old ways.'

Nothing.

And then it happened. The whole of the edge of the clearing became alive as men came into the open. They were all armed and ready for anything. Antinous was on his feet again.

'Sit down!' I yelled at him. He sat, even more reluctantly than the last time.

The men advanced on us and I steeled myself to continue sitting. Then I recognised Chad. I stood and moved towards him.

He pointed a sword at Antinous and looked at me.

'He's OK,' I said. 'He's with me and there are only the two of us.'

Chad turned and said something to his companions. They all visibly relaxed but noticeably did not put their weapons away. He turned back to me.

'We were told that you were dead. Been killed – what is your word – executed.'

'He didn't have that authority, but I could have died by other means. Starvation for one. Brutality for another. My God was with me, I had some good friends, and there were others who hated Tiberius.'

He laughed loudly and many, but not all, of the weapons were put away.

'So, you are here. What do you want? I have a guess.'

'Go on,' I said.

He squeezed up his eyes and looked at me. 'Food!' he said.

It was my turn to laugh.

'Today?' he added.

'If that's possible.'

'I don't know. We will see. How will you take it?'

'Can you bring it? Or shall I go and fetch people to carry it?'

'We will bring. Oh, it's good to see you back, Marcus. Now we can get back to "business as usual" and we can all eat!'

With that he came and gave me a huge bear hug that in my weakened state I could barely withstand. Iden did the same but without quite so much force.

'You know, you are a wise young man,' he carried on. 'You came on your own, or nearly so. If there had been many of you we would have killed you all!'

'I guessed that, and I only brought Antinous here because he can run like the deer to get help, or at least say how you killed me!'

Again he roared with laughter and all weapons were sheathed by now. It was safe to offer our thanks, say our goodbyes and see what they brought us to eat.

'By the gods, Marcus, you're a miracle and you've got guts with it,' exclaimed Antinous when we were well out of earshot of the native village. 'How on earth did you do that?'

'I've always treated them fairly,' I said nonchalantly. I could afford to do that! 'And I've gone along with their way of doing things. Like the time I got their druid to approve the trees I wanted to cut down. That surprised a few and stood me in very good stead with them.'

Antinous shook his head in wonderment.

'You're a bloody miracle,' he kept repeating to himself and when we were close back to the mine went off at the double to announce that food was coming and, no doubt, what a marvel I was.

Food did indeed come later in the day. The villagers were apologetic that there was no meat with it but they had not had time catch and kill any of the boar that roamed the forest. However, they brought flour and vegetables, so that at least all would get something to help build them up again. I took a small quantity for Clio and myself and no one objected.

Back at the house I found Clio exhausted but brighter. She had brought some order to the house, had washed herself and her clothes, and was generally looking more her old self. She also flung herself round me, nearly knocking me down in the process.

'Hey, steady on,' I said. 'You're the third person to do that and I'm not strong enough to stand it.'

She looked at me with questioning eyes and I told her about Chad and Iden. She laughed.

'Oh, it's good to see you back even if you are thin as a stick. Now I want to hear all about what happened and how Julius Octavius came back to save you.'

'You shall, but first go and do something with this food so that we can eat at least a little. Then I have a lot to tell you – most of it direct from the man himself.'

Her eyes widened. 'Really?'

'Yes, really.'

She bustled about and came back with a gruel which, whilst not very appetising, at least filled a few corners.

'So?' she said with even wider eyes.

I had no choice but to wade in. 'He's been playing pater to me and wants us to get married. How about it?'

She leapt up and flung her arms around me again, but then drew back.

'We can't. He must know we can't.' She held up her hand, fingers splayed. 'One, we're slaves so need his permission. Two, we neither of us have parents, so who can give us away? Three, we haven't lived together long enough to claim it that way. Four…'

She ran out of reasons and I laughed. She gently slapped my face.

'I'd love to marry you, Marcus, but we can't. Not yet anyway. Doesn't your new pater understand that?'

I laughed again. 'I said more or less all that to him and Aemelia…'

'To Aemelia as well? Was she in on this?'

'Very much so. In fact I'm not sure that it isn't all her idea.' I paused.

'Well go on!'

'Yes. He is quite adamant. We have his permission. He knows we have no parents and, by doing some very strange arithmetic, as far as he's concerned we've been living together for a year!'

'There's got to be a snag. What's Aemelia's role in all this?'

'She just sat and smiled and nodded her head at all he said. She's sent you a present, although actually it's for both of us, I think.'

I went and got the parcel that I had carried all those long millia from Ariconium. She pounced on it. Inside were two very smart new tunics in fine material with the edges bound in red and two Egyptian cotton dresses in a delicate shade of blue.

'What on earth...?'

'She said they were to display our new status. She even wanted me to wear mine when I left Ariconium! I would definitely have been robbed, or at least laughed at, wearing something like that.'

Clio continued to stare in wonderment. 'You might be important, what with running all this.' She waved an encompassing hand in the general direction of the mine. 'But I'm only Julius Octavius' skivvy, sent over here to be your skivvy!'

'Much more of that nonsense and you'll be getting a good spanking,' I said.

She just looked at me and giggled.

'You know, I think those two have been working up to this for a long time. Those,' I pointed at the contents of the parcel. 'Must have come from Rome. I'm sure there's nowhere around here where they could have got anything of that quality.'

'Then we must make their dreams come true, mustn't we?'

'And ours!' I said.

Chapter 35

And so it all began to take place, almost as though Clio and I were not part of it. When next Antinous had to go to Ariconium, I sent separate word to Julius Octavius that we wished to take him up on his offer of allowing us to get married. The response was immediate and peremptory: 'Come and see Aemelia and me immediately. Both of you.'

Clio was thunderstruck. 'What's he talking about – "both of us"?'

'For his own reasons he wants to see both of us,' I said. I knew I was being difficult but I had no more idea than she had as to why he wanted to see Clio as well.

'But what am I going to wear?' she wailed. 'That man ruined what few clothes I had. Enjoyed ripping them off me, he did. Gave him a thrill, he said. Claimed he'd replace them with something better, but he never did.'

And she spat on the floor, as though to get any thoughts of him out of her head. I have to say, I was taken aback by this outburst, but I was to learn that the whole Tiberius episode had been very traumatic for her and that this sort of tantrum was to become a part of our life.

'We could wear our new clothes,' I ventured.

'You didn't.'

'That was different.'

'How?'

'I was supposed to be dead, for a start!'

'I suppose.'

'And because I would have been very conspicuous walking back here.'

'Hmm.'

'We could change when we get there. We could use Helen of Troy's hostel.'

She brightened at this suggestion but it was not to work out. When, some days later, we arrived at the guardhouse, there was Julius Octavius' messenger boy waiting for us with strict instructions that he was to take us immediately to his dominus' house. His orders were that this was not business so I was not to go to his office or anywhere else, but straight to the house. We had no choice, tired and dirty though we were from our long walk. The boy led us to the front door of the house.

'Not this door,' I remonstrated with him. 'The slave's door at the back.'

'No, dominus,' he said, 'I was particularly told to bring you to this door.'

He shrugged and spread his hands, as if to say that orders were orders, daft though they might be. And in the split second before we entered I realised that he had called me 'dominus' – me!

It was Aemelia who greeted us.

'Welcome,' she said. 'Come in. Come in.'

'But domina,' began Clio, who was patently overwhelmed by the situation in which she found herself. I had assumed that she was familiar with Julius Octavius' house, but it transpired that she had never even been there.

'No, no. Not domina, it's Aemelia from now on!'

Clio was lost for anything to say, so I had to intervene.

'Domina...' I started.

'And the same goes for you, Marcus,' she said abruptly, and held her finger to her lips to imply that this was the end of the matter.

She surveyed us.

'It looks as though you've brought your new clothes. That's good.'

At least we'd got something right!

'Now Clio and I will go and bathe. Marcus, you will have to wait until Julius gets back.'

Clio continued to remain dumbfounded and I wasn't much better.

'Come,' she said, leading Clio off I knew not where. Clio cast a plaintive look back at me as she went.

I was left standing, very ill at ease. Yes, I had been in this house before and, in fairness, Julius Octavius had always treated me as an equal when here, even if it had been different in his official office. Also when here I had been largely on business, despite some of the subterfuges to which I had necessarily become a party. But this time I was here for him to become my substitute pater. This time I was to become part of his family! And what did that mean? He had always had quite remarkable faith in me. True, I had always obeyed his commands, as I suppose any good son should, but in my case it had been as a slave to his dominus rather than through any family loyalty. Frequently of recent days, I had tried to remember what it had been like to have a pater and what my duties to him would have been. Slightly to my shame I didn't remember what having a pater had really been like. I remembered getting into trouble – occasionally – and that he had taught me to read and write. And it was these skills that had brought me to the position in which I now found myself: the wheel going full circle, you might say. So I supposed, all in all, that having a pater was a good thing. But, and it was a big but, I was still a slave, so if he wanted to play with my being his surrogate son then there was absolutely nothing I could do about it!

I ruminated on all this for what seemed like an eternity. His boy did bring me some food and drink, for which I was grateful, but it also added to my anxiety because I wasn't sure of my status in this household. Of Aemelia and Clio there was no sign. Eventually Julius Octavius appeared. He seemed to be unusually flustered.

'Ah,' he said, 'glad you're here. Got delayed, so later than expected. Did they bring you a drink? Yes. Good.'

He did not seem at all his usual suave self.

'Yes, dominus,' I began.

He waved a finger at me.

'Marcus, Marcus, didn't Aemelia tell you? No "dominus" here. Julius from now on!'

'Yes, indeed she did say so.' I certainly didn't want to give her a problem. 'But I needed you to tell me. I could not presume such a thing.'

He eyed me and smiled.

'Always trying to get it right. Eh?'

'Yes, dom – yes, Julius.'

'Come, we have a lot to talk about.'

He led the way along a passage to his bathhouse. I guessed he must have one but I had never seen it. It was not large but it had all the proper pools – hot, tepid and cold. We didn't have such things at Clearwell. If we needed to wash, the local stream had to do. I had realised that Gaius Maximus had started to add baths to the house but I had not bothered to rebuild them; there had been more important things to do. I had occasionally used the communal one at Helen of Troy's hostel, but that tended to be full of loud-mouthed soldiers who resented my being there at all.

We started in the hot pool and I have to say it was sheer bliss. Perhaps my house needed baths! But Julius quite obviously had something on his mind.

'Now, Marcus,' he began, once we had got ourselves established. 'I know you wrote that you were, but are you and Clio definitely going to get married?'

'Yes,' I said.

'Good,' he said, 'No ifs or buts? No second thoughts? Or other reservations?'

'None.'

However, I was mystified by this casting of doubt on what Clio and I had wanted to do almost ever since we first met.

'Good,' he said. 'Because we have a lot to talk about. First, Aemelia is going to act as mater to Clio. She should know this by now.' (So that was why I hadn't seen them since we parted!) 'And I am going to act as pater to you.'

I bowed my head in acquiescence. I couldn't speak!

'So now you both have your respective mater and pater's permission to marry, and if I've been doing the arithmetic correctly...' (He hadn't!) '...you've been living together for over a year, so in theory you can do what you like.'

I bowed my head again in grateful acceptance.

'And as dominus to both of you, you also have my permission to marry. How's that?'

'That takes care of all the legalities,' I said, 'and very tidily. Thank you, Julius, Or should I say Pater!'

Perhaps I was getting used to this form of address, for he laughed and certainly looked as though a weight had been removed from his mind. He held up his hand.

'There's more,' he said.

There was? Had he not settled all that needed to be settled for us to marry?

'From the moment when you are officially deemed to be married you will both become freed.'

'But, dominus…' I began. I was flabbergasted. Of all the things I might have hoped for, that was beyond my wildest dreams. Every slave dreams of the day he will be freed but…

Julius Octavius was carrying on as though he had to get all this said before he could relax. 'You know and I know that I've always trusted you, and you've worked wonders with the mine, the house and the local population, so you deserve it. And if Clio is to be your wife then she must be so too, quite apart from the fact that she survived that rascal Tiberius.'

I was overwhelmed. 'To say "thank you" just doesn't seem enough,' I said.

'And to say "don't mention it" is about the same!'

We both laughed and relaxed. Then he became the Julius Octavius that I knew and not my pater, which role I was beginning to think didn't really suit him.

'Quickly into the cold pool,' he said. 'And then we must join our respective wives.' And he winked at me!

My, the cold pool was cold! We were in and out of it in a flash. We were soon dressed and on our way when a thought crossed my mind.

'Does Clio know about all this?' I asked.

'Aemelia will have told her all about the wedding, but the other – no. I'll leave you to tell her that good news.'

Then he added enigmatically, 'If it *is* good news.'

There was no time to quiz him on that before we were in their reception room. As we came in, Clio jumped up and ran to me.

'Has he told you the good news?'

'He has, and more besides.'

She was radiant and bubbling over, and therefore missed the second bit of what I had said.

'For the first time in my life I shall have a mater,' she said, dancing round me. 'And you will have found a second pater!'

She danced round me again and I was embarrassed. This was all very fine, but Julius Octavius was still very much my dominus, and for the time being at least we were both his slaves. Aemelia smiled beatifically at her protégé, while Julius Octavius wore a resigned expression.

'We're both delighted for you,' said Aemelia. 'Aren't we, Julius?'

'Indeed we are.'

I noticed that he didn't sound wholly convinced. What was that slightly barbed remark he had made earlier, about whether it really was good news?

Whilst I had served at table in my youth, I had never reclined at table as was the way in high-class houses, and I wasn't sure whether Clio had ever even seen it done. We were a bit out of our depth, but Aemelia was the perfect hostess and had anticipated our likely problem.

She smiled and said, 'I will explain.'

And she did, so we were soon one happy family.

Later we were shown to the room I had used when Julius Octavius had rescued me from the clutches of Tiberius. As he did so, he became mysterious again, saying that tomorrow he would talk to me about far more serious matters than we had discussed today. He must have seen or sensed my alarm because he added, 'Don't fret, Marcus – it doesn't really affect you,' which hardly put my mind at rest.

Of course Clio and I had been sleeping together ever since Clio first came to Clearwell, but we were slightly taken aback that it should be assumed to be the norm in someone else's house. Especially when that house belonged to Julius and Aemelia, even if they were now technically mater and pater to both of us. And did that make it worse, or better?

***

Clio and I did not have a very good night. We were both jumpy and wondering what in the world was happening to us. She would wake up suddenly and say something like, 'What if he makes all these arrangements and then it's not legal?' Mostly I had no answers for her and could only soothe her nerves as best I could. I had my own worries too. I was being moved out of the little world that I knew, and might have to find new friends that I could trust. We were jaded in the morning, but the household seemed not to notice, for which we were grateful.

Julius Octavius was as good as his word and took me into his house office to discuss whatever it was that was on his mind. As was his way, he came straight to the point.

'I think the Empire's collapsing,' he said.

I looked at him in total astonishment. Had he gone mad overnight? I certainly didn't have words with which to answer him. The Empire had existed for centuries. Why should it suddenly fall apart now?

He smiled. 'Don't panic too much,' he said. 'It probably won't happen immediately.'

I recovered the power of speech. 'What in the name of your gods and mine are you talking about? It can't collapse. It's too big. It stretches too far. It covers the whole world. It just can't!'

I was lost for real reasons but my conviction was clear. Rome was too big to vanish overnight.

'I've told you you're naïve, Marcus, haven't I?'

'And I've told you that you're not the only one,' I said somewhat peevishly. I was getting fed up with being told this. He laughed, which didn't help my humour.

'Listen to me. As you know, I'm a military man at heart, and just now we won't go into how I ceased to be. That's for another day, if at all. I know how the army works and how it thinks. And what some of its problems are. I've been to Rome recently and, as you know, I didn't like what I saw and heard. Indeed I did not.'

He paused as though reliving what he had seen there, then carried on.

'What you've just said is exactly right. It's too big and it stretches too far. There's trouble on the borders with the barbarians. Mostly with the Huns and Goths in Germania. That's where I got into trouble. Subsequent commanders have tried to do what I did and not done any better.'

He sounded bitter and I held my tongue. He brought himself back to the present.

'We don't get a lot of news as to what's going on here, but we had a cohort of soldiers pass through and use all our facilities a few weeks ago. And eat all our food!' He sounded bitter about that too. 'They were being moved out of Cambria to Corinium in order to replace those sent from there to Gaul to replace those sent to fight the Goths, or whoever it was. And so on, and so on! That reduces army strength to the west of us in Britannia Prima, and that could spell trouble.'

'But we're fairly safe here, aren't we? The local population here depends on us.'

'Perhaps. I've also heard, and through something better than just army rumour, that troops have been withdrawn from the wall that Hadrian built.'

'Well that doesn't affect us at all.' I was getting quite heated about this nonsense he was talking!

'You're right – it doesn't affect us. Not directly, and not now, at least.'

I was a little consoled.

'The thing is – and this is where it hurts, without the army here in force we're out of a job! No army, no swords, no spears, no ironwork for ballista, no body armour, no nothing. We can't exist on making a few hinges, boat nails and the odd plough.'

I began to see his point. 'So?'

'It may not happen for five, ten, maybe twenty-five years, but for absolutely certain, unless something changes we shall have a problem. I'm getting to be an old man, but you have your life in front of you.'

He was getting maudlin now and I was about to tell him so, but remembered in time that I was still his slave. In any case, he stopped me from speaking.

'All this is one reason why I've freed you, and it will be your job to free others – that is, unless we all find ourselves without our Roman masters and slaves are thus automatically free. Marcus, I don't know what the future holds but I'm worried. As you know, this is home to me now and I can only wait and see what happens, but you, you have the chance to arrange your life so that you can take any opportunities that may or may not come.'

I was overcome by his perception. I had noticed that the demand for ore, and therefore presumably the demand for iron, had been a bit less of late. He could just be right.

'And one final thing, Marcus. Make friends. Make friends where it matters. You're good at it. Make the most of your skills.'

Chapter 36

On this second night we were in a whirl of thoughts. Clio was faced with the enormity of suddenly becoming the matron of a household and all the responsibilities that this would entail, not to mention the prospect of motherhood and the risks and pleasures that that might bring. I had never asked her if, in her rough and tumble life, she had ever given birth to a child, and if so, what had happened to it. I'm not sure that I wanted to know the answer to either question. For myself, I was seriously concerned with what Julius Octavius had been telling me and his foretelling of what the future might bring. If he was right, and in my experience he nearly always was, then the future looked bleak indeed. And here was I about to take on a wife, a house (although that had not been mentioned), hopefully a family and, now as a freed man, on what sort of income? It didn't look good.

As might be imagined, we talked long into the night, each telling the other what our respective mater and pater had said.

Finally Clio put her arms around me and said, 'Marcus, we will survive.' Then she looked me straight and hard in the eye and said it again.

I smiled at her. I was certain she was right but just at that moment I could only see problems.

'We will. We. Both of us together. I know we will.'

'You're right,' I said, with more confidence than I felt was justified. 'Anyway, nothing's going to change overnight, so we'll have time to think.'

Whilst I was right in so far that nothing changed during the night, changes came thick and fast, were momentous in the extreme and came much quicker than any of us might have expected.

***

The next morning we were all a bit the worse for it, so I could only guess that Julius and Aemelia, sorry, Pater and Mater, had been discussing us and the future as well. In fact Julius had already gone to his office. The military tradition of starting the day at dawn dies hard. Aemelia was her usual kindly self but seemed a bit distracted.

I started as I meant to go on. This was going to be a new and more forthright me!

'As soon as we've eaten we'll get on our way back to Clearwell,' I said. 'There'll be things for me to catch up with there. I'll call on Pater in his office on the way.'

I thought the Pater bit was quite clever of me.

Aemelia looked under her eyes at me, smiling broadly.

'Good boy!' she said and laughed.

Clio remained obviously nervous but it did feel a bit like what I remembered of family breakfasts, both our own and for the lawyer family, when I was a boy in Rome. Putting it that way made me feel old as well. I wanted to get away.

As we were about to leave, Julius reappeared, but not at all the Julius in command of all that surrounded him that I knew so well. He was again flustered and out of breath.

'Thank the gods you haven't gone,' he panted.

'But I was going to call on you on my way out,' I said.

Aemelia was puzzled too, and Clio just kept looking from one to the other of us with the occasional glance at Aemelia for good measure.

'Has something serious happened?' I continued.

'No. No, not really, but after all we were talking about last night, the future is being foretold before our very eyes. Enough to make a man want to sacrifice something to his gods.'

'What is?' said Aemelia flatly.

The tone of her voice seemed to bring him back to us, as I suspect she intended.

He drew a deep breath.

'There's another cohort of soldiers passing through, and not just going to Corinium like the last lot, but all the way to Gaul and then the frontline with the Goths. Helen's swearing at anyone who gets in her way. They've eaten almost all the food we had in stock and they reckon there's another lot not far behind them. I tell you the place is collapsing!'

'Calm down,' said Aemelia.

'Calm down? All you can say is calm down? When the world is falling in on us? Here and now? In front of our eyes?'

I had never seen him like this.

'Dominus,' I said. At this moment it seemed appropriate to call him that, both as my master and as my pater. 'Let them pass through. For all you know there may be replacements going the other way but not through here. Or coming from the North or somewhere.'

He looked vacantly at me before his vision actually focused.

'Marcus, you could be right. You have to be right. The gods be praised. Yes, you're right, you have to be.'

I wasn't at all sure that I was, but it was necessary to say something and it seemed to be pulling him out of his despair. Indeed, within minutes he was his usual upright self and in charge again. Aemelia looked relieved.

'So you're off, are you?' he asked, as though his outburst had never happened.

'Yes,' I said. 'I'll send word of how we want to organise this wedding, and we'll come and see you again as the arrangements progress. To report progress – to be official about it.'

It was not much of a joke but it seemed to break the ice and we all laughed.

'Get on your way then, and I suggest you avoid going through the camp. Far too many boisterous soldiers about. Find a back way.'

'I know one,' I said, and I did, from creeping in and out of Ariconium surreptitiously in the past. There was much hugging and kissing, which was again embarrassing, and we finally left.

'What was that all about?' asked Clio, almost before we were out of earshot, let alone out of sight.

'I'm not sure. He's obviously very worried about what's going on. Even if he likes it here, as he says he does, I think he doesn't like not knowing the larger scheme of things. I've never known him worry about anything much – except us producing enough ore, but this seems to be getting to him.'

'Why?'

'I don't know.'

'How did you know what you said about soldiers coming from somewhere else?'

'I didn't. I just had to say something.'

'Do you believe there are? Some coming, I mean.'

'No.'

'So what about us?'

'Us?'

'Yes. Us.'

'We just keep on as though nothing was happening.'

'And the wedding?'

'We start arranging it, as he said it should be done.'

She considered this. 'And us being freed?'

'Either through Julius, or by default if the world as we know it collapses around us.'

'That's all right then.'

Clio could treat life very simplistically. If her wish of the moment was going to be fulfilled then all was right in her universe, and nothing else was of any consequence. So we talked about the wedding. I have to say I wasn't terribly excited about the event itself but it gave Clio something else to think about as we walked back along the tracks I knew so well. She was excited about it. I suppose it made her feel a legitimate person for the first time in her life, instead of being a cast-off child available for the likes of Tiberius to treat as dirt. As far as I was concerned she could arrange it all however she wanted, but there were two quite big 'buts'. Whilst I had a little money put by that I had scraped from various sources, most of them best not talked about, I was in no position to be lavish with the festivities, and I doubted if Clio had a sesterce to her name. Second, and to my mind more serious, was how were we going to do anything, anything at all, that would remotely recompense Julius Octavius and Aemelia for the faith they had shown in us? Particularly Julius, who had shown it for many years now, and indeed as good as saved my life. By the time we were back, whilst we had some immediate ideas, we were no nearer solving the two 'buts'.

Then the mine took over.

The place was unusually quiet when we arrived.

Polonius, Sparticus and Trojan were standing in the yard as though in conference, the latter two with whips in their hands and Polonius looking ready to murder anyone who crossed him with his own enormous bare hands.

'Trouble?' I said, already knowing the answer.

'Yeah,' growled Sparticus. 'Fellow called Meta took exception to his soup and threw it in the face of one of the cooks. Burnt him quite badly, but that's the least of it.'

'Go on,' I said.

'All Hades broke loose. Just like that.' And he snapped his fingers to make the point. Polonius nodded in agreement. 'In minutes they were all at it. Fighting. Throwing anything they could lay their hands on. Punches. Kicking. Mayhem it was.'

Polonius continued to nod his head. Trojan said nothing, but then he never did say much.

'So what did you do?'

'Fought our way out and left them to it. Cowardly I know but there's only three of us to twenty-five or more of them. They're locked in, we'll clear up the rubbish later, maybe tomorrow. Maybe find out who was behind it, had a grudge or whatever.'

'Why?' I asked.

'No idea.'

'None at all? Food, work, injuries, what?'

They, all three of them, shook their heads violently. It was Polonius who spoke this time.

'It's been good. We've had no trouble for a while. I think they were all so pleased to see the back of that idiot Tiberius that anything was better.'

'Well, we stand guard tonight in case they've got ideas of getting out.'

'Going to be a long night.' It was the first time Trojan had spoken. 'Could make a difference you being back.'

Polonius nodded again. I was flattered but it gave me an idea.

'Let them know I'm back,' I said. 'In the meantime I'm going to take Clio here back to the house and I'll see you later,' then adding as an afterthought, 'Then we can plan.'

I had noticed Clio standing well apart from us and looking lost. Like me and the mine, she and the house had to be together again. We left the others looking anxiously at the mine entrance and made our way towards the house. We were subdued and this had taken the shine off our happiness.

'Remember what you said,' I suggested.

'What?' she said, with no intonation in her voice.

'We will survive. You said.'

It seemed have an effect. She walked a little more quickly and held herself a little straighter. 'You're right,' she said. 'We will.'

'And see what tomorrow brings.'

She shivered. 'That could be bad.'

'It could,' I conceded.

She shivered again but we had reached the house and she was soon back in her element, ordering Lupus around to light fires and lights, and Gallus to get us a meal. After we had eaten, I went back to the mine to find the three strong men more or less where I had left them.

'Any change?'

'Trojan and I went down to the inner gate and told them you were back. Think they'd fought themselves to a standstill. Brought them up with a bit of a jump it did. They know you don't stand no nonsense with them so they're worried now.'

'Let them worry,' I said. 'We won't be in any rush in the morning. I'd stay with you but I don't think I'd be much use if it came to a fight.'

Polonius laughed. 'True. Very true. Can't see you with a whip and a sword – or your bare fists.'

And he balled his up to show what he meant. Frightening.

Sparticus managed a timid smile. 'He's right but even that lot…' and he jerked his thumb in the direction of underground, 'respect you for surviving the cage.'

'Yes, well,' I said, 'I had a bit of help because nobody liked Centurion T.'

'Take the credit. You survived. How doesn't matter!'

This was getting embarrassing.

'OK. Get some sleep between you if you can. I'll see you at first light.'

And I left while the going was good.

***

The next morning Sparticus, Trojan and I presented ourselves at the inner gate. I was unarmed but they each had their whips, swords and daggers. We were astonished at what we found. We had expected chaos, with broken artefacts and men all over the place, but instead… instead all the slaves were sitting quietly waiting for us. Anything not broken was back in its proper place, the rubbish was all piled in a heap, and there was calm as though nothing had happened! I was taken aback but said what I was going to say anyway.

'Within five minutes I want one of you out here to explain to me what happened and why. Sparticus and Trojan will escort you.'

I turned to walk away and out of the corner of my eye saw one of them move – as though they had pre-empted my thinking. Perhaps they had, as I heard the gate being opened and shut, followed by the sound of feet behind me. We went out into the yard and we stood round him making it very obvious that he had no chance of escape and that this could be his last sight of the daylight.

'It was my fault,' he began before I could say anything. 'I suppose I started it but I never expected that to happen.'

I held up my hand. He stopped babbling.

'First, your name?'

'Meta, dominus.'

'How old are you, Meta?'

'Fourteen, I think, dominus.'

I didn't think he was that old, but then he may not have known how old he was. Many didn't. Or he might have wanted to seem older than he was.

'And how long have you been here, Meta?' I was being sweetness and light.

'About a calend, dominus.'

'I am told you threw your bowl of soup over the cook. Is that right?'

'Yes, dominus.'

I think he was surprised that I knew this. 'Why?'

I shot the word out at him, loud and very clear. He jumped, and hesitated.

'I'm listening.'

He was close to crying, but had made up his mind what to do.

'Dominus,' he said and looked me straight in the eye. 'I lost my temper. I'm not used to this hard work. I came from the family that served the prefect at Corinium. He was sent to Gaul and the procurator got rid of all the slaves. Split up the families and I got sent here.' And almost to himself he added, 'Strange really, because I would have thought there would be another prefect sent out.'

'Go on,' I commanded.

He looked surprised and at the same time managed to look like a dog that knows it's in deep trouble. He gulped.

'Even I could make better soup than what we get. I was so annoyed about it I just threw it back at the cook and told him to learn his job properly. It was just me and I knew I'd get whipped, but I never expected everyone else to start fighting and smashing the place up. We've cleaned up a bit,' he added hopefully.

I caught sight of a wry smile on Polonius' face and I knew just what he was thinking.

'Trojan, lock him up,' I ordered. 'I'll talk to him later.'

Trojan hustled the lad off and none too gently, which was good from my point of view.

'Sparticus, how many are hurt down there? How many can work?'

'From what I can see, it's mostly bruises, black eyes and bleeding noses. I think we could have a broken arm, but apart from that they can work. Yeah, they can work.'

'OK. Get them back to it. No food till midday and split the gangs up so they can't gang up against us. And drive them hard for a bit.'

'Got it, dominus.'

And he went off whistling to gather up Trojan and obey my orders to the letter.

Polonius, when I turned to him, was rocking backwards and forwards on his heels and toes and staring at the sky, innocence written all over his face.

'You and I need to talk.'

'I thought we might,' he said.

Chapter 37

I led the way to Polonius' so-called office. Almost before the door was closed he said, 'You got a problem, haven't you?'

'Yes,' I said, 'and I don't know quite know how to solve it.'

'Your problem.'

'You're not being helpful. You know that?'

'Well, the gods were with you, and you got me out of what could have been a very nasty hole. And you seemed to hit it off with the big man just when it mattered most and you've done well for yourself. I'll allow you that. And you've been good for the rest of us here. It's not an easy life but it could be a lot worse. But this lad isn't going to do nothing for you.'

'For you that's quite a speech, but I know all that.' I thought I'd get my own back just a little.

'Thought you might.' He looked smug.

'I'll let him sweat and talk to him in the morning. Maybe I'll think of something.'

Polonius gave one of his grunts that suggested he thought that this was a good idea.

'By the way, how old do you reckon he is?' I added.

'Don't know. Not more than twelve, I'd say.'

'That's about what I thought.'

'Can he cook, like he says he can?'

'No idea. Sparticus might know but I doubt it. He hasn't been here long enough for anyone to find out anything much about him.'

An idea was forming in my mind but I wasn't telling Polonius. 'And what of the rest of them? Why did they go berserk?'

'We spent most of the night asking ourselves that question.'

'And the answer was?'

'Haven't got one. The only possible is that they're getting fed up with getting out more and more ore that just sits in the yard. Sounds a bit daft, I know, but we all like to think we're doing something useful, slaves though we may be. And while we're talking about it, why is it piling up like it is?'

'That, my friend, is something I was going to talk to you about, but now is not really the time. However…' I paused.

'Well?'

I continued to think just what I was going to say. Once I said anything, Polonius was going to want the whole story. So why not now while it was all fresh in my mind? I would have to caution him as to how much he told anyone else, or we could have even more trouble on our hands, although Julius Octavius could be wrong, even by his own admission.

'Have you seen or heard of any soldiers passing through this way?'

'What's that got to do with anything?'

I held up my hand.

'The boy said the prefect his family worked for had been moved to Gaul, and it seems he wasn't replaced.'

'So?'

'There's been two lots of soldiers pass through Ariconium. Withdrawn from Cambria and sent to Gaul to hold the frontier against the Huns, or the Goths. Nobody knows which. Not that it matters.'

'And what's that got to do with us?'

'That's where Julius Octavius got into trouble, so I think he knows, or guesses something about it.'

'And?'

'Hold on and I'll tell you! The key thing is that these soldiers are not being replaced – as with the boy's prefect. Now do you see?'

'No.'

My, Polonius could be difficult when he wanted to be!

'It looks like Rome is trying to hold the frontier in eastern Gaul by withdrawing soldiers and administrators from Britannia and not replacing them. In other words we're being sacrificed to keep Gaul in one piece. Now do you see?'

At least he had the humility to look puzzled. 'So they're taking soldiers from here to help Gaul,' he pondered. But still hadn't caught on.

I had to spell it out. 'No soldiers, or fewer soldiers; no demand for swords, weapons and all the other things they make for the army at Ariconium.'

'So less ore required?' He sounded pleased with himself.

'Exactly.'

I decided that I was going to leave it at that for the moment. We could talk another time.

'Think about it,' I said. 'I need to report this to Julius Octavius, so send Antinous to me when you see him.'

He grunted, got up, and shifted his immense bulk in the direction of the mine entrance. I could almost see his brain digesting what I had told him and wondered how long it would take for him to realise the implications. Not long I suspected. I called after him, 'Make sure the boy stays locked up, but also see he gets a minimum of food and some water.'

I had learned what it was like!

We now had paper, or papyrus, to write on, a material that I had heard came from Egypt. It was better than the wax tablets but had the disadvantage that one couldn't alter what one had written like on a wax tablet. On the other hand it was lighter for the runner to carry. When Antinous appeared I told him he was going to Ariconium immediately but that I would be following him the next day and he was to wait for me before returning. I hoped Julius Octavius would accept my suggestions and sent Antinous on his way. I then went down the mine to see how things were there.

'Pretty fair,' was Sparticus' assessment of the situation.

'No troubles? No fights?'

'No. They're scared stiff of what's going to happen to Meta. By the way what is happening to him?'

'I'm going to take him to Ariconium in the morning. He doesn't know that yet.'

Sparticus turned and looked at me very sharply. 'They'll kill him there,' he said. 'In days. Do you have to? It wasn't that bad what he did, and the soup's pretty horrible at best. I'd do the same.'

There was real concern in his voice. Not like him at all.

'I'm taking him first thing tomorrow. Myself.' And I tapped the side of my nose.

'Oh,' he said, and changed the subject.

It was time to talk to the culprit and see if all the plans I had laid were right. I had Trojan fetch him out to the office and then stand in front of me like a boy at school, which in truth was what he was. I sent Trojan away. I wasn't sure whether that made him more nervous as to what was going to happen to him or less. I began amiably enough.

'Now, Meta. You told me that you lost your temper about the soup. Why?'

'Dominus, I did try to explain—'

I cut him off. 'You said you could make better soup yourself. At your age? And by the way, just how old are you, really?'

He paled significantly. 'Oh, dominus, I'm twelve in two calends' time.'

'I thought so. You lied to me. Not good.' I let it hang in the air. 'Let's go back to the soup.'

He brightened a bit. 'Well, dominus, I could make it better. Especially if I was allowed to get some of the right things to go in it.'

'What do you mean, the right things?'

'Out in those woods, especially, there's lots of things I could add that would give it a bit of flavour. Make it easier to eat.'

He realised that he was getting into deep water and shut up.

'To do that would give you the chance to poison all of us,' I said.

'Oh, no, dominus, I wouldn't do that.'

'Tell me about your family.'

He relaxed.

'We were slaves, of course, but worked for the Prefect in Corinium. He got sent to Gaul unexpectedly to take over from one who was killed in a raid by the Huns. I don't know where. Word was that the prefecture wasn't going to continue so we would have no incoming prefect to work for. So he gave us as a family to a friend of his where we could continue doing what we had always done. Trouble was, this man didn't want us children, so he sold us in the market there. Nobody wanted me so I just got put in with some slaves who were coming here.'

It all came out in a rush but that was the gist of it. I had to admit to wondering how he had got here because I certainly wouldn't have taken him.

'So you say you can cook?'

'I can make good soup, at least, dominus.'

'Can you read or write?'

'A bit, dominus.' He looked hopeful.

'We'll see about that tomorrow,' I said, and shouted for Trojan to take him back to his cell.

I had other things to do for the rest of the day and Clio wasn't exactly pleased with my going back to Ariconium when we had only just got back from there.

'Can't you send him with one of your bully-boys or put him on a cart or something?' was her not unreasonable argument.

'No, because if I do that, he won't get to precisely where I want him to go.'

'Marcus, you're talking in riddles. Just what do you mean?'

I considered. I explained. She approved.

***

First light saw me gathering up a length of rope and waking Meta from however little or much sleep he had had.

'We're going to Ariconium,' I said.

It had the desired effect. He nearly fainted. I made a great show, for the benefit of Sparticus and others, of tying the rope round his neck. I had taken the idea from the soldiers that had marched me along this way. It was intended to intimidate Meta, and it did.

Once we were clear of Puzzlewood, I released him from the rope but told him very firmly that if he made a run for it he was as good as dead.

'Anyone who sees you round here will know where to take you. You'll get flogged at best and put to work that will kill you. I shall just turn round and go back to the mine. Got it?'

'Yes, dominus,' he quavered.

When we could see the smoke of Ariconium in front of us, I put the rope back round his neck and we marched up to the gatehouse and straight through without stopping. There was a lot of jeering from the soldiers on duty about what sort of lapdog I had brought them, to which I replied in kind. It made Meta realise just what he had come to.

We went straight to the hostel where I hoped Helen of Troy would be around. She was. Standing with her huge arms across her bigger breasts, she looked down her nose at Meta.

'They said you were bringing me a boy,' she shouted, 'not something that's still on its mother's milk.'

'Calm down,' I said. 'It says it can cook, soup anyway.'

'Hey, are you trying to do me out of a job?'

'Calm down,' I said again.

'It's all right for you now you're high and mighty and going to get married to that little girl of yours. Knowing your luck you'll be a freed man in no time at all, and then you'll never speak to inferiors like me – even if I am free anyway!'

She just had to get the last bit in!

'You know me better than that,' I expostulated.

"Course I do,' and she ruffled my hair like a child – which would not be good for my standing at the mine if anyone found out about it. 'Come in and bring that with you, if you must.'

We retreated into her kitchen, from which she casually threw out a couple of slaves. Meta looked totally bemused, as well he might.

'Tell me the tale,' she said resignedly. 'And it better be good.'

'How much do you know?'

'Best part of nothing.'

'OK. This boy here, Meta by name and not yet twelve, said he could make better soup and threw his bowlful back all over one of our cooks. For reasons unknown it created a rumpus with everyone else. That in turn made for a lot of bruises and a broken arm.'

She looked at Meta, who was looking at his feet.

'Bad boy,' she said. 'Could get you into big trouble.'

Meta continued to look at his feet and could have been crying.

'So what's all that to me?'

'I have been extremely lucky since I've been here. I came from almost the same background as this boy, but I had the advantage of a leisurely walk from Rome to break me in. He didn't. By sheer chance I happened to help Polonius out because I could read and write. You know the rest. I'm passing the luck on to someone else.'

'So where do I come in?'

'By the gods, you're thick today!' I said.

'So you want me to take this on?'

She looked distastefully at Meta.

'You've got there at last.'

'I was there a long time ago,' she grinned. Turning to Meta she asked, 'Now if you were going to make some soup that was worth eating what would you want?'

I think that at that moment, Meta finally realised what was happening and came out of his trance-like state. He rattled off a list of ingredients, some of which were new to me, and finished off with a desire to go and see what he could find. Helen was patently impressed.

'Where did you learn all that?'

Meta went off into what I had already heard with a few extra details thrown in.

'I'll take him,' she said. 'The gods only know why. We're not that busy these days except when a lot of soldiers pass by, but I expect we can use him.'

I turned to Meta. 'Now you've been very lucky. Helen here is not as bad as she looks.' (A glare from Helen.) 'And she'll look after you. You do anything stupid… Well, I told you earlier what would happen to you. And both she and I will walk away.'

He was as good as crying again but hopefully not from fear. 'Thank you, dominus,' was all he could manage.

'And give him something to eat. He's had next to nothing since it happened.'

Helen nodded and immediately started to show him what was what. My priority was to get back to Clearwell that night, but first things first I needed to report to Julius O that Helen of Troy had taken on Meta. That done I found Antinous and, having eaten well, we set off for the mine.

On the walk home I explained to Antinous what I had done, and why I had done it, and found him enthusiastically in favour. He also assured me that the others underground would be too. Nobody blamed the boy for what he had done, but neither did he have any idea as to why the consequences were so dramatic. We both puzzled over that, but I made a mental note to improve the food, or at least the cooking!

Chapter 38

I was dog-tired when I got back to Clio. I seemed to have spent the last few days walking and had to admit that I was out of the habit, added to which Antinous walked very fast, which was of course why I used him as a runner. Clio was bubbling over with ideas about the wedding but I was in no mood for that or anything else, which disappointed her. To eat and sleep was all I wanted.

In the morning I felt much the same and raised her wrath by postponing such discussion until I had the mine working to my satisfaction again. She was not pleased. Perhaps I should have stayed overnight at Ariconium but I didn't want to be any further involved with Meta. As I had expected, Antinous had broadcast just what had happened to the boy and also, as he had predicted, there was general agreement that it was a good way out of a difficult problem.

'He wasn't doing much. The rest of us were carrying him. More than likely we should have thrown our soup over him!'

This seemed to be the consensus of opinion.

I told Sparticus to lay off the pressure as it didn't actually help if we had too much ore in the yard. Very soon we shouldn't know where to put what we were digging! He looked disappointed but didn't comment.

When I caught up with Polonius it was another matter.

'Been thinking about what you were saying,' he began.

'And?'

He was struggling for words. 'Does your friend over there,' he said, jerking a thumb in the general direction of Ariconium, 'think that all we've worked for is going to fall apart? That all we've lived for is for nothing?'

This was putting me on the spot. I knew full well that whatever I said would certainly get to Sparticus and Trojan, but I didn't want it to become general knowledge. At least not yet. Maybe I had to trust him.

'Polonius,' I said, 'to be more truthful than I really want to be, the answer to that is yes.'

He flinched as though I had hit him.

'But,' I carried on, 'and it's a very big "but", he says he doesn't expect it to happen soon. Maybe five years, maybe twenty-five, maybe never.'

I felt rather than saw him relax.

'The problem from our point of view is, as I said before, no army, no military iron goods.'

'So what do we do?'

Despite his huge bulk he looked deflated, almost beaten, like a disappointed child.

'Come,' I said, 'there is some good news at least.'

'And what's that?'

'Clio and I are to be married with full honours from "him over there", as you describe him.' And this time I jerked my thumb towards Ariconium. 'So at least we'll have a party to look forward to!'

'Well, I suppose that's something to think about.'

'And I must now go and see my wife-to-be or she'll be getting rid of me before we even start. And don't make too much of what I've just said: it may never happen – in our lifetime at any rate.'

He smiled and grunted, which I took to be an acceptance of both situations. I left him so that I could go and find Clio.

Little did I know it at the time of this conversation but within a calend we would be working as hard as ever and the ore disappearing from the yard faster than we could replace it.

***

When I finally got back, Clio wasn't so much angry, as I had expected, but sarcastic, which was more difficult to deal with.

'So Polonius, who really rules the mine, has graciously allowed his dominus to go home to see his abandoned housekeeper!' was her opening remark.

'Don't be silly,' I said.

'Silly, is it? When you're the abandoned housekeeper it feels very much as though the dominus of Polonius has greater allegiance to his slaves than to his only woman.'

'Now you really are being silly,' I said again. 'For a start you're not my housekeeper but shortly to be—'

But she didn't let me finish. 'Oh, but I am, I am. I was sent here by he who is greater than Polonius and greater than the dominus of Polonius to look after the said dominus!'

This was a game that two could play.

'Housekeeper that you say you are, slave that you definitely are, I shall have no alternative but to treat you as the slut that you pretend to be and put you over my knee and spank you – hard.'

'Oh, goody, goody!' she cried and ran away towards the bedroom.

So that was another hour spent not making any plans towards this wedding.

When we did get down to the matter seriously it came to be fairly straightforward. We had to decide on how many people were going to be there, officially or otherwise. There would be the likes of Polonius and Sparticus from the mine, but it would not be everybody; that was too much. I had decided that it would be a day off for all, but that most would be only onlookers, although they could join in the fun. I wanted to invite a few of the local population, particularly Chad and his wife Modron, Iden and his wife, whose name I did not know, as part of my efforts to keep them in with what we were doing. At least I assumed she was his wife. Did they have wives, or just women? I didn't know! Also a few from Ariconium such as the redoubtable Helen of Troy, Petrus and the blacksmith, to which three I perhaps owed my life. I hoped there would be no problems unless a cohort of soldiers turned up at the wrong moment.

As far as food and drink were concerned we thought that Gallus and Lupus would rise to the occasion, only allowing that we could provide them with enough food with which to work. Helen might help if necessary. It was another reason for inviting some locals, who might then be more helpful in providing food.

However, there were two areas that were going to be tricky. The most serious concerned Julius and Aemelia – Pater and Mater. In all the years since Gaius Maximus was killed, Julius had never visited the mine; he had taken my word for everything. Whilst I had rebuilt the house at his directions it had been done so that there was no spare accommodation in it. In normal circumstances Clio and I would have vacated the only bedroom for their use. But for the wedding that was not possible as the bed was an integral part of the ceremony and the world would want to know that we had used it properly. Never mind that we had proved it to our own satisfaction within the last couple of hours! We didn't have an answer other than that he brought a military tent, if there was one, that they could stay in or we could use as a bedroom if necessary. We would have to talk to them about all that.

The other was the nature of the ceremony itself. Clio had her own shrine in the house to various gods and could not understand why I was happy with my two bits of wood tied together in a cross and then not take much notice of them either. She could not understand that treating others as I would wish to be treated was more important to me than the two bits of wood themselves. And I knew absolutely nothing about what Christians did for a marriage. Benedictus had left before telling me. In any case very few of those attending had much time for Christianity, so there was not really any choice. It would have to be done in the name of the gods that everyone knew about. Tough on me, but there it was.

All these things would have to be approved by Julius Octavius. This was because until we were actually married we were still legally his slaves, not to mention him and Aemelia being pater or mater to us. There was much to think about.

So I sent word to Julius Octavius with Antinous the next time he went to Ariconium that we wanted to see him and Aemelia about some of the arrangements for the wedding. To my surprise I had a somewhat peremptory message back saying that he was sure I was quite able to organise it all without his help. Well, he was right of course, except for the major conundrum of what we were going to do with the pair of them. I had to more or less spell it out to him and then had a rather austere note saying that he saw our point and we could go and discuss it.

We had eaten very well before we got to the reason for being there. He approved with a wave of his hand all the other ideas that we had.

'So what will you do?' I asked.

'Have you any ideas?'

I knew he was testing me, just as he always did.

'We could build a temporary hut or you could bring a military tent – if there is one.'

'And who's going to use it?'

'Well, naturally, we are, but there are problems.'

He cocked an eye at me, again as he often had in the past.

'Knowing the rough and ready nature of that lot, if we're secluded in the hut they'll either break it down or set it alight in order to be sure that we're doing what tradition demands. And if it's your tent, the same may apply and it might not be much use as a tent afterwards.'

They obviously hadn't thought of these possibilities, and the ideas I had suggested caused a good deal of laughter, which at least broke the slightly strained atmosphere. He pondered, stroking his chin, and looked at Aemelia in hopes of inspiration from that quarter. She became very interested in the table.

'Suppose we only come for the day?' he said. 'Or you had it here?'

I was appalled, but I still had to realise my position. 'Having it here would prevent quite a lot of the people that I really want to come from coming. I can't see Polonius and his family coming this far, for example. The same goes for the locals, with whom I'm trying to forge better relationships. As you suggested,' I added for emphasis.

'Fair point. Maybe it's just a day's journey then.'

'But you'll have to leave just as the fun is beginning and that'll put a damper on it all.'

Aemelia, and Clio for that matter, were both keeping well out of this discussion. Julius – I still couldn't quite think of him as Pater – continued to mull this over.

'If we come in a light chariot, which we probably should anyway, we can leave again so that we're back here before it gets dark,' he mused. 'Then all that has to be done can be done while we're there and we can leave all your people to drink the night away without us to cast a shadow on the proceedings.'

I was about to comment that that would be a shame when he carried on.

'Yes,' he said with finality. 'That will work. The bed bit you can do, or pretend to do, at any time while we're there or after we've left. After all it's not as though either of you are new to what you're supposed to be doing.'

He grinned, Aemelia smiled broadly, and Clio and I blushed to the roots of our hair. He was of course, as always, absolutely right, but it was the very businesslike way of putting it that was unnerving. It settled the matter, and we could make our way home the following day knowing that a major burden had been lifted, even if it was not quite what we had in mind.

The only thing that then delayed us was seeing those at Ariconium that we wanted to invite. Petrus was the first we came across.

'I should love to come,' he said diffidently, 'but I'm not sure if the rules allow it.'

I laughed.

'Petrus,' I said, 'you are due to retire very soon. Yes?'

He nodded.

'When you do that, there won't be any rules and your shop won't survive if you make too many to force yourself to live by. Pretend there aren't any this time, and just come. Julius Octavius is coming so you'll be in good company.'

He looked at me dubiously and finally agreed to see what he could manage – which meant he would come.

Helen of Troy was overjoyed and enveloped me in one of her usual bear hugs that I barely survived. She was a little less spontaneous with Clio. She shouted her congratulations in a voice that I thought even Julius O might have heard back in his house!

'Do you want any help with the feeding arrangements?' she asked.

'I hoped you might offer.'

'Well, you just let me know.'

'I will.'

So that was something else solved. I enquired where I might find the blacksmith and she volunteered to go and look for him. While she was gone, Meta sidled out of the kitchen area.

'Thank you, dominus,' he said, and scurried back in again.

It appeared that my subterfuge in that direction had worked.

The blacksmith was nowhere to be found, but Helen promised faithfully to pass on my invitation. So it was back to Clearwell to prepare for this wedding.

Chapter 39
Tacitus

I know what they say about me even if they think I don't. Tacitus by name and taciturn by nature. Get it? It's true, I know. And I know they laugh at me. But life's been hard on me and I've never been the life and soul of any party. I know that too.

I was a Pilus Prior once! Would you believe that? Shouldn't think so to look at me now. Bit like the bulla man here, I got chopped down a peg or too – no, a lot of pegs – when a campaign against the Huns went all wrong. Wasn't the same one as his though, but the effect was the same. Wasn't my fault, in the same way it wasn't his – or so he says.

Almost anyone who had any sort of rank was demoted back into the ranks. There wasn't many ranks left to be demoted to! And even less in the line of centurions to demote to what there was. And we got scattered around all over the place so we couldn't lodge any complaints about what a bloody shambles it had been. Nobody takes any notice of one man's grouse – it's just soldiers grumbling like they always do. Now if there'd been twenty or thirty of us, and we couldn't have mustered many more than that, then somebody somewhere might have had to take notice. And the world might have found out who got it so badly wrong. Could have been embarrassing!

And this place? How did I get here? Well, I suppose that's my fault. Like I said, soldiers are always grumbling and my grumble was the poor state of the equipment we were provided with. Armour that didn't fit or fell apart when you needed it most. Swords that wouldn't sharpen or bent at a critical moment.

Now my pater was a blacksmith and had worked in a place like this. One thing I didn't want to do was follow in his footsteps but that doesn't mean that I didn't learn a thing or two from the old codger. I could temper a sword or weld two bits of iron together in the fire if I had to. Might not have been a beautiful job but it was better than we were getting. So I started a little line of my own making swords do what they were supposed to do. Made a few sesterces out of it and could have helped my own promotion when I sorted out the same things for one or two officers.

Well, word got round and when my world fell apart I got sent here. Pretty good mess the place was in with nobody really knowing what was what. That was before Julius got here. His predecessor was just incapable. Relied on the slaves to know what to do and most of them didn't – or said they didn't. Just like the army – anything for a quiet life. I knew their way of thinking, see, and we soon came to an understanding, shall we say, that their lives would be a lot worse if they didn't do the job properly. It could be half decent if they did it right. Well that's a bit of an overstatement, they just wouldn't die quite so quickly.

Then this Julius comes along and we have something in common. Same problem for both of us. Created a bit of a bond, it did. It didn't change much though. He had his orders to fulfil and the rest of us had to follow, but he's OK, he is. Have to be a bit more careful now though. Slaves aren't as expendable as they used to be. But at least he explains how it is and you do understand his problem. Better than him just bawling his head off at you, army style. Guess he could have been a good man to serve under – but that's the army for you!

Chapter 40

Life became a dream. I know that is an overused phrase beloved of writers, but in the case of Clio and myself it was true. Particularly for me. She was rushing about, chivvying Gallus and Lupus around, ordering this and arranging that. I was almost an onlooker. Fortunately the mine had some problems which kept me occupied and also the requirement for ore from Ariconium had come back to something like previous levels. Maybe some new soldiers had arrived in the area or some battles had been fought requiring them to be re-equipped. Either way it kept my lot busy, which was the best way of preventing trouble.

Somewhere along the way I must have told Polonius about the promise of freedom for Clio and myself once we were married, but in all the chaos exactly when had escaped me, so I was surprised when Polonius cornered me one morning.

'We've been watching you…'

I took a guess at what was coming and cut him off.

'We?'

'The wife and I.'

'OK, go on.'

'The way you're setting up this wedding, anyone would think you were a freed man already. Are you?'

'No. But I will be once we're married.'

'And will you be?'

'I sincerely hope so, or we're all going to be in the proverbial. Could even be the wrong side of the law. Wouldn't Tiberius be pleased?'

I laughed at my own humour, but Polonius was serious and wagged a meaty finger at me.

'You be careful,' he said. 'If you carry on as you are and something happens to your big friend, or he doesn't stick to his side of the bargain, then you're in real trouble.'

'I know but I'm only obeying his orders, which, and you know it as well as I do, as his slave I'm bound to do.'

'And who else knows about those orders?'

'You,' I said, largely in jest.

'Just my point,' he said.

'So?'

'Listen to me, Marcus, will you! Suppose he drops dead or gets himself murdered. He's not everyone's best friend, and you've already had a taste of what some would like to see done to you.'

I eyed him narrowly.

'Polonius, are you trying to tell me something? Or, more to the point, tell Julius Octavius something?'

He went all baby-faced and innocent on me.

'No,' he said, 'not at all. Nothing to tell. Just as long as you're sure you know what you're doing and what the consequences could be if it all goes wrong for you.' We parted, but he had given me something serious to think about.

That evening I managed to calm Clio's excitement down enough to talk to her about what Polonius had said. She looked pensive.

'But we will be freed, won't we?' she said.

'I'm sure we will be,' I said, 'but as Polonius says, if anything happens to Julius Octavius, then what?'

'Is it likely to?'

'I wouldn't have thought so, but maybe Polonius knows something we don't, or has heard some rumour or another.'

'He could always just drop dead,' she said, joining in the morbidity.

'At least in that case there'd still be Aemelia.'

'She wouldn't count for much amongst all the men and soldiers.'

'Hmm, you're probably right.'

'So what do we do?'

'I think I should either go and see him again or write to him. We weren't that welcome last time so it might be better to write. Might even be a warning to him. He could be grateful. I'll think about it.'

I was almost talking to myself, not to Clio at all, but at least a sort of a decision had been made. In fact it took me several days thinking about what to say and how to say it but I got there in the end. I had a go at Polonius to see if he did actually know if anything was in the wind. I got nothing new and came to the conclusion that if there was, then he didn't actually know about it. Perhaps it was as simple as that – he was quite genuinely concerned on my behalf!

In the end I wrote Julius a fairly long scroll explaining what I had heard and from whom, my conclusions, and explaining, a bit timidly if truth be told, that I thought Polonius had a valid point. I also took the liberty of suggesting that he and Aemelia should be careful, especially when they were travelling. I hoped I hadn't overdone it.

I sent it with Antinous and was more than a little worried when he wasn't back for four days. Had I incurred the great man's wrath?

Antinous was full of grumbles when he did get back. 'Kept me there, he did. Said your letter had given him a lot to think about. Whatever did you say? Bored stiff I was. Nothing to do and nobody much to talk to. Hey, and where have all the soldiers gone? There's hardly any of them left. And only Petrus sitting in the guardhouse, on his own, mind. Looking very smug he is. Only got a couple of calends before he retires.'

I learnt a lot in a short time from Antinous. More importantly he handed over a large parcel, saying that there was a scroll inside it. In fact it was a series of parcels within parcels.

First was a formal letter from Julius O thanking me for writing to him, suggesting that my information was probably wrong but that I should open what he had sent me in the numbered order.

Second was another letter, also very official, stating that from such a date in the near future I would be a freed man and attaching all the necessary papers to make me such.

Third was a similar letter and papers for Clio. That was a relief. For a nasty moment I thought he had forgotten to include her.

Fourth was a lovely letter written by Aemelia wishing us all the best in our future lives together, that they were hoping to be at the wedding on the same date already mentioned, and hoping the enclosed would be useful.

Fifth was their gift. Just as they had given us new tunics, they now presented me with a real toga and Clio with a dress that any girl would be proud to wear for her wedding. All of which had to have come from Rome.

The scheming pair had been working this out for calends and calends! We really would be Roman man and wife now! But for how long, if there was any truth in his foretelling of the future?

I had to send Antinous almost straight back with a suitable letter of thanks. Again he grumbled mightily, but I simply said I could not explain why just now. I assured him that he would soon be back. I also caught up with Polonius.

'I think you were right,' I said. 'And the man himself obviously thinks so too. He, and may your gods bless him, has fixed a date for *my* wedding and sent the papers freeing both of us from that date.'

Polonius grunted, as only he can grunt.

'When?'

'Just before midsummer,' I said.

He nodded his head with satisfied approval, gave another mighty grunt and went off to do whatever it was he was doing.

At least all was well in that quarter.

***

The next few weeks became difficult and worrying, and it had nothing to do with the fact that Clio and I were getting married. Well, of course, it did and there was a great deal to organise with instructions coming on a regular basis from our respective pater and mater in Ariconium. The obvious change there and, for all to see, was the decline in ore required over there. I did tackle Julius O about it in one of my letters. He suggested that I should come to see him.

We discussed the general situation, which was depressing. Whilst not many soldiers had passed through Ariconium, those that had told endless tales of their numbers being reduced and all but the oldest, the infirm and those nearly retired being sent to Gaul in order to hold off the Goths.

'But,' he said, 'enough of that. You need to make friends with Tacitus.'

I was startled. I knew Tacitus, of course I did; he was effectively my opposite number at Ariconium. He operated the furnaces that turned our ore into iron.

'Why?' I asked. 'He's never got two words to say for himself. Hardly speaks!'

'I know,' he said. 'It's not easy, but you two are going to need each other if the sky falls in on us.'

I was even more startled.

'How so?' I asked.

'Oh, Marcus. I've told you you're naïve and, added to that, you live in your own little world over there at Clearwell with not a clue as to what's going on around you!'

'That's hardly my fault.' I was piqued. 'I am a slave, after all, and I have to do as I'm told.'

He grinned. 'Not for much longer. And then you're going to have to wake up as to what's going on.'

I was fed up with being told off like naughty schoolboy.

'So what's taciturn Tacitus got to do with all this?'

'You and Polonius know how to get ore out of the ground and Tacitus and the blacksmith know how to turn it into ironwork that people want.'

I began to realise what he was getting at.

'So you're saying that if the demand for swords and armour disappears, leaving only a small need for iron goods for building, then we could build a small-scale business doing just that.'

'Well done, Marcus.'

He beamed but I didn't like the sarcasm in his voice. Nonetheless I was a step ahead of him.

'Working on a small scale he could smelt ore at Clearwell without having to cart it for millia. Or anywhere else that we can find ore, for that matter.'

He laughed. 'You see, you can think when you have to!'

But a thought had struck me. 'Why are we so far apart?' I asked. 'If you think about it, it doesn't make sense.'

'History,' he said. 'I believe that several generations ago ore was mined near here but then better quality was found further away, but the smelter didn't move. Eventually it was proved that yours was better, even if it was further away, but still the smelting process didn't move. But you have that choice.'

'Have you told Tacitus what you've told me?'

'Not in so many words, but the man's no fool and, unlike you,' there was that note of sarcasm again, 'he's here and as near the centre of things as it's possible to be in this out of the way place. He's more than likely guessed what's going on, and for sure seen the soldiers disappearing from here, not to mention the ones just passing through.'

'Antinous told me about that and I think Petrus is the only one I've seen.'

'He's not quite on his own but it's getting close to that. They've ordered away all the young and fit ones.'

He sounded depressed himself. Perhaps removing his soldiers was robbing him of his life-blood, despite his protestations about liking it here. I left him and went to find Tacitus.

'Hello, stranger,' he said in his lugubrious voice. 'What brings you here?'

'I've been told to come and find you.'

'Still obeying orders then? Thought you were free to do as you liked nowadays.'

'Not till I'm married.'

He nodded but didn't say anything. It seemed that I had to make all the running.

'He says that you and I ought to get together.'

I presumed he would know who I meant by 'he'.

'Why?'

This was hard work. 'Has he told you that all this is about to fall apart?' I swept my hand around his domain.

'Not in so many words, but I'm not stupid. I can see what's happening.'

Julius Octavius' words almost to the letter.

'Then you'll agree that the man usually knows what he's talking about?'

'He's all right, he is.'

I took that for a 'yes'.

'Well, he says that you and I ought to get together. Along with your blacksmith and Polonius at my end.'

'And where does he fit in?' He nodded in the direction of the great man's office.

'He doesn't.'

I could use a minimum number of words too, if it suited me!

'So what's his big idea then?'

'That if the army goes away totally, which it appears to be doing, then we set up a small-scale operation over at Clearwell to smelt a bit of iron for the locals and make it into whatever they want – probably swords and the like so that they can fight each other instead of us.'

'Kill us, more likely.'

'No, I don't think so. From what I've heard, the barbarians have respect for people who can work iron. More likely we'd find ourselves protected by whoever was on top.'

He didn't say anything, but I could see his mind working. I'd heard all I'd just said from Mahout, who had come across the phenomenon in Iberia.

'I'll think about it,' he said.

'Include the blacksmith in your thinking,' I said. 'We can't do this on our own.'

He nodded and turned away. That was the end of that conversation. I could see he was going to be a difficult man to work with, but his knowledge was going to be crucial. So that gave me more things to think about on my walk back to the mine and home. When I got there Clio was all excited and dancing about like a small child.

'Steady on,' I said. 'What's all the excitement about?'

'Guess,' she said, looking at me under her eyelashes.

'Couldn't possibly.'

I was tired and not in the mood for games, even if I did have an inkling of what might be coming next.

'I'm expecting a baby!' she said.

Chapter 41

Wedding Day. I was fed up and cynical about the whole exercise. Not the least of this was because of Clio and the child she was now expecting. I knew precious little on this subject, but I did know that she should not work too hard if she was to survive. But she hadn't stopped one little bit. Because of Julius Octavius' intransigence about spending a night away, the whole thing had been shoved together so that he could get back to his beloved Ariconium the same night. And it was the following day that all the fun would take place – the eating, the drinking, in fact all the things that made a wedding worthwhile. Added to that, why were we going through this charade anyway? After all, Clio and I had been living together for quite long enough for us to be legally classed as being married. I supposed that the important thing was that once this had all been gone through, then we should be free people and could do whatever we wanted. For what that was worth in present circumstances.

So I was not in a good humour when I went outside for some fresh air and a change of scene that morning. Therefore I was more than just astonished to find Benedictus sitting cross-legged on the ground within a few paces of my door, looking very much as though he might have been there all night. I was pleased to see him and it lightened my mood.

'By all that's true, my friend, how do you manage to be here this morning, of all mornings?'

'I'd heard a whisper,' he said. 'So I thought I'd come and see if it was true.'

'Oh it is, and am I glad to see you! This is all happening under the old gods because I don't know what you Christians would require.'

He seemed to ponder this for a moment. 'In truth,' he said, 'neither do I!'

I was aghast. I had considered him to be the fount of all knowledge where this Christian bit was concerned.

'So what do we do, or rather, what do you do?'

'I'll do what I've done sometimes before. You go through the ceremony with the old gods because that will keep most people happy, and then I'll give you a blessing in the name of Jesus Christ and that keeps you and me happy. How's that?'

'Isn't there more to it than that?'

'Not unless you want to write a complete ceremony and there's hardly time for that.'

He had a point.

'OK, that'll have to do. We'll decide in a while just when you do it. Anyway, welcome, I should have said that before. I'll send food out for you.'

He bowed his head in acceptance and said, 'Peace be with you.'

And it was. I felt much happier and more able to cope with the coming day. I had to smile too. I could hear Helen of Troy in the kitchens with Lupus and Gallus. Despite it being their kitchen and that they had done all the basic preparation, she was ordering them about in a loud voice and with language that would make the entire Roman army blush. I knew the eating would be good – when we got to it.

In the middle of the morning Julius Octavius and Aemelia arrived. Aemelia took Clio off to see her dressed properly. Julius suggested that he and I should get away from the mayhem that was, as he described it, 'ladies' work', and take a walk in the woods.

'Provided we'll be safe,' he said.

I was surprised. Was he taking my previous warning seriously?

'I think so,' I laughed. 'If they do anything they shouldn't, some will lose out on a good feast and many more will lose out on what they've sold us over the past few weeks.'

We strolled in the woods and chatted about nothing in particular, eventually returning so that we were almost too late, earning us a scolding from his wife and my wife-to-be. A quick change of clothes and we were ready. Because Clio and I didn't have homes or parents of our own it all had to happen from the one building, which was a bit odd for any of those present who knew how it should be done.

Thus Aemelia brought Clio out of the door all dressed in the finery that her 'mater' had provided for her, so that Julius and I could go in through the kitchen door and then pretend that it was his house and the formal wedding contract could be signed. Then Clio was brought forward and said the traditional words: 'Ubi tu Gaius, ego Gaia.'

This had to be translated for those who were not of Roman origin, which was most of the assembled company: 'Where you are Gaius, I am Gaia.'

I knew this was part of the ceremony but I wasn't too happy about it, knowing what had happened to the previous holder of that name. But it was tradition and it was a new house so I could only hope for the best.

At this point Benedictus stepped forward and, holding his staff beside him as a badge of office, proclaimed in a voice so loud that it surprised everyone as it echoed around the trees: 'I bless you both in the name of Jesus Christ.'

And as he did so he raised his right hand and made a huge sign of a cross. He then stepped away and back into his usual humble self.

We then made a sacrifice of a small pig. Most thought this was the right thing to do. I thought it was a waste of good meat! I retreated into what had now become my house again. Clio then brought grease from the pig to smear on the doorposts, followed by a blazing brand from the sacrificial fire, which she then turned and threw into the crowd. They were ready for it and nobody got burnt. My job was then to carry her over the threshold into her 'new' home. And then the fun could start!

She tried to run away. I caught her. She tried again and her bridesmaid exhorted her to go to the bed with me. She ran again, this time right out of the house. I ran after her, cheered on by all the men present. I grabbed her again.

'Come on, wife,' I said roughly to her. 'You know what you have to do now.'

More cheers. More exhortations to Clio. Much laughter as well.

'But husband,' she cried, somehow managing to make real tears stream down her face, 'you are so big!' More laughter. 'And you will hurt me.' Even more laughter. 'What is a girl to do?'

'Come,' I said, very sternly, 'and I will show you.'

More cheering and laughter.

She went all coy and shy. 'I will come with you, if you will come to me,' she said.

That really roused the cheers!

I picked her up again, ran for the door and we were ushered into the bedroom by the bridesmaid. She took one look at Clio's belly and decided that we already knew what was expected of us, and that we knew what to do and didn't need any help from her! There was a great deal of cheering and shouting of ribald remarks from outside the window, which was not how we were accustomed to make love, but it was fun and we managed some appropriate grunts and shouts for the benefit of those who were checking on our progress. After a suitable interval, we reappeared looking flushed and dishevelled and ready for the meal that had been so long in the preparation. It was hard to believe that it was still only mid-afternoon.

We ate and we drank for the rest of that day. Julius Octavius had brought a sizeable stock of wine with him, perhaps from his travels through Gaul, and the locals had brought a supply of their ale. Most people were unsteady on their feet by the time the great man left, as the sun began to sink. Both he and Aemelia professed to having enjoyed themselves hugely and wished us well for the rest of the night and the celebrations that would inevitably carry over into the next day. Certainly their departure released any inhibitions that might have still existed amongst those present. It was going to be a long night.

The sun was high in the sky before many were about the following morning. Not surprising really. I was not in the least in the mood for talking business or anything like it, but free as I now was, and knowing what I did, I had to take any opportunity that came my way. So when the blacksmith wanted to talk to me I had no option.

'What's this you and Tacitus have been talking about?' he asked.

'How much has he told you?'

'Huh! You know he never says much. Said I should ask you.'

So I explained what appeared to be happening and the ideas that had been put into my head. He seemed doubtful.

'You're vital to this plan, you know,' I told him.

'Your man Poly… whatever it is. What does he think?'

'Polonius? Come and meet him. In different ways you're two of a kind. About the same size if nothing else!'

He looked sideways at me very much as though he did not believe me.

So we went to see Polonius, who was definitely a bit the worse for too much ale, and talked the whole thing through in some detail. I think the two of them had a bit of a problem understanding each other, but that may have been the drink. At the end of it the blacksmith said, 'Yeah, I think that's going to be OK. I'll go back and tell Tacitus properly what he was trying to explain to me. It might make more sense that way.'

My second business operation of the day, more advisory in nature, was with Petrus, who wanted to talk about his shop.

'Where should I have it?' he asked.

'I don't know,' I said. 'Did you have anywhere in mind?'

'I was going to have it at Ariconium but that hardly exists now, so I had wondered about Lydney. Somewhere near Nodens' temple. Lots of people must go there.'

'They do now but that could change.'

'Take a long time though won't it?'

'Probably.'

I had no idea really, so I said, 'You could try Glevum.'

'Not sure about that. Too many shops there already.'

'But lots of people there all the time.'

'True. I'll have to think about it.'

Poor Petrus. He had spent too much time in the army obeying rules – to the letter – and now having to think for himself was becoming difficult.

Finally I found Chad, who had walked up from his village to ask very much the same questions.

'The elders have sent me,' he apologised. 'They said I knew you best and you would probably tell me the truth.'

'I am honoured,' I said, 'but I don't know anything official, even if there's anything official to know. You do realise, don't you, that part of all this is that I'm now no longer a slave but a free citizen of Rome – for what that's worth at the present time.'

'I had guessed that, and you deserve it, but what's all this rumour about your soldiers all going and the mine closing, even Ariconium itself?'

I drew a deep breath. Should I tell them how it really was or take the official line?

'I have to say again that I don't know,' I began. 'Nobody's saying, but the rumours you're hearing, what you're seeing and what you're guessing are likely to be true. Where that leaves us and the long-standing arrangements we've had, the mine and Ariconium – well your guess is as good as mine. My opinion, for what it's worth, is that something will continue but on a much smaller scale.'

That, at least, kept my options open.

He pondered this a while. 'Thank you for being honest with us,' he said. 'I'll take that back to the elders and you can be sure I'll be sent back to talk to you again. Enjoy your feasting today.'

'But you'll be joining us of course?'

'Ooh yes!' And he grinned right across his face.

'And bring any more who would like to come. It's open house tonight until we run out of food and drink!'

'I will,' he said, and went.

It might cost me a bit, but if it kept relations between us good, then that could only be valuable for the future.

So for Clio and me it was a quiet day. We weren't expected to do anything and if we did attempt to do something, other than just sit around, we found that someone else jumped in and took over whatever minimal task we happened to have thought of. We both found it irksome.

When evening came it all changed. There was food and drink for all. It was only a few days from midsummer and the locals always made much of this, so our party was something of a taster for their own annual celebrations. I had never been invited to that before but hoped that I might be now. Again my increasingly mercenary mind was thinking that I might understand them better for the future, if indeed there was a future. In fact they turned up in force, even bringing wives and daughters with them. I was fearful of it being too much temptation for all my lone male slaves in the mine, but could only hope for the best.

We sat round an enormous fire. We sang. We ate. We danced, after a drunken fashion. Clio and I were chased off into the bedroom with orders for a repeat performance of yesterday for those who weren't there. We obliged – twice! We drank more. Some snored. Some made love. Eventually all slept.

Nobody was going to be starting very early the next day but that was a minor irritant as Clio and I looked forward to a new future for us and our child to be. We were not to know that that future was to be changed out of all recognition before that child was even born.

Chapter 42

It was a few days later, by which time we had all had time to sober up, that Sparticus came to me.

'You need to speak to that lot.' He jerked a thumb in the direction of the mine.

'Oh?'

'Since your party the other night they've heard all the rumours that are going round. They know the ore's piling up again. They want to know what's going on.'

'I wish I knew,' I said.

'If you don't know, then who in Hades does?'

'I don't think anyone does.'

'That's no help.'

I knew this was coming but I hadn't had time to work out an answer. I had been more concerned to get my own freedom sorted out, and be sure of it, before worrying about anyone else. First things first and look after number one was becoming the order of the day. I was learning – fast!

'Tell them I'll talk to them tomorrow or the next day. Will it wait that long?'

'It'll have to.'

I thought I knew what I was going to do and I was going to tell Julius Octavius, not ask him. He had never queried what I did in the past, so why should he now? I was going to be within my rights and I feared we would have another riot on our hands if I didn't. That wasn't going to help anybody. Either way, the principle was settled, but I wanted to let it ride overnight in case I changed my mind on the details.

The next morning I called everyone together, even the cooks and house slaves, all the way up to Polonius, who grunted and grumbled about being included.

'I know a very few of you are not actually slaves,' I started. That covered Sparticus and for some unknown reason one of the mine cooks. 'I hope you all had a good time a few days ago.' Some rubbing of heads. 'And that you enjoyed the show put on for you.' Laughter and pointing at me. 'But you have also had the chance to hear all the rumours.' Deathly quiet. 'I'm sorry but I don't know the answers. Nobody does. Not even Julius Octavius over at Ariconium. He has been anticipating this and it's one of the reasons that he made me a freed man when I got married. As you well know from the piles in the yard the demand from Ariconium for our ore has dropped off again. Each time it does that it rarely returns to previous levels.'

It remained eerily quiet; all I could do was plough on.

'Because you have been loyal to me, and we none of us know what will happen next, I am going to arrange for any of you who want to be freed, to be freed. I can't do it on my own authority yet, but I will get the necessary papers sent over within a few days.'

There was a muffled cheer.

'But be warned. You will have no rights. I will employ as many of you as I can, but only in exchange for food – no more. If you remain a slave then I shall have to keep you, but if necessary I may have to sell you, and be assured that I shall. The final alternative is that you stick with it, and if everything collapses then you will automatically find yourself freed because there will be nobody left to own you. Let Sparticus know by tomorrow night what you want to do and I will arrange things accordingly.'

It was a sombre group that broke up and went back to work after that.

As I turned away I found Polonius blocking my path.

'And what should I be doing?' he asked.

'You know the plan?' I said.

'Yeah. But…'

'But what?'

'You never said anything about this.'

'I know but I would have thought it was obvious that you can't remain a slave and be part of my scheme.'

'Can't I be your personal slave? I've been a slave all my life and don't know no different.'

Because I knew his character, he seemed pathetic in his distress.

'I think you should go for freedom. I'll want you around as a bodyguard if nothing else!' I was only partly joking.

He grunted.

'Then if this scheme of mine gets going you can be part of it. If the old ways come back you'll have the choice of being able to do something else if you don't like who's in charge.'

He saw the logic of that, nodded his head almost vigorously, and grunted his way off.

In the end, twelve out of the twenty or so slaves that we still had took the option of being freed. To a man they all agreed to stay where they were, as they were, until I got the official documents through from Julius Octavius. That simplified things. I sent Antinous off with the list of names and didn't expect him back for a few days.

When he did come back he brought the official papers and a letter from Julius O complimenting me on what I had done. I was relieved that my first major decision as a freed man had met with his approval. The twelve were then free to go, but they were like young rabbits leaving the burrow. They would walk a little way and then scurry back and it was a week or more before any moved more than a mile from the mine. It was almost funny.

Life then settled down to a sort of existence that I think everyone thought was strange. I employed what freed slaves I could. The carters came on an irregular basis to take what ore was required by Ariconium. Nobody said so, but all and sundry, from myself to the local population, seemed to be waiting for something to happen. Would the army return and life go back to how it was? Or would we find ourselves on our own? And more difficult, we, classified as the Roman oppressor, would have to learn to live with a population that considered itself the rightful occupants of Britannia, without the authority and power of Rome to protect us. And all that, despite the locals being in a perpetual state of near or actual warfare amongst themselves!

This state of being in limbo carried on for a couple of calends before disaster struck in a most unexpected way. One day there was a commotion at the gate and I found Petrus and one of Julius Octavius' house servants wanting to get in and see me.

'Petrus,' I said, 'what are you doing here? I'd have thought you would have started your shop somewhere by now.'

He ignored my banter, having much more serious matters on his mind. He had patently been hurrying as he was very out of breath.

'It's Julius Octavius, dominus. He's been murdered! And his wife!'

'Murdered!' I yelled. 'Who by?'

That was a pretty stupid reaction. Petrus was unlikely to know!

'Sorry, Petrus. Just tell me what happened.'

'Dominus, the boy here went to wake them as he always does. Getting no reply at the door, he ventured in. Both lying in bed with their throats cut. Seems that somebody, possibly two, crept in without them hearing and…' He paused. 'Killed them.'

'But who…?'

Then my brain began to work again and I could straight away think of two likely suspects – and Julius Octavius had a reputation for having enemies.

'I may be able to guess,' I carried on. 'So what have you done about it?'

'Well, dominus, I spoke with Tacitus, as he's the only other person with any authority over there, and he said to go and fetch you. He said you would know what to do!'

This was becoming the story of my life. The world seemed to think that I would always know 'what to do'. So what was I to do? I needed to get over there quickly but Petrus was in no state to start walking back there at this time of day so it would have to wait.

'Come to the house,' I said. 'Eat and sleep and we leave at first light.'

Clio was as horrified as I was and we spent a lot of time talking about it. The biggest mystery was why.

The next morning I set off as it was just about getting light, with Petrus and the boy, on what had become a tiresome walk to Ariconium. Clio was to follow later with Antinous for company and security. He was under strict instructions to walk slowly and stop if Clio wearied. She was after all getting close to having her baby, but, with her usual determination, was going to see her 'mater', whatever it took.

Tacitus was waiting for us.

'I've kept everyone out,' he said, 'And I've left it how it was. So you can see it.'

We went to the house. I wasn't sure I wanted to 'see it' as Tacitus so succinctly put it. However, it seemed that I was in charge, if only by default, so I had to do whatever was required of me.

'It' was certainly a mess. Cutting someone's throat always creates a lot of blood as the dying body pumps it out. It's the same with animals and is why slaughtermen are always covered in blood. As Petrus had suggested, it had to be the work of two people who had synchronised their actions so that there would be a minimum of fuss and less chance of the victims raising the alarm. There was a good chance that the murderers could not have got away with it without being covered in blood themselves. But I would come back to that. I turned to Tacitus.

'You're sure you haven't moved anything?'

'No. It's exactly as it was found this morning.'

He turned to the boy, who nodded his head vigorously in confirmation.

'Was this here?' I asked.

'Yes, dominus,' he said in a tight voice.

'You're sure?'

'Yes, dominus.'

It was his turn to look to Tacitus.

'It was,' he said.

I picked up the scrap of papyrus and looked more closely at it. It was a drawing of a stubby branch on a tree with two apples falling from it. I was right! The eunuch had left his mark. Of course he would not have done it himself; he was incapable of that. But he could have paid someone very well indeed to do his dirty work and would be well pleased with the result. He had the advantage of knowing the layout of the house and the routines of its occupants. He had always been devious, so with no soldiers on patrol nowadays, there was absolutely no chance of anyone catching either him or the murderers. Conceivably Tiberius could have been involved, but I thought that he had been long gone.

It was decision time again.

'Tacitus,' I said, 'I know who was responsible but we can forget that. We need to bury them, and quickly.'

'Yes, Marcus, but where?
'Here.'
'Here?' he queried.
'Yes,' I said. 'He loved this house and this place. They both did. So we'll bury them here.'
'But just where?' he persisted.
'Here, under the atrium floor!'
He looked totally baffled.
I spelt it out. 'If we bury them here and lay the floor back over them then there's no chance of anyone finding the bodies and thinking there might be valuables worth digging for. Or of any animals digging them up.'
'I'll get men,' he said and went off.

Conveniently Clio and Antinous turned up at this moment. She was overcome by what she saw, and lit lights to her gods and arranged the house shrine as it should be in these circumstances. I went off to find Helen of Troy. We would be needing a funeral feast within a few days for all who lived or worked here.

The floor took more breaking up than I had expected, but eventually it was done and a grave dug under it. We laid them in it side by side as they had been in their bed. Clio was overcome with tears again and I have to confess I was very close to it myself. I had seen plenty of violent death, even ordered the death of unsavoury people, but this was different. This man had had confidence in me from, it seemed, the first time I made my way through the woods to his presence. Such as I had achieved was entirely due to him. He had appeared in the nick of time to save my life, or at the very least to prevent my being a cripple. He had provided a house for me, and a wife to go with it. Aemelia had been graciousness itself in helping Clio and me become what we now were.

I knew even less about Christian burial than I did about marrying, but I made a sign of the cross over the grave and said a prayer to myself and then went off to do my best to enjoy the meal that had been prepared. There had not been many at the burial but I thought a goodly number would turn out for the meal. In any circumstances a free feast is not to be missed. But, no, there were not many there; even some from Ariconium itself chose to avoid it. Having got on with Julius Octavius so well myself, I had never really believed that he'd had enemies. But it would appear that it was so.

The next day I had Tacitus fill in the grave, ram the earth as hard as possible and relay the floor over the top. It was never going to be a precise job, but then it was highly unlikely that anyone would live in the house again. Clio did whatever she considered right with the shrines and I shut the house up, and that was that.

It was time to talk to Clio. 'When we get back…' I began.

'I know,' she said. 'What's to prevent us going the same way?'

'Exactly. There are a few reasons but they may not count for much in these times.'

'Such as?'

She turned her nose up at me in a disbelieving manner.

'For a start, I haven't made the enemies that Julius O did. I haven't had the opportunity apart from anything else.'

She considered this. 'True, but whoever did this may…'

'We know who did this, or at least was responsible for it. His downfall is not directly my fault, but…'

'Always a "but".'

'There is,' I agreed. 'Which brings me to where I started. When we get home, we're going to have to barricade the doors and windows, and have Polonius or someone like him on guard all night.'

She shivered and I took her in my arms. Over the last few days we had lived in Julius and Aemelia's house, but for safety in numbers we now moved into Helen of Troy's hostel. I then sent Antinous back to Clearwell with instructions for Polonius to start strengthening the doors to our house and for Sparticus to find us a guard.

Over the next days Tacitus and I had to effectively wind up the smelting operation at Ariconium. And those who were not already free had to be freed, though this turned out to be a much smaller number than at Clearwell. We both agreed that the whole place had to be abandoned. Any who cared to come with us might have something to do, or they might not. The latter was more likely. Perhaps because there had always been something of a passing population here, a largish number were willing to take their chance and make their way to Glevum, where there was more likely to be work. I hoped the papers I had signed would stand up if they were queried. Clio and I set off as soon as we were able and the remainder, which included Tacitus, the blacksmith, Helen of Troy and perhaps eight or ten others, would follow in due course.

It was going to be the start of a new life for all of us.

Chapter 43

Polonius and Sparticus were not pleased to see me back.

'What are we going to do with all this rabble that you've invited back here?' was their unanimous opinion.

'I really don't know. I have to decide.'

'Well, don't be too long about it. They'll be here in a day or so.'

'Not as quickly as that!'

'You just wait and see.'

And they both grumped off.

And they were right.

The first few did indeed arrive within a few days, led by Petrus, 'because he knew the way'.

'I'm not staying,' he said. 'I'm going on to Nodens' temple. See if I can start my little shop there.'

'And good luck to you,' I said, and meant it.

'Good thing I didn't start it in Ariconium, now isn't it?'

'You'd have been out of business before you started!'

'Too true.'

I was glad he was moving on. Even if I was doubtful about his plans, it was one less person I had to worry about. By now I had decided on a plan. We would create a new village around my house. That way I would get some protection if the eunuch and his henchmen came looking for me. In addition the water supply just there was adequate and never stopped running, and there was plenty of timber to be had.

'But no big trees to be felled without my permission,' I ordered, knowing that I needed to consult the local druid on that subject.

Next came some of Tacitus' men with a request for carts to bring the materials and tools of their smelting trade. I got in touch with Chad, asked him to send some of his carts over to Ariconium, and explained what for. Unsurprisingly he was not too pleased about this. He was going to lose income by not having ore to transport, and his quiet world in the forest was going to be taken over by a crowd of incomers. He also knew how the forest had been devastated by the endless quest for wood for charcoal to burn around Ariconium. I had foreseen this and as yet did not have an answer. However, with ill grace he went.

Thus the blacksmith, more men and I knew not what else arrived. They unloaded all the stuff – there was no other word for it – in the mine yard. Finally Tacitus, Helen of Troy and the remaining hangers-on came a few days later.

'I burnt the whole place down before we left, except the house, of course,' announced Tacitus with what sounded almost like pleasure in his voice.

'You did right,' I said.

'Now what?' he asked. No words wasted!

'We become builders.'

He grunted. 'Another Polonius,' I thought.

'Where?' he asked.

'Around my house.'

He smiled. A rarity.

'Protection, huh?'

'Correct.'

'You're in charge.'

With that he wandered off and I was left wondering just what he thought or meant. I hoped no more than he had said.

I found Polonius and we followed Tacitus in the direction of the house. Once there we decided who was going to live where, and how the place was to be laid out. Primarily it was to be a collection of huts built along the stream that would provide us all with water. They would initially be of light wooden construction but could be strengthened and rebuilt with stone if it became possible. Personally I was of the opinion that this was only going to be a very temporary village despite the solidity of my own house. It would give us mutual protection and time to sort out just how many actually wanted to stay here and how many would want to move on. Even I was dubious about staying.

'Don't think I want to move here,' said Polonius. 'I'm very happy where I am and as I am.'

'You've got to,' Tacitus told him.

'Why?'

I could see problems coming between these two. 'Polonius,' I said, 'we've been through this.'

'I know but you never said anything about moving house.'

'He's right. We all need to live close together,' answered Tacitus before I had a chance to get a word in. In a way it carried more weight if it came from someone else.

'I don't want to move. The wife don't want to move. Nor the kids neither.' He was definitely grumpy.

'If you'd seen the blood over there…' and Tacitus jerked his hand towards Ariconium, '… you wouldn't be arguing.'

'I can look after myself.'

'In a straight fight maybe, but when they creeps up on you in the night?'

Polonius gave one of his mighty grunts that said a multitude of things and went off, hopefully to persuade his family that life wasn't as bad as it might seem.

'Thank you,' I said to Tacitus.

And he grunted as well and went off to start making a furnace. This lot were getting as bad as the boar that roamed the forest with all their gruntings at each other.

It took us the best part of a calend to get ourselves organised and enough charcoal made out of the waste wood from our building works to even think of smelting some of the ore stockpiled in the yard. Then it was over to Tacitus and his men to do their bit. We were all fascinated to see the intensity of heat they created, pumping at their bellows, and eventually the small stream of molten metal they poured from the pot. It didn't seem much for all their effort, and ours – for mining the ore in the first place. Then the blacksmith set about it and made some hinges for doors but much as we wanted these for ourselves I was adamant that I had to take them off to New Hamm to sell and thus get an idea of how viable this operation was going to be. I was disappointed. Drusius, who had built the roof of the house, bought them in the end after a lot of haggling.

This little exercise proved that I was not going to have a choice. Much against my will I was going to have to sell all those who had decided to remain slaves. To make matters worse, I gathered that slave prices in Glevum had sunk to rock bottom as owners moved away to what they hoped were safer areas.

First I gave all those remaining the chance of freedom, but only two took me up on it. I almost had to attempt to restrain Polonius from wanting to be sold. I told him very forcibly that he was a freed man, whether he liked it or not, and so were his family. He didn't like it! Thus Sparticus, Trojan and I first gathered all the relevant information we had on those to be sold, and with a heavy heart set off for Glevum. We took the road that paralleled the great river and it was new to most of them. I did my best to make it something of an outing as I had known many of these men for a long time. Just to sell them, for who knew what, went against the grain. We crossed the river in the usual place and took the road into town. The slave market adjoined the cattle market and had improved slightly since I had passed through it. Although of course I and those with me were being sent to the mines as a punishment not as a profit for some greedy slave trader.

We set out our wares and the auction followed on without a break from the cattle being sold in the yard next door. Our slaves were sold, as expected, at abysmal prices, but I was glad that all went to individual buyers rather than to dealers who would just sell them on while starving them along the way. They all took it stoically; it was after all just another part of a slave's life.

'Didn't like that,' said Sparticus as we started on our way back.

'Nor me,' I said.

'Rather flog a man than do that.'

Trojan nodded his agreement.

'Did you see anyone you knew?' I asked, in an effort to change the subject.

'No. Should I have?'

'Just wondered. I thought I saw a face I recognised in the cattle market.'

'Who?'

'No idea.'

'Can't help you then.'

It was the end of that conversation but it broke the spell and we went on our way with a slightly less morbid view of life. From my point of view it put a little bit of cash in my pocket and I could see that money, or lack of it, was going to be the next problem. Well, I was wrong there too, because I got back to find that Clio was about to give birth, and that was something I knew nothing about. We were very much an all-male group and the only ones who did know anything were Helen of Troy and Polonius' wife, Irna. And how those two hit it off quite astonished me.

I went to see Clio, who was thrashing about on the bed with the two women trying to restrain her.

'This shouldn't be happening!' she screamed. 'I thought I had another calend to go.'

And she collapsed into a heap breathing heavily.

'Babies can be early,' I said, trying to soothe her.

'And then they're small, or sickly and don't live,' she whimpered.

'But if you've got it wrong…'

'I haven't got it wrong!' she yelled as the pain came back.

Helen of Troy nudged me and nodded her head to the door. I took the hint and left. This was definitely women's work and I was best out of the way. But I couldn't settle to anything. I didn't want to be with anybody. Their concern, sympathy, worry, whatever, was cloying to me. I couldn't just walk away into the woods, which is what I would like to have done, because I might be needed. But for what? To see my firstborn child was the best hope, but every man knew that childbirth could be a disaster for both mother and child. I tried sitting in my office to do some work, but that was no good either. Then I spotted the cross on the wall. Why hadn't I thought of it before? I prayed to my God and to Jesus Christ. It calmed me, if it did nothing else. I could still hear Clio, my Clio, screaming as the pain took her, but somehow it didn't seem so bad. Maybe praying really did do some good.

And then there was silence. The quiet hit me worse than the noise. And then… and then, I heard the faint wail of a baby crying for life. I was on my feet in a flash and went to tap on the door, but Irna beat me to it. She had the door open and was on her way to fetch me. Helen of Troy had a bundle in her arms, which she showed briefly to me and then handed to a pale, worn out but radiant Clio.

'It's a boy,' she said softly.

There was suddenly noise from outside, as of people banging around, followed by shouting and more noise. Irna had obviously passed on the good news to those hanging about my house that I hadn't even noticed myself. I smiled.

'We have to think of a name,' whispered Clio.

'Time enough for that,' I said.

'And the shrine?' she said with horror in her voice. 'It wasn't prepared before, and it'll be even more wrong now.'

'Helen or Irna can do it,' I said.

She looked at me in horror.

'No. No. It's my shrine and I have to do it.'

And she started to struggle to get up.

'Oh, no, you don't,' came the very firm voice of Helen of Troy as she pushed her down onto the pillows. 'If it needs doing, we can do it, and it's thanking the gods that you need to be doing, not fretting about the shrine.'

Very well put was my thinking.

'Anyway,' I said, 'I've been praying to my God and it must have worked because you've produced a beautiful baby for me and you've survived it well yourself.'

'Oh.'

But at least she consented to stay where she was without trying anything silly.

My problem was that convention called for yet another celebratory meal. I had given a little thought as to how we would celebrate this event assuming that it had all gone as it should, which indeed it had. But as Clio had said there was another calend to go I had made no efforts to do anything about it. I went to find Polonius, who could usually be relied on to do the necessary in that direction. As I expected, there was much sucking in of breath but he would see what he could do. Gallus and Lupus had already started to make some food, and others were working the same way. We had a few hours to prepare but it was going to be quite a night!

Chapter 44
Letter to Lucius

My dear brother Lucius,

It is good news indeed to hear from you, but you say little of yourself and still less about how in the name of all your gods you should have heard how I come to be a freed man and so quickly too. I know it is what all slaves want above all else, and I was no exception, but it is not as easy as it sounds. Let me explain.

As to whether you stand any chance of being freed, or being promoted as a slave, it is ultimately a case of being in the right place at the right moment. Luck, or fate, or the will of the gods – or in my case one God, as I have become a Christian. You remember Pater insisting on teaching me to read and write, and my hating it? And you could wait a year or two? Well that was what did it for me. It's a long story with lots of ups and downs but, yes, I was in the right place with the right ability at the right moment, and the rest followed on from there. I guess from the style of your letter that you have had to have someone else write it for you, so my advice is to learn how to do it yourself.

You don't say, but I have the idea that you may be thinking that you could come to Britannia and I could help you or use you, or even buy you. Don't even think about it. I can only imagine you have heard about me from soldiers passing your way from here. Well, that is just what is happening. There are hardly any soldiers left here now; they have all been sent to fight the Goths or the Huns or whoever it is that is threatening the borders of Gaul. A high proportion of the non-military population is following them as well. Because of that, nearly all the slaves have been freed because there is no work for them to do. And because there is no prospect of them being sold, they will automatically become freed within time. I employ a few of those who were slaves and we make a bit of iron occasionally to forge into something we can sell. The future does not look good for any of us. The local population has not yet quite realised what is happening, but when they do, the tribes will start to fight each other again and mayhem will ensue. There are certainly not enough soldiers left here to prevent it.

No. Stay where you are. It is safer, and, be warned, I can be a hard, and if necessary, a very hard dominus if the need arises! It is better that we write to each other occasionally, provided of course that letters continue to get through.

Your loving brother,
Marcus

Chapter 45

The following morning the only people who were sober and able to do anything constructive were Helen of Troy, Clio and Justin. The decision to name him that had been hurried, but we were in agreement about it. Where the name came from we neither of us had any idea, but we thought it suited. In practice Justin was not able to do much except make a noise demanding to be fed. Helen of Troy became like a nurse to Clio and started to teach her the mothering skills that Clio had missed out on as a child. I was going to be very grateful indeed to this brash, outspoken woman. Not only had she seriously helped to save my life in the Tiberius affair, but she was as good as going to do it again now, by looking after Clio in her hour of need.

How Helen was sober I had no idea, as she seemed to have been drinking as much as anyone else last night. Clio and baby had put in a token appearance, and been cheered loudly for doing so, but everyone understood when she did not stay long.

Tacitus, despite also suffering from the night before, came to me looking worried.

'Dominus,' he began. (I never did manage to get him to call me Marcus.) 'I had planned to smelt some ore today but…'

He shrugged his shoulders and spread his hands. It saved speaking.

I laughed. 'You'll not get much done today,' I said. 'It wouldn't be safe anyway with half of them not knowing what they're supposed to be doing.'

He drew himself up. 'In the old days, they wouldn't have been drinking and if they had then they'd still have to work. If they got hurt, well, that was tough.'

'But now, does a day make any difference?'

'Suppose not. But the blacksmith's got some swords to make, mind.'

I nodded.

'Let it ride for a day,' I said. 'OK?'

I clapped him on the shoulder to show there were no hard feelings, and by the way he winced I didn't think he was that sober himself. Just as well if they didn't work today, I could ill afford having Tacitus injure himself.

Like Polonius, he grunted and went away.

He had a point though. We were all very new to this idea of working to meet our customers' demands. In the past we produced iron, wrought it into something, mostly for military use, and the army took it without question. Presumably they then paid Julius Octavius and the process started again, or rather, carried on relentlessly. Now I would have to have enough men who knew what they were doing available to do what was required. And for that we would have to have men who could mine, could make charcoal, could smelt the ore and be able and willing (that was most important) to do all the other chores associated with the process. I was going to have to plan in advance – a whole new concept.

It was a short while after this episode that Polonius came to me. He had in his own way foreseen the problem.

'Marcus,' he said, 'we've got a problem.'

'Oh, yes?' I said, and he started on a diatribe more or less along the lines on which I had been thinking after my discussion with Tacitus. I held up my hand to stop him.

'I know, I know,' I said. 'You been talking to Tacitus?'

He looked a bit sheepish but admitted he had.

'Have you got enough men to mine ore in reasonable quantity?' I asked him.

'Depends what you call reasonable. We've still got plenty in the yard anyway.'

'Not the point. Can you mine, say, a quarter of what we did before?'

'Oh, yes. Easy.'

'Good. Because that's all we're going to need – at most.'

He looked aghast.

'But…'

'Look, Polonius, my old friend, we have to sell what we make.'

He looked blank.

'Somebody has to buy our iron goods,' I persisted. The army isn't here any more to take all the iron we can make.'

'Oh.'

I still didn't think he really understood, but I carried on regardless. 'You've got to use the best of our men to mine the ore, then let Tacitus have them to smelt it, and then use them to clear up afterwards. And if they're not either mining or smelting then they have to be burning charcoal. And if there's still no need for them, they're out of a job. Got it?'

He nodded his head. 'Going to be hard,' he said.

'I know, but it's the only way we're going to make this work.'

He nodded again and lumbered off alternately nodding and shaking his head as he went whilst he digested this whole new concept. I thought he would very soon be talking to Tacitus about what I had said, and I was right. I had the same conversation with him the next day, and with the same reaction.

But my prime concern at this time was my family – Clio and Justin. I really need not have worried though, with Helen of Troy having effectively taken over my house and my household, and everything in it.

'Where does she get the energy from?' grumbled Gallus.

'And I've never heard such language!' marvelled Lupus.

Nevertheless, they would both do any mortal thing that she asked of them. Clio was soon getting about again, although Helen of Troy would only let her feed Justin.

'You look after yourself,' she would bellow if she caught Clio doing any serious work. 'We can do that for you.'

'I'm getting bored,' Clio complained to me.

'But she's right,' I said, trying to soothe her pride.

'But how would I have got on if the world hadn't collapsed and she hadn't been suddenly available?'

'I don't know,' I said, 'but I expect we'd have managed somehow.'

'But how?'

'It doesn't matter how. We would have.'

She wasn't satisfied. 'She does everything. And if she doesn't do it herself she gets someone else to do it.'

'She has a certain charm, and it works wonders.'

She grunted. Another one!

So over the course of a year or so life shook down into a sort of normality. It wasn't very organised and there were times when we had little work on hand. This was not good because it led to trouble between our men, who started to grumble if they had nothing to do, grumble if we demanded work of them, and either way complain that they couldn't live on food alone. Never mind the cost of keeping our ex-slaves and labourers, it was getting harder for the rest of us to survive. I made another trip to Glevum to see what I could buy that I could resell at a profit. I bought some corn and made a little, a very little, from it.

One evening I found Polonius singing mightily and almost dancing a jig in the yard.

'I found it!' he shouted.

I had to think for a minute. Then I realised.

'You have?'

'Yes and nearly where I expected it!'

'And is it good?'

'Looks it, but I shan't know until Tacitus smelts some.'

He had found the new seam of ore that had caused us so much trouble, effort and anxiety for so many years.

'Calls for some celebration,' I said.

'Oh no,' he countered, 'Wait till we know it's good.'

'Very wise,' I said.

What I didn't dare tell him just now was that it was too late. The demand that we had been so anxious to fulfil was gone, along with the army. However, if it was as good as he seemed to think then at least we would have a ready source for what business I could find. And that was the next thing worrying me. It looked as though I was going to cease to be in charge of a mine. Now that we were all together and demand was minimal, Tacitus and Polonius could look after that. In fact Tacitus, despite his gruff manner, was a good manager, and I could see why Julius Octavius had had him in charge at Ariconium.

It seemed that the plans that had been working their way through my head for some time would have to see the light of day. I would have to become a dealer, or a merchant or businessman of some sort, but being stuck in the middle of the forest was not a good place to be for that. Perhaps I should move to New Hamm? It was time to talk to Clio, and I wasn't at all sure how she would react.

But she got there first.

'Marcus,' she said, 'I'm expecting another baby!'

I suppose I should not have been surprised, should even have been expecting it. Justin was getting on for a year old and she had not been feeding him herself for a while, so it was more than likely that another would be on the way.

'Marvellous news,' I cried, but was mentally having to rearrange my plans to accommodate this new development. 'Who else knows?'

'Silly, no one yet. You had to be the first to know.'

'Not even Helen of Troy?' I teased.

'Least of all her, but she could have guessed perhaps.'

'She's pretty astute.'

I held off my ideas for a few days but eventually I had to explain what I was thinking about to her.

'I thought you had something on your mind,' she said. 'You've not really been with us just recently, and from before I made my announcement.'

'Has it been that obvious?'

'My dear Marcus, I always know when you've got something, good or bad, on your mind!'

I ignored the jibe, if there was one.

'More to the point,' I said, 'if I'm going to do this I think we ought to move to New Hamm.'

'Do what?'

'Ah. I haven't explained, have I?'

'No.'

'Like it or not, I'm going to have to become a merchant if we're to survive, and to do that I need to be in some place, not stuck in the middle of a forest.'

There, I'd said it, and I wasn't at all sure how she would react. She didn't immediately, which caused me to start to panic.

'That, I think,' she said, 'is the best idea you've had since I first came here!'

'Really?' I was genuinely surprised.

'This place hasn't got very good memories for me, you know. Or have you forgotten what happened to me here?'

'I most certainly have not, but it's some time ago now.'

'There are places in this house that I still don't like to go. A slamming door can set me on edge. If we get short of food or supplies I expect to get beaten for it.'

'But why haven't you said this before?'

I was thunderstruck that she should have been keeping all this to herself.

'To run the mine, you had to be here, didn't you? I was your wife, so I had to be here too, didn't I?'

'Yes, but…'

She put a finger to my lips. 'No buts. Life will go on and I shall be delighted to come to New Hamm with you. After all, as I said to you a long time ago, I'm a town girl at heart and hate all these trees, but we'll have to do it before this next baby turns up. Oh, and we'll have to take Helen of Troy with us.'

'And Gallus and Lupus?'

'If we can afford it.'

Ever practical is my dearest Clio.

***

Extraordinarily, history then repeated itself. I went to New Hamm to see what the possibilities were for a house to live in, with my first call to be on Drusius. He was bound to know if there was a house for sale or a site where I could build one.

'Ah,' he said, 'there's just the one for you.'

'Oh?' I said.

'Yeah. Used to belong to one of your lot. Got a bit too big for his sandals and, accidentally like, the roof got burnt off it. Nobody hurt, and damage nothing like as bad as yours. Not a big place but it might do you.

It's on the higher ground, so it won't get flooded when the rest of the town does. Go and have a look.'

I did and liked what I saw. It was in the main street with a big room to the front, which would be good to sell things from. It had a bit of garden ground behind with its own well, which was important as we were accustomed to clean fresh water. As Drusius had said, it wasn't bad but it was open to the sky.

'Two problems,' I said.

'Go on.'

'Who do I buy it from and for how much? And knowing what the roof on the house at Clearwell cost, I can't afford it.'

'First one's easy,' he said. 'Just move in and claim a right to be there. The man's gone, and in a big rush. Heard tell that he was following the army. Didn't feel safe round here any more. He'd heard of someone getting their throat cut in the night. Frightened him.'

'I know about that,' I said. 'And in that case there were other reasons, but how can I claim it's mine?'

'That's easy too. Take possession and live in it for a year and a day without him chucking you out and it's yours! 'Tis the custom round here.'

'Might he? Come back and chuck me out, I mean.'

'No chance. He's gone for good. Nobody liked him anyway. But you, you're different. Everyone knows you're OK, so you won't have any trouble.'

'OK,' I said, 'but what about the roof? That's still going to be expensive.'

He pondered this for a moment. 'What's going to happen to your present house?'

'Don't know. Could fall down. Tacitus or Polonius might move in but I doubt it. I think they'd be afraid to. Some nasty things have happened there.'

He drew a deep breath.

'Well,' he said slowly, 'we could take the roof off that and remake it to fit this one.'

I was astounded.

'Can you do that?' I asked.

'Probably. It'll cost of course, but not as much as starting from scratch. No trees to fell for a start.'

It was a happy man who returned to Clearwell and came back again a few days later with his wife and son to look at their 'new' house. As I expected, Clio was delighted.

'At last I'll be able to live as a free person in a proper place,' was her benediction on the project.

And so it happened. True we had an uncomfortable spell when we literally did not have a roof over our heads, and even after we'd moved in, the house was even more basic than the Clearwell house had been at the beginning. But slowly we pulled it together and installed our servants (note, servants now, not slaves), plus Helen of Troy, who now seemed to be part of the family.

To make it a bit easier, at least Clio was a little bit late this time with the birth of our daughter – called Aemelia, for obvious reasons.

Chapter 46

We had barely settled into this new life when a down-at-heel Petrus turned up on our doorstep. He started straight into what he wanted to say.

'I'm sorry, dominus, but my idea of a little shop hasn't worked out. Can I come and work for you?'

I wasn't surprised but I was worried. Here was I about to try doing much the same thing but on a larger scale. I could only fail on a larger scale too.

'What went wrong?' I asked him.

'With the army all going and the hangers on going with them, there's no one understands what Nodens' shrine is about. Not interested. It's starting to fall down!'

'Not your fault.'

'Then I heard you were setting up as a merchant here so I thought I'd come and see if I could help.'

'I'm sure you can,' I said. I did in fact need somebody to look after my so-far empty shop when I was away. 'But I don't know how I'm going to pay you.'

'Oh, don't you worry about that,' he replied airily. 'Just feed me for a start – that'll be enough. And I'll bring along what bits I've got to sell and that'll give us a start.'

'At least I'll have something to put in this empty room,' I said, laughing.

So it was arranged. I knew he would be honest; it would be against his rules not to be! All I had to do was to decide how I was going to go forward.

But it was a time for being distracted.

A man, a man from Glevum, turned up wanting to see me. He had been to the mine and been sent on here by either Tacitus or Polonius. He was a bit cagey about which one it was, but he had refused to be intimidated. He wanted to see me, and me only. If I had gone to New Hamm, then so be it, he would follow me to New Hamm, and here he was. Petrus advised me not to see him and to send him on his way immediately. However, curiosity got the better of me and I let him in. When he was sure that I was the Marcus he wanted, he handed me a scroll that, he said, he had written for someone who couldn't write and it was especially for me. He also hoped that I realised that he was taking an awful chance in bringing me this scroll, and that I would treat him accordingly.

I unrolled the scroll, which was of poor-quality material, and immediately realised what it was. I called for food and drink to be provided for my visitor and settled myself down to read. I also gave instructions that he was not to be allowed to leave until I said so.

Dear Marcus,

If you ever receive this then I shall be dead. Hopefully I shall have died naturally but there's always a chance it may not have been so. Also, if you do read this it will be due to the very great kindness and courage shown to me by one man, and particularly his daughter. I've never learnt to write, so this has been written down by another brave man and I can only hope he's put down what I said and not invented something else of his own. How it will get to you I have no idea.

I've seen you three times since we last met – officially that is. Twice you saw me but weren't sure enough to do anything about it. Once was quite recently across the market when I could just see the idea that it was me ticking in that clever little head of yours, second was only across the street and I had to vanish pretty quick because you definitely recognised me that time. Third I was driving some cattle and you were walking in the opposite direction talking to one of your friends and you never saw me at all. I would have liked to have spoken to you but I didn't know how you'd react, and I'd heard what had happened to some of the others that went back. See?

I did see and was glad to have it confirmed that I had seen him because it had always bothered me as to whether I should be believing my own eyes. I was also glad that I hadn't had to decide what to do about him. In his way he had been good to me. He had protected me from his fellows and from the worst that the mine could offer. I would have found it very hard to mete out the justice that he would rightly have deserved. So what had he been doing?

Yes, I started the riot. You probably guessed that.

I had.

After you disappeared as an errand boy I got so fed up with it in there. For me the work was not impossible but those stupid gang-masters just kept picking on me. I could have killed them – very easily – and at least once very nearly did, but that wouldn't have helped. I had to get away. I had spent my life fighting the system but now it was just grinding me down, as it was meant to do. So I hit on the idea of a riot. There were enough silly sods in there to think they could get away with murder but I was only interested in one thing. Me. Surprised? Surely not. You knew me better than that.

As he expected, I was not surprised

Anyway I told them that once we were out, they were on their own because I had no idea what was out there other than trees, and also because more than one or two together was going to be obvious to the locals. All partly true, especially the first bit. But I knew what I was going to do and I didn't want any hangers-on. Also I didn't think so many would break out. I thought it would be just the bad guys and if they got what they deserved – good.

Interesting and it makes sense. Mahout wasn't that stupid after all. Create a diversion and do what he wanted in the ensuing mayhem.

My plan was to get to the river. The big one that you call Sabrina and some of the locals call Hafren. Then somehow I had to get across it. I had no idea how I was going to do that, but in the end I was lucky and it was quite easy. You had spoken of tides, and I had an idea that when the water was what you were told was 'out' it might be possible to walk across. I spent two nights watching the river and at its very lowest it is quite shallow and I happened to come to it at a point where there's like a rock ledge all the way across. I discovered later that it's a well-known point for the locals and they use it quite regularly. Even then, the current's strong round your legs and you have to be careful. Anywhere else it might, but only might, have been possible to cross. Anyway, make it I did. I had reckoned that the river would be like a dividing line and life would be different the other side and I was right. Here there are hardly any trees, the locals live by raising a few cattle, and it's wet and horrible in the winter. However, nobody much comes here. We're unlucky if we see a Roman taxman once in a year! And the land's flat so you can see anyone coming from millia away. It was all better than I'd dared hope.

So having got across, what next? Mostly I was hungry. I had taken a bit of bread with me but what was left was tiny so I needed food. But I had to be careful. To get violent, which was what the old Mahout would have done, would surely have landed me in trouble, so I had to take a chance. All your gods must have been with me that day! On a bit of higher ground I came to a hovel of a place but it was obviously lived in because there was smoke coming out of the roof. A dog barked and a wild-looking man came out of the house, if you could call it that. It was pretty obvious what I was and that left the man with choices.

His duty would have been to turn you in, for which he would have been amply rewarded, but obviously he didn't.

He could have turned me in and I would almost certainly have killed him if he had tried, and anyone else who tried for that matter. I had decided I was not going to be anyone's slave again even if I got killed myself in the process. I would fight so that it was a quick death too.

Well, that's one way of looking at it.

The man pointed to an even smaller and rougher hovel, indicating that I could shelter in there while he thought about it. He also brought me a bit of food – a peace offering perhaps! It transpired that the man's wife had died and he was trying to carry on with only his very young daughter to help him. He knew he should hand me in but he needed help in the form of muscle power and I had plenty of that. Well-honed from loading carts! So it came to be that I moved in with the two of them. Quite by chance I had another advantage on my side, and again the gods must have been with me. The people who live this side of the river are much darker-skinned than the lot your side, and have curlier hair. I'm not very black and I don't stand out over here. Maybe that's why they took me in – thought I was one of them! Either way it's a lonely place and they seemed lonely people with not much contact with anyone else. I've often wondered if they had something to hide as well and we had another unspoken bond between us. So I became a farmer – of sorts.

My first job was to learn the local language and learn it well so that it wasn't too obvious that I came from somewhere else.

I can see you having trouble there Mahout. Speaking to me was hard enough.

Oh, but he was a good man, Marcus! He mothered me like a dog with her pups. Whichever bit of heaven he has gone to, may the gods act kindly towards him. He showed me what to do, how to manage the cattle without upsetting them, how to milk, how to help a calf out of its mother. And then how to watch the weather so you know when the grass will be ready to cut and when the land will flood in the winter. I would do and did do anything he asked of me. Willingly. I was his slave, but by my own choice.

Doesn't sound like you at all, Mahout! But then, with the extremely nasty alternative staring you in the face, you had to be sensible.

And it got better. Once we all trusted each other, to the point that I knew he wasn't going to hand me in and he was confident I wasn't going to beat his brains out, he more or less handed me his daughter! 'She's a bit young for you yet, but you'll get together in due time and good luck to you. Keep the place together, it will.' Those were his very words. Matilde – that's her name – was as anxious to 'keep the place together' as he was. And so we got together ourselves and have been that way all these years. Anyway, to be realistic there wasn't anyone else within millia. And, Marcus, can you imagine this? We've got two children!

No, Mahout, I most certainly can't. This Matilde must be pretty special to bring you down to earth like this. Mind you, I do know from experience that you can be very gentle and very persuasive when the mood takes.

Sadly the old man died before the second one, a boy, was born. I think the cold and wet of this place probably got to him in the end, as I guess it will get to me eventually. Will have done already if you're reading this.

So I had to run the farm after that and that's how I came to see you in Glevum. The man always took any cattle to market because I was too scared…

You, scared?

… of being seen, but after he died I had no choice. No cattle to market, no money to buy the few things we had to buy. Simple, really. By that time I had reasoned that you were possibly the only person alive who might know who I was and I almost, but not quite, trusted that you would be good to me too if you allowed me to tell you this story. Would I have been right?

I'm really very glad you didn't ask that of me. I was worried stiff that you would have come back with the others after the riot and I would have had no choice but to put you to death. I was pretty certain you were behind the trouble and, certainly just then, I would have had to do what was right in order to keep my head up amongst the rest of them. Even by the time we saw each other I was still a slave, even if I was the dominus of my own little kingdom at Clearwell. Again, I would have had to prove my mettle. Now? Well, now's different, but be grateful you made the right decision at the right time, Mahout.

So, now? Well, like I said, I'm a farmer with a wife and family. Or maybe a dead farmer. If that, then the place is in good shape and Matilde should be able to manage it until the children can help her and take it on themselves. Life has been good to me even if I do still have to keep an eye over my shoulder for trouble coming my way.

I've heard a bit about you, here and there. Done very well for yourself by all accounts. I always said you were bright, and good luck to you. In our ways the gods have been good to us. May Mars, Venus and all the rest bless us both.

Mahout

And of course you don't know that I've put all those gods behind me now and have become a Christian with only one Lord and God to worry about. And He would have wanted me to forgive you even if the system wouldn't. You are definitely a lucky man, Mahout!

I sat looking at the scroll for some time after reading it and then reread parts again in order to make the best sense of it. I called the messenger in.

'Did you know this man?' I asked him. I held up the scroll to indicate who I meant.

He hesitated.

'Don't worry,' I said. 'The man is dead. Whatever he may or may not have done is now of no consequence. He was a good friend to me a long time ago.' I felt no need to elaborate. 'And I should like to know more of him.'

'I'd not say that I knew him,' the man replied.

'How then?'

'Well, it was like this. To look at him he was a stranger but at the same time he wasn't, if you get my meaning, and yet again he seemed to belong.'

Very true. By his own account even, Mahout had a very swarthy dark skin.

'He started coming to market with an old man what farmed by the river. Then I heard he died, the old man I mean, and this fellow, Aiden he called himself, seemed to take on from him. But he couldn't read or write, see. The old man could, just about enough to get by, so this one came to me to write whatever was needed. Never used to be required, but since you lot came there's been a lot more of it. If you'll pardon me saying it.'

I nodded. After all it was that ability and that requirement that ultimately got me out of being a slave.

'So we met now and then when there was something needed doing in the scribing line, until he says to me one day, he says, "Faron, there's something long I need written down, more like a story than anything, and it needs to be delivered into the Forest after I'm dead. I'll make it worth your while."

'By Jupiter, I says, that's being a bit morbid, but I expect we can do it. Anyway over a summer we got it down and I wrote it out fair on some of this newfangled paper. Eventually I got word that he had died. I think the damp and the wet of where he farmed got to him. So here I am keeping my side of the bargain that he paid me for. I do hope I did right.'

'Very much so, but obviously as you wrote it, you know what's in this?' Again I held up the scroll.

'Oh my. Yes and no. Yes I wrote it, and no, it's so long ago that I can't remember the details.'

'That's probably a good thing and its best that you don't try to remember. Doing that just might cause you trouble.'

I looked at him very straight. He got my meaning.

'As you say, dominus, I have no recollection at all of what was in that scroll.'

'Keep it that way, Faron.' I rewarded him handsomely for his lack of memory and he went on his way a very happy scribe. Even if our world was collapsing, this man could be in trouble if he fell foul of the wrong person

***

I was glad to have heard from Mahout. I had often wondered about him and I had been more or less right as to what had happened – I could believe my own eyes – I had seen him. So what does the future hold now? Many would say that I have achieved all I could hope to achieve considering the point from which I started. I have my merchandising business, which is beginning to work out, and I have to admit this, Petrus must have been sent by God. He seems to have a nose for what I should buy and at what price, but then maybe he's learnt the rules of this game!

I like to stand on the headland at New Hamm, as I did with that centurion years ago, and contemplate the world. By all accounts Britannia is falling into chaos as the power of Rome moves rapidly away. Will there be a resurgence, or will the local tribes fight each other to the death? The river comes and the river goes. It comes quietly and it comes crashing. My life entirely. Periods of quiet, like when I was a runner or living with Clio. Periods of crashing, like the riot or Tiberius. As for the future? Who knows?